Surviving The Fatherland

A True Coming-of-age Love Story
Set in WWII Germany

ANNETTE OPPENLANDER

First published by Oppenlander Enterprises, LLC, 2017
First Edition
www.annetteoppenlander.com
Text copyright: Annette Oppenlander 2017
ISBN: 978-0-9977800-4-8
Library of Congress Control Number: 2017902204

AWARDS FOR
SURVIVING THE FATHERLAND

2017 National Indie Excellence Award
2018 Indie B.R.A.G. Honoree
2017 Winner Chill with a Book Readers' Award
Finalist 2017 Kindle Book Awards
2018 Readers' Favorite Book Award
A Discovered Diamond Historical Novel
An IWIC Hall of Fame Novel

"This book needs to join the ranks of the classic survivor stories of WWII such as "Diary of Anne Frank" and "Man's Search for Meaning". It is truly that amazing!" **InD'tale Magazine**

"This novel is fast-paced and emotively worded and features a great selection of characters, flawed and poignantly three-dimensional." **Historical Novel Society**

"...eye-opening and heartbreaking..." **San Francisco Review of Books**

"I would heartily recommend this book as an engrossing and well-researched story with two of the most engaging protagonists I've read for a while." Jessica Brown for **Discovering Diamonds - Independent Reviews of the Best in Historical Fiction**

"I for one am glad she shared her story with us as it gives us a look at a different perspective from those who endured this tragic time in history. "Surviving the Fatherland" by Annette Oppenlander is highly recommended reading!" Carol Hoyer for **Reader Views**

"...simply beautiful." **Readers' Favorite Five Stars**

"...a book well worth reading as it shows you a different side of the war, it shows it from the eyes of children during the war and how things shaped for them when they grew up." **EskieMama & Dragon Lady Reads**

"I highly recommend this book!" **Long and Short Reviews**

"...one of the best World War Two memoirs I have read." **The Death of Carthage**

"Highly readable." **Janette M., Librarian**

"...absolutely fascinating." **Cathy H., Educator**

"Amazingly touching, vividly described and masterfully written, this book leaves a strong impact on you." **Read Day and Night Blog Review**

DEDICATION

For my mother, Helga, a strong woman
who triumphed against the odds, and
For my father, Günter,
whose brave soul is my inspiration.

ACKNOWLEDGMENTS

I want to thank my father, Günter, and my mother, Helga, whose willingness to visit painful events in their memories never ceased to astound me. Without them there would be no story. I also want to thank Helmut's family for allowing me to share his part of the story. Over the past fifteen years I've had many people help me make this novel possible: Alexander Weinstein who helped me through a first version of the manuscript when I still had much to learn and who instilled in me the belief that I could one day become a novelist; my writing buddies Diane, Susan and Dave who've read several versions of this story over the years; the Stadtarchiv Solingen for sharing my hometown's history; Sara from Yellow Bird Editors for pointing out what was still missing and helping me arrive at a meaningful end; and finally my husband, Ben, who's stood by me and endured endless discussions, the occasional tears and many readings.

BASED ON A TRUE STORY

"When these ten-year old boys join our organization, [...] then they join the Hitler youth four years later, and there we keep them for another four years, and then [...] we immediately take them into the party, into the labor front, in the SA or SS [...] Their further treatment will be furnished by the military and they will not be free for the rest of their lives."
—Adolf Hitler

"Woman's world is her husband, her family, her children and her home. We do not find it right when she presses into the world of men."
—Adolf Hitler

"Hope is the thing with feathers
That perches in the soul
And sings the tune without the words
And never stops at all."
—Emily Dickinson

BOOK ONE: MAY 1940 – APRIL 1945

CHAPTER ONE

Lilly: May 1940

For me the war began, not with Hitler's invasion of Poland, but with my father's lie. I was seven at the time, a skinny thing with pigtails and bony knees, dressed in my mother's lumpy hand-knitted sweaters, a girl who loved her father more than anything.

It was May of 1940, my favorite time of year when the air is filled with the smell of cut grass and lilacs, promising excursions to town and the cafes in the hilly land I called home.

Like any other weekend, my father came home that Friday carrying a heavy briefcase of folders. Only this time, he flung his case in the corner of the hallway like it was a bag of garbage. You have to understand. My father is a neat freak, a man who keeps himself and everything he touches in absolute order. And so even at seven—even before he said those fateful words—I knew something was different.

My father had been named after the German emperor, Wilhelm, and Mutti called him Willi, but to me he was always Vati.

Ignoring me, he hurried into the kitchen, his eyes bright with excitement. "I've been drafted."

At the sink, Mutti abruptly dropped her sponge and stared at him. Her mouth opened, then closed without a sound.

I didn't understand what he was talking about. I didn't understand the meaning of a lie, yet I felt it even then. Like others detect an oncoming thunderstorm, pressure builds behind my forehead, a heaviness in my bones. There is something in the way

1

the liar moves, his limbs hang stiffly on the body as if his soul cringes. His look at me is fleeting and there is something artificial in his voice.

At that moment I knew Vati was hiding something from us.

"They want me there Monday. I'll be a captain." His voice trembled as he sank into a chair, still wearing his coat and hat.

"But that's in three days." Mutti picked up Burkhart, my little brother who was a just a toddler and had begun to whine. "It's fine," she soothed as she paced the length of the kitchen, the click-click of her heels like an accusation.

I frowned and moved closer to my father. Since my brother's birth, Mutti had been spending every minute with the baby. No matter how well I behaved, how I did what she asked, I rarely succeeded drawing her eyes away from my brother. It annoyed me to no end that I couldn't stop myself from trying.

"Vati, where are you going?" I asked, secure in the knowledge that my little brother wouldn't draw away his attention.

My father's cheeks glowed with excitement. As if he hadn't heard me, he rushed back into the hallway and knelt in front of the wardrobe. I followed.

One door gaped open, revealing a gray military uniform. He was rummaging below.

"What are you looking for?"

"Just a minute." He emerged with a pair of shiny black boots.

He knelt at my level and to this day I remember smelling the cologne he used every morning, a mix of spice and citrus.

"I am packing."

"Where are you going?" Vati had never been away, not even for one night. In fact, he and Mutti had strict routines, and these were dictated by the clock. We ate every night at six thirty sharp. Even on Sundays. Breakfast was at seven in the morning. Clothes never ever lay on the floor, each item brushed and aired and returned to its spot in the closet. Life was laid out in rules, washing hands before dinner, carrying a clean handkerchief at all times and always, always looking spotless when leaving the house.

He smoothed the pants of his uniform. "I'll be helping out in the war."

"Will you be back for my birthday?" My birthday was on

June fourth and I worried about our customary visits to town. In the window of *Wiesner*, our local toy store, I'd discovered a *Schildkröt* doll. Her name was Inge and I wanted her badly. Vati said she looked just like me, with blond hair and this pretty red-checkered dress with a white apron and white patent shoes you could take off.

As Vati lifted me in the air and turned in a circle, I shrieked in surprise and delight. I was flying.

"They want me after all! With all my experience, they should be glad."

Mutti put Burkhart on the floor and leaned in the doorframe to the kitchen, her arms folded across her chest. "I wish you didn't have to go."

"It's not so bad, Luise." Vati gripped her shoulders as if he wanted to infuse his excitement into her. "I'll be back soon. We're so much stronger than last time."

"All I see is Hitler sending more men into battle. Do you at least know where you're going?"

Vati shrugged. "Probably France or Scandinavia."

"Will you be back soon?" I tried again.

He patted my head and returned to his chair at the head of the table. "I'll be home before you've found time to miss me." As he began to whistle, something nagged my insides like a tiny clawing animal.

A screeching wail erupted. Sharp and metallic, it cut through doors and walls and echoed through the streets. No matter that the siren blasted every day, it made me shiver.

I watched my mother freeze, her eyes filled with something I would soon learn to recognize as fear. The siren continued—up, down, up, down. Another wail erupted. This time it sounded like the foghorn of a ship, signaling the end of the alarm.

Relieved that the horrible noise was over, I climbed on my father's lap, running a forefinger across the bluish stubble of his jaw. "Vati?"

"Not now, Lieselotte, we are talking," Mutti said.

I looked up in alarm. Mutti had said Lieselotte when everyone called me Lilly, a sure sign she was mad. I slid back off, keeping my hand on Vati's arm.

Mutti tucked a strand of pale hair behind her ear and

slumped into a chair. "I hate these air raid sirens."

Vati didn't look up from the newspaper. "It's just a test... a precaution."

Mutti abruptly straightened. "I should work on dinner. You *do* remember that my brother is visiting tonight?" Two red spots that didn't quite match her lipstick glowed on her cheeks. "Lilly, there's honey all over this table. Wash out the dishrag and wipe this down."

"Yes, Mutti." I clumsily scrubbed the surface, glancing back and forth between my parents. Vati's eyes, usually a watery blue, sparkled like an early morning sky.

"Don't you see that this is important?" he said, letting the paper sink once more. "We're fighting against England and France, even Scandinavia! Our country needs us."

"You mean they need you."

"Everyone has a role to play."

"They didn't ask me if *I* wanted to play a role." Mutti's voice was shrill as she set a pot on the stove and began to peel potatoes. "I'll be stuck with two children to take care of."

"That's exactly what the Führer wants you to do. Girls are meant to be mothers and take care of our families. We take care of the rest."

"Like your war?"

Hearing my parents argue made my insides turn knotty. I wanted them to stop, yet I finished cleaning and said nothing. All I did was return to Vati's chair as their arguments continued flying like knives above my head.

"We have to make sacrifices," Vati said. "You're a strong woman. Besides, isn't the government taking care of things? Every family receives rations, even for clothes. They're thinking of everything."

"These ration cards are so cumbersome. And the sirens drive me crazy."

Vati got up and patted Mutti's back. "Don't worry, everything will work out fine.

During dinner, I continued watching my parents. Heavy silence lingered except for my brother's babble and the scraping of spoons across porcelain bowls.

I didn't taste much of the soup. My eyes were drawn to the stony faces on either side as I recalled the events of the afternoon, wondering if I had done something to make them angry. In that stillness of the kitchen, I sensed that my life was about to change. Something dreadful lingered like a wolf lying in wait behind a bush ready to pounce. You didn't see it or hear it, yet you knew it was there.

"Tim says that women who wear lipstick are whores," I said, my gaze lingering on my mother's mouth where the remnants of lipstick clung to her lower lip.

"Who is Tim?" Mutti snapped.

"A boy in my class. His older brother is in the Hitler youth and they say girls should not paint their faces and listen to the men—"

"Young girls like yourself are pretty just the way they are," Vati said.

I was sure Tim had talked about all women and though I burned to know what a whore was, I decided to keep my mouth shut. My teacher's probing eyes appeared in my vision, and I remembered my earlier mission.

"Vati, will you read with me tonight?" I was a terrible reader, hated it, especially when I had to read aloud in class and Herr Poll slammed his ruler on my desk when I got stuck.

Mutti's mouth pressed together in a straight line as she headed for the window to pull down the blackout shutters. "Not tonight," she said. "Clear the table while I cover the other windows and change your brother. Then you get ready for bed."

Vati jumped up and disappeared in the living room. "We'll do it another time," he said before he closed the door.

As I watched Mutti carry Burkhart to bed, I felt as transparent as the air around me. But not in a comfortable way—more like a sore throat that sticks around and reminds you off and on that you're still sick.

After stacking our dishes in the sink, I followed my father, who was studying a file of papers.

"Vati?"

"What is it, Lilly?"

I hesitated. Was this a good time to ask about *Inge*, the doll? Vati was acting so strange. Even now his face had a damp shine to it as if he'd run to catch the streetcar.

"Nothing," I said. *Gute Nacht*, Vati."

"Sweet dreams."

Disappointed, I quietly closed the door, stopping halfway to my bedroom. No sounds came from the kitchen.

I was about to climb into bed when the doorbell rang. I froze. Something bad was going to happen. Was the war coming to get Vati?

But when I heard voices in the corridor I recognized Mutti's brother, August, my favorite uncle. He always brought me gifts, a chocolate éclair, a flower from his garden or a bowl of sweet cherries.

I breathed again, growing aware of my icy feet on the linoleum.

By the sounds they'd gone into the living room, a perfect opportunity to see my uncle and find out more about Vati's plans. If I pretended my stomach ached, maybe, just maybe I could visit for a while. I bent over my brother who was lying on his back, his mouth relaxed in sleep, blonde curls framing his face. In that moment I envied him. It wouldn't be the last time.

On the other side of the wall, Vati shouted. Alarmed, I tiptoed into the hallway and peeked through the living room door. Uncle August, his legs stretched long in front of him, lounged on the sofa next to a young woman I didn't recognize, while Mutti sat on an armchair by the window.

"I don't believe this. How can you be so enthusiastic?" August's voice rose as he spoke, at the same time patting the young woman's knee. "Don't you remember the last war? You of all people."

"Nonsense," Vati said from somewhere beyond the door. "This war will be over quickly. Our weapons are superior. I mean, Poland practically fell in a day and France and Scandinavia aren't far behind."

August shook his head, his eyes squinting. "I don't understand how you turn your back on your family." His voice was filled with disgust. "Aren't you worried about leaving your wife and children? This damn thing gives me the creeps. The SS and Gestapo are watching our every step. Just the other day—"

"Shhh," the woman next to him said. "August, please be careful. What if somebody listens?"

"I'm not turning my back," Vati shouted. "We've got to do our duty. Besides, the Führer is taking care of everyone."

August threw a glance at Mutti. "Since when can we trust

the government?"

Mutti leaned forward. "The apartment below is vacant. When Willi leaves, I won't even have a neighbor to talk to," she choked, her eyes glistening. "You want me to ask Herr Baum? He's older than Methuselah and can barely walk, let alone help if things get worse."

I cringed. I liked the old man next door, especially his knobby hands that were brown and gnarled like miniature tree trunks. He always listened when I spoke as if what I said were important.

"I'm convinced this war will be over before the year is up." Vati sounded irritated, and there was that darkness again, that fakeness in his voice. "I, for my part, am proud to help out."

August jumped up so suddenly, I nearly banged my head against the doorframe. "Well, I'm not." His eyes narrowed. "I thought your job at the city was highly important. Strange they let their top civil engineer walk off like that."

The silence that followed reminded me of dinner when my parents hadn't spoken, yet I could hear their anger as clearly as if they'd screamed at each other. I no longer wanted to go inside, yet I couldn't leave, my legs as rigid as Herr Poll's ruler.

"Either way," August continued, "all I wanted was to introduce my fiancée, Annelise. I'm sorry I came."

Mutti stood up, wiping her eyes. "Please August, don't go yet. I'm sure it'll all work out."

"That's right," Vati said, sounding calm again. "Let's drink to your engagement. I'll get a bottle of wine from the cellar."

I rushed to my bedroom and curled up tightly the way I did during thunderstorms. It took me another hour to get to sleep, my mind firmly on the image of Vati handing me the doll, Inge, for my birthday.

CHAPTER TWO

Günter: May 1940

"Attention! Feet together, arms down, hands at your pant seams. Look straight. Stand still," the boy shouted. He was no more than sixteen, and the khaki uniform hung in folds around his narrow chest. The hair around his ears, shaved to the skin, left a tuft of blonde on top like a bird's nest.

He paced up and down in front of us, a row of eleven year-old boys, his eyes narrowed into angry slits. "Men," he yelled, "you are the future soldiers of Germany. You don't fight to die, but to win." He yanked open a book. "I quote. Nothing is more important than your courage. Only the strong person, carried by belief and the fighting desire of your own blood, will be master during danger." The book snapped shut. "I expect absolute obedience."

I stood next to my best friend, Helmut, at the sports stadium where the local Hitler youth met for drill. We'd lined up in rows of three deep in the middle of the grass-covered field. Another boy with red and blue patches on his shirt appeared in front of us.

"Tuck in your shirt, pull up your socks," he said, pointing at Helmut. "Look at the filth on your shoes. This is no way to dress. Show some pride."

From the corner of my eye, I watched Helmut adjust his shirt and rub his shoes. Helmut sometimes forgets about these things. Thankfully my own socks stretched to just below my knees.

8

Still, I held my breath as the boy passed by. Earlier today we'd bought a uniform: black shorts and beige shirt, neckerchief with leather knot, armband, and the best part, a brand-new knife. Mother had grumbled about spending so much money.

"But Mutter, all boys have to go," I'd argued after we left the store. "They told us at school. It's our duty." I didn't tell her how excited I'd been about my new outfit. Most of the time I get the hand-me-downs from my older brother, Hans.

"What're they going to do with you?" she'd said, her voice stern with irritation.

"Make fires and camp." I didn't tell Mother that I couldn't wait trying out my new knife and going on adventures with a bunch of boys.

Now I waited in a line and couldn't move a muscle. Stupid.

"Attention! Turn left, march! One, two, one, two, follow me." Birdsnest headed down the field while the other youth observed, waiting for us to trip and fall out of line. We marched back and forth, left and right, crisscrossing the field. What a bore.

The air smelled of early summer and warmth. Dandelions and forget-me-nots dotted the grass like a colorful carpet. Imitating my classmates, I fought the urge to look around, keeping my head straight toward the horizon as if I could see what was coming a mile away.

A man in a brown uniform with a red armband watched from the sidelines. Distracted for a moment, I stepped on the heels of the fellow in front.

"Ouch," the boy yelled. "Watch yourself, idiot."

"You're the idiot. Why did you stop?" I said.

Birdsnest materialized in front of us. "What's going on here?"

"He stepped on me," the other boy said.

My cheeks felt hot. "He suddenly stopped."

"Name."

"What?"

"Your *name*."

"Günter Schmidt."

"Listen to me, Günter." Birdsnest's eyes narrowed. "Quit playing around. You're training to become a soldier. On the ground. Give me twenty pushups, quick."

"Yes, sir." I hurriedly dropped to the grass and hid my face because my head had turned into a super-heated balloon ready to fly away.

Out of breath I returned to the row, swallowing the choice words choking me. The marching continued, followed by singing:

> *"Our flag flies in front of us;*
> *To the future we trek man for man,*
> *We march for Hitler through night and adversity*
> *With the youth's flag for freedom and bread.*
> *Our flag flies in front of us,*
> *Our flag is the new era,*
> *Our flag leads us into eternity,*
> *Yes, the flag is more than death.*

Birdsnest continued reading from his book about becoming heroes, but my thoughts, sped up by the gnawing in my stomach, wandered to the dinner waiting at home. On dismissal, Birdsnest gave me a nasty look before reminding us to practice marching and standing to attention. He never mentioned camping or making fires. *Boring.* We weren't allowed to use our knives either. Worse, we'd have to go again Saturday.

By the time I arrived at my house, it was late and I was in a rotten mood. Helmut is much more of a talker, but he was grumpy, too, and we'd walked home in silence.

I lived on the first floor of an apartment house on *Weinsbergtalstrasse*, one of a row of identical three-story homes. Recently built of brick and stucco, they were considered modern, each house painted the same pale green except for an occasional flower box in a white-framed window. I loved our new water closet. You pulled on the chain, which I was strictly forbidden to play with, and the water released from a tank under the ceiling, flushing everything away. Helmut still had an outhouse.

Entering our flat, I tossed my cap in the corner and headed to the kitchen. "I'm hom—"

The words stuck in my throat because the table, set for five, was untouched, the room deserted. A sense of unease crept up inside me, quickly forgotten because of the delicious smell emanating from the cast-iron pot. I lifted the lid and let out a sigh: bean soup with ham and smoked sausage. I glanced at the clock, seven-thirty. No wonder I was starving.

We never ate later than six. Something was wrong.

Reluctantly, I turned away from the soup and tiptoed down the hallway. Voices came from my parents' bedroom.

Stopping at the threshold, I knocked. "*Vater*?"

"Come in."

I cracked open the door. "Are we going to eat?"

Mother sat hunched over on the bed, my father kneeling in front of her. I wanted to enter, but something in their expressions held me back.

My father straightened with effort. "I'm leaving tomorrow."

"What do you mean?" I looked back and forth between my parents.

"I've been drafted."

I stared at him as his words echoed through my head. "But you said they needed you in the factory. You said you had more work than you could handle, making those fancy swords for the officers."

"That's what I thought." My father's voice remained steady but his jaws were tight.

"Can't you tell them you're too busy?"

My father sighed and put an arm on my shoulder, his expression serious. Despite being short, he could carry a hundred kilo sack of grain as if it were a small child. He wasn't the hugging type, but tonight he held on to me.

"That's not how it works."

"Where will you go?"

"Don't know. Maybe to Scandinavia."

Wiping her eyes, Mother stood up. "Why don't you get your brothers and eat? We'll pack and be in soon. And take off those clothes."

During the night, despite being tired, I tossed and turned. I'd burned my tongue on the soup at dinner, and my stomach was making weird noises. By the sound of it, my older brother, Hans, wasn't sleeping either.

While the radio proclaimed victories daily, news of fallen soldiers had begun to arrive, and announcements appeared in the newspaper. A square black cross was printed above each obituary and Mother grumbled and shook her head, reading the names and ages of the dead. I envisioned my father stumbling blindly toward a sea of barbwire, his head and eyes wrapped in bandages, his arms stretched in front.

Time stood still in the early morning hours as I wondered if my father would return with limbs missing or not at all. I imagined the obituary in the paper: Artur Schmidt, died in battle. I considered asking Hans what he thought would happen, but before I could, a soft snore came from the other bed.

I turned on my back and stared into the darkness. The apartment was silent, but not the silence of peaceful sleep, rather an artificial stillness of cries muffled by pillows and of thoughts that whirled without end. I turned again, facing the wall, my last thought of my father waving to me with a rifle.

In the morning I awoke with a start. My brother's bed was a pile of sheets and blankets. Remembering last night, I sighed. Soft murmurs drifted in from the kitchen—my father's voice. I wanted to stay in bed and listen, and at the same time I wanted to be near him.

With a sigh, I jumped out of bed.

"Günter, you sleepy head." My father opened his arms. "Give me a hug."

I buried my face in the folds of my father's shirt. "Are you leaving now?" My father smelled of shaving soap, reminding me of his ritual, the razor, a single sharp blade, swiped back and forth across a leather strap to sharpen it further, the soft foamy soap and the thick brush made of badger hair, my father disappearing under a layer of white bubbles before taking the knife to scrape away the stubble.

"It's time."

Everybody crowded in. I sobbed, my throat tight and achy.

My father grabbed me and Hans by the arm. "You two need to take care of your mother and Siegfried."

I swallowed hard, the lump in my throat threatening to expand to my eyes. I knew that Hans was upset by the way his shoulders trembled. My baby brother, Siegfried, was only three and had no idea what was going on.

"I don't want to hear of any mischief. Do what you're told."

"Yes, *Vater*," I said. "When will you come back?"

"As soon as they let me."

"Promise?"

"I'll write." My father moved toward Mother. "I'll see you soon, Grete," he whispered.

Wiping his eyes with the back of his hand, he turned. For a moment he looked around the living room, the leather sofa, his favorite chair in the corner, the walnut table and matching sideboard.

A bright morning sun beamed into the room, throwing patterns on the wood. A starling trilled high of summer and new beginnings. With a final nod, my father hurried to the door—and was gone.

Mother dabbed her eyes where fresh tears kept arriving. "You heard what your father said. We better talk about your new responsibilities."

"Can't we do it after school?" My legs were heavy from lack of sleep.

Mother resolutely picked up pen and paper. "Who wants to help with laundry?"

"That's girl's work," Hans said. "Besides, I'm too old for that."

"Not me," I said.

"Enough." Mother smacked a fist on the table. And though she was a short woman and even at eleven I was taller than her, I bowed my head. "You heard what your father said. Günter, you'll help with laundry. Hans, you'll do the ovens. I also need someone to clean the hallway stairs and sweep the sidewalk." I tuned out.

Life was going to be one big chore.

CHAPTER THREE

Lilly: May 1940
Early Monday morning when I returned from the outhouse, the front door to our two-family home was propped open.

I was deep in thought, scheming about how I could get Vati to myself one last time and how to work in a reminder about Inge, my new doll, when I almost collided with two men maneuvering a sofa through the entrance. As if Mutti's wishes for a new neighbor had been heard, a horse carriage loaded with tables, chairs and assorted boxed stood in front of the house.

Like Mutti I'd secretly wished for a family to move in downstairs, another child I could play with. My best friend, Lydia, lived five blocks away, but I wasn't allowed to visit because with all the sirens and threatening notices in the paper, Mutti wanted me home after school.

Bouncing from foot to foot, I took up position beneath the red beech tree in the front yard. In summer, the red beech held out its arms to shade me and hide my climbs to the top. It rustled and whispered into my ear with a thousand voices. It was steady when my arms trembled, it was solid against my skin like a caress, and most of all, it never went away.

As the men unloaded a wooden trunk, straining under its weight, Mutti's voice echoed through my head. *Don't talk to strangers.* But what could it hurt? At last somebody wanted to live here.

We lived on *Wachtelstraße*, a quiet street on the south side

14

of Solingen, the kind of neighborhood where cars were a rarity and people knew each other by name. Vati liked it because the streetcar was only three minutes away and because our home was respectable. The flat below us had been empty for months, its windows bare and dark even during the day. I'd imagined the house watching, invisible eyes following me across the front yard.

Now the windows stood open to release the stench of musty air. A gray-haired woman who wore a surly frown like an ill-fitted dress was hanging lace curtains on rods. The woman looked like a maid. She couldn't possibly be my new neighbor.

The stream of movers continued snaking in and out of the house. Like ants, the men scrambled back and forth, their faces strained from the weight in their arms.

"Are you down there, Lilly?" Mutti called from upstairs. I often wondered how she saw through things and knew what I was doing, especially anything she didn't like. And the list of unacceptable things was long.

"I'm watching the new neighbors," I shouted, keeping my eyes on the movers.

"Time for breakfast." Mutti's voice had the edge.

"Coming..."

A man materialized at the entrance of the sidewalk. Unlike Vati's cropped head, this man's hair was longish and shiny under a layer of pomade. Slicked back, it hung over his collar, revealing a square forehead. His skin reminded me of the dough my mother prepared to make sweet bread.

He was talking to one of the movers. While I tried to decide whether to go upstairs or move closer to the man, he turned and walked toward me.

I jumped up. "Are you our new neighbor?"

The man's eyes, a watery blue against his pale skin, focused on me. A curious expression moved across his face like a sudden change in the weather. It made me uneasy.

"And who might you be?" the man said.

"I'm Lilly. Are you moving into our house?"

"Yes."

I looked past the man in search of his kids. "Where's your family?"

"Lilly, is it? My name is Karl Huss. I live by myself." Huss leaned forward and placed a hand on my shoulder. "Come and visit me soon." He smiled, revealing a row of yellowed teeth.

I wrinkled my nose. The man stank of cigarettes.

When Huss began patting my cheek, I pulled away "I've got to go."

By the time I entered the kitchen, my breath caught in my throat. "I met the new neighbor," I blurted. "He doesn't have a family."

"I hope you aren't bothering him." Mutti took in my grass-stained hands. "Wash up and make yourself a sandwich. We're nearly finished with breakfast. I need to take care of your brother."

"He lives alone." I remained in the doorframe watching Vati, whose nose was buried in the *Solinger Tageblatt*, our city's daily newspaper. Mutti was feeding my brother. Like a bird his mouth opened rhythmically waiting for another spoonful. For a moment I wanted to be him, feeling my mother's closeness, capturing her attention.

"Why does he need a big apartment?" I said aloud.

"We'll find out soon enough." Mutti cooed as she wiped Burkhart's mouth. "Tummy full?" Kissing his head, she lifted him into her arms, her eyes on Vati. "At least now I have someone to talk to."

When Vati didn't answer, she shook her head and left the room.

I ran to Vati's side. Now was my chance. "Vati?"

Vati reluctantly let his paper sink. He looked distant in the gray uniform with the silver buttons. "What is it, Lilly?"

"Can you read with me now? Class isn't till nine. I've got to practice two chapters and you know Herr Poll always shakes his ruler at me when I get stuck," I hurried. "Lydia says he'll hit my fingers one of these days." I took a breath.

Vati looked at me, but his eyes focused on something behind me as if he could see straight through my head. I tugged on his sleeve. What was the matter with him?

"Please."

He abruptly straightened and picked up a bag. "Time for me to go."

"Give your father a kiss." Mutti reappeared in the door, clutching Burkhart to her chest. I tapped against Vati's knee-high boots. They were so shiny, I saw my face.

Vati hugged me tight. "Be a good girl and help your

16

mother."

My heart hammered in my throat. *"Tschüss,* Vati."

I knew this good-bye was different, but how could I fathom what war meant? All I knew was that my insides were twisting, that this leave-taking felt all wrong, my grasp failing to stop Vati's shiny legs from moving out of reach.

Following him into the stairway I yelled after him, "Come home soon!" I waited for him to look up or yell something back at me, but the front door slammed shut with a bang.

"You better get ready for school," Mutti said, sticking her nose into my brother's hair as if she wanted to hide in there.

As I shouldered my book bag, I glanced at Vati's desk. Like him, it exuded neatness. His papers lay untouched beside the leather pad and the gold-tipped fountain pen I was forbidden to touch.

I hesitated. There was something cold and abandoned about the room—a stillness like a frozen lake in the middle of a forest. I jumped when I heard Mutti's voice from the kitchen, fussing at my brother. I'd be late for school.

With a sigh, I opened the door. Herr Poll would be angry with me today.

CHAPTER FOUR

Lilly: July 1941
Vati had been gone for over a year, and my life had worsened a little more each day. Sirens blared day and night as the lines at stores grew longer. Our bakery closed, followed by our favorite butcher. From one day to the next, signs appeared in their windows, their doors padlocked.

Over the course of the war, Hitler would close hundreds of thousands of stores and service businesses, forcing their owners to enlist or join the production of war-related materials.

They were small changes at first, certain foods missing, fewer clothes available on ration cards, walking farther to find an open bakery…

Every day I caught myself listening for Vati's footsteps. My breath would slow each time I heard the front door, a part of my soul rejoicing. Every day, he remained absent.

And something else changed. Fear moved into my life. Before Vati left, I hadn't experienced dread other than a bit of uneasiness when going to the dark basement.

Now I had this shakiness in my legs that wouldn't go away. In school we practiced climbing under the desk and lining up against inside walls or marching to the basement, teachers producing enthusiastic smiles as if we were playing a game. It was a vague feeling, a discomfort I couldn't define except that it made my sleep restless and my daily routine tense.

Mutti grew increasingly nervous and her temper, no longer

buffered by Vati, flared.

I took the brunt of it.

The thing is, I mostly accepted Mutti's wrath as normal. I'd surely done something to deserve it. In the end, I didn't know any better, and I accepted my new neighbor's peculiar habits in the same way.

It was late that evening as I hurried downstairs. Cigarette smoke crept into the hallway through Huss's door. I squeezed shut my nose with two fingers and rushed past, all the while wondering what he did for a living. All the men I knew worked or fought in the war like Vati.

To get to the outhouse in the backyard, I had to pass through the cellar from where a door led out back. In the *Waschküche*, the basement room where everyone did laundry, ropes stretched across the ceiling. A sack of clothespins sat in the corner next to the stepstool I used to reach the tall lines. A single bulb threw shadows across the stone floor and the drain covered by an iron grate. I avoided the spot on my way, imagining hands edging out of the black hole and gripping my legs.

As I ran to the backdoor leading into the garden, Huss appeared out of the gloom and stepped into my way. "*Fräulein* Lilly, up so late?"

I froze, leaving a few feet of distance between us. "Forgot to pee."

"I see." Huss made no attempt to move.

I wiggled, my bladder demanding release. "I need to go."

"I like your hair." Huss managed to touch my pigtails. A mixture of tobacco smoke and unwashed skin wafted across. In the gloom of the basement his face swam above me, his chin gray with stubble.

"I really need to go."

"Of course." Huss shuffled to the side, but not enough for me to pass easily. Forced to move closer, I squeezed through the opening. For a moment, Huss's hand touched the crown of my head, his touch heavy as if his fingers were filled with rocks. I rushed to the door, my heart pounding against my ribs.

By the time I reached the outhouse, my underwear was damp. Mutti would be angry. I wasn't supposed to be up at this hour, and now I'd need fresh pants.

I hated the outhouse: the wooden platform with the

circular opening sat above an abyss filled with waste. Flies swarmed unless the air outside froze. Maggots crawled below. Toilet paper had become rare, and for the past few months we'd used scraps of newspaper, torn into strips that hung from a nail. A smile spread across my face as I imagined lighting the paper on fire and roasting the maggots alive or better yet, stuffing them into Huss's mail slot in the front door.

I closed the cover with a thud and opened the door to catch fresh air. A half-moon hung above me surrounded by the first handful of stars. It was hard to believe Vati had left more than a year ago. Did he see the same sky? Was he even thinking about me, Burkhart or Mutti?

Walking quietly, I scurried along the house wall. The basement door stood open. I couldn't remember how I'd left it. Huss was gone but I still smelled him. From now on, I'd be quieter.

I tiptoed to my bedroom when I noticed Mutti sitting like a statue behind Vati's desk. She held a glass in her hand and seemed far away.

"Why are you still up?" she asked, noticing me. "It's after nine."

"Forgot to pee. What are you doing?"

When she didn't answer, I went on. "Herr Huss scares me."

Shaking her head, Mutti headed for the window and lifted the blackout shade. "You didn't bother him, did you?"

"He's horrible. I don't want to have anything to do with him."

The air raid siren began to wail. For a second I stood frozen, watching Mutti leap from the window into the bedroom and return with Burkhart on her arm. Nearly four, he was old enough to walk, but Mutti carried him everywhere.

Air raid warnings were no longer an empty threat. German cities were bombarded on a large scale, what was later confirmed by the Royal Air Force as *morale bombing*, the widespread bombing of inner cities intended to 'break' the morale of the German people. As if people like Mutti and I would've been able to stop Hitler's madness.

"Quick! To the basement!" Mutti shouted over the din of the siren.

I kept my eyes on Mutti's back as we hurried downstairs. The noise drilled into my body, my heart thumping in my neck and my bones reverberating with the sound.

In my haste, I slid on the concrete steps and crashed onto the stone tread in front of Huss's door, the fall sucking the air from my lungs.

Hot knives stabbed my spine as the sirens stopped. Eyes blurry with tears, I sat up slowly. My head swam. In the distance there was thunder. Those were the bombs Mutti talked about. I leaned against the stone step. Panic kept me in place as securely as if I'd been tied down. The thunder grew bolder. I glanced up at my neighbor's door, worried he might appear, worried he might pull me into his place.

I looked at my fingers, then my feet in the scuffed shoes—I was an island on the cold steps. As my breath returned to normal and each second stretched to eternity, I began to comprehend that this was my body, my life. That there was separation between me and Mutti and Burkhart and each of us took individual steps. And that I was ultimately...alone.

Getting to my knees, I hummed, "*Ein Männlein steht im Walde ganz still und stumm.*" I'd learned the song in first grade and Vati used to sing with me.

I looked back at the door with the milky glass. Nothing moved. With a sigh I straightened, ignoring the ache in my back. My legs felt as soft as the jello Mutti used to make.

"Lilly?" Mutti called from the cellar.

"I'm coming." I commanded my feet to take each step slowly. As I descended into the basement, the explosions grew muffled in tune with my pulsing spine.

Mutti held out a blanket. "Why aren't you answering? What happened?"

"I fell."

"Are you all right? You'll need to be more careful."

"My back hurts."

"I'll look at it once we get upstairs. It's too dark down here."

"When is Vati coming home?" I asked looking around carefully, the gelatin in my legs firming. Huss was nowhere to be seen.

Mutti shrugged, her lips set in a firm line. I knew better

than to say any more.

The entrance door opened and I quickly sat up in bed. Vati's voice floated into the room. I had to be dreaming.

"Luise?"

Then Mutti said something and Burkhart cried out. I flew to the door. "Vati!"

My father stood hugging Mutti while my brother held on to his leg. "Hallo, Lilly." Vati extended one arm to embrace me. "Look how you've grown."

As we settled in the kitchen, I noticed the stubble of beard on his face. He looked thinner, his uniform and boots sprinkled with mud.

"I missed you." I climbed on his lap. "Will you stay home now?"

Vati shook his head, his eyes serious. "We aren't done yet." He glanced at Mutti. "I've got great news, though. Did you hear about the *Führer's* new children's program?"

"Sending kids to the countryside?" my mother said.

"They've organized camps and host families so our children can live without bombs, study better and eat well." Vati straightened, distractedly petting my head like you'd pet a stranger's dog. "I found a family for Lilly. Since she's only nine, she can live with them. It's just for a few months until we've sorted out this war. It'll free you up, Luise."

I slid off his knee. What was Vati talking about?

"Where do they live?" Mutti said.

"*Thüringen* in the east. It's all arranged. Lilly will leave this weekend."

"Vati?" I cried, my insides twisting. Where was Thuringia? "I don't want to leave."

"It'll be fun," Vati said. "You'll get to eat better and be safe there."

"But Vati," my eyes filled with tears, "I live here."

"Of course, you do. It'll be only for a short time."

I fervently shook my head. A great big cloud descended on me. Vati was lying again. Though I knew by now what a lie was, I didn't want to believe it. Surely, I'd misread the signs. Made a mistake.

I stomped my foot. "I'm not going!"

"Don't be silly, Lilly," Mutti said. "It sounds like a perfect plan to me. Remember how you fell tonight when the bombers came? You won't have to be afraid anymore." The pressure in my head grew. Mutti was lying, too.

"I don't care." I placed my hands on Vati's. "Please, Vati, let me stay."

"I'm sorry, Lilly, it's settled."

CHAPTER FIVE

Lilly

The train station at the Solingen *Hauptbahnhof* bustled with families. Children ran and screamed, some cried, their parents chatting and trying to look happy. Whistles blew as trains arrived and departed, sucking streams of youngsters away or expelling new crowds onto the platform.

I struggled to keep up while my parents searched for the correct platform. Elbows shoved and pushed. Though it was sunny outside, my body felt frozen in the shade of the roof. For three days I'd tried to convince Vati I needed to stay home. To no avail.

"Here it is—third class." Mutti pointed at the rust-colored carriage with the number three painted on the side. I followed her gaze to the train car that would carry me away from all I'd known.

The train headed east to *Erfurt* and from there to *Arnstadt*, a small town to the south.

"Let's go, Lilly." Vati sounded impatient. "We don't want to miss it." *As if he were going.* I ordered myself not to cry, but my eyes didn't obey. Tears dripped off my chin, my cheeks icy.

I followed Vati into the carriage. "Here is your seat."

"I'm coming," I said, my voice swallowed by a whistle blowing.

As I struggled to squeeze onto the bench and Vati hugged me, I realized Mutti had not followed.

"You're a big girl now," Vati said. "You can help make Germany strong. Work hard, help your foster mother and one day

24

you'll become a mother just like Mutti…" Vati continued. I didn't hear what else he said because I concentrated on remembering the sound of his voice.

It is a strange thing, the quality and timbre of a voice. After a while, the mind plays tricks, and no matter how we press replay in our heads, we cannot recall what we heard years ago.

He was gone before I managed another word. Other kids leaned out the window by my seat and though I tried to catch a glimpse of my parents, every inch of the glass was plastered with waving, screaming and kissing children.

I thought I heard Mutti yelling, "We'll see you on Christmas."

The train lurched. I slumped into my seat, thinking they hadn't mentioned when I'd return home. Christmas was months away, and tears flowed once more. I didn't pay attention to the other children who were stuffed next to me. Some talked excitedly, exchanging names and what little they knew of their new homes.

I stared out the window where scenes raced by in rapid succession: military convoys clogging streets, woods and farmland dotted with red-clayed roofs and whitewashed buildings, church steeples green with patina, gardens with orderly rows of beans and berry bushes, flowerpots brimming red and golden, and the ragged silhouettes of bombed homes.

Certain of its destination, the train chugged me away. Somewhere in the back of my mind, I wished for it to jump off its tracks. I didn't want it to be so sure and fast. I wanted it to halt and reverse—to take me home.

My thoughts grew disconnected, whisked apart like the locomotive's steam in the wind. Vati reading to me in the kitchen, Mutti holding my baby brother after they came home from the hospital, pulling Mutti to Wiesner, the toy store after my birthday, the doll, Inge, gone from the display window…vanished from my life like Vati.

The train whispered with iron voices, the vibrations lulling me to sleep.

Someone tugged at my sleeve. "Little girl, the train is arriving." A young woman pointed at the piece of paper pinned to my chest. I jumped as the realization of my journey flooded me with new dread. "Come on, I'll help you find your foster parents."

The train station was mayhem. Children and families

mingled, but the dynamic was different. Instead of parents sadly sending off their children, strangers were searching for their visitors. Once in a while, a shout rang out as a foster mother discovered her charge. A troop of Hitler youth marched past, collecting boys for camp. Everything blurred into a glob of colors, bodies running and voices mixing.

"What's your name?" The young woman from the train bent low, her face inches away. She wore bright red lipstick, the kind my mother liked. I could smell her perfume… roses.

"I'm Lilly Kronen," I answered. It came out almost in a whisper.

The woman smiled and took my hand. "Let's find your new family." We stopped several times while she chatted with waiting families. I watched the steam locomotive belch a cloud of smoke as my train slowly left the station.

"I'm Frau Flug. Welcome to *Arnstadt*." The woman in front of me smiled, the corners of her mouth reluctantly tugging upward and away from the drooping lines of her face. She looked old, her skin a sea of wrinkles as if a piece of colorless fabric has been scrunched together.

I felt stiff and awkward. Mutti was no picnic, but this woman smelled like mothballs. "*Guten Tag.*"

"Please take my hand."

I stuffed my fingers into my pockets. "I'm too old for that."

Frau Flug seemed disappointed. "Fine, have it your way, but stay close to me."

The town was small and we soon arrived on *Waldstraße*. Yellow brick walls framed a small garden where hedges and flowers had been forced into an angular pattern of green and white. A one-story home squatted in its middle, windows hidden behind pale yellow shutters.

"Here we are," Frau Flug said, unlocking the front door. "Let me show you your room."

The narrow bed, hidden underneath a comforter, filled most of the space. A dark landscape in oil hung above. An airless brown curtain covered the window.

"You can put your clothes in here." Frau Flug opened the dresser at the foot of the bed. "You want me to help you?"

"I can do it myself."

Frau Flug glanced at her watch. "Fine, I have to start dinner. Herr Flug will be home soon. We always eat at six o'clock...on the dot." She turned to face me. "Remember you can't open the window. We must keep the house hidden, just in case."

I nodded and began unpacking. Unsure of what to do next, I entered the kitchen. Several pots bubbled on the stove and I felt the familiar sting of hunger.

"You can wash up in there." Frau Flug pointed toward a door. "Herr Flug likes it when children have clean hands." Glad to be hidden once more, I disappeared in the tiny bathroom.

"Don't forget," Frau Flug urged when we heard the front door open a few minutes later. "Speak only, if you're spoken to. Herr Flug doesn't like loud children."

Taking great care to brush off my dress, I followed Frau Flug to the dining room. Herr Flug was already seated at the head of the highly polished oak table now set for three. Everything about him was long and thin, the narrow upper body matched by a face with deep vertical lines.

His eyes were surprisingly dark, deep set under gray, bushy eyebrows. He wore his hair short, shaved above the ears and parted on top, copying the style worn by Hitler. Except for the missing mini moustache, he looked a lot like the photo of Hitler above the credenza. Folds of skin hung over the edge of his collar and I watched in fascination as his Adams apple moved up and down underneath the loose skin.

Vati had told me Herr Flug was the principal of the local elementary school. I noticed the red band and swastika symbol on his upper arm, the same kind Herr Huss wore when he left the house.

Despite the heaviness in my body, I looked forward to eating. Herr Flug followed my every move as I climbed on one of the dining chairs. Bowls heaped high with potatoes, green beans and roasted meat in gravy appeared as I searched for clues when I could start eating.

"Hungry, are you?" Herr Flug's voice carried easily despite the whisper.

My breath caught. "Yes, I, we don't get much," I stammered. How could I explain to this man the constant rumbling that made my insides hurt, the lines at the rations office, and Mutti trying to stretch meals from one week to the next?

"Let's pray." Herr Flug lowered his head. I closed my eyes, peeking off and on as my host labored on. Saliva threatened to spill from my mouth, at last forcing me to swallow. A gurgle escaped my throat just when Herr Flug finished his prayer.

"Excuse me." A look at Frau Flug told me I'd failed the first test.

The boiled potatoes were overcooked and mushy, the gravy lumpy and the roast tough, but I didn't care. In my nervousness, I ate fast, barely looking up at the two strangers. By the time dessert came, chocolate pudding wiggling toward me on a glass plate, my stomach revolted.

Willing myself to ignore the milky smell of the pudding, I concentrated on a spot on the immaculate tablecloth.

The heaving got worse, bile rising from my throat like vinegar.

"You don't like pudding?" Herr Flug plunged his spoon deep into the dish.

"My stomach hurts."

At last Frau Flug spoke. I wondered why she'd been silent all through the meal. "Why don't you get ready for bed?"

"You aren't ill, child?" Herr Flug said, a vertical frown between his brows. "You don't want to make us sick." He looked at me as if I were a nasty insect filled with unmentionable germs.

Had I not felt so terrible I would've thought it funny.

Instead I nodded. The rumbling in my stomach grew along with visions of me vomiting all over the perfect table. I jumped up, dislodging my chair and ran out. Trying to remember where the bathroom was, my stomach began to somersault.

After throwing up, I changed and climbed into bed. I dug beneath the comforter and wished never to emerge again. My body ached, my last thought of Vati sitting at the kitchen table in another world.

The veins on Frau Flug's hands moved beneath her skin like blue worms. I didn't want them to touch me, yet I scolded myself for rejecting her. She reminded me of a stick, all wooden and hollow. Oddly, she also reminded me of Mutti and her refusal to be close to me. Disappointment spread through me when I realized I couldn't stand Frau Flug's hugs. The more I rejected my host, the sooner I'd go home. I smiled grimly when she became curt and stopped trying.

School was a different matter.

I struggled to fit in, but the local children teased me about my worn and unshapely dresses. They called me names—the poor girl from the city—their whispers loud in my ears. I hated being an outsider. My thoughts returned constantly to my friend Lydia, who'd stayed home with her mother.

Herr Flug was so imposing, I never spoke in his presence. The words simply didn't form and I was glad when his cold gaze passed over me. I learned he was in the NSDAP party, and because he ran the school, didn't have to enlist.

Every night he listened to the *Volksempfänger* radio, another one of Hitler's inventions. Every family I knew owned one.

Right now they were commenting on the army's advances.

"Wonder if they bombed Solingen yet," Herr Flug whispered to his wife. I was in the middle of setting the table and almost dropped the plates when I heard my hometown mentioned. I didn't listen to Frau Flug's answer but from then on I worried.

Every night, I thought of Mutti and what would happen if she died. Would I have to stay here forever? The thought was so unbearable that I had trouble sleeping. And there was Vati, who fought some place far away. Now I always hovered near the radio, ready to listen to the news, heart pounding in my throat.

Five weeks into my stay, I received a letter from my parents. They'd gone to Berlin on invitation from the government. Mutti had enclosed a photo of the three of them smiling at me.

I stomped to my room, cheeks flushed with anger. Not trusting myself, I stuffed the letter under my pillow because I wanted to tear it to shreds. They were living happily without me.

I had to find a way to get home.

An opportunity soon presented itself. Just like my parents, the Flugs were creatures of habit and strict schedules. Every afternoon after returning from school, Herr Flug emptied his pockets onto the sideboard in the kitchen and took the seal ring off his hand.

The following night, I kept myself awake reading *Pucki's First Grade* by Magda Trott, a series about the daughter of a forest ranger who gets into lots of adventures. It was one of the few things I liked about Frau Flug who'd bought all twelve volumes just for me, something my own mother would never have done.

As soon as I heard the Flugs enter their bedroom, I tiptoed into the living room. Feeling around in the dark, I took the wallet and ring and hid them under my mattress.

The next morning I went to school as usual. Dinner was exactly at six o'clock. When I appeared with washed hands, Herr Flug's conversation with his wife abruptly stopped.

"How was school?" Frau Flug said, the lid beneath her right eye twitching.

I shrugged, dipping my spoon into the soup. "Fine."

"Not happy here, are you?" I felt Herr Flug's dark-eyed stare burn a hole into my skull.

I kept my gaze on the bowl. "I miss my parents."

Herr Flug threw his spoon on the table. "They didn't teach you any manners. I was told you came from a respectable family. Otherwise I would've never…it was all a lie."

I sat up straight. "My family *is* respectable!"

Frau Flug patted her husband's arm. "Lilly, you wouldn't know—"

Herr Flug shook off his wife's hand. "Let me take care of this. It's a straight question. This is my house and I have a right to know.

"Lilly," he said, his eyeballs drilling into me, "have you seen my wallet?"

"Nnnno," I mumbled.

"Look at me, child. Look me straight in the eye." Herr Flug's voice was strained.

"No!" I shouted.

"Listen to this." Herr Flug addressed his wife. "If you weren't barren, we'd have children of our own instead of this…this!" I watched in fascination the spittle fly off Herr Flug's lower lip. I felt a bit sorry for Frau Flug, who was sobbing into a pink handkerchief. I later figured out why Herr Flug had been so nasty to his wife. Frau Flug had failed the most important contribution to the Reich, bearing a bunch of kids.

Herr Flug smacked down a fist. "She's guilty, if you ask me."

I kept sitting at the table as he marched to my room, Frau Flug running after him. My heart pounded and my legs refused to move.

"You thankless child!" Herr Flug stood in the door, his voice quivering in fury. "We take you into our home and this is how you thank us?"

Even with my eyes down, I saw Herr Flug's hands opening and closing below his long arms, his fingers twitching with suppressed rage. It wouldn't matter if they beat me. It was worth it. They'd surely send me away now.

A week passed, then another, and nothing happened. I now ate alone in the kitchen but was still required to go to school. With all the time spent inside, my reading slowly improved. Every afternoon I escaped along with the heroes in my books.

"You can pack your things tonight," Frau Flug said one evening as she put a plate of mashed potatoes, white cabbage and fried sausage in front of me. "I'll take you to the train in the morning."

Once Frau Flug left, I stuffed myself. I was smiling.

When the train arrived in Solingen the next afternoon, Mutti waited for me. "What did you do?" she said, giving me an angry pat on the cheek. "Why did you steal from the good people that took you in?" Mutti shook her head. "You've never done anything like this!"

"I wanted to come home."

Mutti adjusted the collar of my coat and nodded, "You gained a little weight. We better hurry." She placed a hand on my back and guided me toward the exit with such speed, I barely kept up. "This is a dangerous time."

"Is Vati home?" I asked.

"Vati is on his way to Russia."

CHAPTER SIX

Günter: Spring 1942

Mother scanned the *Tageblatt* for the latest news and obituaries. "They're telling us to use the new bunker. It says to seek immediate cover during air raids."

I was more interested in the lone pot on the stove. "Helmut and I saw it yesterday. It's nasty. What's for dinner?"

Like mushrooms, bunkers had sprung up all over town. In our neighborhood, Brühl, the new bunker was a five-story monstrosity of concrete and reinforced steel.

I didn't mention I'd gotten sick to my stomach when Helmut closed the bunker's door. It was dim inside, and the walls seemed like they were moving in on me. The few window slits weren't enough to see out or allow sufficient airflow, just enough to give the illusion of a way out. I couldn't breathe. Shadows crept along the walls like ghosts, demanding my soul. The white enamel bunks along the walls reminded me of hospital beds.

"Barley soup." Mother looked up. "What do you mean you saw it?"

"We stopped by. The bunker is dark and stinky."

"Better that than bombs on the house." Mother's forefinger traced the article in the paper. "They're talking of total war. I thought we were already doing that." She sighed. "Göbbels says Germany can deal with the truth, that we're strong. We need to fight England and the Russians and it will shorten the war. I'll believe that when I see it."

"I wish *Vater* would come home," I said. "He'd know what to do. Or at least he'd help us find food." "It doesn't look like he'll be back anytime soon. Not according to the news." Mother folded the paper and smoothed a hand over the small stack of letters piled on the table.

My father had written regularly until a few months ago. We thought he remained in Norway and, aside from a few skirmishes with the locals, hadn't seen any fighting. I was glad my father was in the north rather than Russia as the paper now listed pages of notices of dead soldiers from the Eastern Front.

Though we sometimes visited my uncles' families—my father had three brothers—my cousins and aunts struggled just like we did. We weren't exactly close and the lack of food made it impossible to join in celebration. So, we stuck to ourselves, each family trying to make it through the day, one at a time.

"Do you think we'll get another package soon?" I asked. I missed the rich food my father used to send. In Norway he'd befriended a shopkeeper who loved to drink, so my father had traded his schnapps rations for cans of elk meat, sardines and herring in oil, smoked fish, butter, dried sausage and fragrant yellow cheese. Anger roiled my stomach when I imagined some other family feasting on our supplies.

"It's been at least three months. Looks like we have to fend for ourselves."

"Helmut and I will scrounge after school."

"Please be careful. People shoot when you take things."

I grinned. "Surely we can find a few potatoes."

Mother closed the paper and patted my younger brother on the head. "Come on, Siegfried, we better pack a suitcase so we're ready for the bunker."

My stomach growled when I went to bed. Our bread was already gone and new rations unavailable till Monday. I dreamed of my father who stood on a rowboat, waving at me. A rope hung from the tip of his rifle and dangled in the water. "Want to fish?" my father kept asking.

Sirens screamed, and I sat up with a start. "Want to fish?" my father's voice echoed.

Mother turned on the light. "Quickly."

I rubbed my eyes. "I'm going to the basement."

"We'll try the bunker. It's safer."

"But Mutter—"

I looked at Hans who was yanking a shirt over his head.

"You going with me?" I asked.

"Let's go." Mother jingled the house key. "Now. Both of you."

I shook my head. Who cared that the door was locked when our house was bombed anyway.

In the darkness outside, I could make out people running. We passed Frau Baumann from next-door hobbling along with a cane. Ahead, the bunker loomed. Like a mouth, its doors gaped open ready to swallow me. People pushed and shoved me forward. As we rushed through the door, a suitcase hit me in the knee from behind and somebody stepped on my heel. The faint odor of paint mingled with the smell of people in fright, a mixture of sweat, unwashed clothes and something underneath, something deeper and rancid—raw fear.

"Over here." Mother pointed at a spot on a bunk. More people crowded in. Beds filled, the spaces in-between, the floors. Many stood. Somewhere in the background bellows cranked to pump air into the bunker. Still, the air was thick with too many lungs competing for too little oxygen. Sweat dripped from my forehead, and yet I felt cold. Hundreds of people blurred in the gloom, trapping me.

I tried to get off the bed but there was no room. Every inch of floor space was covered with frightened humanity. The doors sealed with a bang, reverberating through the stone floor.

"I can't breathe," I managed, my chest tight as if I'd run a fifty-meter sprint. "I need to go outside."

"We have to wait until they sound the safe alarm." Mother was clutching our suitcase in one arm, Siegfried in the other.

Hans patted my arm. "Calm down."

"I need to go outside *now*," I was saying when the sound of explosions reached my ear. An exclamation of fear escaped the people around me, a collective sigh of terror.

"Günter, you can't," Mother whispered. "The doors are locked."

Ignoring her, I stood up on the bed and stepped on somebody's hand.

"Idiot," a woman yelled, her eyes glittering in anger. "Stay seated." She held a cross in her hand, rubbing it over and over.

34

"Sorry."

"Stay put." Like iron vises, hands seized my shoulders from behind and shoved me back on the bed.

I wanted to scream, but there was no air in my lungs. I had to concentrate on my breath or I'd pass out. In, out, in, out. The air turned thicker, an invisible fog laced with lead. The faint noise of plane engines vibrated through the walls. It was impossible to tell where they were or what direction they were headed, yet some people still looked up as if they could see through iron and stone. Explosions began to thunder, ten storms unleashed at once.

Somebody whimpered as blast followed blast. The air stopped in my lungs, refusing to move through my throat. Who cared about the explosions? I needed air. In, out. The bunker was a coffin, its walls moving, pushing against me, taking my breath and turning everything black. Nothing mattered, not even the bombs hitting homes. In, out.

By the time the siren buzzed the all clear, I was ready to throw up. Like molasses, the crowd moved slowly, too slow for me. I had to get out now. Not waiting for Mother, I squeezed through the endless bodies.

Legs trembling, I stumbled outside, filling my lungs with cool night air. A few stars twinkled above, distant and cold. No matter what Mother said, I'd never return.

Around me people vanished into the darkness. Eyes to the ground, we returned home, worried about what awaited us. Even though my house was unharmed, my gut told me that nothing was quite the same—something beyond our view had begun to crumble.

CHAPTER SEVEN

Lilly: May 1943

It was a bright day at the end of May except for a haze brewing on the horizon. After a third record cold winter, spring had arrived reluctantly. Daffodils and purple crocuses still bloomed in the front yard and the young leaves of the beech tree glowed crimson.

I was wiping down the living room table, sofa and windows. The couch with its yellow cushions still reeked of smoke. Last night Mutti had had guests. As usual I'd peeked through my bedroom door.

They were all strangers, and Mutti's voice had floated above the rest, loud and animated. A woman sang something while the deep baritones of men reverberated through the walls. How could Mutti enjoy herself when Vati was away? I squeezed out the cloth and slapped it on the floor, spraying water all over the linoleum. It felt wrong, this cheeriness. It was as though Mutti was working hard to forget about Vati.

Working my way around the room, I daydreamed of Vati's return. He would embrace me and swing me through the air, just like he used to. Three years had passed since he left and the memory of him was fading. I don't know when it happened, but one day I just couldn't remember what his voice sounded like. It scared me because it felt like a part of him was gone from my life. In reality, all of him had long gone.

So I clung to the things I remembered best. The way he'd sat behind his desk, bent over his files. The way he'd held his fountain pen, carefully writing in a neat script, and the smell of his cologne.

I always took longest to clean Vati's desk, sometimes pausing to sit on his chair. Removing the leftover bottle of schnapps, I wiped the desk now bare except for the leather pad. Inside the top drawer sat Vati's folders as if it were just a matter of days until he'd return. Wiping carefully, I dusted the items inside the drawer, then rested my cheek on the leather pad.

When I opened the window, Burkhart was playing with a toy truck near the entrance to our yard while Mutti swept the sidewalk. I cringed. Herr Huss leaned against the fence next to her.

I couldn't tell what they were saying, but Mutti smiled and nodded as Huss patted her forearm. Something about the way he touched her gave me a sick feeling and I wanted to shout at him to let her go.

All of a sudden Mutti's expression turned grim. Herr Baum lumbered toward them, his legs stiff on unbending knees. I leaned farther out the window as Mutti mumbled something like "thinks he's so smart" to Huss.

"They bombed *Wuppertal*," Herr Baum yelled, nodding in the direction of our neighboring town ten kilometers away.

When neither Huss nor Mutti answered, he continued, "The black ash...they say, it's from the people that burned. It's covering the land like a shroud." He paused, catching his breath. "My sister wrote from Berlin. They're getting bombed up there. They'll turn this country into a graveyard."

I carefully inspected the sidewalk and lawn, imagining a black cloud descending over the house. Despite our growing food shortages and increased bomb alarms, it was hard to imagine such destruction.

"I'd be careful making such sweeping statements," Huss said.

Mutti nodded. "At least we have the bunker nearby." She turned her head, looking at the enormous structure looming less than a hundred meters away.

Huss smiled at Mutti. "Our Führer thinks of everything."

It reminded me of Vati's words before he left. What sort of man allowed bombs to fall on his people.

Herr Baum shrugged. "My knees are too stiff to make it before the doors close. I just sit in the basement." He squinted at

Huss and stepped closer to Mutti. "Any news from your husband?"

Mutti bit her lip. I knew it well. Every time I asked when Vati was coming home, Mutti got this look, a mix of anger and frustration. Lately, I hadn't asked.

"Nothing but an occasional letter." Mutti wiped the sweat from her forehead. Unable to get haircuts, she'd put her hair in a bun. The government now barred hairdressers from serving women with hair more than six inches.

"Our army has been making great strides," Huss's gaze fell on Herr Baum, his tone cold. "Too bad you're so slow or you'd be first up at the front."

To my surprise Herr Baum ignored him and waved at me. I ducked, but of course it was too late.

"Lilly, I thought you were cleaning," Mutti shouted.

I reappeared in the window. "Almost finished, Mutti."

"If it's all right," Herr Baum said, "I could use Lilly's help."

Mutti seemed to waffle, but at last she nodded. "Just for a bit."

No longer listening, I raced downstairs.

"I need you back here in an hour," Mutti said as soon as I came to a stop outside. You'll have to watch Burkhart while I pick up our food." She turned to Herr Baum. "Can you believe these rations? Four and a half pounds of bread and a half pound of sauerkraut for an entire week." She shook her head.

The supply situation had indeed gone from bad to worse. We had ration cards that bought nothing, entire sheets of coupons for potatoes, sugar and flour, but the stores were depleted, shelves empty. More shops closed, their workers needed at the front and for the production of arms.

Waiting in line at the bakery, I'd heard people whisper that the war was lost after the winter in Stalingrad. They muttered to each other, figuring I didn't hear. I also knew people caught listening to enemy radio transmissions were shot, and that Sophie and Hans Scholl, the leaders of the student resistance group *White Rose,* had been executed.

Of course, the propaganda continued. Cheered on by fanatical followers, Goebbels had announced *total war,* meaning that the Reich was ready to engage with more enemies more forcefully while the home front—us—was supposed to provide every resource still available. That meant women entered the production of arms, well, all remaining resources went into the support of the army. The bleeding out of the country had reached a new level.

"Surely things aren't that bad," Huss said with a tight smile. As if by chance, he patted the red armband with the swastika. He was all decked out this morning in a brown suit and long black boots. "You should watch the new movie *Baron Münchhausen*. It'll take your mind off things."

Waving a dismissive hand, Herr Baum turned away, mumbling, "What nonsense. Not enough to live, too much to die. We starved two terrible long winters during World War One. It'll come to that. You'll see." He abruptly turned to me, his voice softening. "You ready, Lilly?"

I nodded, trying to match my steps to the old man's.

Behind me Huss mumbled to Mutti, "He is lucky I don't turn him in. If he weren't so old and decrepit, he'd be arrested."

I don't think Herr Baum heard him. At the time I didn't realize how brave the old man was in the face of the obvious mole burrowed in our home.

"How's school?"

"Boring. Our new teacher is really old." I hesitated, worried Herr Baum would be angry. When he chuckled I went on, "I like getting lunch. Potatoes and parsnips, and sometimes milk."

"I see."

To my surprise, Herr Baum unlocked the wooden gate to his yard. I had never been in the back.

"Let's go around," he said, closing the door behind us. A twenty-foot apple tree shaded the lawn, which was cut short except for a patch of long grass dotted with dandelions and daisies. A wooden table and two chairs sat next to the house. I scanned the yard to discover the work that needed to be done.

Herr Baum stopped in front of a wooden box near the basement door.

"Over here, Lilly."

To this day I remember the feeling of pleasure, the warmth that spread through my middle like a bowl of soup on a winter night. A smoky gray rabbit squatted inside the enclosure. It had long floppy ears and white spots on its front paws, and its dark brown eyes peered at me.

"A bunny," I whispered, placing a palm against the wire

part of the cage.

Herr Baum unlatched the door. "Do you want to hold it?"

Softness touched me as the rabbit snuggled into my arms. "It's warm." I rubbed my cheek against the fur.

"Her name is Anna," Herr Baum said. "I was hoping you'd help me take care of her. She needs to be fed and handled every day. She'll need cleaning, too."

"I'll help you." I couldn't take my eyes of the sweetness in my arm. "I'll come every day after school."

"She loves dandelions." Herr Baum pointed toward the patch of long grass. "Why don't you pick some? I'll hold her for you."

I rushed to pick clumps of yellow flowers and leaves until my fingers turned green. "Is this enough?"

Herr Baum's eyes twinkled. I had never seen him smile before.

"That's plenty. Here, put it inside the cage so Anna can eat."

I stuffed the pile inside the box. He carefully put back the rabbit and latched the wire loop.

"How about a piece of cornbread? I'll bring it out here and we can eat with Anna." Without waiting for an answer, Herr Baum disappeared inside the basement door.

"Does Anna like cornbread?" I asked through bulging cheeks a few minutes later. We had pulled the two chairs in front of the enclosure, watching the rabbit.

"Anna only eats greens and vegetables. She likes carrots, but I don't have any right now."

"Where did you get her?"

"My younger sister raises them on her farm and gave me one." I looked at the old man whose voice had turned grave. "One more thing."

"What is it?"

Herr Baum looked over his shoulder as if somebody were listening from behind the apple tree. "Promise me to keep this a secret," he whispered. "It's just between you and me."

I fervently shook my head up and down. "I won't tell anyone."

"Lilly?" Mutti called from a distance, her voice irritated.

Herr Baum straightened to collect the plates. "You better

go. We don't want to get you in trouble."

I rushed toward the gate when I remembered something. "How will I get in?"

Herr Baum followed. "I'll leave it unlocked during the day. You can visit her anytime.

Make sure you come alone."

I smiled as something wonderful embraced my heart. "*Danke*, I'll be back tomorrow."

CHAPTER EIGHT

Günter: May 1944

Another May arrived with warmth and blue skies. Flowers bloomed and fresh green covered the land. I always loved spring and tried to tell myself that things were getting better, but that only lasted until I saw the pinched faces around me. Everyone was waiting for news from their loved ones—us included. One of my uncles had died somewhere on the Eastern Front. Seeing my cousins and aunts crying at the funeral made me wonder if my father would be next. He hardly wrote these days and when he did, it was a reminder of how much I missed him. A constant picking at a wound that refused to heal.

Mother had developed a worry line on her forehead, reaching down to her nose. Hans was grumpy most of the time. His voice had changed, sinking deeper then jumping up and lowering itself again.

"Why is he so cranky?" I said to Helmut as we hiked the woods in search of something to eat. "I ask him a harmless question like what he's up to and he about bites my head off."

"Don't know. Maybe he's getting a boner."

"What's that?"

"You know, when your dick gets big and... you know."

My cheeks burned, but Helmut didn't seem to notice. "I see," I managed.

"It happens when you dream. It feels really good and your underwear gets sticky." Helmut wrinkled his forehead but wouldn't say anymore.

I remembered the crude jokes from school and had experienced the occasional dream myself. No way would I say anything. I'd find a book to read about it, though with all the school closings it was getting more and more difficult to get into the library.

It didn't really matter anyway. I just wanted to score food or find something valuable to trade. These days rations were so short that my stomach rumbled constantly.

We were hiking along the narrow valley of the Wupper River where grassland, small farms, a few houses and gardens competed for space. On both sides of the valley, oak and beech, cedars and firs shaded the steep slopes.

Helmut eyed a black and white bull grazing on the other side of the barbed wire. "We better walk around. That fellow looks mean."

I nodded toward the gray band of water in the distance. "Maybe we can catch fish."

"What're we going to catch them with?"

"No need to be so negative. You have a better idea?"

"No."

We walked on silently. Lately we disagreed a lot. It wasn't really arguing, just a general mood of discontent. I couldn't quite put my finger on it, but I was angry most of the time. It wasn't just the lack of food. My entire life was going to pits, school interrupted, the paper full of doomsday notices and almost no news from my father.

Helmut wasn't doing any better. In addition to being stick-thin, he'd picked up smoking and was always on the lookout for the next drag. But cigarettes were expensive and rare. I, for one, would've much preferred a nice piece of bread with butter and sausage or cheese. We had no fat to eat anymore, not even margarine and certainly no oil or butter.

I'd always enjoyed being outside, exploring the woods and hiking the hills and valleys. Instead, the intense afternoon sun stung my eyes, and my stomach felt like an empty pouch.

Helmut pointed at a field. "What about the fruit trees?" The small orchard behind one of the houses looked peaceful, but the pears and apples were still small and green.

"They aren't worth eating," I said, not bothering to stop.

I'd stolen unripe fruit before, but even after cooking they were too sour. Mother, not wanting to waste them, had added them to the bread and nearly ruined the dough.

"Do you have a better idea?"

"Let's check the restaurant. Maybe they're throwing out leftovers."

The Rüden restaurant, named after a famous dog who'd rescued a wealthy duke, sat adjacent to the Wupper river and was a popular destination for foot-worn hikers. A long time ago, I'd been here with my parents, happily chasing my brothers around the tables. We didn't have much money even then, but we had each other. No—we'd had normalcy. A normal outing on a Sunday afternoon. The new normal was bombs and starvation and losing fathers in the war.

As we neared the restaurant, I knew instantly something was wrong. It was quiet, too quiet, the side yard deserted. Not even a bucket or a flower pot sat out.

"Let's look in back," Helmut said.

We peeked around the corner. The restaurant garden was empty except for a couple of tables, three chairs tossed alongside, the once white paint gray and chipped. Grass covered part of the furniture. The bleakness of the garden sent shivers up my spine. Everything I knew was beginning to look rotten and dead.

"We might as well go."

"Who's there?" a gravelly voice called out.

I turned. For once, I couldn't muster the energy to run. A man studied us from a side door. At least I thought that's what he was doing because with the sun in my eyes, I only made out a silhouette. "Sorry, we were looking for something to eat."

"You boys in trouble?"

"Just hungry."

"Come here."

As I drew closer I noticed a rifle against the man's shoulder. A bandage covered his throat. Blood had soaked through and dried, making his neck look rust-colored. His right arm was missing, the sleeve of his shirt tied into a knot. How did he manage anything with one hand?

His eyes were unreadable, his face without emotion as if his features had frozen in place.

"Shouldn't we go?" Helmut whispered into my ear.

I ignored him. A strange curiosity was taking hold like seeing a circus act and wondering what crazy stunt the acrobat was going to do next. I imagined my father standing like this, with injuries to his throat and arm, and worse to the unseen parts of his soul. The idea of coming home empty-handed scared me worse than the man.

"We're looking for food," I blurted.

The man was silent for a moment and remained still as marble.

I glanced at Helmut who looked ready to bolt. Mother's voice whispered, *"Don't trust anyone. People are dangerous."*

"You live nearby?"

I nodded. Close enough. If you hiked across the hills, I'd be home in forty or fifty minutes.

"You boys want a job?" The man's voice sounded like pulling metal across a rasp. "I need help cutting wood. I'll pay in food."

"What do you have for us if we cut your wood?" I said.

"Potatoes. A bit of cheese. I used to make cheese and sausages for the restaurant."

The man disappeared in the entrance.

"You sure," Helmut said. "What if he shoots us when we're inside? He may be one of those sickos who kill for fun." He ticked his temple with a forefinger.

I hesitated. What if Helmut was right? Half of me wanted to run.

"What're you waiting for?" the man called from the inside.

"Coming," I shouted, relieved when I heard Helmut follow.

We passed through the kitchen, a giant stove with lots of burners, past tables and pots, the man's foot dragging *clunk-clunk* across the tiled floor.

"Through this door. The chopping block is to your right. You'll see the axe and saw. The wood is under the overhang. The well has good water if you're thirsty." The man's instructions sounded chopped like the wood.

I wanted to ask where he had fought, how he got injured, what his specialty had been. Most of all I wanted to ask if he knew my father. But I never said anything, not even when the man gave us bread and a cooked rutabaga. There was no butter, not even salt, but oh, it was warm, glorious heat sliding through my throat filling my insides. I could've eaten ten.

As my muscles grew tired and heavy, all I thought of were the potatoes and cheese and Mother's face when I entered the kitchen.

It was long past dinner when we headed home. Each of us carried a sack with a week's worth of potatoes and a piece of hard cheese. I cradled mine like a child. Once in a while I lifted it to my nose, sniffing the cheese, pungent and sweet at the same time. I hadn't tasted cheese in a year.

That night, I dreamed my father returned. His clothes were torn and covered in grime, his right arm was gone, covered by a knotted shirtsleeve.

CHAPTER NINE

Günter: June-August 1944

I lay on my bed watching my brother pack. Hans's face was stoic. He moved faster than usual, but his arms and legs kept bumping into things. Picture frames and clothes tumbled to the floor, and he forgot to pick them up.

I looked around the room we'd shared for as long as I could remember. How I had wanted a place to myself. Now I just wanted my brother. I'd share the room until I was an old man rather than see Hans go off like this.

"Can't you say you're sick?" I pleaded.

Hans stuffed socks into a canvas bag. "When they say you're drafted, there's no arguing."

I stared at him, wanting to say more. Why didn't he yell or complain or kick something? I could have dealt with any of it—anything but the outward calm, the acceptance of fate. Instead I just asked, "You think you'll see Father?"

"Unlikely."

"You could ask." What I really wanted to know was if Hans was scared and to remind him to be careful. In the stuffiness of our room, the words refused to come. The feeling of helplessness was paralyzing, and I knew my words meant nothing. They were a mere scratch on a mountain.

I wrapped my arms around my knees and closed my eyes. It wouldn't be the last time I wished to jump out of my skin.

In the kitchen, Mother paced back and forth. "You're only

seventeen," she wailed as she put out Hans's last breakfast, two slices of cornbread and blackberry jam we'd saved from last summer. "First your father, now you. What are we going to do? They're going to kill us all."

Hans took Mother's hand. "I'll be fine."

Watching my brother, something icy curdled my stomach. Each day The *Tageblatt* was filled with pages of obituaries, and Mother poured over them, searching for familiar names. My father had been transferred to the Eastern Front in the Balkans. He'd written once, but we'd heard nothing in months. His care packages were a distant memory.

For the rest of the meal we sat in silence, my brother's eyes shiny. Tears pressed against my skull, begging to come out.

Hans punched my arm as we headed for the door. "Stop acting like a stupid girl. Don't worry, you'll be next."

I cringed. Was that supposed to make me feel better? I felt torn between shouting an insult and hiding Hans in the attic.

We hugged and I watched my brother, trying to memorize his features. What did you say to somebody facing death? No words were right, so I said nothing.

As he took his leave, Hans's eyes, shiny with grief and longing, burned themselves into my memory like a scar.

"Just us now." Mother wiped her face.

I scanned the deserted kitchen table, my little brother watching us. At seven, he still didn't know what was going on. It was a good thing.

"I'll take care of you," I said, clearing my throat. "I'm going out to look for food." In truth, I needed time away from the apartment where everything reminded me that my family was shrinking. My father had left four years ago. I'd gotten used to that. At least I didn't always look at his empty seat now. But with Hans, it was as if a new hole had appeared in my life.

It was easier to be outdoors—to keep myself busy. Then I wouldn't think about how much I'd relied on my brother for support. Not the physical kind, but an emotional bond that had given me strength. In the absence of our father, we'd stuck together. Entering my room, I stared at the vacant bed, shadows filling its emptiness.

At that moment, I decided to stop reading the paper and listening to the radio. It was maddening to hear nothing but propaganda and listen to speeches about how we were supposed to fight for honor until the end. What did that mean anyway? All I cared about was getting Father and Hans home and food into my stomach. The only good thing was that I'd escaped the drills of the Hitler youth because I played accordion. Helmut hated every minute of it. As part of the youth band we visited hospitals and nursing homes, appeared at dances and festivals. The music allowed me to escape, if only for the time I played.

Hans wrote once and sent photos. He'd finished training and was waiting for marching orders. He looked strange in the uniform and fancy cap—older and somehow detached.

July and August were hot, water often rationed. The city's reservoir, a vast lake in good times, was nearly empty. With the schools and pools closed, I spent most of my time roaming the neighborhood with Helmut.

Thirsty and sticky from the heat, I arrived home from a fruitless search for food. I'd scoped out a row of almost ripe blueberry bushes behind a house, but people were watching and I'd given up.

Mother rushed at me, waving a letter with a swastika in the upper left corner, her eyes anxious. "You have mail."

Without comment, I ripped open the envelope. "I have to report for muster," I said frowning.

Mother sank onto the bench. She opened her mouth but nothing came out.

"I guess I don't have a choice," I mumbled more to myself. "I have to go."

That night I rolled around in my bed, staring into the darkness. I'd discovered masturbation and it occasionally helped me relax. But not tonight. Instead I wondered where I'd sleep and what the Front was like. Maybe I'd see Hans.

I imagined myself next to my father, carrying rifles and running along barbed wire fences. My father nodded at me, his face covered in black grease.

I blinked away the tears, pooling behind my closed lids and felt them dribbling down my cheeks. It was dawn before I dozed off.

Boys crowded in front of the muster office, a squat one-story building and former school on *Wiener Straße*. Most of them were classmates or neighborhood kids, bony like me with shirts patched together above high-water pants. I swallowed, but my mouth remained dry as cotton.

Even Rolf Schlüter, the loudmouth in my class, looked pale and tightlipped. I wondered if Helmut had been here earlier today. How I wished my best friend were by my side now.

Two military officers, grim and still as statues, stood guard at the entrance. They wore the traditional grayish-blue uniforms of the SS with knee-high black boots, red armbands and the zigzagged silver double S on the collar.

"Enter!" A deep voice yelled as the doors opened.

The yellow painted room would've been cheery under normal circumstances, but the vinyl of the single examination bed in the corner, the covered windows and the gray, speckled linoleum made the room stark as the halls of a morgue. A scuffed brown desk stood along the wall, the man behind it reviewing a stack of files.

An officer entered. Beneath his reddish mustache, trimmed in Hitler fashion, his lips were pressed thin and bloodless. The officer wore a military cap, his head shaven above the ears. I wondered if the man had hair as I worried that my own was too long.

"Form a line!" the officer shouted, his voice surprisingly high.

I shoved through the crowd to find a spot along the blue tape on the floor. The room turned silent.

"Strip," the officer barked. I hesitated when I felt the eyes of one of the officers narrow. I yanked down my pants, forgetting to untie my shoelaces. Because we couldn't find new ones these days, they were knotted and my shaky fingers couldn't undo them. Frustrated, I kicked off my shoes, yanking my shirt over my head at the same time. I didn't want to be last.

Next to me, Paul, a classmate of mine, was struggling with the top button on his shirt. His chapped hands trembled. One of the officers strode over, his boots loud on the linoleum. Without a word, he yanked Paul's arm down, grabbed the collar and savagely pulled at the button, which catapulted against the opposite wall. He smacked Paul across the cheek, the slap echoing in my ears.

"Maybe you'll be faster next time," the officer said. "You're an embarrassment..." His eyes narrowed as he glared at Paul. I kept staring straight, fighting the impulse to put an arm around the boy's shoulders. He was inches shorter than me and looked more like twelve than fifteen. The room had turned into a tomb when I heard another smack, followed by a sob.

"Quit your crying," the officer's voice seethed.

"Attention!" someone shouted from the door.

I risked the tiniest peek at the man in a white coat who carried a stethoscope around his neck. He looked ancient, his skin wrinkled with folds under his eyes and neck. Wisps of gray formed a thin ring of hair around his skull.

After a brief whisper with the officer, the doctor stopped in front of Paul, whose nose had begun to bleed. "Name?"

"Paul Mans," the boy whispered.

"How old are you, *Herr* Mans?" The doctor squinted at his clipboard.

"Fifteen," Paul said, his voice barely audible despite the stillness in the room.

"Louder."

"Fifteen."

"At fifteen you should be able to undress?"

"Yes." Paul tore off his shirt, an angry welt spreading across his cheek.

Handing his clipboard to the officer with the bloodless lips, the doctor walked to the beginning of the line and pulled his glasses, which had balanced at the end of his nose, closer to his eyes. Then he planted his stethoscope on the chest of the first boy. "Breathe. Again."

The other officer made notes, compared names, dates and registrations. "K.V...Approved for battle," the doctor rumbled one after another.

Two boys picked up their pants.

"Do you have permission to dress?" the officer hollered.

The boys threw down their clothes as if they were poisoned.

"Answer me!"

"No," both stammered.

"The answer is *nein, Unterscharführer.* Don't forget that you

51

are under orders of the SS now. Do I make myself clear?"

"Yes, *Unterscharführer!*" both yelled.

My throat tightened the way it did in the bunker. With every inhalation, the doctor drew closer and my breathing grew louder. If I passed out, I'd die. In...out. The doctor appeared in my peripheral vision. Not now. Breathe. I didn't feel my feet or my hands, nor did I notice the icy linoleum.

"Name?"

"Günter Schmidt."

"Breathe." The cold rim of the stethoscope slid over my chest as I sucked air. "Fit for battle."

I gulped and the doctor moved on. Why didn't Paul stop sucking up snot? He was liable to get hit again.

A higher-ranking officer entered, his chest decorated with assorted medals and stripes on his sleeve. The heels of his boots clicked as he took position in front of us. How could the man stand there and feel comfortable? None of us wore a shred of clothes.

"The Führer has asked for your help," the officer said coolly. "At last you can honor your fatherland and fight for a strong *Aryan* Germany. I assume all of you will volunteer for the Air Radio Troup?" His voice adopted a threatening tone. "Of course, you could join the *Weapons-SS* instead." Nobody spoke and I tried to figure out what I was supposed to do or say. "Members of the Weapons-SS are sent to the Front and serve in our elite units."

I suppressed a shudder. Three years and two months ago, four SS-men had shown up next door and dragged my neighbor, Herr Baumann, into a waiting car. The man had been a communist, some had whispered. Since then more and more people had disappeared, like the man with the crooked spine who'd worked at the kiosk, and the family of Jews who'd owned the department store downtown. Nobody had seen any of them since.

"But if you volunteer," the officer rambled, "You get to choose your regiment. Who will volunteer?"

One after another we raised our hands. Despite the frigid air, my skin was clammy as I slowly lifted my arm.

"Very good!" The officer's mouth curved into a smile that didn't reach his eyes. "For now your enlisting orders are to prepare yourself and be ready when called upon. You're now under the direct orders of the SS and the Führer. Dismissed!"

Without another word all but one guard left the room.

My head whirled as I dressed. I was a soldier. A knot formed in my throat, an invisible noose tightening. What did the officer mean to be ready?

I'd have to tell Mother. Today. Ignoring the excited buzz and the curious stares of my classmates, I followed Paul outside. Unlike them I didn't feel like talking. All I wanted was to run. Where to was the big question.

CHAPTER TEN

Lilly: November 4-5, 1944

When the sirens began to blare on Saturday afternoon, I was washing socks in the sink. The sound always pounded my nerves, but after five years of incessant air raid alarms, this appeared to be another false warning.

"Mutti?"

My mother emerged from her bedroom. "Let's go," she said, clutching my brother to her chest. Though he was in second grade, Mutti couldn't stop herself from carrying him around like a baby.

Hands dripping, I grabbed my suitcase. The door slammed shut behind us as we rushed downstairs and up the path to the street. The siren screeched much louder here, drilling into my head. I wanted to plug my ears, but my arms were heavy with a bag and coat.

But this time, the drone of airplanes snuffed out the sirens. Shrill and high, they buzzed like a swarm of killer bees. Only to be outdone by the whine of falling bombs. And then...explosions.

There is no way to adequately describe the high-pitched buzz and the inevitability that comes with this sound. There is no backing out, there is no running away. If you are in the wrong place, the bombs will get you.

Somewhere in the recesses of my mind, I registered the explosions coming from downtown. But unlike other times when the bombers had turned away after hitting a factory or other specific target, this time the noise continued to grow. This time they were coming for me.

I trembled, my eyes fixed on Mutti's back.

She turned and I saw her mouth open, but I could not understand her. A stitch pierced my ribs, making it hard to breathe. Fear propelled me forward—fear so powerful I felt my heart pound in my throat as I gasped for air.

The blasts roared closer together and melted into a continuous boom.

Cold metal glinted in the cobalt sky. Closer.

A huge boom, followed by a sudden gust of wind, threw me down. Glass exploded above me and struck my face. My ears rang as I scrambled to stand and get my bearings. I was confused—couldn't feel my body. As people rushed around me, their faces pale and rigid with panic, I picked up my case and followed them.

The bunker doors were open, its lights faint as a dim fire. If a bomb hit nearby, there would be no escape. Another roar.

The sound tore at me, drilled into my head like metal screws. I was shoved inside by the mob of bodies. The screeching above intensified as more bombers flew overhead, the sound muted through the bunker's walls.

Did I scream? It's the only thing I don't remember. I wouldn't have heard my own voice.

I stumbled across legs and arms, suitcases and boxes, trying to keep up with Mutti, touch her, just her sleeve or the hem of her dress. All beds full, I collapsed along the wall.

Bodies squeezed together closer than anyone would ever walk or sit. Now we touched each other. Strangers close as lovers.

I saw nothing, unable to move. Only my chest heaved. Mutti had gathered a crying Burkhart on her lap. I wanted to crawl in to join him. I wanted to let go of my tears. I didn't, though. I couldn't because I was too busy sending nasty thoughts to the pilots in the sky.

The bunker shuddered.

Cold crept through my coat. I shivered despite the heat around me. It was not the nice warmth of a fire or lying underneath a comforter. It was a stinky heat, full of sweat, hot breath and too many bodies shoved together. I closed my eyes and covered my ears. The ground moved, became liquid, as if skating on tiny wheels.

The air grew thicker, filled with dread and whimpers. I could feel it, taste it. I had heard Mutti speak about carpet bombs. We'd walked home from the store when she chatted with a neighbor, an older woman who always looked sour, as if she disapproved of life itself.

Mutti spoke in a low voice, but I'd learned to listen more closely whenever adults whispered. The neighbor mentioned bombs falling on cities in such large numbers that they covered the ground like a carpet. Such a harmless word, a piece of furnishing we all had in our houses.

I squinted through half-closed eyes as Burkhart buried his face under Mutti's arm. I pulled my legs tightly against my chest, wrapping my arms around like a ball.

I wondered where Vati was and if he was being bombed, too. And for the first time I asked myself what he did and if he was doing the bombing of some far away place.

Suddenly everything grew still.

I listened, trying to ignore the whispers. I wanted them to be quiet so I could hear. Hear the bombers.

Nothing.

I grew aware of my body, how it ached, my legs stiff and cramped. Bloody cuts covered my arms, but I didn't feel pain.

I couldn't have said if the bombing lasted five minutes or an hour. I later learned 580 bombers had dropped their load in fifteen minutes, a lethal mix of carpet bombs, steel-tipped bombs, phosphor burn bombs, and air mines.

The silence continued, my ears filled with cotton balls. I sat, unable to move despite the ache in my limbs. Maybe I would stay here forever and become one with the bunker.

"Is it over?" Burkhart asked, his voice higher than usual. The murmurs inside the room grew louder.

"I don't know." Mutti's trembling hand smoothed the hair on my brother's head. By now I was used to her one-sided affection toward by brother. It still hurt, but it was something I'd accepted and buried as another ache in my heart.

So just hearing her voice was enough. The tension in me released and I looked around. To my left and right, people straightened and peered upward as if they could see through the ceiling. I wanted to sleep and never leave.

The doors opened, fresh air filtering in as more people

arrived. Pale and shaky, they carried boxes and suitcases, pillows and blankets. I kept listening for planes but nothing was moving outside.

"Let's stay here tonight," Mutti said.

Despite my discomfort, I was glad. I'd rather starve than go outside. I didn't care that it was cold, the ground hard. I leaned against the wall and closed my eyes.

A weak November light filtered through the window slits when I awoke in the early morning. It was barely more than a shadow.

Mutti straightened. "We'd better go home."

My legs were weak from lack of sleep and the horrific air inside the bunker. My feet dragged as we walked, the suitcase a lead weight in my hand.

The air was filled with smoke. A house down the road burned, the roof collapsed under purple flames. To my relief, our home stood, but its stuccoed wall ornaments had crumbled, leaving hand-sized holes in the plaster walls. Windowpanes and frames had vaporized, green wallpaper visible inside my neighbor's living room. A piece of lace moved in the breeze like cobwebs.

Inside was worse. Glass and wood splinters covered everything, even my bed. The light looked dull and somehow fluid as it entered the glassless windows. The blackout shutters had torn away.

Mutti ran her hand through her hair as she took it all in. "What are we going to do?" she asked, more to herself than to me.

I shivered inside my coat. Our kitchen stove would be no match for the cold that had already moved in.

"What are we going to do about the windows?" I asked.

"Give me a hand," Mutti said. "We'll slide the wardrobe in front of the window. Then you sweep the floor."

I didn't want to clean, I wanted to rest. No, I wanted to leave. I longed for a safe place, a house where it was quiet, where I could play or go to school. "I want to go somewhere else."

Mutti's lips were pressed together in that certain way, and I braced myself for another outburst. This time it didn't come.

"We'll go to the city offices when they open and ask for a new place. Right now, I need your help with the firewood so we can heat water for coffee. Get us a load from the basement. Then

57

you sweep."

When Mutti said coffee, it really meant some fake roasted grains. Coffee was no longer available. I suppressed another comment, the basement nearly as much of a trap as the bunker. In the staircase I tried the light switch. It remained gloomy.

With shaky hands, I lit a candle and held my breath as I made my way downstairs, passing by my neighbor's door. Nothing stirred and I hurried past. Maybe a bomb had dropped on Huss.

The woodpile was nearly gone. I'd have to find more tomorrow.

"I wish Vati were here," I said, stuffing kindling into the stove. "He'd know what to do." For a moment I envisioned him walking into the door with an armful of supplies. If there was one thing I remembered, it was his reliability. He was always punctual, his briefcase under his arm, he'd adjust his hat in front of the mirror and leave for work. The image was replaced by him lying in a field hospital, white as dusted flour and unable to speak.

"But he isn't," Mutti snapped. She continued pacing, looking at the shredded curtains. "They won't keep out the cold. We'll move the heavier curtains from the living room and close the door. And we need wood or glass."

"This is the rest," I said. "It won't warm us if the windows are broken."

"I know, Lilly, we'll have to fix them."

We huddled around the stove, my back icy as if I were still in the bunker.

"Here." Mutti handed me a piece of bread and a carrot. "The water lines are out. We'll need to go to the well." She pointed at the bucket under the sink. "I'll show you the way and you can get it next time."

"Why can't Burkhart help?" I looked at my brother who was brushing glass shards off his wooden toy truck. It was in moments like these I felt the inferiority my mother had been nurturing in me. Even though my brother was five years younger he was always better, an exceptional human being compared to his ordinary older sister. The injustice of it rose in my throat like bile, but I swallowed it down.

"Careful, dear," Mutti said, inspecting Burkhart's palms. And to me, "He's too small. Let's go."

The street was covered in debris. Smoke rose in the

distance, but we were heading in the other direction. "Remember the way, so you know for later."

"What are we going to do about baths?" I asked. I'd always enjoyed the time by myself though lately I had to share with my brother to save water. The zinc tub was small and we had to heat pots on the stove, but it had been fun to sit in the warmth.

"We'll have to wash with well water until they repair the pipes."

We joined the line in front of the spring. The sky was hazy despite the sun. Nobody spoke. People looked scared. Some had bloody cuts. A woman in front of me bled from one ear. It was shady beneath the willows and I shivered. The November sun had no strength.

The soup we cooked for an early lunch was thin and the potatoes only half done. "You better cut wood when we return," Mutti said, "unless we find another place tonight."

"I'm tired. I want to do it tomorrow." My arm ached from the water bucket.

"Let's go then and find out about a room." I detected a note of uncertainty in Mutti's voice as she grabbed her overcoat, her breath a white cloud. Surely, many people were looking for new homes.

Schools had closed months ago and the local elementary school had been reassigned as a rations and communications office. Shreds of paper with missing person photos and wanted ads, trades, lost and found and classified ads plastered the walls.

"Lilly, look for apartment rentals while we wait in line," Mutti said as we weaved through the crowd. Nobody moved. Clothes in different states of disrepair, everyone waited in line, sitting on the floor, along the walls, the desks and stairs. The gray linoleum, still shiny and smelling of wax, was covered with glass and shreds of window framing.

I recognized one of my former classmates. Careful to keep my distance from the snaking throng of people, I asked, "how long have you been waiting?"

"All morning." The girl was my age but looked much younger. An old linen grocery bag dangled from her arm.

As I walked back to Mutti, somebody screamed and the hum of voices stopped abruptly. Everybody looked around—out the glassless windows and up—unsure whether to leave the precious spot in the waiting line. Like fly poop, dots of gray speckled the horizon, growing quickly larger.

In the darkening sky, the drone of hundreds of engines mixed with the cries of the crowd. Then followed the sound that froze my blood, the high-pitched whine of thousands of bombs dropping to earth.

The ground began to shake beneath my feet. Explosions found their targets, fell with ease through roofs and walls, and dug themselves deep into the earth, pulverizing everything in their wake.

My limbs were numb as I watched people scatter. A sound sang in my ears, of destruction, of danger. Fear made my knees soft as pudding as the air turned into something thick and unyielding, too difficult to breathe. My lungs bucked and I gulped.

"Where's the basement?" Mutti yelled, tugging my arm. At least that's what I think she said. The noise was deafening. People ran this way and that, nobody sure where to turn. An old man stumbled to the ground. I stepped on his coat and caught myself. Nobody helped. Thinking about Herr Baum, I wanted to stop and pull him up, but Mutti yanked me forward.

The basement stairs appeared to the left. Bodies pushed from behind and I grabbed Mutti's sleeve to keep from tumbling down the stairs. The hallway below was thick with people. The mob from above kept pushing. Hysterical cries echoed.

The blasts drew closer until they turned into unending roar. The stone floor beneath me vibrated and skipped. My stomach lurched as I imagined being buried down here. It was as if the earth had opened up to swallow us, punishing us for the years of terror Hitler had inflicted on neighboring countries.

I lost Mutti's hand and stood with my nose pressed against a man's wool jacket, my breath filtered through the fabric. Somebody prayed aloud. Other voices joined.

The air turned hot and poisonous. More explosions—the second wave. We waited as planes whined overhead and the carpet-bombing continued on the other side and to the south.

When it finally stopped, I felt dizzy from lack of oxygen. The man next to me moved and I was able to see Mutti on the other side.

"We'd better go," she said.

My legs wanted to buckle. "What if they return?"

"If we hear something, we'll run back down." She picked up Burkhart.

"Can't we wait a little longer?"

"Don't you remember? We need to look for a room or apartment?"

"Yes, but—"

"Enough, Lilly." Mutti turned and walked toward the stairs.

I followed, terrified to lose sight of her again. A new line had formed upstairs, but I kept listening and scanning the sky for planes. Beyond the neighboring houses, smoke billowed.

When it was finally our turn, the woman shook her head. There were no places to stay. Too many houses had been destroyed and were unlivable. We added our name to a waiting list and left.

Mutti gritted her teeth. "We'll have to manage somehow."

We stumbled past bricks, mortar, glass, broken roof tiles and tree limbs until a mountain rose in front of us.

Two houses had collapsed across from each other and though they hadn't caught fire, they had crumbled. Some of the walls had broken away. More bricks, wood framing, furniture pieces, a sink littered the street, creating a wall of loose rubble. A doll, its torso burned, its legs gone lay in my way. It looked like a cousin of Inge, the doll I'd never received. All of a sudden I was glad, and from the depth of my throat rose a giggle.

The sound bubbled its way upward until it burst from my mouth.

"What's the matter with you?" Mutti said, exasperated.

People looked dazed, but all I could do was giggle as if I were insane.

Blood pooled where the front door of the house had once been. A woman lay on the ground, her feet bare and her skirt torn to shreds. Her head and face were covered under a flowered pillowcase, gaudy against the red.

A man lay in the debris, his head and half his back faced down, his legs and feet at an odd angle as if he'd dived into a pool of rubble. Blood oozed from a cut in one leg where the fabric had torn.

A girl knelt in front of a small boy and kept touching the boy's face, talking and crying at the same time. There was no blood, but the boy's open eyes stared straight at me, his expression frozen in surprise.

I looked away. The boy was Burkhart's age.

"We'll have to climb across," Mutti said. "It's still faster than going back and all the way around."

When I looked over my shoulder for Mutti, my eyes lodged on an object in the rubble, gray and indistinct, yet somehow familiar.

A man's hand, black hair on thick fingers, stuck into the air as if in greeting. Dusted gray with mortar, the gold band on the ring finger glinted.

I shrieked.

"What is it?"

"The hand!" I pointed, my eyes drawn back to the stillness of the hand.

"Over here, quick," Mutti yelled. "Somebody is buried." Two youths and an older man began to dig, pulling away stones.

I hurried in the opposite direction, my legs machine-like, carrying me up the hill toward our apartment, away from the still fingers and the smells that grated my throat like acid.

My sides ached as I came to a stop in front of our house. I hadn't even waited for Mutti.

Glassless windows greeted me like hollow eye sockets, curtains drooping limply. The beech tree looked sad, its limbs black tentacles.

"What are we going to do?" Mutti said, catching up to me. "This is impossible."

I scanned the darkening sky. Until that moment I'd somehow thought my parents would protect me from evil. That they provided a shield I could hide behind. But I'd lost Vati to the war and Mutti had no power to protect me. Bombs did not care about me or my family. Like their makers they had no soul. They had only one task: to destroy.

I was on my own.

"You think they'll be back?"

"I don't know. We can't stay but we can't move. What are we going to do?" Mutti's voice quivered.

"Herr Baum may have supplies," I said.

"Herr Baum doesn't want to talk to us. Besides, I haven't seen him in ages. He may be—"

"I'm going to check," I said. "Maybe he needs help. He

said he wanted to stay in the basement and his house is still there."

"Fine, do it your way. I wish you weren't so stubborn," Mutti yelled after me.

I knocked on the old man's door. The shutters on his front windows had blown off and broken. One hung by its hinges at an odd angle.

"It's me, Lilly," I yelled, banging on the door. Herr Baum didn't hear well and since the doorknob turned, I walked right in. "Herr Baum?"

"Is something wrong?" Herr Baum was climbing the stairs from the basement. He was coughing and moved very slowly.

"Are you hurt? Is Anna okay?" I said, looking at obvious signs of injury. Herr Baum's clothes were intact.

"We're fine. Just old and rickety. It's nice of you to check, though. Or did your mother send you?" I knew he didn't like Mutti because every time he saw her he had this squinty look in his eyes. Somehow I knew it was because of me, which made me like him even more.

"I wanted to ask you for help."

Herr Baum had reached the floor level and held on to the railing to catch his breath. His chin grizzly with stubble, he wore a colorless hat and wool scarf.

"Why don't you come in so I can rest?" Herr Baum motioned at his door. "Go on, I'll catch up in a minute."

We passed through cold and drafty rooms and entered the kitchen. A thick candle threw dancing lights against the walls.

"We have to stay here. I haven't had time to repair anything. I wish they'd quit this nonsense. I can't stand it. I'm getting too old for this." Herr Baum shook his head. "You want some bread?"

I eyed the loaf of *Schwarzbrot* sitting on the kitchen table and licked my lips. I was ravenous.

"Of course you do." Herr Baum cut a thick slice and handed it to me. "Sorry, I don't have any jam or butter but it's good bread."

"*Danke.*" I sniffed the crust before taking a bite.

Herr Baum sat down with a sigh. "You said you needed my help."

"Yes, I was wondering," I said chewing, "if you have any materials to cover windows. I know you need some, too. But

Mutti… we don't have anything to cover and no tools. So I thought, I remembered your toolbox."

"You remembered my toolbox," Herr Baum said, shaking his head. "I can't remember what day it is, but you remember my toolbox from five years ago."

"Yes, you had hammers and nails and some other metal things."

"You're absolutely right. Smart girl!" His deep-set eyes rested on me. "I tell you what. Tomorrow, we'll fix windows. You can be my assistant. I'm too tired now, but we'll find something to cover your windows. Don't you worry." Herr Baum's gnarled hand patted my arm.

"I better tell Mutti. I'll be back in the morning."

"Wait." On Herr Baum's palm lay an apple.

"It's from my garden. Maybe you can help me make applesauce sometime. My fingers don't want to cooperate." Herr Baum grimaced as he looked at the knots on his hands.

"I can peel apples really well." I held the apple to my face, the fruity smell heady in my nose. Then I took a bite and closed my eyes.

"It's a Jonathan. I keep them in the basement. Anna likes them, too."

"See you tomorrow." Still chewing, I wiped the juice off my chin and carefully shut the front door behind me.

CHAPTER ELEVEN

Günter: November 4, 1944

On my way home from trade school—I'd managed to get a spot as a day student—I trudged through the mountains of dried leaves the November wind had blown across the streets. It was Saturday and I planned to meet Helmut and catch a movie in the evening. Not that I cared for the *Wochenschau*, the weekly shows about Germany's military advancements that preceded every movie, but I'd finally get to see *Die Feuerzangenbowle*, the new film with Heinz Rühmann everyone was talking about.

One of Germany's most gifted actors, Rühmann played a famous poet, posing as a high school student and creating lots of mischief. It sounded like just the right thing to forget about life, Hans and my father, and my rumbling stomach. Most of all, I wanted to forget about the looming military service.

The letter had arrived shortly after muster.

"Günter Schmidt, born 12/20/1928 – KV...deferred." How soon I'd be going was anybody's guess. Everyone at muster had been approved for battle. Hitler's war machine was ever hungry.

Mother cried and I'd felt relieved. The speeches and news from the government no longer spoke of victories. Instead they urged us to be strong and fight to the end with honor. I wondered what the end meant when things felt like an end already, when all I could think of these days was to get my father and brother home.

"Mutter?" I said, unlocking the door to the apartment.

"I'm taking a nap." Mother's tired voice sounded from the

65

living room.

"Sorry, did you fix my pants?" I whispered. "I'm going out tonight."

"Not yet. I'll take care of them this afternoon. Lunch is on the table."

Lunch was an overstatement. I wolfed down the broth with a handful of potato pieces and onion, barely calming the gnawing in my stomach, thinking about my weekly bath. After five years of war we were lucky to still have running water and gas. *Köln, Wuppertal* and *Remscheid* had been bombed a year or two earlier and survivors collected water from wells.

"What're you doing?" Siegfried leaned in the door to my room.

"Nothing much," I said, unbuttoning my shirt. "Taking a bath."

"My pen broke." Siegfried held out a palm with the stump of a pencil, its lead tip missing.

"What did you do? Throw it at somebody?"

"Stefan stepped on it. He's mean."

"Aw, let me take a look at it." I tussled Siegfried's hair and pulled out my pocketknife, the only prized possession I still owned. I cut away the wood at an angle, creating a new sharp edge. "Here you go."

"Will you go off to war too?"

Siegfried's question caught me by surprise. In fact, I was speechless.

"Not if I can help it."

"But Hans and Father went. Mother says she doesn't know when they'll return."

If they return. I cleared my throat. "I don't know either, but for now I'm here. Better let me get to my bath, all right?"

Siegfried hesitated for a moment and then left me to my thoughts.

Why hadn't Father written? Or Hans? It was worse than not getting any more care packages. That we'd manage somehow. We always had.

The gas boiler on the bathroom wall hissed, sending a gush of hot water into the tub. White clouds steamed the air as I slid in with a sigh. It was two in the afternoon, and I'd have a few hours to myself. I dunked low, inspecting my bony knees. I'd grown again this summer and wondered if I was now taller than my father.

We'd run out of shampoo a long time ago and the bar of soap was down to a nub. Brushing furiously at the dirt under my fingernails, my thoughts returned to the evening ahead: checking out the black market that had sprung up on an abandoned lot and meeting Helmut and his new girl at the movies.

Helmut had had his eyes on her for months and finally succeeded in inviting her. Her name was Gerda and she was our age, sixteen. Helmut had met her at Ullrich, the printing company where he apprenticed as a typesetter. He seemed to think she was special.

I wondered how far Helmut had gotten with her. His eyes had turned dreamy when I'd asked him to describe her. Supposedly she had beautiful brown hair like a doe, and she seemed to know what she wanted.

If I was honest, I resented Helmut's new interest. I was used to getting all of his time. Gerda sounded like a nice enough girl and all, but nothing special. Really, no girl was special. I didn't care, being much too busy with school, work and trying to scrounge up supplies. Taking care of Mother and my little brother was a full-time job on its own. I sure didn't look forward to being the third wheel tonight.

A wail rose outside. The siren's sharp blast echoed down the street. No matter, how often I heard it, the sound made me jumpy.

No, I refused to be afraid. Bombers always flew under cover of night. Lately, we'd had a lot of false alarms and people had begun to ignore them.

The knock on the door was rapid. "Günter?" Mother shouted.

"I'm not done yet."

"We're going to the bunker. Hurry. Get to the basement." Mother had long given up convincing me to go to the bunker. The door slammed shut and for the briefest moment it was utterly silent. For some reason that silence frightened me more than the sirens before.

But I didn't want to leave the precious hot water. I tried to focus on the state of my meager wardrobe, what shirts were clean and still fit. Nothing worse than looking like a fool in front of the new girl. Maybe, I'd borrow one from Hans.

The high-pitched drone of engines brought me back to the present. Like a monstrous steam engine they chugged and chomped closer, followed by the whining and whistling of falling bombs and mines. Then explosions. Loud...growing louder, mushrooming into a massive boom.

The ground vibrated. The tub's water sloshed on its own accord. Then the walls around me shifted, a terrible grinding as if the house were coming apart.

I jumped up. Too late.

The ground beneath trembled.

The air roared.

I covered my ears, the sounds barely muffled. Where was my towel? I had to get out. Get out now.

The window above the tub burst, exploding into silvery shards. Freezing wind hit my wet skin like a blast from a winter storm. I shook myself, glass splinters flying as I leaped from the water. Grabbing my pants, I rushed to the door. For a split second I saw myself lying naked, bare skin scraped and bloody.

I hesitated and then stepped into my pants. I'd not die naked.

The ground shifted and I hit my shoulder against the wall, the noise deafening. I had to get downstairs. Now.

The explosions melted into continuous thunder. The hallway expanded, growing longer as each second stretched.

Another wave. Louder.

I reached the staircase, jumping two steps at a time, ignoring the glass crunching beneath my feet. A huge rumble jolted the house as I flew past the oak entrance door.

My heart thumped against my ribcage. This was it! This was the end. I had been too slow.

The basement...Get to the basement.

Something cracked behind me, the sound like a gunshot. As if in slow motion, the heavy oak doors lifted from their hinges and crashed into the hallway. I jumped the last three steps and rounded the corner to the coal cellar, our designated bomb shelter.

"Günter, oh my God." Our second-floor neighbors, a couple in their seventies, sat in fright, protecting their heads with their hands. They looked ashen, eyes wide with terror.

I slumped on the bench.

"You all right?" My neighbor peeked through his hands.

"Your mother and brother?"

"At the bunker." Only when I said it aloud did I remember that it took at least five minutes to get to the bunker. With Siegfried in tow, it was more like eight. I trembled, shaking my head to banish the thought of them lying somewhere outside.

The house was on skids, moving this way and that. Dust and mortar fluttered from the ceiling. Thump, thump, thump.

When I looked down, I noticed my knees knocking. Something brewed inside me, choked me, but it wasn't fear or panic, it was anger.

Fury turned my insides on fire. Boiling now. I'd struggled for five years, helping Mother survive, always searching, always worrying where the next meal would come from.

So we could end like this? Mother and my brother wiped out by bombs, Hans and my father shot and buried in no-man's-land. For what?

A sob escaped me.

The old woman put an arm around my shoulder. I felt her quake against my side. Another crash came so close that things were breaking on the other side of the wall. I covered my head with my arms, bending low.

Still damp, chest bare, a deep chill crawled up my legs. My feet felt funny, but I couldn't think straight. My thoughts jumbled into fragmented scenes—my father in his favorite chair, smiling at me, Hans on the bed and in his uniform, Mother bending over my little brother. Chances were we'd get buried, the house collapsing above us. For a second, distracted from the noise, I grew aware of the glass in my slippers and shook them out. There were no cuts.

Silence.

No all-clear sirens. Just quiet.

I strained my ears. Nothing.

The stillness felt strange, unreal. I looked up. It was almost dark in the little room, the smoky dust of empty coal bins hovering like black fog.

I straightened. "I can't stand this."

"They may return," my neighbor yelled after me.

"Let them," I mumbled, already around the corner. My thighs felt weak as if I'd carried a load for miles.

I smelled the smoke immediately, acrid and thick, mixing with the sharpness of a November wind. In the back of my mind new dread registered. I crept forward.

The cellar doors, leading to the laundry area and shared by the neighbors, had torn out of their frames and now lay on the ground.

A hole gaped where the front doors had been. Wood framing hung splintered, the oak doors half way down the stairs. Glass shards littered the stone steps in the entrance. The plastered walls and ceiling were pockmarked.

I crawled across the door panels and, sniffing like a dog, entered my apartment. Where was the fire? Cold wind hit me—I'd forgotten about my bare chest.

I stood quietly to take in the scene.

Curtains hung in pieces, moving in the wind. All windowpanes were gone, the usually spotless linoleum covered with glass and wood splinters. Catapulted across the rooms, they spread across the sofa, shelves, tables and chairs. The dining table had flown to the opposite wall.

The kitchen was worse.

Like in an earthquake, the house had bucked, opened cabinets and drawers, and expelled everything inside. China and glasses, pots, pans and cutlery covered the ground. Precious spices lay blown across my mother's good china. Midnight blue with a gold rim, it was still pretty, even now. Our meager supplies of flour and salt had settled in-between, mixing with glass and pottery shards into a mosaic of destruction.

I picked up a coffee cup. Inspecting it closely and finding no cracks, I put it on the table.

Remembering that I was cold, I hurried to my bedroom. More glass and wood covered the beds and floor. Books scattered across the room as if somebody had tossed them, some open, pages moving in the breeze. I grabbed a work shirt and stopped.

What should I do? Paralysis gripped me as I thought of the immensity of the bomb attack. My house was a mess. Mother would be shocked. Mother!

Who cared about the house? I had to find her.

I rushed into the hallway and almost collided with my mother who stood frozen, Siegfried on her hand.

"Everything is broken," she said, her eyes unsteadily gazing around the room.

I didn't know what to say. I wanted to wrap my arms

around her, but it didn't seem right. "I'll get the broom and shovel," I said.

"My favorite china." She shuffled to the sofa and slumped down.

"Mutter?" Siegfried pulled her sleeve. "I'm cold."

I draped a blanket around my brother's shoulders and headed for the kitchen to get a drink of water. A hissing sound came from the faucet.

"They must've hit the water lines."

Mother still sat. "You'll have to fetch water from the well. Who knows when they'll repair the lines?"

A long time ago, the newspaper had printed instructions on what to do in case the water or gas lines broke.

Suppressing a shiver, I flicked the light switch. "No power, either." Without the protection of the windows, the air inside was as cold as outside. "Get me two buckets. Right now, I want to fix the windows. We'll freeze if we don't get them closed." Without waiting for a reply, I headed to the door.

"Fetch water first," Mother called after me.

I sighed in frustration. "Yes, Mutter."

Flames billowed from a house up the street. People watched as two women dug in the rubble. I tried to remember who had lived there, but my mind felt as porous as a sieve.

At the well I waited my turn. The water ran strong and cold, filling my buckets quickly.

The walk back stretched impossibly long as I climbed across the wreckage, my arms numb from the strain.

I thought I should feel thankful that the bombs hadn't found me or my mother or brother. Yet, all I wanted was to scream and yell. The endless tasks of surviving had become infinitely worse.

I delivered the water and, without comment, headed for the basement.

In the corner of our private cellar a wooden crate was stuffed with saws, hammers, an old axe with a broken handle, pliers and a few odds and ends. A greasy oilcan stood on a ledge next to two canisters of paint with dented lids. I sniffed.

I remembered watching my father oil the push mower. I'd smiled as he showed me where to apply the oil. A flannel work shirt hung on a hook behind the door. My father had worn it working in the yard. The fabric felt clammy as I slipped it on.

In the corner sat an assortment of scraps, linoleum remnants, an old carpet, broken chairs, and pieces of wood and cardboard. Acrid air filtered through the window, burning my nostrils. An orange glow flickered across the pavement from the house at the corner.

Starting in the kitchen, I worked my way around the rooms, covering each window with a patchwork of wood, cardboard and linoleum. Ignoring the glass splinters on the windowsills, I hammered until my arms grew so heavy, I kept missing the nails. Some were rusty and bent and I had to straighten them again and again.

The work was hardest in the living room. The window was much larger and the cross frames had vanished with the glass. I'd have to find larger pieces of materials tomorrow.

The sky glowed brightly to the north, from downtown. For five years, we'd covered windows and done without streetlights, trying to hide from enemy planes. It had been futile.

Filthy and tired, I headed for the kitchen. I'd have to work on the front door in the morning.

Mother and my brother had gone to sleep. A candle stub burned inside a tin cup with a small chunk of black rye bread next to it. I gulped some water from the "fresh" bucket and stuffed the bread in my mouth.

I'd forgotten what butter and smoked sausage tasted like. The memory of my father's care packages—with their herring, rich fish soup, and real berry jam—was as distant as a forgotten dream.

I pulled off my father's work shirt and eyed my chest where every rib was showing, my skin smudged with dirt and soot. So much for a bath. Sagging on the bed, I wondered if Helmut was safe. My plans to see the movie seemed like months ago.

The face of my father drifted into my thoughts—it seemed the haziest of all.

CHAPTER TWELVE

Günter: November 13, 1944

The fires in town raged for a week, ash snowing and covering everything. It blew with the wind, softened roads and blanketed rubble. It found a way inside through ruined walls, broken windows, through holes in roofs, cracks and entrances.

Then it began to rain. Heavy clouds hung above Solingen, fusing with the gray and black of smoke from hundreds of fires, unleashing the first storms of the approaching winter and turning the ash into sticky mud.

Still, the city burned until there was nothing left to burn. The fire consumed all, melting glass into heaps, cooking bodies in their own fat until they shrank to the size of babies.

The day after the bombing, I'd visited Helmut, feeling great relief that he and his mother were unharmed. Together we investigated the neighborhood in an ever-wider circle as more and more people competed for a place to stay, scavenging for food or anything usable.

"Do you want to go downtown? The fires are finally out." Helmut sat on a pile of bricks stacked along the sidewalk. It was a cold afternoon, and rain drizzled just enough to chill the air without drenching us. We'd worked hard, cutting down roof trusses for firewood.

My stomach rumbled as usual. "Why not." Despite the constant search for food and supplies, I was bored. Schools were closed, most factories destroyed. I'd been unable to find an apprenticeship, not even a simple job, while chores at home grew harder and longer. "You think any of the stores are open?" Ever since the bombing I'd secretly wondered what was left of town, my mood sinking with every day the fires raged.

"Let's find out."

Walking downtown usually took fifteen minutes. Not today. As soon as we crested *Brühlerberg*, we slowed down. It was hard to take it in because the town we'd known was gone.

Solingen's old city downtown had grown for hundreds of years. The half-timbered *Fachwerk*, the typical building style of the region, was made from black wood, the rectangular spaces in-between white. This gave the old homes a fresh checkerboard look. Other houses had shale siding, small, exactly-cut tiles creating a beautiful smooth, glimmering surface, like silvery fish scales.

It was all gone.

In front of us lay Armageddon, an endless desert of crumbled rocks. Walkways had disappeared, replaced by trails across ruins and rubble. The old cobblestone streets lay buried along with its victims, the memories and keepsakes of thousands.

Buses and trams no longer operated, their paths destroyed, rails bent like pieces of wire among square miles of broken concrete, bricks, household goods, and wooden beams.

I wanted to turn around right then. I should've insisted.

Instead I followed Helmut, who hopped from rock to rock as stones shifted underfoot, sometimes giving way, opening deep gaps where one could fall in and be swallowed by a concealed basement. People hiding in their cellars during the attack had vanished, covered and crushed under the weight of the rubble.

If one was lucky enough to be in an air pocket, digging, lifting and moving the debris became a race against time. Families excavated with their bare hands, as neighbors joined and worked through the night. Often victims died long before they were found, the dust and shards of red brick and roof tiles covering them like drops of blood. Naked bodies, their clothes torn away from the air pressure of bombs and fires, were stacked like cordwood along the sidewalks, waiting for pickup.

By now nobody was alive beneath the wreckage and the idea I was stepping on dead people made me go soft inside. My chest squeezed together like it had in the bunker, a weight that refused to lift. This could've been Mutti or Siegfried. I picked up a piece of rock and hurled it into the distance. It hit a piece of corrugated metal with a clunk, the sound as forlorn and helpless as I felt.

"Damn!" I heaved. "There is nothing left standing." Covering my nose with one arm, I scanned the hill toward *Dreieck*, the heart of downtown, where a network of trams used to speed in three directions.

Nearly every house had been leveled with occasional charred roof trusses sticking up like black bones. I looked at my mud-covered pants in disgust, ignoring the heaviness of my heart. *Don't get sentimental. Not now.*

Amid chunks of concrete and brick, something black stuck into the air. It looked like burned wood that had turned to coal. My nose stung from an overpowering mixture of soot, dust and something sweet.

When I realized what I was looking at, I abruptly turned. "I'm leaving."

"What's the hurry?"

I nodded toward the blackness.

"Are those...people?"

I nodded again, my throat too tight to allow airflow. What looked like wooden poles were arms and legs charred into twigs, shrunken and gnarled and reaching for the sky as if asking for help. I meant to turn away and yet I was rooted to the spot.

Helmut scrambled across the stones. "Let's go."

An old woman pulled a cart with scraps of wood past us. Her face was gray and indistinct like the shapeless heaps behind her. A group of women worked nearby, clearing a path, moving debris and cleaning each brick to be reused. They crouched and stood up, their movements mechanical, picking and stacking bricks into neat rows. They were silent, even their work sounded toneless.

That's what life had become. A series of mechanical movements, of tasks lined up without break. Because if you let yourself pause and think, you'd drop to the rubble and break apart like the rocks around you.

"There's nothing for us to scrounge here," Helmut said.

"Nope." My voice sounded high in my head as I slid down the heap, flinging up mud and flies. They swarmed, turning into a green and iridescent cloud. They'd crawled through crevices to find places to lay their eggs. The buzzing pierced my ears like thorns and I wanted to run from the noise worse than the whine of bombers. I knew why there were so many. I knew what they did.

I kept looking straight ahead because if I looked at Helmut I knew I'd ball and never stop again.

Though I hadn't ever been much of a shopper, I'd enjoyed visiting the cafés and bakeries, the old part of town with its small stores. I'd loved the fountain with the old sword smith on top of the stone column where boys let their boats swim. I'd lost my city.

As a cloud descended over my head, I wanted to lie down. The sadness was so intense, my body felt as if it were filled with cement and I had to force my legs to move.

Clearing my throat, I said, "We might as well go to the woods. At least, it's not all scorched and exploded."

"Boys, can you help me for a moment?" A man stood atop a flight of stone steps, the former entrance to a house. Where the doorway and walls had once been, debris piled high.

I took a tentative step towards the old man. "What do you need?" He looked disheveled, his coat and pants crusted with the same thick mud, his hair, grayish white and curly, a halo around his skull. His face was deeply lined and covered with dust and grime. A scraggly white beard covered his chin. His eyes looked crazed as they darted back and forth between me and the rubble behind him.

"It's my wife. She is down there."

"Your wife is buried?"

"I hear her. She's calling me."

I rushed up the stairs with Helmut right behind me. "Where is she?"

"Right down here." The old man's forefinger pointed at the mountain of bricks, shale, cement and beams. "Can you help me get her out?"

The mess of stones was overwhelming. "Do you have any shovels or a pickaxe?"

"No tools."

"But it's been nine days," Helmut said. "I don't hear anything."

The man nodded. "She's calling, my Liesel is calling."

The man kneeled down, picked up a brick and threw it a few feet. I crouched next to him and listened, laying my ear on the ground. Nothing except silence and the overpowering smell of decomposition. I abruptly straightened and patted the man's shoulder. "Are you sure, you can hear her? Because I can't."

Helmut shook his head.

The man didn't answer, but kept picking up bricks and bits of stone. Most of the pieces were too large to lift and he soon sat back on his heels. He looked frail, emaciated as if he hadn't eaten in weeks.

As I turned to leave, the man's fingers closed around my forearm. Sinewy and arthritic, they were surprisingly strong.

"You have to help. I can't do it alone."

"Let go." I tugged at the man's arm. The grip held like a vise.

"Please."

Helmut, who'd already descended the stairs, climbed back up. "Why don't we lift this piece together?"

"Yes," the man nodded eagerly and let go of my arm.

I joined Helmut on the other side of the collapsed wall. "On three," I said. We lifted and strained, but the piece didn't budge. It was like trying to empty a lake with a thimble. "You will need equipment to move this." I rubbed my hands, which were chafed and covered in muck. "Do you have a place to sleep?"

The man didn't seem to hear.

"Do you want us to help you find a place to sleep?" I yelled.

The man shook his head. "I stay right here. This is my home, right here with my Liesel." He petted the rocky ground.

"I'm sorry, I don't think we can help you." I nodded at Helmut. "Let's go."

As we hurried away in silence, I heard the man address someone else. "Can you help me for a minute?"

"Thanks," I said to Helmut after a while.

"No problem."

There was nothing else left to say.

CHAPTER THIRTEEN

Lilly: December 1944

Four and half years after Vati left, I no longer asked Mutti when he would return. By now I knew that men never did. At least not in one piece.

They were being chewed up by Hitler's war machine and as city after city crumbled into ashes, obituaries and missing persons' ads—the local newspaper was discontinued—began to cover walls and public notice boards. They weren't just soldiers, but hundreds of thousands of civilians.

Though I was only twelve, I did the laundry in the large brick basin washer in the basement. Schools were closed and we spent all day heating and stirring, soaking and rinsing. White laundry was laid out on the backyard lawn to bleach and had to be washed a second time.

Many days Mutti sent me to get firewood. Armed with a rather dull hatchet, pulling an old cart behind me, I'd head for the woods.

"I don't want to do laundry." I stood with my arms crossed. It was Saturday and I'd planned to go outside and scrounge. I loved the forest, its smells and the quiet, the whisper of leaves and branches high above, the only untainted place left in my world.

"Don't you mouth off, young lady." Mutti's voice was shrill. "I'll tell you what to do and you better listen."

"Why can't we do it Monday?"

"Because it's been put off too long already."

"Fine." I stomped into the staircase. I'd learned to recognize the impending ambush of Mutti's foul moods. Time to withdraw.

"Don't forget to take the laundry basket."

I ignored her and bounded downstairs.

The *Waschküche* was gloomy because the window was covered with a metal grate to keep burglars out. I tried the light switch. Nothing.

The electricity wasn't the only thing that had changed since the bombing. I had frequent nightmares. In my dream, a hand walked on its fingers, following me on the street. The hand was dusty white as if it had been rolled in flour, but bits of flesh and sinew dragged behind it, purplish-red as the tentacles of an octopus. The hand crawled and crawled and no matter how fast I ran, the hand sniffed me out.

I locked doors and windows, but the hand opened them. It slowly crawled to my bed, across my body to my throat where it choked me. I screamed and woke up. In an earlier dream, the hand belonged to Vati. I'd dug in the rubble and found him underneath, white and pasty, his blue eyes vacant.

My stomach ached, not from hunger alone, but the fear that sat in there. Like a rusty cannonball, it pressured and scraped against my insides.

"Fräulein Lilly." Huss stood in the door to his personal cellar. The iron padlock hung open, showing crates and boxes covered with lids or hidden under tarps. I wondered what he kept in there.

"Hallo Herr Huss."

"Your hair looks very nice today."

"Thank you."

"Is it time to do laundry?"

"Mutti will be down soon." Ignoring him, I kneeled next to the brick basin to stuff shreds of precious newspaper below a clump of twigs.

It was a pain to make a fire beneath the big basin, that's why we did laundry less and less, washing what we had in buckets or the old zinc tub. Only bed sheets and blankets were still cleaned in the basement and we waited until all bedding had been used. The fire caught and I straightened to look for the buckets.

I had to fetch water from the well three times to fill the basin.

"Do you need help?" Huss materialized next to me.

"I can manage."

"It's no problem, Lilly. I'll be happy to help you with the water." Huss's voice was silky.

"I'm fine, really." I looked up, realizing that Huss stood between me and the stairs. I was trapped. Sweat trickled from my armpits.

Moving backwards, I bumped my leg on the iron door of the fire pit.

Huss followed, herding me to the backdoor. I forgot about the bucket, watching him. My insides began to squirm. Deep down I'd always known Huss was all wrong. Why hadn't I been more careful?

His eyes narrowed as he smiled. "If you're a nice girl, I'll help you." His arm shot out and I felt fingers on my hair. "How soft it is," he sighed, moving closer still.

"Please, let me go."

"But I'm your friend," he said, his voice deeper and raspier. He was breathing harder, too. Strangely, I knew he wasn't lying. In his twisted mind he believed what he said.

My shoulder blades touched the back door and I groped behind for the knob. The cold hand of panic crept up my spine.

"If you're my friend, let me get a bucket and do my laundry," I yelled, hoping against the odds Mutti could hear me.

Huss towered close, his fingers wandering past my cheek to my neck. He was more than a foot taller.

My fist flew against his scrawny chest and bounced off uselessly. "Leave me alone."

"How strong you are," he chuckled.

Remembering the knob behind me, I frantically pushed. It didn't budge. The slimy hand moved across my shoulders. "Why don't you come up to my apartment? I have chocolate."

"No, thanks." I smelled his shirt stained with something dark. "My mother will be upset if I don't get the laundry started."

"But you work too hard for such a young girl. How old are you now?"

"I'll be thirteen in June."

"A young woman," he breathed. His fingers moved to my

chest.

For once, I was glad for the formless wool sweater. Not that there was much to see. Not like most of the girls in my class, who looked like real women with curves. "How beautiful your breasts are, like rosebuds."

My cheeks went up in flames. I stomped down hard, my boot grazing the fronts of Huss's open sandals.

He cried out as I shoved past him. "You little witch. I'll get you later." Then he laughed, the echo following me upstairs. With a shudder I opened my apartment door.

I still smelled his hands.

"Are you ready for the sheets?" Mutti stood in the bedroom door, her arms filled with pillowcases.

"Not yet." I rushed into the kitchen, forgetting that I still wore shoes.

"What's taking you—"

"Huss attacked me," I gasped. My head throbbed like an overfilled balloon.

"What do you mean?"

"He touched me."

Mutti frowned as if she weren't sure whether to believe me. "Did anything happen?" she asked finally. "I mean beyond him touching you."

"He came really close, pinned me to the wall and then his hands—he touched my head and my breast." I turned red again.

"I see." Mutti bit her lip.

"I'm not going back down there."

"I'll go with you."

When we returned, Huss was nowhere to be seen. His cellar was locked and the fire had almost gone out. The buckets stood in the corner near the backdoor where they belonged.

As night fell and despite being exhausted, I couldn't sleep. Mutti seemed distracted. I thought it was because of Vati. After the bombing in November, many soldiers had received "bomb leave" to check on their families. Several of our neighbors had come home. Not Vati. He hadn't written either. I burned to ask Mutti what it meant, if something was wrong with Vati.

But looking at Mutti's pressed-together lips made me

swallow my questions.

I knew we were struggling when I watched Mutti divide up our meager rations. We'd eaten corn bread and watery soup for a week. Burkhart often whined about being hungry. I kept my mouth shut, keeping the gnawing in my middle to myself.

I got up and tiptoed into the hallway. Mutti would be angry if she saw me walking around. Anymore, a little thing set her off and she yelled for an hour. Or I'd get the silent treatment, her not speaking to me for days. Of course, it was never Burkhart. My brother could do no wrong.

"Your brother is too little," she'd say. "Burkhart needs his rest." And when Burkhart whined in her absence and pretend cried to get his way, she'd come running. "Leave him be. Shame on you." I lowered my head and shrank away then because I knew arguing would do no good. That's when I dreamed of running away. I imagined packing my bag with a spare set of clothes and a bite of bread, walking out the door without a look back. I'd march down the street…

Somebody's laugh brought me back to the moment and I stopped in the middle of the hallway. The sound was muted, but distinctive, drifting up from below. Huss never had guests, nor did he go out. I always knew he was around by the rancid odor he left.

The kitchen was dark and silent, the living room empty, too, which was strange because Mutti often stayed up much later. I never knew when she went to bed. Another giggle. I opened the door to the staircase. Cigarette smoke hit my nostrils and something frying. Carefully setting my feet, I slipped downstairs. Another laugh and the air was filled with the delicious aroma of soup. My mouth watered.

Light shone through the milky glass of Huss's new door, never mind how he'd arranged to get new milk glass. When a shadow passed by, I shrank back, pressing myself against the wall.

Nothing. The voices were too quiet to understand, the cold floor making my bladder throb. There was no way I'd go to the outhouse in the dark and without a candle.

Suddenly, chuckles turned to laughter, familiar yet strange. Mutti's voice was unmistakable.

I strained my ears. Somebody moaned. A man's heavy breathing. I shook my head to make the image go away.

When the apartment grew silent, I made my way back to

my room where I kept a bucket for peeing. The soles of my feet were frozen, my legs covered with goose bumps. I'd barely climbed into bed when the front door opened and closed.

In the silence that followed, an image formed in my head. Mutti and Herr Huss. It was unthinkable. Yet...

It was then I realized that Mutti had become a liar just like Vati.

The next day, Mutti was in a good mood. She even laughed when I made a face over Burkhart's antics.

"What's that?" I asked, pointing at a couple of square shapes on the table.

"It's bread, Lilly."

"Where did you get it?"

"It was part of our ration. You just didn't notice." Mutti said, grabbing a loaf. "We better eat it before it gets dry."

My forehead throbbed. My insides churned. I wanted to yell then, ask Mutti why she lied and what she was doing with that despicable man downstairs. I said it in my head and swore to myself that one day, one day, I'd do something about it.

CHAPTER FOURTEEN

Günter: December 1944

Like every month, I headed to the rations office to pick up the supply of cards for my family. Afternoon clouds hung low, tingeing the air gray and threatening rain.

I didn't notice the sign until I tried opening the door: *closed until further notice.*

What was I supposed to do now? The prospect of going home to a handful of shriveled potatoes made me slow…then stop. I couldn't return home. Not like this.

"Günter, wait," Helmut shouted. "Are you picking up cards?"

For the first time I noticed how gaunt Helmut looked, his eyes shiny and clothes draped loosely. Despite the lack of food, we'd both grown during the summer, revealing bony ankles beneath pants held up by lengths of twine.

"They're closed." I couldn't keep the despair from my voice.

To my surprise Helmut's eyes sparkled with excitement. "I just heard about an Army convoy heading through town. Maybe our dads are with them." Helmut lowered his voice. "My neighbor says they're retreating."

Against my will, I imagined myself in a tight embrace with my father. We'd still not heard from him, his last letter reduced to short scribbles as if he were in a hurry or didn't want to tell what was really going on.

I worried he'd be lost in one of the terrible battles. Lately men simply disappeared while families waited for news, waited— for a letter, a card or the hero's note of condolence from Hitler's regime. Especially if they had been in battles in the east—like my father was now.

"He won't be there." I shook my head to discourage my own hope.

"But maybe they have news."

"Let's go." At least it was a distraction.

On the outskirts of Solingen, in the blue-collar neighborhood *Höhscheid*, we joined a crowd of women and children peering anxiously down the street. Instead of looking at the Rhine river valley in the distance, we fixated on the men snaking uphill in an endless procession. The soldiers' eyes were downcast in faces expressionless and hidden under a coat of dust, their movements mechanical as robots, their boots filthy and their uniforms torn. I focused on the nearest men a hundred yards away. One of them was leading a horse.

"They're still too far," I said as we worked our way to the front of the line. But no matter how I stared, the faces were unfamiliar.

"Is he waving at us?" Helmut said as the man with the horse pointed in our direction.

When the soldier broke away from his troop, I punched Helmut in the side. "Let's go meet him."

As we got closer the man looked even more haggard and sickly, his eyes glassy, rimmed red from infection or lack of sleep. His mare had seen better days, too. Angular hip bones protruded from the animal's shanks held together by rugged brown skin. Sores festered where the saddle had been, a caricature of a once proud warhorse.

The soldier waved. "Come here—quickly."

We hurried near, but he kept looking back at his troop. His shoulders hunched and he bent lower, whispering, "I need civilian clothes and shoes. Any chance you can spare some?"

I wrinkled my nose as the stench from weeks of unwashed skin crawled up my nostrils. Dirt coated the man's neck and the grayish chin covered with stubble. Behind him the convoy kept marching.

I followed the man's gaze to a vehicle, a VW *Kübelwagen*, an officer visible in the backseat. Brass buttons gleamed like foreign objects in the afternoon light.

"I'll give you my horse," the soldier continued with a trembling voice. "She used to be a fine mare."

Like during our meeting with the one-armed man, I felt a strange curiosity. The man was obviously afraid. After what we'd heard about deserters or people speaking up against the regime, it was no surprise.

"Sure, Mr., I've got clothes," I heard myself say.

"Shhh." The man casually picked a chunk of mud from the horse's flank and glanced at the approaching car.

"From my father," I hurried under my breath. "He's in the war, too. Any chance you know him? His name is Artur…Schmidt."

The man grimaced and shook his head.

"Sorry, son, I don't know your father. There're too many of us." After another glimpse at the car he continued. "Where do you live?"

"Not far, maybe two kilometers. Can you come with us?"

"No!" The man sounded afraid again. "I have to stay with my company. We must meet after dark." Behind us the car's engine roared closer.

My knees trembled, but this was the break I'd hoped for. We could do a lot with this horse. "We'll follow you to town," I said. "On the way we'll watch for a meeting spot."

"Everything all right here?" The well-dressed officer straightened inside the open VW and suspiciously eyed the soldier…and me.

"*Jawohl, Herr Hauptmann*," the soldier yelled, throwing up an arm with the Hitler greeting.

"Sir, he…I asked him about my father?" I said. *Why didn't I shut up?* "He is in the war, too. Maybe you know him. His name is Artur Schm—"

"Not much chance of that." The officer impatiently waved at his driver who immediately revved the engine. As the horse soldier hurried off without another look, I felt my knees go soft.

"Say, you." The officer's voice cut like glass shards.

"Yes, sir?"

"Shouldn't you be serving by now? How old are you?"

"I'll be sixteen in two weeks. They haven't called me yet."

Despite the December wind, sweat dripped under my shirt.

"You'll get your chance to serve our *Führer* soon." The officer whipped an arm across the windshield. "*Heil* Hitler."

I raised my arm but the jeep was already driving away.

"That was close." Helmut's face was pale as flour.

I let out a breath. No time to be afraid. "Do you see the man with the horse?" Uphill soldiers and trucks disappeared in a dust cloud.

"What do you want to do?" Helmut asked as he followed my gaze.

"Catch up to the soldier."

"What for?"

"To trade the horse, of course."

"Are you nuts?" Helmut's voice was shrill.

I walked faster. "Watch out for the car," I whispered as Helmut hurried alongside.

"What are you *doing?*"

"We'll help him."

"They'll shoot us," Helmut hissed. He looked ready to throw up.

I placed a forefinger across my lips and shook my head. There were people everywhere. Most were harmless, some were not. It was impossible to know.

The troop began settling under a stand of oak trees, which had remained standing among homes now reduced to ruins. We were still a few hundred yards away when I noticed an old barn behind a deserted house, its roof a black, gaping hole.

I veered toward the barn. "This should work," I mumbled, inspecting the inside.

"What if the officer sees you?" said Helmut, staying close.

I sucked in a mouthful of freezing air and straightened my back. Sometimes I wished Helmut would shut up. "Wait here."

Afraid of losing confidence, I forced my shoulders to drop casually and walked toward camp. Helmut was right, of course. This was insane. But then my stomach rumbled, a dull ache that never seemed to leave these days. I was stinking tired of being hungry…and afraid.

My heart pounded in my throat as I eyed the VW parked along the north side.

Fifty feet away, the horse soldier was on his knees, rolling out a stained military blanket.

"Leave," he said as I approached, sounding irritated and terrified at the same time.

Ignoring the man's fury, I bent low and nodded at the old shack. "We can meet you over there."

"When?"

"Nine tonight?"

"Yes," the soldier breathed.

From a distance I saw Helmut trying to look relaxed while leaning against the barn. "What size shoes do you wear?"

"Doesn't matter."

I slowly rose and, resisting the urge to run, strolled toward the barn, all the while expecting the officer ramming a pistol into my back. My legs and feet were jelly. *Walk.*

Helmut pulled me into the barn. He looked green. "You're crazy."

"Just hungry." Taking a deep breath, I peeked over my shoulder. Somewhere in the fading light I thought I saw the reflection of brass buttons. "Let's go."

Helmut raced off as if a pack of wolves were after him. I had trouble keeping up, hugging myself against the damp cold that seemed to crawl beneath my skin. Six weeks of rain had turned the ground into sticky gunk, staining my shoes and the once clean linoleum of my home.

It was dark by the time we reached our neighborhood. We agreed Helmut would pick me up after dinner.

I burst into the kitchen. *"Mutter."*

"Where have you been? I thought you picked up our rations." Arms firmly tucked at her sides, Mother had the scolding look.

"The place is closed. But listen, I have really good news." Before Mother could say anymore, I explained my encounter with the soldier.

"We need clothes to trade for the horse."

"What in the world are we going to do with a horse?" Mother asked. "A military horse...if the SS sees you..." Her voice quivered.

I bit my lips, hiding my uncertainty. It was dangerous, but I was sick and tired of starving. "We'll find a way."

"Even if you get the horse, do you have any idea how hard

it is to butcher? It's not a rabbit or chicken. You have to hide—"

"I have Helmut. We'll share the meat." I hugged my mother. "Don't worry." I quickly walked into the bathroom to hide my shaking hands. Clearing my throat, I called over my shoulder, "better hurry."

In the basement, Mother held up a sweater and sniffed.

"Mutter, please." If the soldier left or found someone else to help him, all my hard work would be wasted.

"It still smells a bit like him." Mother shook her head. "Maybe I'm imagining things." She held out the sweater. "It'll keep the man warm."

"We need shoes, too."

My mother sighed again. "I only have one pair left—your father's best Sunday shoes." She pulled them off the bottom shelf and inspected the soles. "Like new," she mumbled, tucking the laces inside.

I've got to go, I wanted to shout. "I need pants and a jacket," I said aloud.

"What if he never needs another pair?" Mother was far away. "You know, your grandparents bought these for him."

I imagined the soldier waiting in vain and walking off with my horse. "*Mutter*, pants?" I fought the urge to yank the shoes from Mother's fingers. Instead I grabbed a jacket and pants from the carton and held out a hand. Without a word Mother passed me the shoes.

"Promise me to be careful."

Helmut arrived as I swallowed the last of my dinner, a single slice of cornbread scraped with the last dregs of sugar beet syrup.

We set off into the dark, clothes in a tight bundle under my arm. With every step my insides got more twisted. I heard Helmut's ragged breaths next to me and knew he wasn't doing any better. I wanted nothing more than to turn around. But that would've meant admitting defeat. And my hunger didn't allow that.

After the fires had died a few weeks ago, there was no electricity, the night a shroud of black ink covering the city and people sitting in fear of more bomb attacks. Being outside most nights, my eyes had adjusted to pick up the slightest hint of light.

"You sure about this?" Helmut said after a while.

"Aren't you tired of being hungry?"

"Yes, but what if the officer…"

"We'll be careful." Ahead fires glowed like red eyes, their smoke more noticeable than the light. "Not a word from now on," I whispered.

We snuck quietly toward the barn. It was pitch black and cold as we huddled inside. I rubbed my shoulders, ordering my legs to quit trembling. It didn't work, so I slung my arms around my knees like I'd done when Hans left. My thoughts wandered to my brother as they did every night. And like every night, my heart grew heavy with the lack of news. Well, there was news, plenty of it about courageous battles and fallen heroes. Since the bombing last month we no longer had a newspaper, which kept Mother with one ear attached to the radio.

"What if he doesn't show?" Helmut's voice shook.

"He'll show!" I said, struggling to sound confident. The slice of bread at dinner a distant memory, I was so hungry that my head felt as if it could float into the dark. It was hard to think of anything but the ache in my gut.

"Maybe he already found clothes and is long gone," Helmut whispered, rubbing his hands together. "I'd love to have a fire. They look really nice."

I remained silent as the worry of being discovered made my throat close up. Mother was right and so was Helmut. That *Hauptmann* would shoot us on the spot. And if the SS or Gestapo found us with a military horse we'd be dead, too. A sigh rattled the air. It was my own. I forced air into my lungs. There was still time to leave.

But I had to have the horse. I leaned against the rough-hewn wood of the barn and pulled the collar of my coat to cover my ears, the coarse wool scratching my neck. Though the dirt floor was bare, the faint smell of straw remained. Voices drifted across too low to understand.

"You aren't sleeping?" I whispered. How I hated the war. It had taken everything from me—my father and Hans—all I'd loved and known. My chance at a normal life with school, comfort and decent food.

"No."

"I'm going to—"

I heard faint steps. Then two shadows, one large, one man-sized, appeared in the barn door.

"Boys?" The soldier's voice sounded anxious.

I jumped from my hiding place. "We brought clothes." I thrust the package at the man who seemed to have shrunken since this afternoon. Without hesitation the soldier undressed, the air heavy with his stench.

I listened for sounds, my insides on fire with worry. What if someone had seen the horse walk off? And why was the man taking so long? As the man fiddled with the buttons of his shirt, I tied up the uniform and handed it to him.

"You saved my life," the soldier sighed. "Take care of my mare. She'll die anyway. At least you can use her." He disappeared around the corner and was gone.

I peered out after him. All was quiet. A few fires smoldered—the camp seemingly asleep. I hoped the man would get away. Everything was falling apart anyway. Deep down I wished my father and Hans would do the same. But then it was probably more dangerous being a soldier. The SS never hesitated when they caught a deserter.

"Let's go!" I whispered.

I yanked the reins. The horse didn't move. She'd walked for months without rest, slowly turning from a beautiful warhorse to skin and bones. Now she was ready to take a break.

"You pull, I'll push." I rammed my shoulder into the horse's rump. To my horror the mare neighed. "Shh!" Through the haze of my panic, I heard voices. Somebody was coming. "Hurry."

Terror was taking my breath. I shoved harder. At last, the horse took a step...and another. We rounded the corner and stopped behind the barn when we heard movement on the other side.

"Nobody here." The voice was tired. "I need a light."

I tiptoed to stand next to Helmut, watching the dark bulk of the horse, willing it to be quiet. My fingers shook as I stroked the horse's mane and face. We waited. One of the hooves touched a rock, a muffled clunk. I held my breath. Though I heard nothing, I felt the presence of the men on the other side of the wall.

"Didn't Hartmann want to put his horse up in the barn?" a second voice said.

"Nothing here," the tired voice answered.

"I could've sworn, he said—"

"Let's get some sleep."

As the men's steps faded away, we stumbled into the darkness. I wanted to puke, something sour rising from my stomach. I had expected to feel triumphant, but the feeling of uneasiness remained. My throat ached with thirst.

"You think we can go by the well? I'm burning up."

"The horse could probably use a drink, too." Helmut attempted to scale a pile of debris. "Come on, lazy, let's go." The horse didn't feel like climbing and stood. "We have to find another path."

"What?" I'd been far away, thinking about the upcoming task of horse slaughter.

"Are you listening?"

"*Ja, Mann.* Let's go past the hedges."

The horse whinnied again, looking for her master. I listened in fright, feeling powerless. If we ran, we'd lose the horse, our chance for real food.

I breathed a sigh of relief when we reached the well. As I cooled my burning forehead, the horse slurped in noisy gulps.

We agreed to try the old community kitchen near my apartment house and headed off again. My ears were on high alert, but all I heard were our breaths and the clunk of hoofs.

The one-story building that housed the old kitchen was used for neighborhood events. I knew it would be deserted. There hadn't been anything to cook or celebrate in years.

Shoving and pushing, we dragged the horse inside. The kitchen was filthy, but it had tile walls and a drain in the floor. I lit the small candle I carried for emergencies, its shine barely reaching five feet across. I could make out the horse's front feet, the walls beyond hidden in shadow.

"Maybe we should wait till morning." Helmut sagged on a stack of bricks. "I'm bushed. We can sleep here to watch the horse."

"Someone will see us." I rubbed my arms and legs to fend off the creeping cold that had followed us inside. The horse snorted and watched as if to remind me that I wanted nothing more than to run and forget about the whole thing.

This was going to be a horrific job. It wasn't just that I was bone tired—the idea of killing an animal, not to mention a huge beast—made me faint with worry. And underneath it all I fumed with hatred for the mess Hitler had put us in, forcing us to do unmentionable things like killing a horse.

But we needed food. Why couldn't my father be here to help? Or Hans? I shook off the image of them lying in some ditch, forgotten and covered with weeds.

When I rubbed the mare's long and coarse mane, the soft skin beneath her ears, she snorted and moved her head up and down as if she were talking to me.

"I'm sure you are just as hungry as we are." Massaging my stiff neck, I nodded toward Helmut. "We need a hammer."

"What for?"

"The horse, you idiot. Unless you have a gun in your pocket."

"No need to get mad. We have a hammer in the basement." Helmut stretched his long arms and headed for the door.

"A big one," I called after him.

I leaned my face against the horse's neck. She felt warm and comfortable. I felt her nibble on the sleeve of my jacket and realized how peaceful I felt. How was that even possible?

I rubbed her chest, a mottled brownish red caked with mud. "How dirty you are." The horse snorted. I wondered what she understood. My fingers found a patch of bare skin, an old wound, still pink and shiny. "Looks like you are a veteran, too."

I closed my eyes and dozed, wishing for this impossible night to be over.

A clank roused me. Helmut was dragging a sledgehammer behind him along with a hand-wagon, a wood contraption with squeaky iron wheels. Hidden within were three large knives, wrapped in a towel, an enamel bowl and sheets of old newspaper.

"Who is going to do it?" Helmut asked.

"I don't know." My resolve had evaporated. Despite her sad state, the mare looked huge. Neighing softly she stamped her feet, her hooves clicking on the stone floor.

Helmut's eyes looked huge in his pale face. "Maybe we should draw straws? The shorter stick loses."

"Fine."

"Fine."

Helmut returned with a grass leaf and tore it into two sections. "You first."

I swallowed hard as I drew a piece. Helmut's arm shook as

he slowly opened his fist. I sighed—I held the shorter piece.

I gingerly lifted the hammer and let it sink to the floor. With a three-foot handle, it felt heavy as a boulder.

"Did you see her scars?" I said. "Look at this." A second scar, long and covered with coarse scab stretched along the horse's hind leg. "I wonder what happened." I traced a finger across her flank.

"Are we going to do this or not?"

"I'm getting to it," I hissed, my voice foreign and tinny like speaking into a barrel. I tried to look away, away from the gentle brown eyes and away from the soft nose. I had to do this now. Before I went crazy. "I'll climb on the counter. Bring her over."

"Wait!" Helmut yelled. "Cover her eyes."

"Good idea." I lumbered outside. Anything to avoid standing here thinking about what I was about to do. At last, I emerged with an old rag. Climbing on a broken piece of countertop at the back of the room, I bound the horse's head. "Give me the hammer."

The sledgehammer had a mind of its own as I swang back and forth. It felt impossible to maneuver. My arms were drained, yet I had to do it. Now.

I swallowed, my mouth dry as the desert.

"One, two and three." I closed my eyes.

The horse stood quietly as the hammer hit her forehead with a sickening thud. Something cracked deep inside. A muffled sound crept from the horse's throat, not a whinny or a snort, more like a gurgle. Hooves scraped concrete as her bowels gave and the room filled with the stink of fresh manure.

Helmut's voice drifted into my fogged brain, but I couldn't make out what he was saying. *Quickly,* my mind urged.

I swung with all I'd left. The hammer missed the forehead and slammed into its brow. Blood spurted, skin tore, splattering Helmut's face. Whitish bone fragments appeared in the red mass above the eye. The hammer crashed between the mare's ears.

The horse trembled, ripples traveling through its rump. Then, in slow motion her feet gave, front knees buckled, then hind legs. She tilted sideways and fell, her bulk filling the room, her head hitting the tile. She lay still, but I heard her labored breathing. Blood oozed from her nose. I jumped down and grabbed one of the knives.

"Get the bowl. She must die quickly." I cut the horse's neck as Helmut shoved the bowl below. Blood spewed, covering us in a slimy spray of red. A puddle grew on the cement. Red rivulets snaked toward the drain in the middle of the floor.

"Man that stinks." Helmut held his nose, leaving a bloody print on his face.

"The bowl, hold it close," I shouted. Bile filled my throat, my mind reeling with what I'd done. Helmut tried to keep the bowl steady, but the blood poured fast and hard, drenching skin, clothes and shoes. The bowl filled and spilled over. The horse seemed to have buckets.

Because I wanted to make sure she was really dead, I crawled on top of her neck. It felt warm and still soft. *Don't lose it now.*

There was no pulse.

"She's gone," I said.

Helmut thrust the largest knife at me. It was slightly rusty but very sharp with a curved blade and a pointed tip. "Let's pull her guts out first."

Too tired to argue, I made the first cut along the stomach, then another. I gagged as the knife dug deep, exposing grayish intestines.

"Help me!" I took hold of the skin, pulling it apart. Together we yanked, arms deep inside the steaming belly, guts spilling onto concrete. I heard Helmut swallowing, my own stomach threatening to turn. I had to numb my senses, not think, not now.

I kept pulling, wishing to lose my sense of smell. It was no good. The stench infiltrated my brain, making every breath a chore. Intestines slithered across the floor, seemingly endless whitish strings of entrails making the air steamy and thick. The formerly white walls were splattered red, the floor unrecognizable.

"I'll start with the leg." I pushed the knife against the skin, my breath ragged. Finally the blade took and more blood oozed from the cut. "Get the paper ready."

"I'm right here," Helmut said, unfolding a large sheet of newspaper. "Don't you have to remove the skin first? I used to help my father with the rabbits and we always skinned them first."

"Right. Hand me that paring knife."

I sliced across the back. "Here, grab hold of this." The

skin resisted and made a tearing sound. "You pull while I cut."

At last the mare's side and back were exposed, its meat the brownish-red of old wine.

"Take this." Holding up a first chunk, I felt half triumphant.

Helmut gingerly touched the meat, still warm and seemingly alive. "It's slimy."

I ignored him and cut another piece. "What are you waiting for? Here's another."

"I'm getting it." Helmut grabbed the piece more firmly and wrapped paper around it. "I hate this smell."

We kept going in silence, me cutting and Helmut wrapping and storing.

"I don't think the wagon can hold anymore." I wiped my sweaty face. "We better take a break so we can get this home. You go first."

We'd agreed to take turns, delivering the meat to our mothers. With that much food we'd have to make several runs.

For a while it was quiet as I worked. I carved up a portion of the back and hind leg when Helmut reappeared with the wagon and closed the door.

"You want to take over for a while." I said. It wasn't meant as a question. I needed air. Walking outside, I breathed deeply, the stickiness on my skin turning to instant frost. With a shudder I forced myself to turn around.

Helmut was bent over the horse's back, packing the second load. "We've got at least four more runs. You're next—"

"What are you boys up to?" A man materialized from the darkness of the entrance. I'd seen him before somewhere in the neighborhood, but didn't know his name. The man, inches shorter than us, stared from watery blue eyes. He was older than my father, his face puffy and soft, shining pale like kneaded dough.

In my gut warning bells began to ring. Why wasn't the man in the war. He didn't seem to have any injuries.

"We butchered a horse," Helmut said.

"A horse, eh." The man glanced at the carcass on the floor. "Did you steal it?" He licked his lips like a hungry animal. They were dark with flakes of skin in the corners as if he'd chewed his mouth. His chest and shoulders were bowed, making him appear hunched underneath the oversized coat.

"We traded it fairly." Helmut placed himself between the horse and the door—his knife, dripping with blood, firmly in his hand.

"Not likely—two boys getting a horse like this." The man's eyes were full of greed as he glanced at the meat. "Maybe I should call the authorities." He tried straightening his shoulders to look important.

I sighed, stepping next to my friend. "Look, mister, we traded the horse as we told you. You know us, we live down the street."

"Nobody gives a couple of boys a horse. I think you stole that horse from our military."

"We didn't." My voice shook, but I grabbed the other knife. Cold anger spread as I watched the small man eyeing *our* meat. Even at fifteen I'd seen his kind before—opportunists who stole from their own mothers to get ahead.

"You know my father, Artur Schmidt?" I said, wishing I were strong and tall. "And my grandfather Egon Schmidt—he owned the scissor factory."

"So what?" the man said. We were silent for a moment, looking at each other. "Give me some pieces or I'll report you."

Helmut looked at me and we nodded to each other.

"Sure." I straightened my shoulders, looking at my bloodstained hands. "We'll give you the bones."

"Bones? Give me meat or I'll go to the SS office right now." The man smiled for the first time. "You're lucky I didn't get here earlier. I'll be back in a few and you better be gone by then." Without waiting for a reply he disappeared.

"*Scheisse*," I said. "I wish we could carry it off."

"You think he'll report us?"

"Doubt it. He wants the meat. *Our meat*," I growled.

The man was back in minutes. "You're still here."

"We'll take what is ours." I looked up from the carcass, the knife heavy in my hand. "I'll finish this piece. Then we'll go."

The man squinted, something wild in his eyes. He opened his coat to reveal an axe and a large knife. "Get out of here, before I miss." He swung the axe in a wide arch, forcing me to jump back.

Helmut cowered behind the rump, eyeing the blade as it sank deep into the flesh. On the second try the axe hit concrete. Sparks pierced the gloom. The man began to move quickly, sending chunks of bone and meat flying, his arms surprisingly strong.

I flinched. "Hurry," I whispered, keeping my gaze on the swinging axe. We cut along the back end as the axe moved closer. We had nowhere to go.

"We are leaving," I hissed, piling the last chunks of meat on the wagon.

The man didn't look up. He was cutting apart the front leg. "Good, and don't come back."

We pulled out quickly and as I gripped my knife, fresh heat brewed in my veins. Never before had I wished to be grown as much as tonight. Never before had I wished so hard to have my father home.

"He's stealing our food," I choked as we dragged the cart down the street. Above us, a steely dawn colored the sky like worn metal.

"I wish my father were here," Helmut said. "Both our fathers. They'd beat him up."

The chunks of meat wrapped in newspaper still quivered as I turned into my street.

"I'll stop by later for the cart," Helmut called after me.

Two minutes later, I sneaked upstairs and knocked, my arms loaded with meat.

"I've got more downstairs," I announced when the door opened.

Mother's eyes grew large . "What happened? Where are you hurt?"

I grimaced. "It's horse blood. Today we'll eat well."

Mother clapped her hands, a rare smile on her lips. "Look at all this food."

"We would've had a lot more. A man stole it all. I wish *Vater* were here." To my embarrassment, my throat tightened. I angrily wiped my eyes with a blood-soaked sleeve.

"You did well, Günter." Mother put an arm around my shoulder when I returned with the remaining meat. "Things will get better. I'll set up the grinder. You better find my largest pot." Mother threw me another glance. "On second thought, why don't you wash? We still have clean water in the bucket."

Most of the blood had dried on my skin. Pulling off my shirt and pants to soak in the remaining water, I took out my good set kept for Sundays as the smell of frying meat reached my nostrils.

"Here." Mother placed a plate of raw ground meat in front of me. "Just promise me to eat slowly or you'll get sick. When you're done, I'll need help heating the stove. We'll can the rest."

We covered the front door with blankets so as not to alert any neighbors who would be attracted like ants to our kitchen. It didn't matter that we didn't have any oil or butter, eggs or spices. Burger patties piled a foot high on plates, and canning jars lined the table.

By the time I went to bed, I was utterly drained. My stomach was full for once, but I couldn't enjoy it. I couldn't enjoy anything anymore.

I'd killed an innocent horse. I loved animals, but instead of honoring her, I'd torn her to shreds and given her up to some low-life thug. The war was turning us all into animals—Hitler, the SS and Gestapo, the men at the front, the bombers, spying neighbors and now me...a murderer of horses. I turned on my side, bitter tears in my throat.

The last thing I saw were a pair of brown eyes with long lashes.

CHAPTER FIFTEEN

Günter: December 1944

The rain didn't stop. It drizzled and dripped, splattered and poured. Low clouds hung above our town like a veil of sadness as the people below tried to pick up a life that was no longer.

Deliveries stopped, production ceased, water and gas lines were empty. Mothers and children buried their dead. Often other mothers and children. Many unwilling or unable to fight for survival lay down and gave up.

I gathered wood, sawed and cut it to fit the stove. I carried water from the well, sometimes two and three times a day. By the time I came indoors, my clothes were soaked and filthy. Instead of washing, I took them off to dry near the stove. Some of the dust and muck just fell off. It was too hard to muster the energy to wash. Since the bombing in November, Solingen was experiencing the worst housing conditions ever. Apart from the thousands dead, so many homes had been destroyed that families were forced to squeeze together. And that included us.

It was almost Christmas, and I paced the floor in Helmut's room. "I can't stand it. It's maddening to have to work all the time, get firewood, get water, get this and do that. You wouldn't believe how it looks in my house. It's a pigsty. My uncle sleeps on the table. The kitchen table where we *eat*." I threw up my hands. "And my cousins, what do they do? Nothing. They just whine and complain."

Two days after the bombing, my two remaining uncles

who'd returned with injuries, their wives and three children had moved in. With their apartments gone, they'd had no place to stay.

"My cousin Bernd," I continued, "*always* takes my bed. Every time I come in, he's there. I'm so darn tired of it."

"You can always—"

"Tomorrow is my birthday," I kept going. "I'll be sixteen, but who really cares. We don't have enough food. And what am I going to give Mother? Nobody has anything." Mother and I shared the same birthday, December 20.

"You can always come here to get away." Helmut's family had been lucky. Nobody had lost their home, and he still had his own room.

"Sorry, man. I sound like my aunt, like a whiner."

The next morning I woke early. I climbed out of bed and across my sleeping cousins sprawled on the floor. Mother was already in the kitchen. On the table, a candle stub burned next to a plate covered with a shred of wax paper.

"Happy birthday." Mother opened her arms, her head resting against my collarbone.

"Happy birthday to you."

"I would've loved to bake a cake." She pointed toward the plate. "Maybe, we can make up for it next year." Underneath the paper rested a piece of cornbread, thickly covered with strawberry jam. I sniffed the fruit, its aroma making my mouth water.

"*Danke.* That's very sweet."

"I traded for the jam with Frau Baumann. I've got something else for you." In her hand she held a sweater. "I made it when you were out."

I choked back the lump in my throat. I knew it had taken weeks, unraveling old pullovers, washing and stretching the wool.

The sweater was a bit long in the sleeves, but nice and warm. These days our house was always damp. We kept a steady fire in the kitchen stove, and though the rain had finally stopped, everything was wet and the mud and ash held the moisture much longer. I felt vindicated and thankful for my mother's resourcefulness.

"I've got nothing to give you. I'm working on Christmas but—"

"As if I care. You're already helping so much," Mother sighed. "My only wish is for your father and brother to return home safely. I have one more surprise."

My mouth was full and I had my eyes closed to savor the jam.

"Your uncles are finally moving out this week."

"When?" I said through the sweetness. I knew Mother was tired of hosting her in-laws. Tempers had flared over the last seven weeks and she'd worn herself thin.

"In three days, I think the 23rd. Thank goodness it'll be just us for Christmas."

I wore my new sweater when I picked up Helmut because we wanted to scavenge for Christmas 'gifts.'

"Happy birthday! Looks like you got a new sweater," Helmut said.

"It's really warm." I patted the wool near my throat. "Why don't we go and check the fields? Maybe something is leftover from the harvest."

"Potatoes would be great. Do you remember how we used to eat *Bratkartoffeln*?" Helmut loved fried potatoes and his eyes looked dreamy. "Mmmh, roasted potatoes with onions and eggs."

I tried to remember the last time I'd had a big meal with my entire family. It seemed like a century ago.

"You think we'll ever get to be normal again?" Helmut said as if he'd heard my thoughts.

I shrugged. "How much longer can this war take? Every man I know who isn't already hurt is gone somewhere. I can't see how we can continue much longer."

"We're losing."

"That's what my uncle says. And remember the soldier with the horse? How could we win if they are bombing the entire country?"

"I hope it's over soon."

My uncles and aunts moved out the morning of Christmas Eve, leaving behind inches of mud. Brown and sticky, it had dried and left a crust of filth on the furniture. Bed sheets and carpets were stained, our good towels ruined. I kept lugging water from the well and helped Mother scrub the floors. Finally, I cut a tree and we set it up in the living room. I'd searched a long time until I found a beautiful blue spruce with thick greenish-blue needles. I helped my little brother make straw stars and acorn ornaments.

As Mother patted the wood carving by her plate, an angel I'd made for her with wide wings and a small halo above its face, Siegfried whinnied and galloped along our freshly cleaned floor. I'd carved a tiny horse from a holly tree and smoothed it with sandpaper until it looked more like a donkey. Siegfried's gift to Mother, a painting of our house and a family of five stick figures, hung on the wall near the tree.

I received a new winter jacket. It wasn't really new, but Mother had managed to trade and alter it. It was made of felted black wool with a large collar I could push up to protect my ears.

We enjoyed some of the canned horsemeat and a few potatoes, onions and carrots, which were now roasting in a large pan. For desert, Mother baked honey cake covered with molasses made from sugar beets that Helmut and I had recently 'found' at a farm.

"I'll stop by our old neighbor for a minute," Mother said after the meal. "I'm sure she'd like a piece of cake."

"No problem." I had trouble speaking, the sweet molasses hurting my teeth.

"Maybe we can play checkers when I get back?"

Alone in the kitchen, I looked at the empty chairs at the table. Did Father and Hans remember Christmas, or they did they just fight and sit in dugouts, horribly cold and wet? It was our fourth Christmas without Father and the first without Hans. What if they blamed me? Were they mad at me for staying home and taking the easy way out? Well, it wasn't exactly easy.

I thought back to the holidays before the war when we'd been a family. I'd taken it for granted and worried about the *gifts* I was getting. Now I just wanted everybody home.

"Günter, come quick," Mother yelled from the front door.

"What's the matter?"

"Our neighbor—it's awful."

The first thing I noticed was that the tiny apartment next door was freezing. Our breaths hovered in front of our faces in white puffy clouds. Faded light trickled through the windows, which were covered in an assortment of cardboard and wood. It cast an icy gloom over the room.

Frau Baumann sat at the kitchen table, fully dressed, wrapped in her coat and gloves. The room was tidy, the counter clean and void of containers, pots or pans.

I bent low to look at the woman's face. She was dead—her skin tinged greenish gray—staring straight at the wall with sunken eyeballs that had lost most of their color. I had no idea how long she'd been sitting here.

To my surprise, I couldn't muster being sad. *Animal. Where is your compassion?* All I wanted was to go back and close the door. "I'll run to the police station in the morning," I said aloud.

Silent tears rolled down Mother's face. "Why didn't I check sooner?" she mumbled, shaking her head.

Putting an arm around her, I led her into the hall. "There's nothing we can do here tonight."

"I should've stopped by more often. She had nobody. I should've given her more of the meat."

I made plans to meet with Helmut to celebrate New Year's Eve. I wanted to surprise him, having scraped together a few potatoes and an onion. Helmut had access to carrots, garlic and herbs, which his grandmother grew in the garden and stored in their cellar during the winter.

When the newly revived siren sounded that afternoon, Mother pulled Siegfried out of bed from his nap. Without comment, they disappeared and raced toward the bunker. As the streets filled with running neighbors, I pulled on my coat and moved to the basement.

I was alone. Since the two-day attack in November, my neighbors always went to the bunker. I felt strangely detached as if I'd worn out my fear. So many bomb threats, so many bombings, so much death. If it was going to happen it would. And yet...

Engines whined as hundreds of detonations erupted in sequence. Though they were farther away, the noise was deafening. I covered my ears and looked at the coal chute, wondering if I'd have time to climb out if the house collapsed. With my hands pressed tightly on either side of my head, I could hear the quick hammering of my pulse.

I thought of the bombers and why they always attacked when I'd made plans, on weekends and holidays. It was as if they planned on people being home, their houses easy targets.

When it turned quiet, I listened for the safe alarm. It didn't come. Minutes trickled by in slow motion. At last, I couldn't stand it any longer and hurried upstairs. Everything seemed in order—there was no more glass to break, after all. I climbed to the attic and opened the wood-covered window to look across the roofs of Solingen. Less than two months ago, the city had burned to the ground. Still they were returning to bomb more. Clouds of smoke billowed to my left, but not close enough to worry. I sighed.

When Mother hadn't returned after dark, I began to worry. To pass the time, I fetched water from the well and repaired one of the windows. It was almost time to meet Helmut, and I was impatient to go. Helmut would be hungry and we'd asked his mother to use the kitchen.

No shells had landed very close, but how could I be sure?

The street was deserted when I stepped outside. My feet crunched on the gravel, sounding even louder on the frost-covered road. Dampness crawled into my skin, and I was thankful for my new coat. I forced myself to slow down. The sidewalk and roads were like snares with holes and debris. I banged my knees on a stack of bricks in front of a house.

"Damn," I yelled as a dark mass loomed ahead. The bunker. Why were the doors closed when the bombers had long disappeared? I listened. Nothing.

The silence was oppressive. Without any wind, the air hushed like invisible breath. I knocked twice, my knuckles complaining from the cold and the impact. Still nothing. I waited, knocked again. Silence.

At last I yelled. "Let me in! Please! I'm looking for my mother."

"Who is it?" A voice seemed to come from far away.

"Günter Schmidt. I live on *Weinsbergtalstrasse* 20," I yelled.

The door creaked open. "Quick, come in." It was almost warm inside, but I was hit with the stench of body odor. The lower floor was full of people, illuminated by two candles that burned along the wall. I moved through the crowd, aware that with every step I got farther from the door. The place was crammed, and though nobody spoke, I sensed their fear—smelled it in the air.

"*Mutter*, where are you?" I'd almost reached the other side of the room when I saw her resting against the bedpost of an iron bunk. The lump in my throat eased, but the sweat beneath my shirt kept coming. "Let's go home." I grabbed Mother's arm to help her up. She appeared dazed.

"What if they come back?"

"Then you return if you want. Right now we should go home." I pulled up Siegfried and threw him over my shoulder, taking deep breaths when we reached the outside.

It was after ten by the time I arrived at Helmut's house.

"Where have you been?" Helmut looked grumpy. "I thought we were going to cook. Instead I ate with my mother. Great!"

"Mother didn't return from the bunker. I had to get her out. I brought you something." I held up my sack. "Potatoes and onions."

"It's kind of late now."

"Come on, we can still cook. It will be a New Year's dinner." Though what there was to celebrate or look forward to I didn't know.

Church bells tolled midnight as we sat down to eat.

1945 had begun.

CHAPTER SIXTEEN

Lilly: February 1945

I was on my way to the forest getting firewood and the stupid wagon I pulled along got constantly stuck on the uneven road.

"Come on," I cried, lifting the front wheels across yet another pile of debris.

This morning I'd realized that Mutti gave Burkhart the same amount of food as me though he was five years younger and a foot shorter. Needless to say I was fuming. And she had the nerve to send me to chop wood with a little hand axe, hours of work that took huge amounts of energy while Burkhart sat around the house playing games and reading.

I was tired by the time I reached the forest behind *Eichenstraße*. From here the land fell into a valley, its slopes covered in a mixture of beech, oak and the occasional conifer. I preferred cedar or pine because I loved the smell of the sap, but more importantly the wood was softer and easier to cut.

The ground beneath the trees was swept clean with not a twig or limb in sight. Every time I had to go farther because people were felling trees by the thousands. Near the bottom of a ravine I spotted a young cedar and made my way there.

The work was backbreaking. In order to chop down the tree, I had to swing the hatchet into the same spot over and over. After ten or fifteen minutes my arms grew soft as overcooked potatoes. I slumped down on the wagon and caught my breath, contemplating whether I should eat the piece of cornbread I'd brought for lunch. It was the size of my palm and I'd be hungry again within an hour. So I waited.

After a few minutes I straightened once more to resume cutting, when I heard a noise. The ground was soft from weeks of rain and covered in soft needles, but being on the lookout for Huss had sharpened my senses. Somebody was near.

I slowly turned and lifted the axe, the feeling of unease sending shivers down my back.

Nothing.

Above me the cedar whispered. Somewhere in the distance a blue jay squawked. I stepped to the right, hoping to catch a glimpse of something or someone hiding behind the thicker trunks of beech and oak trees.

Nothing.

Feeling silly I shrugged and turned back to my tree…and nearly fainted.

A man stood next to it. At least he sort of looked like a man. The whites of his eyes were the only unsoiled part on him. He wore military pants, the stripes still visible, and an old blanket fashioned into a poncho. His face and hands were covered in so much filth, I had trouble making out his features. Not that I cared to.

I shrieked and raised my hatchet, blood pounding in my neck. "A step closer and I'll hit you."

"I'm unarmed." The man's voice was soft as he slowly raised his arms, palms out.

"What do you want?" My hands shook, but I kept the axe in front of my chest.

"You have any food?"

I shook my head. "None to share. Please go."

But instead of leaving, the man sank to his knees and then slumped over on his side.

"Hey, mister, what are you doing?" I cried. He was lying right in front of my cedar.

The man didn't move. *It's a trap*, my mind whispered. He's trying to get you like Huss. Except this man looked genuinely sick. And he stunk like rotten garbage.

I wrinkled my nose and took a step forward. Then another. "Hello? Please get up? It's too cold on the ground."

The man's purplish lids fluttered and he slowly opened his

eyes. "Let me be."

"You're in front of my tree." Hatchet loose in my hand, I took another step, right to the prone figure. If he'd try anything, it'd be now.

The man groaned. "I'm sorry," he whispered.

"Can you at least move over, so I can finish my tree?" I said. "I'll help you."

The man's lids fluttered open again and he half-heartedly leaned on one elbow. I took hold of his arm and tried to lift him higher. "You've got to help me," I panted. "You can watch me cut the wood."

Apparently that did the trick because he pushed himself up with his other arm and with my help scooted to the next tree. He sighed heavily and leaned back, closing his eyes again.

"I'm sick," he mumbled. "So sorry."

I was about to resume chiseling at the tree when my hatchet paused midair. I looked at the half-dead man leaning against the tree. Then at my wagon. And back.

Ever so slowly I picked up my cornbread and carried it to the man. I broke the chunk in half and held one end under his nose.

"Here, eat."

The man's eyes opened, a trembling hand taking the bread. He sniffed and ever so slowly lifted it to his lips. Our gaze met and I nodded. The next second he'd stuffed the piece into his mouth, chewing like a crazed animal.

I slowly bit into my half, thinking that the hunger I'd so far experienced was no match for this man's.

"I'm Lilly," I said.

"Erwin." I didn't really want to take the hand he held out, but I shook it anyway.

"What are you doing in the woods?"

"Hiding," he breathed. Our eyes met again. "I…was a soldier. Couldn't take it anymore."

"Do you live in Solingen?"

"Darmstadt." He hesitated. "I've got a little girl. Just like you. Her name is Magda."

I straightened and stuffed the remaining bread into my mouth, the man's eyes following my move. *Who was he calling little. I was almost thirteen.* "Are you going home then?"

He nodded. "Don't know if I'll make it. I've been on the road since December."

I bit my lips, trying to conjure up a map of Germany. Darmstadt was somewhere south, at least two hundred kilometers. The way he looked, Erwin wouldn't make it out of Solingen.

Silence settled between us. I wanted to ask what had made him stop the soldiering, but Erwin had closed his eyes again. I remembered my job and gripped the axe, my stomach an empty pouch.

All afternoon I chopped and rested, chopped and rested while Erwin slept leaning against the tree. It was dusk and I was drenched in sweat by the time I loaded my wagon with two-foot logs of fragrant cedar.

Erwin hadn't moved much, so I patted him on the shoulder. "I'm going home now."

His lips grimaced into a smile. "Thank you, little girl. Lilly, it's a nice name."

"Be careful," I said, leaning forward to pull against the steep grade.

Nothing happened. I stood rooted like one of the trees. What if Vati sat some place in the woods like Erwin? He needed a place to sleep, a warm place and he needed food. *You can't take him home. Huss is watching.*

But there was somebody else, somebody I trusted implicitly. I returned to the tree and resolutely shook Erwin's shoulder.

"Oh, hello again," he smiled softly.

"Let's go. I'm taking you to a safe place."

Erwin's eyes opened wider. "It's all right. Too dangerous."

"No!" I yanked at Erwin's sleeve. "You're going to die here."

Erwin chuckled. "I'm already dead."

"Not while I'm here," I insisted. "What about Magda and your wife?"

"Probably bombed...dead."

"But you don't know that." I punched him in the chest, the anger giving me strength. "It's never too late. Let's go."

For a moment neither of us spoke. But at last Erwin got to his knees, and slowly, even slower than Herr Baum, he straightened.

"I can't help you walk, but I'll be very slow."

Erwin nodded. "Very well, Miss Lilly. You are the boss."

With a grimace I leaned forward again for the trek home.

It was dark by the time we reached my neighborhood. I'd stopped every fifty yards because Erwin was even slower than I was pulling the loaded wagon. Mutti would be pissed, but right now I had no time to think about that. I needed to get Erwin off the street without being seen. The blackout helped, but it also made it impossible to see holes and debris, which gave me an idea for later.

When we reached my house, I tucked my wagon behind the fence and grabbed Erwin's sleeve.

"Just a few more feet," I whispered.

"You live here?" he asked as I led him up the road. "Why—"

"You can't stay with me." Eyeing Herr Baum's front door, I listened. Considering there were people behind the walls of all these homes, it was eerily quiet.

I rang the doorbell. If Herr Baum didn't hear me, we'd be in deep trouble. Seconds ticked by, a minute. I rang again. Erwin slumped on the bottom step and leaned his head against the cast-iron handrail.

When nothing happened, I tried the door handle. Locked.

Panic rose in me, red-hot flames igniting my veins. I began to shake. I'd promised Erwin a place to stay. What if Herr Baum had gone somewhere or he'd died? I hadn't seen him in a few weeks. Erwin would be in danger in my house. Even at my age I knew Huss was the type of man who'd take great pleasure in turning in a deserter.

Precious minutes ticked by as I imagined Mutti pacing back and forth in the kitchen, her eyes squinting from rage and maybe a little worry. I had to get home. But Erwin...

That's when I remembered the gate. I was such an idiot. Herr Baum often left the gate unlocked so I could visit Anna. I rushed over and tried the handle. Locked. Damn.

The ground crunched under my feet. I was making too much noise. Rocks! I quickly bent down and grabbed a fistful.

"Stay here," I whispered, making my way to the front of the house. It was a risk to be in the open in front of Herr Baum's house, but anybody walking by wouldn't think too much about a girl, trying to alert a neighbor.

Just as I thought, a faint sheen seeped along the edges of the kitchen window. I hurled a handful of rocks at the shutters. Then another.

The window creaked open a bit. "Hello?"

It was Herr Baum. Relief flooded me, until I remembered what I had to do.

"It's me, Lilly," I said quietly. "Can you open the door?"

"Lilly? One moment." The window closed and I raced around the corner. Erwin sat frozen in place. I didn't even know if he was awake.

The front door opened and Herr Baum stuck his head out. "What's wrong?"

"Nothing," I said. "Can I come in?"

"Of course." He opened the door wider and I slipped inside. His rheumy eyes scanned my face. "You look terrible. What have you been up to? Is your mother all right?"

"Yes, I...they're fine." I took a deep breath. "I have a favor to ask."

Herr Baum nodded solemnly. "Why don't you come into the kitchen? It's too cold out here."

"No," I cried. "I mean, maybe in a little while. I was in the woods today and there was a man there."

"He hurt you?"

"No," I said again, wishing Herr Baum would let me finish. "He's a German soldier. Very sick and hungry. I—"

Herr Baum gripped my hand. "You didn't."

I nodded slowly. "I couldn't leave him there. He'd die. And you know how Huss would turn him in."

Herr Baum's eyes bored into mine. "He's here?"

"On the front step." I looked at my old friend. "What else was I supposed to do? It could've been Vati."

The hallway turned silent. Somewhere in the distance a clock ticked.

"You know what happens if they find him?"

"He'll be shot."

"That's right. And any person helping him will be dead as well."

"We'll be careful," I hurried.

Herr Baum's gnarly hand patted my dirty one. "All right, then. Let's take care of him." He paused. "But Lilly."

"Yes?"

"Promise me, this is the last time. It's too dangerous. For all of us. The Nazis are getting crazier by the minute. They know the war is lost. They know it and they don't care." His voice turned into a whisper. "They are happy to take us to hell with them." He straightened his shoulders and opened the door. "Let's take him to the basement."

We settled Erwin on a mattress under a heap of blankets. While Herr Baum went to warm up soup, I washed the man's grimy hands. He mumbled something unintelligible as our dirt mixed together in the bowl.

"You better go home," Herr Baum said, a steaming bowl in his hand. "I'll take care of him."

I nodded, the aroma of the soup reaching my nostrils. I was about to fall over myself. Now that Erwin was settled, the energy I'd mustered this afternoon, evaporated and I was about to face the wrath of the century.

"I'm home," I announced as I dropped an armload of cedar wood next to the kitchen stove.

"What happened?" Mutti cried, rushing up to me. "I was worried sick."

Were you, I wanted to ask. "I twisted my ankle and had to stop. There're holes everywhere."

Mutti looked me up and down. "Better let me take a look."

I nodded, stealing a peek at my scratched-up calves, hoping my alibi was convincing. "Can I eat first? I'm starving."

"All right. But wash your hands."

I quickly turned to the sink. Mutti would surely wonder why my fingers were so clean.

The next morning right after breakfast, I mumbled something about visiting Herr Baum and hurried down the stairs.

"How is he?" I said when the old man opened the door.

"Weak, but all right, I think."

I entered the basement storage room, its shelves empty

except for a few glasses of applesauce.

Erwin leaned onto his elbow when he saw me. "Lilly."

"How are you?"

"Much better. Friedrich has been very nice to me."

"Friedrich?"

"No need for last names," Herr Baum said from the door. "Erwin here was a teacher just like me."

I looked back and forth between the men who acted like old friends.

"Erwin will need different clothes. Mine are way too short. It'd be suspicious. I'm burning the military pants. Besides, they're beyond repair."

I looked at Herr Baum who was about my height of five feet. Erwin was almost a foot taller. "But our clothes ration cards no longer work," I said.

"I know," Herr Baum said. He scratched his grizzled chin. "We'll have to come up with a different solution."

"I can't stay long," Erwin said. "It's too dangerous for you."

Herr Baum limped to the bed. "You will as soon as you're strong enough."

"But I'm taking your food."

"There's enough," Herr Baum said. "In fact, why don't you go upstairs, Lilly? I've got bread for you."

I was just finishing my slice when Herr Baum entered the kitchen. "He looks a lot better," I said.

"It'll take a while, but he'll mend." Herr Baum slumped on the bench across from me. "I'm afraid I'll have to take a trip to Cologne to see my sister. We'll need to get him something decent to wear."

"But there are hardly any trains," I said.

"I've got to sleep over it."

I straightened reluctantly. Mutti was waiting for me to watch Burkhart while she went to get rations.

As I reached the door, Herr Baum called after me. "I'm glad you helped him."

It made me smile.

During the following week I stole over to Herr Baum's place as often as I could.

"You sure like that old man," Mutti commented one afternoon when I returned from another visit.

Erwin was making good progress. He now took his meals in the kitchen, the outside shutters firmly closed. Herr Baum was much more cheery than I remembered. He even smiled sometimes when Erwin retold stories from his classroom.

The only problem was that Herr Baum's trip to Cologne was no longer feasible. He'd received a hastily scribbled note from his sister who'd lost all her worldly possessions in a recent bombing and was staying with a cousin. And Erwin wanted to leave to check on his family. More so, he was worried about putting us in danger.

"He is always nice," I said simply, the issue of Erwin's outfit weighing on my mind.

"I'm going to see Annelise," Mutti said when I didn't answer. "She's awfully worried about August."

Of course, my uncle had been drafted soon after Vati and was supposed to be somewhere in France.

"Make sure Burkhart goes to bed by eight. I should be home around ten."

I nodded absentmindedly. An idea was taking hold. An idea that had simmered for a while, but now that Erwin was stuck and Herr Baum couldn't help, it was my job. Even if it'd get me in deep trouble.

As soon as Burkhart went to sleep, I tiptoed into the bedroom. His cot was beneath the window while Mutti's big bed sat across from the wardrobe. I stole a glance at my brother's peaceful face, before opening the door to the closet. One side contained Mutti's dresses and skirts, the other my father's clothes. But where my father's suits had hung, now gaped a hole—except for one suit, a charcoal gray with needle-thin black stripes. Vati's best Sunday outfit.

Over the course of the last couple of years, Mutti had bartered or given away Vati's things. The government demanded all civilians to give for the *Winterhilfe*, the annual request to donate clothes and furniture to the needy and as of late, our soldiers. The drawers were empty except for a couple of pairs of socks and underwear.

The cot by the window creaked as Burkhart turned on his

side. I waited for a moment, and when Burkhart didn't stir, slipped the suit from its hanger. At least I knew which soldier was getting the suit, I thought grimly.

Ever so quietly I closed the wardrobe and returned to the kitchen. I folded up the suit and stuffed it into my school satchel. I'd pretend to go to Herr Baum for a lesson. After all, everyone knew he was a retired teacher.

I carefully locked our door and slipped downstairs.

"Who is it?" In Herr Baum's voice swung anxiety. It was something I'd never heard before.

"Lilly."

The door opened and I rushed inside.

"He's in the kitchen," Herr Baum said, leading the way.

I couldn't keep myself from grinning as I entered the small room. Erwin was wrapped in a couple of blankets, wearing one of Herr Baum's slouch hats.

"It's late," Herr Baum said. "Where's your mother?"

"Visiting my aunt." I couldn't contain my excitement and opened my school bag. "I've found something to wear for Erwin."

The suit was a bit crumpled, but even in the dim light it was clear what a nice suit I'd brought.

"Lilly, you can't." Erwin's gaze hung longingly on the rich fabric.

"You took your father's suit?" Herr Baum shook his head. "Your mother will have your hide. Better take it back."

I folded my arms across my chest. "I'm not."

"Lilly, listen to me." Herr Baum leaned forward. "What happens when your mother finds out?"

I stubbornly shook my head. "She'll give it to the next winter campaign anyway. At least I know a friend is going to wear Vati's suit." I bit my lip. "Vati isn't coming back any time soon."

"How do you know that?" Erwin asked.

"I just know." Of course, I didn't. But at that moment, a feeling of warmth spread through me. Erwin needed something I could give and it made me feel incredibly important.

Herr Baum looked at Erwin who looked back at me.

"All right, then. I guess I'll try it on." Erwin unfolded the pants and slipped them on under his blankets. The waist was baggy, but the length perfect. Tossing away his cover, Erwin tried on the jacket. It was loose as well and the arms slightly too long.

"This works." Wonder swung in Erwin's voice. He sank on the chair and covered his eyes with his hands. "I'm going home now," he cried, his shoulders shaking.

I patted his back. "I'm sure glad you'll see Magda soon." In the back of my mind I imagined Vati returning home in a new suit.

Erwin wiped his face and enveloped me in a hug. "Thank you," he whispered. "You saved my life."

The feeling of love lasted exactly until I entered the kitchen of my home where Mutti was pacing up and down.

"Where have you been?" she asked.

Momentarily at a loss for words, I held up my satchel. "Herr Baum helped me with a math problem." My bag was empty, of course, but Mutti luckily didn't look.

"I can't believe you go out at night for tutoring and leave your brother unattended," she yelled.

"He was sleeping."

"What if there'd been bomb alarm or a fire?" She bit her lip and I knew she was working on punishment. "You are not to go back to that man. I don't like you spending all this time there."

"But Mutti, I—" Tears sprung to my eyes. Not because I was afraid of Mutti, but because Erwin was going to leave tomorrow. And I'd promised to be there to see him off.

"Get to bed this instant."

I crept into bed, exhausted, my last thought of Erwin in his new suit.

I awoke to Mutti's face hovering above my bed. "Where's Vati's suit?"

I was trying to wake enough to get my thoughts straight. Judging by the gray light trickling through the patched-up windows, it was early morning. I'd not come up with an excuse, hadn't really expected Mutti to find out so quickly.

She took hold of my shoulders and shook me. "I asked you a question."

I rubbed my eyes, trying to buy time. Nothing came to mind, my brain as empty as my stomach. I thought of Mutti's visits downstairs and knew that I would never tell Mutti about Erwin.

"I gave it to the *Winterhilfswerk*," I blurted.

"What?"

"They came by the other day when you were getting rations. They needed more clothes, so I gave them Vati's suit. They said they'd send it to the soldiers who return home as invalids."

Mutti's eyes were still glued to mine. I felt them digging around in my mind. I didn't blink. I didn't breathe.

At last she straightened. "Never ever take something from our home again."

I turned to the wall, swallowing the sigh rising up from my throat. "Yes, Mutti."

Remembering Erwin, I jumped out of bed as soon as Mutti left the room. He was going to take off early. But there was no way for me to go. Not now.

The suit had been the last straw and Mutti immediately put me to work washing windows. And so I cleaned and dried the panes of the living room, my gaze directed to the street beyond.

Around nine I noticed movement behind the fence—a figure in a suit with an old-fashioned suitcase passed by slowly. Erwin had shaved and cut his hair—a bit shaggy, probably courtesy of Herr Baum.

I placed a palm on the windowpane and for a moment, he paused and looked up at me. Our eyes met between the bare limbs of my beloved red beech. He gave the tiniest nod and then he was gone.

I closed my eyes and began to cry.

CHAPTER SEVENTEEN

Günter: March 1945

I sat on my hands to keep them from freezing when our teacher, Herr Leimer, entered. After the citywide bombing in November when just about everything had shut down, I'd finally managed to get back into a vocational school that accepted new students.

Leimer was old as dirt and had been pulled from retirement after all the real teachers had joined the war. It was March and our classroom, windows carefully plastered with assorted vinyl, cardboard and tarpaper, was as gloomy and cold as the frozen landscape outside.

Like my classmates, I wore a coat and a wool hat Mother had knitted from an old sweater. Frustrated about the stiffness in my fingers, I had been opening and closing my fists because technical drawing was my favorite subject.

But instead of going to the board and suggesting a quick-draw to warm up, Leimer repeatedly cleared his throat. His cheeks, rugged from age and too many cold nights—or as some rumored, too much drink—burned unusually red.

When the shuffling of chairs and bodies finally ceased, I forgot my icy hands. The old man looked as if he'd fall over any second. He even swayed a bit. Still, he didn't speak. Instead he looked at us with his watery blue eyes, holding everyone's gaze until the chair shuffling resumed and everyone began to whisper.

"Boys," he said at last. "I was asked to tell you..." Leimer's voice choked a little. "You've been summoned for

119

another muster. Let me read what it says." He labored to unfold an official looking document, his hands bony and covered with bluish veins.

"Every man, born 1928 or 1929, must report for muster." He paused, his breath loud in the silence. "If found fit for battle, your orders are as follows: Travel to *Marburg* by next Monday, March 12 and find the office of the Hitler youth." The paper sank. With it Leimer's voice. "That gives you a week. But first you have to report for muster to update your papers. Everything else will be explained there."

I scratched my jaw and took a look around the room. This couldn't be happening. Not now. I'd been sure the war would be over soon. Last December when we'd met the horse soldier, he'd said the end was close. I wanted to hurl my paper at Leimer.

"How will we get to Marburg?" somebody asked.

"Where's Marburg? Are we all going?" Excited voices filled the room.

Leimer raised both arms. "Silence." The chatter subsided reluctantly. "There is no official transport to Marburg. It's maybe two hundred kilometers southeast. You must find the way yourself. Look for a truck or try catching a train. Most likely you'll have to walk."

"Why do we have to go now?" Paul Mans was still as small as last summer when the officer had slapped him around. I was sure he dreaded another visit. So did I.

"The Führer needs everyone's help." Leimer hesitated as if he wanted to say more. But then he simply shook his head.

"What about uniforms?" somebody said.

"And weapons?" another boy yelled.

Leimer frowned. "I assume you'll receive everything when you get there. Class dismissed."

The room erupted in chatter, voices in various levels of development, deep baritones, mixed with scratchy adolescents. I watched Rolf Schlüter who always bragged and shoved people around. You were either in the Rolf Schlüter club or you weren't. I definitely wasn't.

Right now Rolf was surrounded by a throng of eager listeners. They all leaned in close while Rolf was explaining his strategy. "It's easy, you'll see. If we all do our part we'll be there in no time."

Funny, I thought as I carefully placed the pencil stub in my pocket, Rolf is good at taking credit for other people's work.

Honestly, I couldn't believe how these boys could be excited. Had they not been around for the past five and a half years? Their chattering was getting on my nerves and all I wanted to do was leave—get away from them and their foolishness.

"What about you, Günter?" Rolf looked at me expectantly.

I swallowed a curse, forcing my expression into neutral. At least I hoped it looked that way. "I'll see if my friend Helmut is going. We'll head out together."

"Come on. Get your friend to join us. We're meeting in *Höhscheid* after the muster."

"Why there?" I asked, immediately regretting it. Now he'd think I was interested.

"Dieter says military convoys pass through all the time. We can catch a ride real easy."

How confident he sounded. "I'll try to make it, but I'm going to wait for Helmut," I said.

"What do you mean *try*?" Dieter asked. "You should be more enthusiastic. Didn't you hear the Führer *needs* us? This will be fun."

I attempted a smile though I wanted to shake my head. How could Dieter consider this war fun? Even a blind man could see that Germany was lost.

"Find your own way then," Rolf said. "But you'll look pretty stupid arriving days late while we catch ourselves some Russians." As if on cue, his friends laughed.

"My brother knows somebody in the *Partei*," one of Rolf's friends volunteered.

"My uncle is a major. He might know something," another boy chimed in.

How could these brothers and uncles be home when my father had been gone for years? Four years and ten months to be exact. I didn't know much, but I knew that joining the war wasn't a smart idea. *You'd do what your father and Hans are doing. You'd be one of them.*

Standing back, I watched the group. Despite his strong words, Rolf looked small among his classmates. Several inches shorter than his friends, his voice didn't carry, as if it were snuffed out by the bodies around him.

"I bet we'll arrive early," Rolf said. "Who is coming with me?" All hands in the group shot up. "Let's go and prepare. See you at muster." He stormed out, followed by his buddies.

I stayed behind along with Paul, who was slowly packing his books. Herr Leimer still sat at his desk on the podium. He seemed to have aged overnight. I wanted to ask him what he was going to do now that the class had been dissolved, but then I remembered the muster. I couldn't be late, especially when it took forever to get there. The roads were still buried in rubble.

That afternoon I saw my classmates at the old elementary school where the military had set up another office. The other location had been destroyed during November's attacks. We all had to strip again and stand in line.

The commandeering officer looked grim as we stood shivering in the frigid air. This muster was even shorter than last time, the ancient doctor hardly looking at us. We all received marching orders to Marburg.

On my way home, I went to see Helmut who had received the same orders.

"I'm not going. At least not right away," I said as I plopped on Helmut's bed. "Remember the soldiers we saw in December? They said we should wait it out. The war will be over soon."

"I don't want to go either," said Helmut. "But we can't stay here. You know what they do if we get caught." His voice quivered as he sagged on a wooden chair by the window. He was usually pretty laid back, but this afternoon his forehead shone with sweat despite the chilly room.

"Of course, we can't stay, but we don't have to go to Marburg quickly. We could take it slow and wait. They said we should *try* to be there by Monday. How will they know who is going and how long it takes? I bet, they just estimate."

"You mean we hide?"

"For a while. See how things develop."

"What if someone checks our papers?" He got back up and began to pace around the room. "I'm not telling my mother. She'll go crazy with worry."

"She'll go crazy either way." I pushed the thought of

telling my mother away. "We could have *problems* and take much longer. Maybe I hurt myself. Or we get lost."

"You don't want to meet this Rolf?"

"No way."

Helmut grinned. "He sounds like an idiot."

"I'll see if we have an area map."

"Let's meet tonight around seven and be ready to go," Helmut said. As I headed for the door, he called after me. "We leave in case anybody is watching."

I hurried home along the inky road, carefully picking my way. We hadn't had street lanterns in five and a half years. The knot in my stomach expanded with the thought of telling Mother.

Determined to remain calm, I longingly looked at the scrubbed kitchen table, "I'm home." No pot sat on the stove. We barely ever had enough rations to cook something warm these days.

"You're late," Mother said, emerging from her bedroom with a patchwork-darned sock in one hand. "I have cornbread and a bit of jam." She rummaged in the breadbox, the hollow sound echoing my stomach. "Better sit while you eat."

My stomach growled as I slumped on the bench. I was hungry, but then I was not. I searched Mother's face for clues, but she showed the usual strained face from years of holding together her fears.

"I've been drafted." How weird that sounded.

The sock dropped on the table. "What do you mean?"

"We got mustered and I'm ordered to report to Marburg."

"What? Today?"

I nodded, hoping my voice remained strong. "I'm supposed to go to Marburg on my own. My entire class does. Helmut, too. I've got a week." I swallowed the last of the bread. The crumbs stuck in my throat. I abruptly straightened, keeping my lips pressed tight. That's how Hans had acted when he left.

"But you're barely sixteen." Mother's eyes were dark with tears. "Do they want to kill us all? You have to be careful, Günter. Promise me."

I nodded, resisting the urge to climb onto her lap and bury my head.

"*Mutter*, listen." I sat back down and took her hands. "I…we've decided we won't go straight there. We'll take a really long time. We'll go slowly, walk around in circles."

Mother squeezed my fingers. "You *must* be vigilant. The SS…they'll shoot you on the spot if they even suspect—"

"Don't worry, we'll make it," I said, wishing my voice sounded more convincing—to her, and to myself. I straightened abruptly and headed to my room. Time to pack.

"Will you see Father and Hans?" Siegfried's voice seemed so high as he hovered in the doorframe.

I hurried over and kneeled in front of him. "There are lots of men out there, but I'll definitely look for them." How could I explain to my eight-year old brother that I had no intention of following my father and brother? *Traitor*. They were out there fighting a war they couldn't win and what was I going to do?

Siegfried leaned his cheek against my shoulder. "Will you write?"

I squinted my eyes shut to keep them from leaking and patted his back as an answer.

It was dark when I snuck out of the house. Mother was tearful but quiet, clutching Siegfried to her chest. I swallowed repeatedly, the knot in my throat the size of a soccer ball. All the words I'd wanted to say didn't come. All I could think of were my burning eyes and my damp palms until I thought I'd choke. Had father and Hans felt the same when they'd marched off? I abruptly turned and closed the door.

It was an unusually cold night for early March, the ground frozen solid. Helmut waited at the corner, his breath steaming in the air. A half-moon colored the sky in burned orange and purple. Scattered clouds threw shadows across our path.

We walked silently, each carrying a small sack with a set of extra clothes, a blanket, some bread and a few potatoes. It was hard to comprehend we'd not go home tonight or any night soon.

I hadn't found a map, so we headed south into the woods. Leaves rustled underfoot and a frigid wind blew. We'd hiked the *Wupper* River hills a thousand times, the landscape as familiar as my backyard. I'd never realized how much I'd loved it here. How I'd taken things for granted.

"You all right?" I said to distract myself.

"Sure."

"You don't sound *sure*."

Helmut didn't answer.

"Why aren't you talking?" I couldn't keep the anger from my voice.

"What about?"

"Idiot."

Suddenly, Helmut stopped and hurled his pack to the ground. "Who are you calling an idiot? Have you thought what happens if they catch us? Everyone is heading to Marburg. What's going to happen if we don't show up?"

"We just have to hide. If anyone asks, we say we got lost."

"What if we're wrong? How do you know the war will be over soon? I mean, it's been going on for five and a half years. What if it isn't and they'll find out we..." Helmut lowered his voice. "We'll get executed."

"Shut up. The way you're going, we'll be dead in ten minutes." I wanted to smack Helmut in the nose. "I don't know what's going to happen, but I know that I don't want to go. People are dying everywhere. Everyone..." I swallowed to push away the thought of my brother and father, "is getting killed. This is stupid."

"I say we go close to Marburg. And then wait."

"Wait for what?" I scratched my forehead. "For the SS or the Russians to find us?"

Helmut remained silent.

"We'll just watch our steps and go where there're fewer people. We can always head to Marburg later."

Helmut didn't answer, but he picked up his bag and began to walk.

The trees grew denser and darker as pines and cedars mixed with oaks and beeches. We found shelter in an old hunting stand about six kilometers from home. The small box, built on twenty-foot poles overlooked a field, was one of thousands sprinkling the landscape. Not daring to make a fire, we huddled in the corner, the wind claiming free reign through the open window.

I couldn't sleep, nor could I feel my toes. It was early morning, the hour before dawn when thoughts of hopelessness and doubt whisper. Dew soaked my hair and blanket. I tried pulling my coat across my knees, but it was too short. I'd grown again over the winter.

Above me, branches moved like giant fingers. Something rustled on the ground below, the sounds magnified by the darkness. The knitted gloves Mother had given me allowed too much airflow, so I stuck my fingers between my legs. I longed for my bed, the familiar sounds of home, and my mother. I dozed, but sleep refused to come.

Helmut was right. What if the war continued much longer? Never mind the handful of soldiers we'd met who whispered of certain defeat. Who knew what was true? All we heard came through the radio, the barrage of announcements, the constant flyers. Not that I listened anymore—at least not on purpose.

What if we were stopped by a patrol? Or we ran into Russians? We had no weapons and no training. Not even enough to eat to last a couple days.

I shivered.

At dawn, it began to drizzle. I looked over the fields, trying to decide on a direction. Two deer grazed below, beautiful and out of reach. Helmut was leaning back, his mouth relaxed in sleep, his wool cap covering one eye.

I punched my friend in the arm. "We better go."

"Let me sleep," Helmut mumbled, turning in search of a more comfortable position. Unable to find it, he opened his eyes. "*Scheiße*, I'm freezing."

"Get your lazy butt moving then." I was in a rotten mood. Helmut was capable of sleeping anywhere, day or night, while my own mind refused to shut off.

Heads low, we trudged into the countryside. The land rolled in soft hills and wide valleys, sprinkled with forests and open spaces, and dotted with an occasional farm or village. The wetness softened our steps but crept beneath our clothes. We walked carefully, avoiding streets and houses, jumping off the road as soon as we heard a sound.

Sometimes, we found a barn filled with straw or hay and crept inside after dark. It was easier to find or steal a bit from a farm. While most farmers had to deliver their harvest to the cause, they always seemed to have reserves. After all, it was easier to grow and hide food when you had land and outbuildings.

"I wonder when we can go home," Helmut said as we walked along a narrow trail. Hard to believe we'd been on the road for a week.

Ferns sprouted, their rolled stalks unfolding through last year's layer of leaves. The forest felt empty, void of anything edible except for the animals we couldn't catch. A ray of sun appeared, adding sharp colors but no warmth to the afternoon. What did I expect? It was only the middle of March.

I pulled off my hat and scratched my head. Everything itched. "Let's rehearse again and make sure we say the same thing." I couldn't help myself thinking about being caught. It was as if a thundercloud followed me ready to strike.

"We're going to Marburg?" Helmut volunteered.

"Maybe we should say we got turned around. Lost our way in the woods."

"We better say I turned my ankle. Who's going to believe we're lost for a week?"

"All right. Fine." I couldn't keep the irritation from my voice.

"If we'd followed *my* idea, we wouldn't have to constantly think of different excuses. We'd just wait in the wings."

I bit my lips. Maybe Helmut was right. But the thought of going south and getting near the very people who would execute us if they knew made me shudder. "Let's wait a little longer."

Helmut sighed. "You think the others arrived?"

"They might already be shooting people." I imagined Rolf with a rifle, his face covered with mud, taking aim at an invisible enemy. I thought of Paul Mans, the small boy who always seemed afraid even in class. Doubt crept up in me, and I abruptly left the trail.

"Where are you going?" Helmut yelled after me.

I shrugged and scratched my neck where the wool coat had left a circle of raw skin. I had to distract myself. My armpits reeked and my crotch itched. We'd soon pick up lice or some other vermin if we didn't wash. But that wasn't what bugged me. The aimless wandering was driving me crazy. Helmut's frown was driving me crazy. Worst of all were my own indecision and doubts.

With a sigh, I thought of my bathtub. Even if I had to haul water and warm it on the stove, it had been pure luxury compared to living in the woods.

"You want to wash?" Helmut's expression was incredulous as if I'd suggested flying to Africa. Helmut dipped a forefinger into the water. "Liquid ice."

I ignored him and stared at the stream that gurgled across moss-covered rocks. This early in the year, the water was knee-deep. Light reflected off its surface in brilliant colors. Ordinarily, I loved all bodies of water, but I'd only gone swimming when it was hot. I pulled off my coat and sweater, unbuttoned shirt and pants, shed shoes and socks, toes curling against the cold dampness of a long winter.

The air pierced my skin. Goose bumps spread. Helmut didn't move.

"Are you going to watch or what?"

"Fine." With a sigh Helmut tore off his jacket.

I turned my back and waded into the stream, splashing myself. "Damn, it's freezing." My feet were numb, making it impossible to keep my balance. I slipped and took a dive.

When I reemerged, Helmut was down to his underwear, his lips blue. "We don't have any towels," he stuttered. His collarbones stood out, his ribs lined in perfect order below like the keys of a piano. Why had I never noticed? Before the war we used to go swimming in the public pool. A lifetime ago.

So, why go on? Why not lie down right here, right now? Or better yet, march to the next HJ office to turn ourselves in. I couldn't answer that question. All I knew was that I'd continue as long as I could walk. I had to believe a new life waited somewhere beyond the horizon. What was another day or week after five and a half years?

"I can't wait to take a real bath again," I said as I rubbed myself down with my shirt, pulling the spare underpants from my bag. A thousand needles pricked my feet and legs and, had it not been for the hollowness in my middle, I'd felt refreshed.

"Let's go," I said as soon as Helmut was dressed.

My urge to move was greater than my need to rest.

Ten days had passed and we were getting into a routine. Every time we reached a road, we watched and listened for several minutes before crossing, only to disappear into the next thicket. With the forest virtually void of food, farms and fields were the only place to score: a handful of potatoes or rutabagas, sorrel and half-rotten apples, a few soggy grains. Not daring to make a fire, we chewed our few finds raw.

We hiked cross-country until we came across a small, well-kept farm far back from the road. I scanned the grounds for signs of political expression, a swastika or the German flag.

There were none. The house stood quietly. Not even a rooster crowed.

"Let's ask for food," Helmut said.

"You think it's safe?" I scanned the windows of the farmhouse, imagining eyes behind the curtains. The farmhouse was small, with red brick walls and clay shingles. The barn next to it was modest too, with one low-rising stall. Nobody was in sight.

We rehearsed quickly... on the way to Marburg, got lost, needing supplies to get there.

I knew Helmut was afraid by the way his upper lip trembled. Just in the last two days I'd noticed my own legs turn shaky. It was like walking on half-cooked spaghetti. My stomach hurt most of the time, and I had trouble sleeping even though the nights had been warmer.

"You want to ask?" I whispered.

"Maybe we should wait till dark and look for something to steal."

"We need to eat," I hissed. Anger reared inside me like a vicious animal, another side effect of starvation. Yet, I didn't move either.

"First I'd like to know how many people live here," Helmut said, settling himself against a tree stump.

Out of nowhere a dog the size of a German shepherd raced straight at us, black fur bristling. It growled and showed impressive white fangs.

"*Guter Hund*," I whispered, feeling my leg muscles tighten, wondering if we could afford to turn our backs without being eaten for lunch.

The dog drew closer, paws silent on the packed dirt, its snarl vicious. As I began to tremble, Helmut cried, "Move slowly and climb the tree."

"What do you want?" An old man had appeared in the entrance of the farmhouse and pointed a rifle at us.

"I wonder if you could..." Helmut said.

"Spit it out, boy. I don't have all day."

"We're hungry…and unarmed," I offered. That was technically untrue, because I never went anywhere without my pocketknife. My knees remained frozen in place.

"Up to no good, are you?" The man waved the rifle.

"We just wanted to ask for something to eat," Helmut said. "We better go now."

"Not so fast. Come out of the bush and show yourself." Had the farmer's voice softened or was I hallucinating? "Hungry, eh?"

We slowly approached. I had one eye on the dog, which had stopped growling, the other on the barrel of the gun. I felt Helmut next to me and considered giving him a sign. But whether to run or advance was anybody's guess.

"Come here, Rudi." The dog trotted to the old man, tail wagging.

"I can see you haven't eaten in a while." The old man's gaze came to rest on our mud-covered boots. "A shame what this country is coming to." He shook his head and walked inside. I hesitated and looked at Helmut.

"What are you waiting for? Come in," the old man said. "Take off your shoes."

The kitchen looked worn like the man's knobby hands, but the oak table was polished clean. The man set his rifle in the corner by the sink. "Let's see what we have," he mumbled as we halted halfway into the room. "Sit, boy."

Was the man talking to his dog or us?

The man rustled around his cupboards. "Sit down, boys," he nodded at the table now loaded with bread, butter, cheese, homemade jam and dried sausage. We sank on two chairs across from each other, my throat dry and my stomach knotting with hunger and worry.

I smelled bread and smoky meat. It was impossible to tear my eyes away. Helmut gulped saliva.

"So, who are you?" The farmer's eyes, sunken within the folds of lose skin, were hard to read.

We're in hiding, I wanted to say. We're running away from the war.

I sighed with relief, hearing Helmut say, "I'm Helmut. This is my friend, Günter. We're on our way to Marburg to enlist."

The farmer studied our faces. "How old are you?"

"Sixteen," we both said at the same time.

The kitchen turned silent. Somewhere in the corner, wood settled in a stove. I was trying to breathe shallowly. My hands shook under the table. All I could think of was the food in front of me, and our lie hovering like an evil ghost in the kitchen.

Strawberries, my brain announced as a whiff of jam slammed into my nostrils.

"...better be careful?" The old man's eyes were on me.

"What?" I said.

The old man shook his head as he sagged on a bench next to us. "I said you boys are much too young to fight. You must be careful."

I nodded slowly, watching the old man's expression. Things sat between us. Unspoken things, yet I was no longer afraid.

I reached for a slice of bread and forgot our misery.

The man watched in silence as we stuffed ourselves. At last I leaned back with a sigh. We'd said little, the old farmer's face relaxed, his eyes twinkling beneath the shadows of humungous gray brows.

"You can sleep in the barn if you want. Just stay out of sight during the day."

I nodded, pulling my gaze away from the bread. My stomach bulged and yet I wanted to eat more.

"I'll give you breakfast and something for the road tomorrow." The old farmer nodded and straightened with a grunt. "Promise me to be careful."

I attempted a smile and shook my head. The man sounded like Mother. Better not think about home. Not now, not any time soon.

But when we sank into the hay, which smelled fresh and felt warm to the touch, and the wind's whispers lulled me away, my thoughts wandered to my parents and Hans, and how they were all scattered. I longed to be with them.

In the beginning, I'd counted the number of days: 192 days since my father left, 33 days since Hans had been drafted, 97 days since I'd last eaten a decent meal. Now, five years later, I counted in years.

Most of the time I didn't count at all.

We stayed two nights, helping the old man with cleanup, stacking wood and straw. On the thirteenth day, with bread and cheese in our bags, we were headed south again on one of the main roads when I heard the rumbling of engines.

Jumping over the embankment filled with a foot of brackish water, we slid into the dense brush. I peered through the leaves as the ground began to vibrate and the noise grew to a roar.

A German military convoy crawled toward us at a snail's pace. Cars, horses, wagons, trucks and people clogged the road. The men looked grim, their uniforms filthy. They shuffled along on foot. The luckier ones were riding high on top of flatbeds. Many were injured.

I couldn't help but scan the men's faces inside the medical trucks. I saw their dulled eyes and bloody stumps. How still they lay. Some moaned. I felt relief when no one looked familiar. Maybe my father was long dead, lying frozen and forgotten in some mass grave.

"You think we should show ourselves?" Helmut said into my ear.

I shook my head as I stared longingly at the provisions trucks and wondered if these soldiers knew about Marburg. All it took was one zealous officer and we'd be turned in.

"I want to go home," Helmut said two days later as we hiked yet another forest path. "We're starving, and my shoes are falling apart."

"What if someone sees us?" I said, trying to ignore my own eagerness for a warm bed.

"We'll be careful."

"Just for a day, then?"

Helmut nodded, a grim smile on his face.

It took us two more days to reach our neighborhood. Under cover of darkness, I snuck through the basement door and tiptoed my way upstairs. Muffled voices drifted into the hall. I had to be absolutely sure nobody saw me. I tried the entrance door. It was locked.

"Who's there?" Siegfried asked from the other side.

"I'm back," I whispered. The door flew open. I slipped

inside just as Mother ran from the kitchen.

"Günter!"

With a sigh I relaxed into her warmth.

"What're you doing here?" she said. "It's not over, is it?"

"No, *Mutter*. But we overheard some soldiers—the Americans are already in *Siegen*. The Army is retreating everywhere."

Mother shook her head. "You can't stay. If someone sees you..."

"I know." I'd never wanted anything more. "Have you heard..." From Father and Hans I'd intended to say, but my voice didn't obey.

"Nothing, no letter." Mother hurried to the breadbox. "I'll fix you something to eat."

Like I'd done at the old man's farm, I closed my eyes as I ate the cornbread. Mother seemed thinner than two weeks ago and I wondered if I was eating her ration. Still chewing I walked to my room. My bed looked warm and inviting. I wanted to curl up and sleep forever.

Mother followed. "You better stay in the basement. I heard the SS just shot several people for picking up leaflets."

"What did the flyer say?" I asked, wandering back into the kitchen.

"That we should surrender when the Americans come." Mother sagged on the kitchen bench. "Hitler wants to kill us all first. Promise me to be careful. I'll get you an extra blanket."

When no footsteps or voices could be heard above, I quietly opened the entrance door and snuck downstairs. I was hungry again, but that couldn't be helped. I locked myself into the coal cellar and spread out on an old mattress we kept down here for bomb alarms.

I awoke from the rapping on the door.

"Better get up," Mother whispered. I unlocked and snuck upstairs. After the warmth of my bed, the kitchen felt like an icebox. "We're short on wood," Mother said as if she'd heard my thoughts.

It would've been easy for me to scrounge firewood, but I couldn't risk it. The SS often appeared out of nowhere, and many people had disappeared after being turned in by spying neighbors like the man who'd stolen our horse. With a sigh, I pulled on my coat and sat down to a piece of cornbread and peppermint tea. I left the next evening at dusk, picking up Helmut on the way.

The air had warmed, the beginnings of spring tinged bushes and trees with fresh green. We kept hiking, some paths familiar, but it was hard to tell anymore. Entire forests were disappearing, either bombed and burned or cut down for firewood.

I was losing track. The first three weeks I'd counted every day, but the monotony of our journey was softening my brain.

"It's been four weeks," Helmut said as if he'd heard me. We were hiding inside an abandoned barn, its walls nearly collapsed around us. "What do you think Rolf is doing right now?"

"Wonder." I inspected my fingernails. They reminded me of the chimneysweeper who was always covered in soot and came by the house twice a year to remove coal dust. It had been in another century.

"I think we made a mistake," Helmut said, avoiding my eyes. "I mean, not going down there."

"Don't know." I imagined my classmates exploding with shouts and applause as Rolf Schlüter, his chest full of medals, marched into class. "I hate not getting any news," I managed.

"What if the war continues another year?"

I grimaced and jumped to my feet. "I don't know." I was so tired. Tired of Helmut voicing the same questions and doubts I had myself and couldn't answer. Tired of being hungry and most of all, tired of being afraid. "Why don't you send a letter to Hitler and ask him what he plans?" I sneered. The anger was choking me like the insides of the bunker.

"I just mean, I can't go on like this. My legs ache all the time." Helmut's voice had turned to a quiver.

"We'll have to." I punched the rough wood of the barn with my fist, welcoming the immediate pain. "How many times can you twist your ankle? It's too late to show up in Marburg."

"It's all your fault," Helmut said heatedly. He began to pace up and down the empty barn, his cheeks smoldering. "We should've gone down there. I shouldn't have listened to you." He threw up his arms and abruptly stopped in front of me. "You said the war would be over soon. But it's not. What if Hitler wins?"

"He isn't."

"How do you know?"

"You heard what the men said."

"Men say lots of things. People tried to kill him over and over. He always survived. Maybe he's invincible."

"He's like any other man, except insane."

"Why don't you admit that you were wrong?"

I shrugged. Maybe I was, but judging by Helmut's fury and balled fists, I wasn't about to admit it.

"Should have and would have," I sneered instead.

"You might as well have pulled the trigger." Helmut sagged onto a pile of moldy straw. "It's only a matter of time before the SS finds us. Or the Gestapo or one of their spies—"

"Shut up. Just shut up," I yelled. "I'm tired of your complaining. Why don't you go back and turn yourself in?"

I didn't want to admit that I felt just the same. My own legs were killing me. My stomach cramped most of the time and I felt surrounded by permanent darkness.

Helmut didn't leave, but after that we no longer talked. We took cues from each other, stopped to pee or take a break. I found myself listening to his breathing and his sighs, the way he cleared his throat. I wanted to say something, but the invisible wall between us held like reinforced concrete. We never looked at each other and we never spoke.

And with every day we got more exhausted until our gait resembled that of old men shuffling and dragging across the woods. We rested more, but the cold weather wasn't finished and we soon had to move again. A few times we risked a fire, the damp wood smoldering and giving off little heat. I worried about the smoke being seen.

More and more convoys clogged the roads. Plain soldiers snaked along in unending streams. I wasn't as afraid of them now because I knew they had little to do with the SS and Gestapo.

"Go home, boys," they whispered when we watched from the side of the street. "We have no ammunition left. The Americans are close."

How close, I wanted to shout. *How much longer?* All I did was nod, afraid to get into a discussion about our wanderings, afraid of looking at Helmut's face. We saw women pushing wheelbarrows with bedding, coffee grinders, pots and assorted suitcases, worn grandfathers with packs and children…small ones with thumbs in their mouths, some school age like my brother Siegfried. Everyone looked hungry and frightened.

On Day 32 of our wandering, at last, we got brave enough to hitch a ride on one of the military trucks of a German convoy. Well, that is I moved out into the line, hoping that Helmut would follow.

"Hop on up, boys," said one of the soldiers walking past.

So we scrambled onto one of the trucks, feet dangling over the edge.

"Did you see the truck behind us?" I shouted over the engine noise, somehow emboldened by our ride.

"No, why?" Helmut yelled back, his gaze focused on one of the soldiers plopping down by the side of the road. The man's boots were torn and he was in the process of taking one off. The sock underneath was dotted with holes.

"They're loaded with food, you know, military bread."

"*Kommissbrot?*"

"We should ask for some." I jumped off the platform. After passing two vehicles, I noticed a soldier marching along with his hands on a rifle. That had to be it. Sure enough, the provisions truck was stacked to its tarped ceiling with dark square loaves like shoe cartons.

"You think you could spare some bread?" I asked, thinking that it felt good to hear Helmut's voice.

The soldier, not much older than I, shot me an appraising look. "Two loaves. We aren't going to slow down for you."

I glanced at the tall truck and the broad tires ready to squash me. I'd wait. "No problem, thanks." Then I yelled over at Helmut, "We can get some, but we'll have to wait till they stop or slow down enough to climb up."

He made a face and ignored me.

When the road turned steep, the caravan decelerated to a crawl. The guard winked as I took hold of the back ramp and pulled myself up. I carefully selected two loaves and stuffed them in my shirt, making sure not to upset the load. Though the *Kommissbrot* was dry and hard, the whole rye, wheat and molasses would fill our stomachs like a real meal. I wondered if the rumors were true that they contained sawdust.

Somewhere in the distance, someone's shout made me

look up. Like in a movie, the soldiers a few hundred yards behind me were jumping into ditches and running for the trees.

I became aware of a buzzing sound, growing rapidly louder as if someone had unleashed a giant nest of hornets. Gray specks appeared in the sky. They grew larger quickly—a squadron of low-flying enemy planes. Before I had time to act, machine gun fire exploded as the back of the convoy dissolved into a cloud of dust.

Terror crept up my legs, the shooting sensation of adrenalin hitting my insides like a fist. I was in the open, ten feet above the road, a perfect target. There was no time to climb down and find Helmut on the other truck.

I jumped and rolled into the ditch as the sky darkened above me. Bullets shredded the bread truck, piercing tarps and metal with ease. I covered my head and lay still. My right ankle throbbed, and the noise was deafening. All I could do was lie there and wait and hope that none of the bullets or shrapnel found me.

When the blasts subsided, I sat up, noticing with relief that I was unhurt. Many others hadn't been so lucky. The sounds of human suffering drilled into my brain—men moaning and crying. My first impulse was to run. Run as far as my legs would carry me.

That's when I remembered Helmut, and cold panic seized me. What if Helmut had been shot? Unable to control my shaking hands, I scanned the road. Soldiers lay strewn between broken-down trucks like throwaway dolls. Most lay still.

I recognized the friendly guard from the bread truck a few feet away. He was on his back, eyes wide open, staring into the sky. His helmet had flown off, and the top of his skull was gone, reddish gray oozing onto the pavement.

Another man lay on his side near the ditch crying softly, "Help me." The front of his army coat had blown to shreds, his intestines visible. I tried to look away, but the man stared straight at me. Since I was still in the ditch we were at eye level.

The man had blond hair, shaven around the ears, his eyebrows brownish caterpillars that didn't match the reddish tinge of stubble on his chin. Blood gurgled from his mouth, and he sputtered as if he were under water. At last, he stopped moving, his gaze frozen.

I climbed out of the ditch. I had to find Helmut. In my confusion, I couldn't remember where I'd left him. My heart raced worse than when I'd run sprints in school. I hurried along the road, turned this way and that. I recognized the truck we'd been on, now broken down, shot to pieces. The wooden bed had splintered, its tires flat. Helmut wasn't there.

"Helmut?" I cried, my voice high in my throat.

Men were running and shouting orders, checking for wounded and dead. I dashed around the broken-down truck. I checked the ditch. No Helmut.

With every step I grew more convinced that Helmut was dead and that I was alone, an island among the frantic activity around me. Until I couldn't walk any farther. I stood amidst the chaos, my mind blank, my body paralyzed.

"Günter?" Helmut's voice drifted through the fog. "Over here."

I turned on my heels, watching uncomprehendingly as Helmut rushed up to me. Mud stuck to his right cheek and temple, but he looked whole.

"I went to look for you," Helmut panted, his eyes huge in his face.

I searched for my voice. "I couldn't find you," I croaked. "I thought you were..."

Helmut patted me on the back, a grim smile on his lips. It was the first I'd seen in weeks. "I'm all right."

I grinned back, then glanced at the sky. "Let's go. They may return."

We melted into the woods, the bread securely tucked in our jackets. During the night, I dreamed about the man with the reddish stubble. In my dream, the soldier sat up, pulling feet of intestines out of his belly. He laughed crazily as he kept piling them on the ground.

I awoke, my face sweaty and cold. I looked to my side where Helmut slept under a blanket. Only a few strands of sandy hair were visible. For a moment I felt intensely thankful that my friend was safe. I wanted to reach over and touch his shoulder, tell him that no matter what, we'd stick together. It was the only thing that mattered, the only thing, Hitler would not take away.

I sat up and broke off a piece of bread. It tasted metallic, as if it were tainted with blood.

Five weeks into our journey and after finding nothing but rotten potatoes in a deserted field, we reached a small village about sixty kilometers from home. A pub was the only official building. No matter how small a village, every place had at least one pub.

Having no industry and being tucked into the hills, it seemed the war had passed this town by, at least as far as we could see. Houses and sheds were intact. Even the church steeple with its bronze bell, white stucco walls and a modest stained-glass window was unharmed. Several military trucks and jeeps parked a couple of hundred yards down the narrow street.

"You think they'll give us something to eat?" Helmut asked, sounding doubtful as we stared at the white-washed walls of the *Gasthof Zum Löwen*. Lights shone from the inside, coloring the windows in a warm glow. The delicious aroma of roasted meat drifted across.

I tasted bile, and my insides churned. We hadn't eaten since yesterday, a handful of shriveled onions from last year. Risking a fire, we'd thrown our find into the wood coals and gulped them down half raw.

"Wait here, I'll go."

I stepped into the street. Nobody was around, though I suspected the trucks were well protected. Trying to keep up my resolve, I slipped into the pub.

With the low ceiling and darkly paneled walls, it felt as suffocating as a bunker. Thick smoke hung in the air. After the brightness of the evening sun, I squinted in the gloom.

A fat man in a black shirt and stained blue apron stood behind the counter, wiping up beer spills. The smell of something sour mixed with stale alcohol filled the air. I wondered how the man could serve food and liquor while nobody else had anything left.

Afraid to lose my confidence, I deftly stepped to the counter. Too late did I notice the military jackets.

I would've recognized the emblems anywhere: a jagged double S clearly visible on collars, armbands and hats: SS officers.

Three men occupied stools to the side of the bar, smoking and talking loudly, a selection of empty glasses in front of them. I silently swore as I glanced back at the entrance, my hunger forgotten.

To my horror, the room fell silent.

"What can I get you?" the barman said, his deep-set eyes

black raisins within folds of doughy skin.

I licked my lips, scolding myself for being sloppy. Why hadn't I peeked through the windows first? Now it was too late. I'd stepped smack into the middle of a nightmare.

If I screwed up now, we'd be done for. I *had* to appear confident.

"My friend and I are looking for a small meal," I said, forcing air through my lungs. "We don't have money, but we can work."

"Another beggar." The barkeeper addressed the officers with a mock grin.

Ignoring the men in the corner, I shook my head. "We'll work for what we get."

"Let's hear him out," one of the officers said.

"What can you do?" The barkeeper asked with a detached voice.

"Chores," I stammered, "like dishes, cut wood, or we can repair stuff. I'm good at fixing things." I looked around the room in search of an obvious item in need of maintenance. The silence grew. I could feel the officers' eyes burning into me.

One of the men leaned forward. "What about fixing our country?"

The officer next to him chuckled. "It'll take more than hammer and nails."

I noticed that the third man hadn't joined the laughter. He looked irritated, his eyes gleaming as coldly as distant stars. Unsure what to do and afraid they'd ask more questions, I stumbled on, "We can work first and you can give us food afterward, as payment."

Why didn't I just shut up and leave? The SS and their obvious arrogance meant nothing but trouble or worse. As I stood rooted to the middle of the pub room, the officers began to whisper.

"Oh, come on, barkeep. Give the boy a break." One of the officers came over.

I did a double take. The man looked like an older Birdsnest, the boy who'd tormented me in the Hitler Youth a thousand years ago. He had the same blond hair, shaved along the sides, leaving a tuft of curls on top. I couldn't be sure. Five years had passed, but for a moment I worried if Birdsnest would recognize me.

"Here, I'll pay for his dinner." The man tossed down twenty *Reichsmark*, something I hadn't seen in a while. The bartender mumbled but took the money. "Better get your comrade, then. Looks like you have a new friend."

"I'll be right back." Now was my chance to disappear. Fast. I turned on my heels and sprinted off, colliding with Helmut outside the front door. Trying to control my panic, I frantically blinked at Helmut, furious with myself for neglecting to set up a distress signal.

"How did it go?" Helmut asked innocently. "I am soooo hungry, I could eat a house."

"I don't—"

"Hello there," someone said behind me.

I flinched. *Breathe.* Luckily I had my back turned. Helmut's eyes widened as the blond SS-man in the immaculate uniform, the high black boots waxed to a perfect shine, stepped into the street.

"What're you waiting for? Your food is ready."

I managed a nod, my throat too tight to speak. *Run away now*, my gut urged. *Run and you'll be shot*, my mind argued. We had to play along. Either way we were dead.

The barkeep appeared as soon as we sat down in one of the booths by the window, his huge stomach hidden behind a white porcelain bowl and plates. "Enjoy."

I swallowed and reached for the ladle. The dark venison stew smelled heavenly. I wanted nothing more than to eat, yet my belly churned with fear. Helmut looked almost green. We had to talk normally or raise suspicion. I managed a weak nod and filled my plate.

To my relief the barman reappeared, shielding us from the SS men. "Bread and beer, courtesy of your new friends."

I eyed the glass before nodding in the general direction of the counter. I wanted to be drunk and forget everything. But alcohol made you careless.

"May I have some water, please?" I asked, my voice foreign in my ears.

I knew the officers were watching us, so I grabbed the fork and slowly began to chew. The rich sauce exploded in my mouth, my taste buds doing overtime. The bread was warm and the crust thick and fragrant. I forgot the men and our situation, my stomach demanding to be heard.

Amazing how you could still eat when your head was already in a noose.

I watched Helmut who was chewing hard, his eyes glazed. We kept eating until the last of the stew had disappeared and the breadbasket was empty. I leaned back and belched. My stomach roiled with a mix of cold fear and too much food. Why hadn't I thought of an excuse to leave? I was just thinking of what to say to Helmut when Birdsnest materialized at the table.

"*Obersturmführer* Kummel, may I sit?"

It *was* Birdsnest. I cleared my throat, hoping that my voice didn't wobble. "Nice to meet you."

"Thanks for dinner," Helmut offered, his gaze hanging on the officer a moment too long. Helmut had made the same connection.

"Where are you boys headed?" Birdsnest asked. I stared at Helmut, trying to decide what to say. Helmut's cheeks were as pale as the tablecloth.

I've got to say something. "We're going to Marburg. Trying to get there on foot."

"Show me your orders!" Birdsnest held out his hand. I scrambled to find my papers. What if the officer asked where we were from? How could we be north of where we'd started when Marburg was quite a bit south.

Instead, Birdsnest ignored our papers and eagerly jumped up. "Did you hear that?" he asked, addressing the officers at the bar. "These two are going to Marburg."

"You don't say." Another officer approached our table. "Didn't they give the order to Marburg weeks ago?" He scratched his head.

I froze. This time it wouldn't be pushups—this time we'd be lined up outside and shot. To my surprise, I still breathed, my clammy palms under the table, my feet cold, toes rubbing against the leather. Why didn't I just fall over and lose consciousness? Get it over with?

"…is your lucky day," the officer was just saying.

"What?" I croaked, coming out of a daze.

Birdsnest jumped in eagerly, "We're heading to Frankfurt. You can hop in the back of our truck and," Birdsnest paused, "Harald, you don't suppose we can take a little side trip to drop off these fine young soldiers?" The third officer, who scrutinized us without speaking, stood up.

"I'm sure."

Birdsnest, now with a proud note said, "You see, you'll get to fight very soon. We need every man."

I choked and hurried to cough. Looking up from my plate, Harald's arctic eyes met mine. Forcing my mouth into a smile, I glanced at Helmut whose upper lip trembled.

"Harald, isn't that great?" Birdsnest chuckled. But Harald didn't speak—he kept staring at me.

"That's wonderful," I blurted. "When are you going? We're pretty tired. We walked all day."

The second officer nodded toward the ceiling. "We sleep upstairs. Meet us here at 05:30."

Birdsnest stood up, snapped his right arm into the air, "*Heil Hitler!*" The other officers followed suit and we raised our arms.

"A little more enthusiasm, perhaps?" Harald wandered over, his voice high, almost girlish.

"Ah, leave them alone." Birdsnest slapped his comrade on the back. "They'll learn soon enough. A few weeks of training and they'll be ready to take on the Russians."

Harald nodded but kept staring as if he wanted to decide whether to shoot or cut us into pieces.

I straightened, thankful my legs were holding up. "We better rest so we'll be ready for the trip."

"You can sleep over there." The barkeeper pointed to a side room with tables and benches. "It's hard but I guess you're used to that."

"We'd be happy to sleep in your shed," I suggested. "We don't want to take up any space." I hoped we might escape if we were outside the building. Especially since it was getting dark.

"No need boys." The bartender smiled. "I'll make room for the young soldiers of our fatherland."

"Thanks," I managed. I had to buy time. We couldn't run out. That would surely raise suspicion. This fellow Harald looked as if he'd enjoy shooting us on the spot.

"We better find the outhouse. Do you have water outside?"

The barkeep pointed to the back door. "Through there,

take a right. The toilet is straight back. There's a faucet next to the house."

"Come on, Helmut." I headed to the backdoor, hoping to look enthusiastic. To my horror, the barman followed and ambled past us.

"Right over there is the outhouse. And here's the water."

Without another word, I entered the latrine. Sweat dripped underneath my shirt. *Breathe.* The stench was overpowering. I needed time to think, but there was no quiet spot. It'd be suspicious if we stayed out too long. My head was numb. The more I tried to concentrate, the more panicky I felt.

I stepped outside, slamming the door shut. Helmut was leaning against the house, his eyes wide with panic.

"Now what," he whispered, his voice shaking with anger. "Why did I listen to you? They'll find out as soon as we get to Marburg."

I just shook my head, my eyes imploring Helmut to be quiet. Somewhere above us a window opened. Our worst nightmare was coming true.

We'd be taken to Marburg and then we'd be executed. I thought of Mother, imagined her pacing the silent apartment, stopping in front of the empty beds. I opened the faucet to cool my burning face. The water was freezing but I didn't feel it. My gamble had failed. Tomorrow we'd die.

To my relief the officers had gone upstairs when we returned inside.

"I'll bolt the doors." The barkeep didn't wait for an answer and the room grew dark. We were locked in.

Heat and cold took turns on my skin. My throat tightened, the feeling of an invisible hand choking the air out of me. I was back in the bunker…in…out…in…out.

"Listen," I whispered, concentrating on every breath, "we have to disappear before morning. If they take us down there, it's over."

Helmut leaned closer. "If they catch us fleeing, we'll be dead, too."

"We'll leave between two and three. That should give us enough time to safely disappear."

"But the doors are locked. How will we get out."

"Through the windows."

"But where are we going? What if they follow us? Or somebody is outside watching? They probably have guards." Helmut's whispers grew louder. "It's all your fault."

"Shhh!" I hissed. "We'll go south." I was mad at Helmut for talking and saying the things I'd been thinking. Most of all I was mad at myself for letting my guard down, for allowing my hunger to lead us into danger.

"They won't expect that," I said. "We'll keep away from the roads. One of us has to stay awake. We'll take turns. There's a clock in the main bar. You take the first watch. Wake me in two hours. It's nine now. DO NOT fall asleep."

Despite my sluggish mind and the unaccustomed beer I'd been too weak to refuse, I had trouble relaxing. I worried about Helmut falling asleep or worse, telling the officers. What if he turned me in to save his own neck? Impossible. We'd been friends as long as I remembered. The bench creaked under Helmut's weight. I nodded off.

I dreamed my father walked into the bar. He was smiling and ordering rounds of beer for the SS men. A hole gaped where his stomach had been. He was laughing as he tipped his drink, beer pouring from his middle. I screamed and awoke.

The first thing I noticed was that I was freezing and the second that I couldn't see Helmut in the darkness.

"What time is it?" I whispered.

Nothing. What if he's gone to tell the officers, the voice in my head commented.

"Helmut?" Relief spread as I detected even breathing nearby. Remembering the clock, I carefully tiptoed into the main bar.

With one hand outstretched I felt my way to the counter. The clock was somewhere on the wall. I walked along the bar, running my hands across the top where I'd seen matches yesterday. Even in the dark I could tell that my hands shook. My fingers caught on the matchbox and the phosphor exploded into flame.

Raising the light toward the clock, I blinked. It was four-fifteen. We'd slept more than seven hours.

Panic gripped me. Fingertips burning I dropped the match. It turned dark as my mind began to race. Any minute the men would be up. I hurried back, shoving Helmut in the shoulder.

"Wake up."

Helmut yawned. "I fell asleep."

I wanted to strangle him. "It's really late."

Helmut grumbled. "What time is it?"

"Hurry," I whispered, "from now on not a word. We'll head straight through the backyard."

"Fine," said Helmut, making the bench creak all over again.

Groping in the dark, I found the window latch and pushed. I'd thought about our escape route last night. With the doors locked, windows were our only chance.

The window didn't budge.

What if the frames had been nailed shut? I hadn't thought of that. We'd be locked in.

Again, I lifted the handle. Something screeched, wood scraping against wood. I pushed harder.

The window reluctantly gave and I held my breath to listen. Any sound would travel. What if the SS had men stationed around the inn? Surely there were guards somewhere close. My breath rattled in the silence. The air outside was windless and absolutely still while my heart pounded in my head so loud that I was sure they heard me upstairs.

I lifted one leg across the sill. Carefully shifting my weight, my foot hit the ground outside. Something crunched and I froze. Ever so slowly I added more pressure. Something beneath my foot broke like a firecracker. New panic rose in my throat. *Run.* I pulled the other leg out quickly and threw myself into the darkness, hoping to land on something soft. Watery grass blades hit my face.

"Wait." I scrambled to my knees and rummaged across the ground. I couldn't see Helmut, but heard his movement in the window. Something jagged cut my hand, a piece of glass or shard, some forgotten flowerpot. I managed to pull away my fingers just as Helmut's foot hit the ground. Again I listened.

All I heard was Helmut's labored breath and my own heart pounding in my neck.

I looked up where I knew the second floor windows to be. It was impossible to tell if any stood open. If someone upstairs couldn't sleep and stood by the window, he would certainly hear us. That grim officer, Harald, was creepy, kind of sinister. I had no doubt Harald would execute us.

I shivered.

The air smelled damp and thick with wetness. It clung to my skin, penetrated my coat, and turned my fingers stiff. Not daring to speak, I stretched one arm to the side, touching Helmut's shoulder. The other hand reached straight ahead. I tried recalling the landscape behind the garden, vaguely remembering trees and bushes. Why hadn't I paid better attention?

A dog barked in the distance, a detached sound, ghostly, impossible to tell how far away. I heard Helmut suck in air, his fear palpable in the darkness. *You've got to be strong.* I carried on, one step…another. It was impossible to tell where we were going. If we wandered off course, we might run straight into a guard or one of the military trucks. I willed my ears, all my senses to lead us.

There was no room for error. Not now. I couldn't let it happen. My thighs wanted to cramp, weak and shaky at the same time. Still, I placed my feet carefully, moved in painful slowness.

A terrible stink reached my nose as my fingers touched something rough. The outhouse. We'd only made it a few yards.

A door slammed behind us and my knees gave. I dragged Helmut with me. A light danced toward us. Somebody shuffled across the lawn. Any second we'd be seen.

We crept around the outhouse away from the light. A loud yawn reverberated, a door squeaked, followed by the unmistaken sound of things dropping below. I tried holding my breath to avoid smelling the stench. I wondered if it was the barkeep.

The dewy grass poked my skin like icy fingers and I began to shiver. Any minute the barkeep would find us gone and tell the SS men. Why hadn't we closed the window to make it less obvious? I was too stupid.

I hardly noticed when the door slammed and the man moved away. He noisily scratched his body as his shadow dissolved into blackness.

Helmut punched my shoulder. "Let's go."

We straightened and wordlessly, one shaky arm outstretched, stumbled forward. It was like walking into a void, a black hole with nothing to guide us, every step a new risk. Brush slapped my face and I closed my eyes. It was just as well. Every minute seemed like an hour, every step a mile. My knees were soft with dread.

Without warning, my hand struck something firm—bark. We went around, stumbling across roots and stones. Another tree rose up. And another. What if we were going in circles?

"Can we rest for a minute?" Helmut whispered.

"Only a minute." I fell to the ground, not caring about the spongy wetness.

"How long do you think since we left?"

"We haven't gone far enough." I envisioned the nasty officer barking orders, saw dogs sniffing, teeth bared and then—

"I wish it were light," Helmut said. "I hope we're heading in the right direction."

"We better go."

After a few feet we ran into another tree. Limbs rustled above, a whisper—it had to be a forest.

Another dog barked. It seemed farther away. We kept walking, last night's dinner a faint memory.

Helmut abruptly stopped and cried, "Ouch, my hand," just as I felt something sharp digging into my waist.

"Barbed wire." I cursed the darkness, blindly feeling for more wires. There were three, the lowest a foot above ground.

"Where do you think this is going?" Helmut asked. "Maybe we should walk around."

"Better go straight," I said, imagining a mad bull charging us on the other side. Cows were a thing of the past. If there were any, the farmers hid them well. "I want to go as far as possible from the inn."

"Wonder how far we've come," Helmut said again.

He always says the things I'm thinking, I mused. We've been together too long. But then I remembered the bombers and how I'd thought I'd lost Helmut. And I knew then that I'd rather stick with Helmut until I couldn't walk another step than to spend one hour alone. "Slide across the ground. I'll hold up the wire," I said aloud.

Helmut dropped to his knees and scooted low. "Now you."

The grass was an icy bath as the wire scraped across my back. The trees had ended which felt like walking in space. We had no reference, no direction. Only the ground sloped lower.

"Let's wait here until dawn," I finally said.

The grass was short with tough blades, the ground squishy and I soon began to shiver. Faintly in the distance we heard sounds.

"You think they're looking for us?" Helmut asked.

"Don't know. You'd think they have better things to do than chase a couple of boys."

"Hope so."

When dawn broke, we found ourselves on a former pasture. Behind us, the land rose toward the trees. Ahead, it fell into a long valley, a patch of woods to our left.

"Let's hide in the forest." I straightened, offering Helmut a hand, all the while fighting the urge to look over my shoulder.

We collapsed in the gloom of a pine stand. Needles covered the ground, and the air was filled with the sharp aroma of pine tar. How I longed for a fire. We were drenched with a mixture of sweat and dew, the skin on our hands hard and dry, fingers bony, knuckles scraped bloody.

I wanted to be home, take a hot bath and go to bed with a warm comforter and clean sheets. I thought of the other beds, my father's and my brother's which had been empty much longer.

Lately, I'd been having a hard time remembering my father's face. Everything was turning blurry, even the memories of how life had been before the war. I thought of Mother standing in the kitchen, looking at Siegfried, the last child, the last person at home and I longed for her embrace, her smile or even her scolding look when I'd forgotten to do a chore.

"I want to visit home." Helmut sat up from his makeshift bed underneath a hazelnut bush. It was too early to carry fruit, but the fresh green was thick. "I could really use a bed for a day or two."

I jumped up. "That's the best idea you've had all day."

Seven weeks had passed since we'd left for the woods. It seemed a lifetime ago. Now that I thought about it, I couldn't stand living this way another second. Even if it meant only for a few hours.

We hiked cross-country until I recognized the hills of the *Wupper* valley.

"Did you see that?" Helmut pointed at a couple of houses in the tiny village of *Wupperhof*. "They have white sheets hanging out the window. You think somebody died?"

"Maybe." I thought of the city bombing last November when white sheets had signaled dead bodies ready for pickup.

Pushing the thought of swirling flies and decomposition from my mind, I concentrated on the happy face Mother would have when she saw me. I couldn't wait to see her.

"I don't know how much longer I can do this," Helmut sighed.

"It should be over soon. Remember what the soldiers said?" How often had I repeated these words? Rolf Schlüter returned to my memory, showing off his medals in class, sneering and pointing his pistol at me. *Deserter*, he said. *Arrest him.*

I walked faster. Anything was better than to think about the consequences of my actions. I was blind to the fact that spring had finally arrived. Though the leaves from last winter rustled underfoot, the trees were bright green, bathing us in shadows.

"There's another sheet," Helmut said, panting and holding his sides. "Do you think they have some kind of disease? The house isn't bombed."

"I can't imagine what it would be."

"What about typhus—you get it from bad water."

"Maybe they poisoned the wells and reservoir." I kept walking. "If the Americans and Russians are close..."

"What're we going to drink?"

"We'll have to get water from a stream and boil it." What if Mother had gotten sick and died? I hadn't been home in weeks. Lots of things could happen, sometimes within an hour or a split second. I quickened my pace.

"Slow down!" Helmut massaged his ribs, panting. "I'm tired."

But I couldn't stop, even if my legs burned and my throat had turned to sandpaper. I had to get home. Now. Never mind it was daytime. That we were in plain sight.

By the time we arrived in the neighborhood, my lungs ached, and I was wheezing.

"Let's meet again tomorrow night. I'll pick you up after dark." I didn't wait for Helmut's answer and sprinted up the street. On *Weinsbergtalstraße* I slowed down. The apartment houses still stood.

The street seemed strangely deserted, and I noticed more white sheets. There was my house. Finally. I scanned the windows of my family's apartment. Nothing. But wait. There was a sheet on the side. I hadn't noticed it at first, but something white hung on the side of the building, my parents' bedroom.

Mother had died.

Dread crept up my spine like icy fingers, sending me to sprint the last bit. The apartment door was locked and I retrieved the spare key from under the mat.

"*Mutter?*"

Nothing. I ran, checking every room—the apartment was empty. They'd taken Mother away. Siegfried was probably dead, too.

I sighed, sitting down heavily, a deep sob building in my chest. Pain spread through me like acid, burning a hole where my heart had been. I'd wait here till the SS picked up or a bomb fell on me. I glanced around the clean and orderly room, my father's favorite leather chair. It'd been empty for five years. Now I was truly alone.

Tears streamed unchecked. Time stood still.

Images of my family danced in my head: eating a meal, Mother baking a pie, my father repairing an outlet, Siegfried galloping around the house, pretending to be a horse, Hans lying on his bed reading a book. They kept circling, drawing me in, a swirl spinning faster and faster, pulling me down and away. The air was turning black.

"Günter?" Mother plunked down her water buckets and rushed to my side.

I looked up, taking in Mother's slight figure, the patched coat and the scarf wrapped around her head. Was I dreaming? Only one way to find out. I jumped up and threw myself into Mother's arms.

"Am I glad to see you," I choked.

"Are you all right?" Mother held me tightly. "What happened?"

"I thought you... the sheets in the window."

"Oh you thought..." Mother shook her head. "This time it's not a sign of dead people. You didn't hear?"

I stared. What was she talking about?

"It's over. The Americans are in town. Solingen has surrendered. That's why we have the sheets out." Mother touched my cheek.

"The war is over."

I watched Mother disappear into the kitchen, yet all I

could see was Helmut's dirt-smeared face, the way he'd looked after the bombers almost got us on the road.

It's over. Over.

No more hiding. No more running through the woods, afraid of meeting the wrong men. After six years, Hitler's foul veil had been lifted. Never again would I need to hide in the basement or sneak out after dark. Helmut and I could walk the street without that creepy feeling somebody was watching.

"Better come and eat." Mother's voice drifted into my consciousness. "Afterwards, I could use some help with firewood."

As I got up to join my family, a chuckle burst from my throat.

I was finally free.

Of course, that moment didn't last. Happiness is but a fleeting emotion. Like a blast of hot air in a cold room, it tends to vanish. As postwar Germany began, it ushered in new pressing questions. How would we survive in the rubble when there was no food, no work and no money? But most of all, what had happened to my father and Hans?

BOOK TWO: MAY 1945 – MAY 1952

CHAPTER EIGHTEEN

Lilly: May-June 1945

The 'morale' bombing continued until May 3rd, the British Royal Air Force and US Air Force dropping millions of explosives on German cities. Dresden, Hamburg, Berlin, Potsdam, large cities and small towns alike went up in flames. I don't know if Churchill didn't understand or didn't care that neither civilians nor soldiers would sway Hitler's war machine. If the war couldn't be won, Hitler was prepared to sacrifice everyone. So he did.

On April 16, Solingen capitulated to the Americans without a fight. We heard about it from a neighbor who came running up the street and knocked on our door.

Mutti just sat down and held her head in her hands. "It's over," she mumbled.

I went to her side, joining Burkhart, and she hugged us both. It was one of the few hugs I remember.

With the war ending, men trickled into town. Wearing assorted clothing to sever any connection to their activities as German soldiers, they stared at the ruins in wonder. Their faces dirty and haggard, they appeared on doorsteps and in living rooms. Some had an arm or a leg missing. Some had all their limbs, but looked sickly and washed out. Some had come and found their houses gone and their families evaporated within.

Screams of surprise and delight echoed in some homes while others remained quiet as women and children waited and watched their neighbors welcome husbands, fathers and brothers. Some men had walked for hundreds of miles; others had been released from POW camps in neighboring cities. Unable to provide food and healthy living conditions, the British and American military were releasing their prisoners by the thousands.

I thought about Erwin and wondered if he'd made it home.

It gave me comfort to picture him enter his house in his new suit, a smile on his lips as he embraced Magda and his wife. Because there was no word from Vati. And that silence agitated me more than the rumors of roaming gangs, mass shootings and hastily dug graves. Like a poisonous cloud, it affected my breathing, clawing my chest with iron gauntlets.

As news of war atrocities spread, the SS killing civilians, death marches, and then the nightmarish discoveries of Jews, either dead or barely alive behind the barbed wire of concentration camps, I was shocked by the magnitude of the killings. But I also was numb. At this point, surviving was a fulltime job. The entire country had turned into a graveyard of carnage, and I wondered what Vati's role had been, remembering the day he had left full of enthusiasm about the war.

My thirteenth birthday came and went. There was no sign of Vati, and no matter how I daydreamed of his return, smiling and hugging me, the front door never opened. Instead I felt Huss's eyes searching for me even if he wasn't home. It was a physical sensation, a creepiness that made me break out in a sweat, a rash spreading across my chest and torso like an allergy.

My body annoyed me—my feet a size ten but my breasts curiously absent. Mutti scolded me about needing new shoes as if I could've told my feet to stop growing.

Of course, new shoes were out of the question. I wore men's boots, formerly black, now gray and scuffed. I hated them.

"Is Vati returning soon? You think he's safe?"

Mutti sat at the table as I scrubbed a handful of shriveled potatoes from last year's harvest.

"Tomorrow I'll go to the Red Cross and ask."

"Wasn't he in Poland?" I was cutting the potatoes in small cubes.

"That's the last I heard. He could be some other place now. Maybe he's walking home."

That's how it went these days, our talks as distant as strangers in a café.

During the night I had trouble sleeping. I wanted to go with Mutti, but it was out of the question because whenever she left the house, I was the built-in nanny. I stared at the ceiling and thought about how I could get my hands on an extra helping of food. Cherries, the only fruit in our backyard, weren't ripe yet and our rations continued to shrink.

The other issue was Huss. I'd changed my route to the outhouse by walking through the entry door into the backyard, therefore avoiding the basement. But every time I left the house, I felt Huss's eyes on my back like a slimy hand.

My room was sticky, my skin clammy. Too broken to open, the window frame was covered with pieces of linoleum and roofing. I turned to my side, kicking away the blanket.

By noon, I paced the floor, watching Burkhart read one of the few children's books we'd saved. Mutti had left after breakfast and been gone for hours.

I jumped when the door to the apartment opened. Mutti looked tired, her shoulders slumped.

"What took you so long?" I cried.

"There were huge lines. Thousands of people are looking for their loved ones."

"What about Vati? Did you find out where he is?"

"I filled out a card with his information." Mutti hung up her purse. "They'll match the card if they can and they'll use it to ask returning soldiers."

"Why is Vati not coming home? Many of our neighbors returned. And they are dissolving the camps and—"

"Lilly, please. I don't know! Can't you let it go for now." Mutti turned and entered her bedroom.

I followed. "What's that?"

Mutti held a couple of crumpled packets. English writing was printed on them.

"Not sure." She tore open the plastic—nylon stockings, translucent and light as feathers unfolded. We hadn't seen stockings since before the war.

"Where did you get them?"

"I stopped by the Americans."

"Why?"

"I thought they could help find Vati."

"And can they?"

"Lilly, I don't know. Maybe." Mutti's eyes turned hard, the way they did when she got mad. "By the way, the Captain will stop by and visit."

"When?"

"Saturday."

"Will he have news then?"

"I hope so."

I wondered why he'd visit if he didn't know anything.

As Saturday approached, I grew more and more excited. I'd received strict instructions about taking care of Burkhart while Mutti seemed agitated, rifling through her closet.

"What are you doing?"

Mutti held up a long navy skirt. Mumbling to herself, she hung it back into the closet. "Too severe."

"When will he visit?"

"This afternoon." Mutti seemed distracted. "This might work." She held up two skirts, one red, and one black. "What do you think, Lilly? I could sew a red border on the black one."

"What is it for?"

"Lilly, I told you, I'm going out and I need something to wear."

"You didn't say you were going out. You said he was coming to visit. Why do you have to go out with him?"

"Why, why? All these questions. I'm going, so be quiet." She wore the new nylons, making her legs appear silky smooth.

My head began to ache. I couldn't get used to Mutti's lies, no matter how many men visited. "Where're you going anyway?" I said.

"None of your business." Mutti inspected her face in the pocket mirror. Our bathroom mirror had broken during the *Angriff*. "How about this one, it was always too tight." She smoothed the folds of a red dress. In ordinary times, it would have been average, but it looked glamorous among the desolation. The thin fabric clung to her body, which had become sharper in its thinness. I hadn't seen Mutti look this good in years.

When the doorbell rang, she flashed a warning glance at me. I was to remain in the kitchen under any circumstances. To my surprise, a man entered, followed by Mutti.

The man looked formidable. More than six feet tall, he towered above us. His eyes were piercing blue beneath blond hair so short, his scalp shone through. His face was deeply tanned up to his white forehead, a reminder of the military cap he now carried under his arm.

"Captain Marks. You must be Lilly."

"*Guten Tag.*"

"You should shake hands, Lieselotte," Mutti said. I stretched out an arm the way you would touching a snake.

"Very nice, *ein junges Fräulein*," Marks said, a thousand laugh lines spidering across his face. He pronounced it Fraulein, his voice deep and booming while his eyes wandered across my body. There wasn't anything to see, but I felt my cheeks grow hot anyway.

"Are you going to find my father?"

"I'll certainly try." He rifled through his pant pocket. "I brought you something." On his palm lay a gold-colored tube. "Lipstick, pink. It'll go well with your face." He grinned.

I snatched the tube from his hand. "*Danke.*" I had never had make-up before.

"I hope you'll find him," I yelled after them. From the living room window I watched Marks open the passenger side of a black Mercedes for Mutti. He walked around easily, like he didn't have a care in the world, like there had not been a war that killed 60-80 million people.

Burkhart pulled my arm. "Let me see."

"Shh." I put a hand over Burkhart's mouth. "Just a minute, I'm trying to listen." Burkhart irritated with the hand on his face, bit my finger. "Ouch, what did you do that for?"

It would be a long evening.

I woke with a start. Somebody was in the hallway. Remembering Mutti's outing, I jumped up, but the door to Mutti's bedroom was closed, and no lights shone underneath. A mix of alcohol and stale smoke hovered in the air.

When I tiptoed into the kitchen the next morning, Burkhart was already there.

"What's for breakfast?" he asked.

I shot back. "The same as every morning."

Then I noticed the cardboard box on the table, the aroma of cheese and salami reaching my nostrils.

"What's this?" Burkhart climbed on top of the chair to get a better look. "Mmmh, that smells good. Can I have some?" Burkhart's hand disappeared inside the box.

"Don't do that." I slapped his arm. Though the cuff had been slight, Burkhart yelled loudly and ran out of the kitchen.

"Mutti, she hit me."

"Quiet." I pulled Burkhart from Mutti's door. "You'll wake her."

Back in the kitchen I carefully selected a peach from the box. It was perfect, unblemished, red and orange with a rich fragrance. I held it to my nose, rubbing the fuzzy skin over my cheeks.

"I wonder where they grow."

"Give me a piece." Burkhart's greedy fingers grabbed my arm.

"Just a minute." I carefully cut the fruit in two perfect halves. "Don't drip."

I closed my eyes as the fruit's flavor spread inside my mouth. I had never eaten anything this delicious. How could I enjoy something I knew came from a man I loathed? A man who'd slinked into our home as if he owned it. A man who wanted things from my mother. Shameless things.

"I'm still hungry." Burkhart scrambled back on the chair.

I pushed away his arm. "Let *me* do it."

Bread, cheese, salami and two bars of chocolate were stacked inside. I tried to gauge if I should take something and risk Mutti's wrath. You never knew what mood she'd be in.

"Let's try a piece of this. Just a small one." I held up a wedge of cheese and the loaf of bread.

"That's really good." Burkhart chuckled as we ate, his cheeks bulging like a hamster. I hadn't heard my brother laugh in a long time. Even if Mutti was going to be mad, it was worth seeing him so happy.

But Mutti didn't yell. She hugged Burkhart and patted me

on the back. It was one of the few times she showed me affection. I soaked up the warmth of her hand like a ray of sun after months in a cave.

I thought of Erwin and how easy it had been for him to hug me close. Why couldn't Mutti be like him? I wished she'd gone off to war and left Vati home. But it wasn't just the physical closeness I had to do without. It was emotional starvation, the coldness with which her gaze fell on me, the way her mouth pinched together when she was unhappy about something I'd done.

"Good. You found the food. Isn't this nice?" She held up the salami. "Here, take a piece."

"We tried some cheese and bread," I said quietly. "We didn't want to wake you."

Mutti gave me a rare smile. "Hopefully, I'll get more. We'll just wait and see."

My brother tried to climb on Mutti's lap, but she pushed him away. "Are we going to the park today?" he asked.

"Not now, Burkhart. I have things to do. Besides it's too hot."

"But are we going later?" Burkhart hovered by her side, wiggling from foot to foot.

"Well, we won't be able to go today. I have to…do something else. I told you that Captain Marks is helping to find your father. I have to meet him today. Besides, he's organized these provisions for us." Mutti straightened.

"When will he know about Vati?" I asked. I knew that her going out had nothing to do with Vati.

"You have to watch your brother this afternoon."

"But it's Sunday. I was planning to visit Herr Baum." I straightened facing Mutti. "I don't want to take care of him."

"I'm leaving at two. Maybe you can take him along."

"Yes, I'll go with you," Burkhart chimed.

I looked at my brother, who had no idea what was going on. The old feeling of envy was back, but I had no intention of sharing the old man with my brother.

Marks walked into the kitchen as if he owned the place. His smile broad, he offered me his hand. "*Hello, mein Fräulein.*"

"Hallo." I kept my eyes pinned to the game I was playing with Burkhart.

"What're you playing?"

"*Mensch ärgere Dich nicht*," I said through my teeth. Mutti appeared in a blouse and skirt, and I turned to her. "When will you be home?"

"Sometime this evening," she answered. "You take care of your brother. I don't want to hear any complaints."

I looked at Mutti's painted lips and then over at Marks, whose eyes were locked on my mother's body. I wanted to hurl the tube of lipstick in his face.

"Shall we?" Marks said. When Mutti held out her hand, he took it and placed it on his arm.

"I hope you'll find out about Vati soon," I yelled after them, but the door had already shut. I rushed to the front window to see the scene from yesterday repeat itself.

When Mutti returned after dark, I shot out from my room. I'd put Burkhart to bed and waited until he fell asleep. He looked peaceful.

I followed Mutti into the bedroom. "Did you find out anything?"

Her dress looked rumpled. Blades of grass fell on the carpet as she took off her shoes. Her lipstick was gone, and she looked exhausted.

"Did you go on a picnic?"

"Lilly, please. Let me rest for a minute. Why don't you let me change and we'll talk later."

"Fine. I'll be in the kitchen."

Mutti never returned. When I checked a few minutes later, she was asleep on the bed. She hadn't even bothered to crawl under the cover. Another cardboard box sat in the hall.

I still had the taste of strawberry jam on my tongue the next morning as I pulled the wagon toward the forest. I'd had no opportunity to ask about yesterday. About Vati.

By now my hand axe was dull as the blunt edge of a knife and even thin limbs took forever to cut. The military occupation had forbidden the chopping and removal of firewood, though everyone did it. What else were we going to use to heat and cook? There hadn't been coal or briquettes in years.

It was past lunch when I returned, my stomach rumbling.

The front door stood open and I was about to enter when I heard voices.

"…have been out late." Huss' voice crept through the opening.

"Karl, please," Mutti said.

"I think it's time for a visit, don't you?"

"Not tonight, Karl."

"Luise, if I were you I'd be careful."

"I said not tonight."

"Tsk, tsk, Luise, why so angry? It was just a question."

"*Guten Tag,* Karl."

All was quiet. I waited for Huss's door to close and peeked around the doorframe.

Huss stood in the stairwell, his body heaving, arms outstretched against the opposite wall, trapping Mutti in-between. "I thought we were friends," he breathed. "Why don't you come in now?"

"Burkhart is alone."

"Maybe I should ask your daughter. She seems like a sweet girl."

"You stay away from her, you hear."

"How about tomorrow? Surely, you won't be too tired then?" He lifted his arm so she could pass. Without a word, Mutti raced upstairs.

I ducked as Huss turned, his gaze passing by the entry. His door closed, leaving behind the stench of stale smoke.

Forgetting to breathe, I flew upstairs. Mutti was in the kitchen, rummaging through the new packages. She seemed far away. My hate for Huss had found new nourishment.

When I returned from the rations office the next afternoon, I heard voices from Huss's window.

"I saw you." Huss's voice seethed.

"I don't know what you saw. It's nothing." Mutti's voice was loud and clear. I froze.

"Do you think I'm an idiot?"

"Karl, please."

"Karl, please," Huss mocked. "I saw you."

"What did you see?"

"You and that American—I thought we had an understanding." Karl's voice grew quiet, and I crept beneath the window to hear better.

"I so appreciate what you did for us."

"If you're playing games, it's going to get ugly."

"I'm not, I need you."

"You better be nice to me."

"I know, tonight, I—"

"Yes, tonight."

In the quiet that followed, I shifted my aching legs.

"Who's there?" Huss said.

I pressed against the wall, my heart doing staccato. The windows above me slammed shut.

I wanted to strangle Huss—and Mutti. All I could do was hurry upstairs.

Burkhart came running. "Where have you been? You were supposed to be home hours ago."

I sighed, trying to catch my breath. Burkhart sounded like Mutti. Ignoring him, I hurried into the kitchen, opening the bread box.

"You're not supposed to take that without asking."

The piece was half the size of my palm, yet I felt guilty. "I'm hungry."

"I'm hungry, too. Are you going to cook?"

Though Mutti had been home all afternoon, nothing was prepared for dinner. "Where's Mutti?" I asked.

"She's visiting the neighbor."

"How long has she been down there?"

"Don't know, a while. She told me to wait here."

"I'm going to get some soup going. Why don't you help cut up these carrots?"

"I'm not supposed to touch knives."

"Fine, I'll do it myself. Get out an onion and two potatoes."

"Lilly?" Mutti stood in the door.

"*Hallo* Mutti." I busied myself with the pot, pouring water from a bucket.

"How long have you been home?"

"Don't know. A while." I hoped Burkhart wouldn't call my bluff.

"She took bread," Burkhart said.

"I was hungry."

"You should ask. We all need to be respectful of our rations."

I nodded, relieved danger had passed. "Will you help me with the soup?"

"Fine," Mutti said.

I cleaned the onion, small and shriveled, its layered outer skin soft. Mutti peeled the potatoes.

"Why did you visit Herr Huss?" I asked, breaking the silence.

Mutti's face remained unmoving, but her eyes darted to me and back so quickly, I almost missed it. She started chopping the potato, her knife digging into the wooden board, two red blotches burning on her cheeks.

"Just saying hello. It's good to have a man around to help with things if we need it."

"What kind of things?"

"You know, fixing stuff and helping with food."

I'd never seen Huss fixed anything for us. "I see." Silence fell over the kitchen.

"Lilly?"

"Yes, Mutti."

"Are you listening? I said, stay away from Herr Huss. Just be friendly, but don't talk to him."

"Yes," I said, opening my mouth to say the things I wanted to say. Instead I remained silent, the issues at hand so overwhelming, I felt if I started my world would implode.

That night, I woke up with a start. I'd dreamed Vati was back. It'd been so real his voice still echoed inside my head. He walked in, old and shriveled like Herr Baum, finding Mutti and Herr Huss holding hands. Vati turned around and left, throwing the door closed without a word, ignoring me and Burkhart.

Anger built inside me then, icy and hot at the same time, constricting my throat and making it hard to breathe. Vati was away, maybe suffering and Mutti—I was furious about Mutti.

I remembered Huss in the hallway, hovering over her like a leech, and the American standing in our kitchen with his knowing smile. I wanted to get up and shake my mother, ask her what she was doing. My mind swirled as I tried to sort out what to feel.

With all this confusion, only one thing was clear. I had to protect Burkhart, keep him away from Mutti's friends and the war's aftermath. Like me, Burkhart had been left behind. Unlike me, he had no memories of Vati. He only knew Mutti and her parties.

"What was he like?" Burkhart once asked when I caught him studying Vati's photo, a small wrinkle on his forehead.

"He read to us," I said, resenting the warmth the memory gave me.

I turned to my side, eyes wide open in the dark as new worries washed over me. I wanted Vati home, but what if he found out and left us?

Maybe it was better he kept away.

CHAPTER NINETEEN

Lilly: July 1945

When Vati didn't come home in May or June, Mutti and I visited Vati's old boss, Dr. Fenning, at the city of Solingen. For some reason, Mutti figured I should go along.

Fenning's face showed mild annoyance because we'd waited in front of his door for an hour, refusing to leave.

"Frau Kronen, what can I do for you?" Fenning said at last, throwing us an indulgent glance as if he were talking to a couple of annoying children.

"This is my daughter, Lieselotte," Mutti said. "We're waiting for word from Willi, my husband."

"Surely, that's not why you came to visit."

"No, I…we are no longer receiving any funds from the government. We need money."

Fenning smiled. "I fail to see where this is relevant." He leaned forward. "The city is not obligated to support the families of missing soldiers." His tone was cool.

"But, Herr Dr., I thought…" Mutti stumbled, "You can surely extend some kind of support. My husband had an important position. He will return home one day soon, and we can repay you." Her voice trailed off.

"Frau Kronen," Fenning squirmed in his seat, fingers drumming the desktop, "I feel for you, but my hands are tied. The city has no funds for this kind of thing. "I wish," he paused.

"What?"

"Your husband, you know—he didn't have to go."

"What do you mean?"

"The director offered your husband a permanent position so he would not have to serve. He had clearance from the city."

Mutti leaned forward. "He could've stayed?"

I felt my fingers curl around the bag I was holding until the straps cut into my palm. *Had I heard right?*

"The city needed him urgently, not that it makes any difference now."

I felt like a fist hit me. Vati had pretended to be drafted and left us because he wanted to be part of Hitler's war machine. The pressure in my head caused me to drop by bag and bend over. I remembered Vati's lie, and my insides twisted anew in the understanding he had betrayed us.

Mutti wasn't doing any better. Her composure broke and tears dripped on her folded hands.

"I didn't know."

With a sigh, Fenning got up and walked around his desk. He put a hand on Mutti's shoulder.

"Na, na, Frau Kronen, it can't be that bad." Mutti kept crying, ignoring the hand edging down her back.

"Maybe there's something we can do." He straightened as if to remind himself that I was there to see his grabbing fingers. Mutti looked up, her eyes swollen. Fenning continued, "What can you do? I mean, have you learned anything…a skill?"

"What do you mean?"

"Do you have a profession, an education? Can you type or keep books or do translations?"

"No, I never—I didn't have to. Willi wanted me home."

"Surely you know how to do something."

Mutti sat up straight. "I can clean and—I can knit. So can my daughter."

I kept staring. The man was a jerk.

Fenning sat back down and put a finger on his lips, his forehead wrinkled in thought.

We waited. Impatient and angry, I watched the soft man behind the desk. My thoughts turned to Vati, who'd worked here a long time ago. He'd been offered asylum from the war. He could have taken care of us, earned a living and remained home. My insides whirled with this new truth as I asked myself what had possessed Vati.

"Frau Kronen?"

Mutti looked up in surprise. Obviously, she'd been just as distracted as I had.

Fenning stared at Mutti. "I said I know a baroness who is always looking for custom knitting. She pays well if she likes your work."

Mutti nodded.

"You have to be very good." Fenning gave us a once-over. "I don't want to waste her time."

"No," Mutti said. "Our work is very accurate. We can do it."

Fenning scribbled something and rounded his desk. "Here." Folding his arm around her shoulders, he handed Mutti the note. "Go to this address and ask for Baroness Warberg. Tell her I sent you."

"Thank you, Herr Dr., thank you very much." Mutti wiggled out of the man's arm and we slipped into the hallway.

"Don't forget," Fenning yelled after us, "use the back entrance, the back!"

I hardly heard him, nor did I pay attention to Mutti or the miles of yarn I'd have to process.

All I thought about was that Vati had deserted us on purpose.

We rushed home in silence. Anger drove me forward as if I could outrun the truth. Only when our home came into view, we slowed. The magnitude of what Vati had done didn't sink in immediately. It was as if awakening after a deep slumber and finding the world unrecognizable. The image of my father, I'd kept in my heart, was nothing but an illusion, a circus trick. It made me wonder if there was truth to anything I remembered.

I was the daughter of a stranger.

I glanced sideways at Mutti. She'd been struggling to keep us afloat and she'd been betrayed as well. Did she feel like I did? Not knowing the man she'd married.

"What are we going to do?" I asked, putting my hand on her forearm.

Mutti pulled away, her head high. "Nothing, Lilly. Absolutely nothing." She turned to me, her expression hard once more. "And not a word to your brother."

As I hung my head, Herr Baum came limping down the street.

"Lilly, could you come over for a moment? I've got a surprise," he said, his eyes strangely shimmering.

Ignoring him, Mutti charged toward the front door. My gaze followed her. Her hat was lopsided and her lipstick smeared. Everyone else saw a woman who'd married up in the world, her shoulders proudly squared as she fumbled for the house key. All I saw was betrayal edged into her being, the fake shell of pretention. Vati's lie hung above her like an acid cloud, ready to dissolve her.

I took a deep breath, swallowing the sadness squeezing my heart.

Herr Baum's voice reached through the fog. "What happened?"

I attempted a smile and took his arm. Some day, I'd tell him about Vati. "Let's go."

The old man was almost giddy as we entered his kitchen. He handed me a card. "Read, Lilly, read."

My Dear Friedrich,

I made it home. Magda and my wife are all right. We are staying with my brother-in-law on a small farm and I will return to teaching this fall. I thank you with all my heart for what you did.

This part is for Lilly:

You saved my life in more ways than I can express. I will never forget you.

Love, always.

E.

My eyes blurred as I reread the card. What a wondrous thing fate was. It had sent my father into the arms of Hitler, had destroyed my trust in him. And yet, fate had sent Erwin because he needed saving. And I had done it.

Herr Baum chuckled. "He's safe."

And like a tidal wave, laughter bubbled up in me.

CHAPTER TWENTY

Günter: July 1945

I squatted near the collapsed walls of a former villa while Helmut dug underneath a sideboard—all that remained of a kitchen. We were searching for valuables, anything suitable to trade on the black market.

When tires screeched and a truck door slammed shut, I flinched. The weeks in the woods had left their mark. I had nightmares of Birdsnest, the SS officer, chasing me through the woods and making me kneel before he put a pistol into my mouth.

I knew Helmut felt the same, his cheekbones even sharper, his fingers like sticks. We never talked about our time on the run, but the memories were always there like some evil ghost lurking over our shoulders.

"What are you boys doing?" a voice yelled in broken German.

I looked up from the rubble. "Searching for stuff."

"It's forbidden to remove items from bombsites." The man wore a British military uniform and waved a rifle.

I kept my eyes on the gun and the man's pistol on the leather belt. "We didn't know."

"This is city property. Read the announcements." The soldier sounded irritated. As Helmut and I scrambled down the street, the officer yelled after us. "Next time I'll arrest you."

"At least he doesn't know our names," I panted as I slumped behind a fence, ignoring the rumbling in my middle.

Dinner was a long time away.

"Or where we live."

"Now, what? I've got to get firewood."

"So we go back?"

I shrugged. I refused to be afraid. "Maybe another place. Surely, they can't have guards everywhere. Half the town is in ruins."

"I can't believe we are *forbidden* to take anything."

"How are we supposed to survive?"

"Exactly."

"Next they'll tell us when to use the bathroom."

"They'll have an administrator of shit," Helmut sneered.

"A *commissioner* of outhouses and water closets."

Helmut scratched his head. "I need firewood, too. We're almost out."

I grinned. "I know a place with a collapsed roof." Unlike trees, roof trusses burned long and hot.

"We'll need saws."

"Wait at the corner, I'll get them." I raced off. At least my house still stands, I mused as I approached our apartment building.

A handsaw and ax tucked under my shirt, I yelled into the kitchen, "*Mutter*, I'll be back in an hour."

The knock on the door startled me. Why didn't Helmut wait at our meeting place as usual? Irritated I yanked open the door.

"What? I thought you were—"

The visitor looked alien. Blackish filth covered his skin as if he'd spent years in a coalmine. His pants, held up by a piece of cord, were ripped, his shirt peppered with holes. Sores festered on arms and chin.

"It's me," the figure said.

With a pang I recognized the voice of my older brother, Hans.

"*Mutter*, come quick," I cried, my eyes glued to the strange figure. "Oh... come in." I motioned my skeletal brother into the house, searching for something to say. My throat was strangely hoarse. "Man, you stink. How are you?"

Hans grimaced through the muck. "Much better now that I'm home."

"Hans!" As Mother hugged my brother, I tried to hide my

shock. Hans looked like a scarecrow left to rot in the field. His once muscular arms were thin as sticks, his skin loose wrinkles. He seemed to have trouble standing.

Mother wiped away a tear. "Let's get you cleaned up. Günter?"

"I'm right here."

"Fetch water, enough to fill the tub. Better go twice."

I dropped the saws and snatched our buckets instead. Anything was better than watching the crumpled figure in the kitchen. I'd catch Helmut on the way. Firewood would have to wait.

Hans had left last October, drafted as part of the early *Volkssturm*, the people's storm, Hitler's last attempts of fueling the war with Germany's adolescents. Six months later I'd been part of that same campaign. But unlike me, Hans hadn't been able to run and hide. He'd joined a radio news troop.... What had happened to him?

We helped Hans into the bath. In former times I would've been embarrassed to see him naked. Now I didn't care. My brother reminded me of a child, helpless and weak.

"Hand me that soap," Mother said. "And get a second brush."

I hurried into the kitchen to get a scrub brush we used for potatoes. "Where is the damn brush?" I cried, digging beneath the sink. I tossed dish cloths and towels on the floor until I found the stupid thing beneath a linen sack.

Hans had closed his eyes and lay back. I counted his ribs as I worked on his shoulders and chest. Everything was black as if he'd rolled in coal dust. Except it wasn't loose dirt, it adhered to his skin like glue.

"Are you hurt?" I asked, picking dead lice from his skin.

Hans didn't seem to hear. He just leaned into my arm like a baby.

Mother sent me back to heat more water so we could wash his head. It took an hour to see skin again. Hans never uttered a word. He only cried out a few times when we'd disturbed one of the many sores. I closed my eyes several times because I didn't want Siegfried, who'd snuck in to take a look at big brother, to see my tears.

We wrapped Hans in a towel and half carried, half dragged

him into our bedroom. Hans's old clothes, mother had dug out of the dresser, hung on him in folds. I gave him my spare belt or he'd have lost his pants. After we fed him a bit of bread and peppermint tea, he crawled under the covers and passed out.

Though I was relieved Hans was safe, I soon longed to be outside and away. With ever dwindling rations, I'd hoped Hans would help *organize* supplies. With an extra mouth to feed, we urgently needed provisions because three months after the war, stores remained closed.

The Brits had taken over the management of Solingen from the Americans in late May and supposedly we were all getting plenty of rations. That is...on paper. We got coupons for everything, but Germany was in such a mess that little food reached us.

But a cloud hung wherever Hans went. At dinner he shuffled into the kitchen as if he were eighty.

"I've got to find more food," I said, poking my spoon into the watery soup with shreds of potatoes and a few onion rings.

"Maybe I should go to speak with the British administration," Mother said. But one of us has to stay with Siegfried. Her gaze fell on Hans who stared into space, seemingly having forgotten his soup.

"Hans?" I said a bit too loudly.

He jumped, then mumbled something before he met my eyes. "What?"

"You think you can stay with Siegfried while we run errands?"

"Sure," he said.

As we continued our discussion about where to unearth enough nourishment to feed four people, Hans remained silent. The next day wasn't any better. Or the next. He slept most of the time or sat forlornly in the living room. Sometimes he picked up a book, but it sat in his hands unopened.

All we knew was that he'd been captured by the British Army in early 1945 and walked home hundreds of miles from somewhere north.

"Helmut and I are going tonight," I said a week later, staring at the kitchen table scrubbed clean and polished as if it demanded food. It was my way of saying we'd steal. What choice did we have? Our pantry was empty and despite what we'd been through, I wasn't ready to starve to death.

Hans nodded. "I'll come."

I glanced at my brother, hoping the dread creeping into my stomach was unfounded. "We go after dark. It's safer. People are roaming all over the place. I'll tell Helmut."

A half-moon threw shadows across our path. The air smelled fragrant of grasses and blossoms, nature's indifference to the destruction around us. Summer had begun in earnest, lulling us with blue skies and warm temperatures. We found a handful of red currants in a front yard, the acidic fruit making me even hungrier.

When we stopped at the edge of a field of dark, leafy plants, I bent low to investigate. "You know what this is?" I whispered, barely containing my excitement.

Helmut sank to his knees. "My feet are killing me." He'd grown again during the year and was much taller than Hans and I.

"Sugar beets." I fingered the leaves. "They've been left for the second season, so they'll be sweeter. Otherwise, they wouldn't be this big yet." I yanked at a stalk. The leaves tore, the root remaining in the earth. "*Scheiße!*"

"Are we going to cook them?" He'd taken off one of his shoes, a big toe poking through the weave.

"Molasses, you idiot," I snapped, tired of being in charge. I'd kept my cool all through the hike, even though we had to stop a hundred times for Hans to catch up.

"Hmmm, molasses." My brother's voice easily carried across the field.

"Shhh," I hissed. "The farmhouse is probably close."

"Let's hurry then." Helmut began rummaging through his pack in search of a sack.

I picked up a pointed rock to dig. It had been dry for weeks and the earth was hard and clumpy. My shirt was drenched with sweat as the pile of beets grew slowly.

I glanced at Hans, who sat motionless. "Why don't you help?"

A dog barked. I froze as memories of the old man and Rudy returned. Chances were we'd be bitten this time...or worse.

There, more sounds: twigs breaking and heavy footsteps. I bit back a curse and crept backward into a stand of hazelnut bushes, dragging the beet sack with me. Helmut followed, remembering his shoe at the last second.

"Who's there? Damn thieves!" A voice drifted through the brush to our right. "You're stealing my crop." A shot rang out.

"Where's Hans?" I peeked through the leaves. Now free of clouds, the moon bathed the field in bluish light. And right where we'd dug, my brother sat unmoving.

To my horror, a man appeared next to Hans, rifle in hand. "What're you doing in my field?" he growled. The farmer had to be in his seventies. He was bald with the ruddy skin of a life spent outdoors. "Answer me!" he said. "I should shoot you on the spot." His dog snarled as if to emphasize the point.

Hans's voice floated across the field. "Why don't you? I don't care. I've had worse."

"What are you doing in my field?" the farmer asked again.

"Taking a few beets."

I held my breath, watching...waiting. Sweat rolled down my temples and chest. I'd never forgive myself if Hans got hurt—even if he was positively crazy. Eyes on the dog, I got to my knees. I had to show myself, confess to the farmer that it'd been my idea.

"Son, how old are you?" the old man was just saying.

"Almost eighteen."

"You alone?" The farmer scanned the dirt which showed the fresh marks of dug-up roots.

Hans remained silent. As I shifted my weight, the dog's ears perked up and it growled. I wanted to run then, but I knew I'd never run again. Hans needed me.

"You been in the war?" The farmer's voice had lost its hostility.

"Yes."

"Thought so." With a sigh the man set down his rifle. "Listen, son. You shouldn't run around at all times of night. You'll get yourself killed. Just because the war is over doesn't mean it's safe."

Hans said nothing.

Why don't you move? Do something. I felt the same sense of paralysis as my brother, my limps fused to the earth.

To my surprise, the farmer stiffly dropped to his knees and

began to yank and twist at the leaves, the bulbous roots pulling out easily. He stuffed the beets into Hans's arms. "Take these and go home. Don't come back. Next time you may not be so lucky."

Hans awkwardly straightened and stumbled into the bushes. He kept walking, having seemingly forgotten about us as the farmer, the dog by his side, walked off in the opposite direction.

"Over here," I whispered.

"I can't believe this," Helmut said. "He got the beets for free. Didn't even have to dig."

"Let's go." I raced to catch up with my brother. "I'll help you carry."

As the gray of dawn crawled across the sky and the air begin to fill with the song of birds, we climbed up a steep hill. I kept glancing at my brother, who strained to breathe and grew slower by the minute. *He used to be strong and order me around. Now I'm the leader.* Somehow I resented Hans's slowness.

When the land flattened, Hans threw himself on the ground, his face pale as the birch bark behind him.

"You all right?" I said.

"Fine."

"You don't look fine."

Hans blinked, his eyes shiny. "Leave me alone." He rolled on his side, turning his back to me.

I tried to control my temper. It didn't work. "You could've been killed," I fumed. "Next time we'll go without you."

"You almost got *us* caught," Helmut said. "And shot."

Hans remained silent as if he hadn't heard.

I shrugged in frustration and grabbed the beets. "Let's go home. It isn't far now." Hans didn't budge. Running out of patience, I tapped him on the shoulder. "Come on."

My brother jerked and slapped hard at my hand, his eyes wild. "Ouch! Why did you punch me?"

Hans's eyes widened as he focused on me. "Sorry. I thought…"

I rubbed my fingers. Hans was a crazy man with slumped shoulders and worn eyes.

Helmut straightened. "I'm starving."

I tapped a foot in frustration. Hans still hadn't moved. It was worse than caring for my little brother.

"Wonder what happened to him?" Helmut pointed a forefinger to his temple.

Hans sighed and mumbled something.

"Why don't you tell us?" I said.

Hans shook his head. In the silence something rustled in the underbrush. Tired of waiting, I straightened. We'd have to take turns carrying my brother. We needed to get home.

But when I looked back down, Hans was muttering. "...Brits got us near the Belgian border. ...marched northeast to *Mecklenburg*." Staring into the lifting darkness, his voice turned mechanical.

"Mostly boys like me without experience—stupid. The older men got treated worse. Some were shot on the spot." He fell silent. It had been the longest he'd spoken since his return.

Helmut picked up the beets. "Let's go."

I glanced at my friend and put a finger to my lips. "Where did you sleep?" I asked turning my attention back to Hans.

"In a field with watch towers and barbed wire. We dug holes in the ground to live. We'd fight over bits of cardboard or fabric to line the bottoms. When it rained, the holes filled with mud."

I spat out a blade of grass. "That must've been terribly cold."

"Sometimes we got wood. We stripped the trees until they looked as bare as black bones."

I slumped down, eyes on my brother's back. "How large was the camp?"

"Thousands. Many died. There were mass graves." Hans slowly sat up and selected a stick from the ground, chewing gingerly. I knew his teeth were loose. "Once you got diarrhea it was over. Men just collapsed in the latrines."

"What did you eat?"

Hans grimaced. "We received a couple of biscuits most days, sometimes a handful of dry beans."

"Beans? What did you do with them?"

"We'd cook—if we had firewood." Hans leaned back with a sigh. "In the beginning when I made it up into a tree I lost the wood. I'd drop the branches on the ground and somebody would grab them and run."

"I would've punched them," I said, a fresh knot of anger

forming in my stomach.

"They threw you in the box for fighting."

"What box?" Helmut interjected. He sat down, his back against a tree.

"A metal container, windowless. You couldn't stand upright or lay down for that matter. Some people were in there for weeks." Hans stared into space, once again in camp. "When they came out, they walked hunched over like old men. I made friends with a boy from Frankfurt. He and I took up house together. It was safer that way because he helped protect our stuff. I'd climb on his shoulder to reach the branches."

"How did you cook?" I thought of our own travels in the spring and the gamble Helmut and I had taken. We'd circled through the woods in terrible uncertainty, waiting for the war to be over while hiding from the SS. Forty-seven days of hunger, forty-seven days of living in fear of being found out and shot.

"A tin can. You'd burn your fingers and we never got the beans very soft, but it was something warm." Hans shivered as if he were back north.

"You're safe now. We'll take care of you." A feeling of warmth spread through me as I realized I meant every word.

"What happened to your friend?" Helmut asked.

Hans turned paler, his chin quivering.

"We better take you home." I held out my hand at a safe distance. Hans ignored it.

"My friend is dead," Hans mumbled. "He was trying to help me and they pushed him down."

"The Brits?"

"Some gang. Rough fellows. They took whatever they wanted. Real criminals. One of them stole my cup. It was enamel and better for cooking. I'd traded a load of wood for it. My friend came to help get it back, but they threw him on the ground. He hit his head on a rock. He lay there, bleeding and nobody did a thing." Hans's eyes glittered.

"Couldn't you run away?" Helmut said.

"Some tried. They were shot." Hans wiped a sleeve across his face.

"Damn war." I watched my older brother whose face looked pinched as if his skull had shrunken along with his muscles. "Let's go home and eat."

Hans ignored me and began to tremble. "Why?" he blurted.

"Why what?" My stomach beyond growling, I wanted to yank Hans to his feet.

"Hitler meant to kill us all." Despite its low tone, Hans's voice seethed. "They knew and didn't care. My friends are dead. My classmates…dead. For what?"

I chewed my lip. What could you say when your own country had betrayed you, sending its fifteen- and sixteen-year olds to be slaughtered, the most evil government of mankind. Looking down at my brother, I felt his sadness and fury like my own. Wordlessly, I held out a hand.

Hans finally took it.

As I sat down for breakfast, the first rays of sun reached their bright fingers through the window. My hands showed traces of mud, my pants were stained, and I yearned for a bath.

"We'll have to keep an eye on him," Mother said after I told her about Hans. "I wish your father were home."

I nodded, not trusting myself to speak. Pressure built in my throat every time I thought of my father. I swallowed, but the lump remained. The war had ended two months ago, and my father had not come home.

What if he'll act like Hans? the voice in my head whispered. *Or not return at all.*

"I can't believe the farmer *gave* Hans beets," I finally said, clearing my throat.

The sugar beet syrup looked like black gold, a heavenly combination of earth and sun melded into liquid sweetness. I licked my lips to savor each drop. I looked around the kitchen, cherishing this moment, cherishing the knowledge that Hans was safe. I would make sure it remained that way, regardless that I was the younger brother.

Across the table, Hans dribbled syrup on a piece of cornbread. His eyes were closed, his face relaxed as if he were asleep.

I smiled.

CHAPTER TWENTY-ONE

Günter: August-September 1945

August's sun scorched the ground, oblivious to the fact that many had no homes and cramped together in tiny quarters, few with running water or electricity. The British military occupation had passed an ordinance to create *Notwohnungen*, miserable leaky apartments to house the thousands of displaced families, or what was left of them.

Though I was happy we had a roof over our heads and that Hans, albeit a new kind of Hans, was safely back, I preferred spending time with Helmut, especially after our near miss with the sugar beet farmer. I'd stolen an old bike from a bombsite and Helmut used his cousin's from before the war. It was too small and his knees touched the handlebars when he pedaled, but it provided a sense of independence.

Like during the war we spent the days in the woods and sometimes made it to one of the lakes. But the lack of food forced us home most nights. We'd hoped that things would get better now that the bombs had stopped. Instead, things were getting worse. We still had no food, not to mention basic products like toilet paper and light bulbs.

Tonight I was particularly agitated. I'd registered for a new year at my school and not a single classmate could be found.

"Nobody is back?" Helmut sat slumped over on the ground, drawing letters in the dust.

"Yet." I no longer envisioned Rolf Schlüter with medals, I

now saw him dead next to the little fellow, Paul, both of them covered in blood and staring with open eyes. "Maybe they're in some POW camp like Hans," I said.

"What are the odds? They're dissolving all the camps."

"Or they're on the way home." I wanted to add that my own father had not returned, but I didn't trust myself to speak without my voice shaking.

At night I worried for hours, tossing and turning and imagining life without him. I heard Mother pacing in her bedroom, the floorboards creaking as she walked back and forth. Dark circles ringed her eyes.

It had been bad enough to have him gone during the war, but we'd held on to the belief that he was fighting somewhere. There was no reason for him to stay away now except for one, and the waiting was unbearable. We never talked about that either, Helmut's father having arrived recently. Sometimes we didn't speak for hours, each of us deep in thought.

When I returned home after six, I was ravenous. Nobody was home and the stovetop was empty. I'd hoped for some kind of soup or a piece of bread.

I angrily threw shut the empty breadbox when I heard laughter. The chatter of several voices filtered through the boarded-up windows. I headed to the basement from where steps led out to the backyard. I hadn't heard laughter in a long time, yet here was another burst of merriment clearly audible through the thick walls of the cellar.

A crowd of people mingled on the lawn. I recognized my cousins and uncles, my brothers. What in the world were they doing out here? Getting closer, I pushed into the throng and there—embraced by Mother, was my father.

"Günter," he yelled. "Son!"

I found myself enveloped in a bear hug. Unable to speak, the pressure in my eyes let go and something released—a thousand knots untwisted. I drew back to look at the man whose arms held me tightly.

I knew in my head it was my father, but it seemed unreal. After five years of nightmares and worrying, what was real now felt like a dream.

Remembering something, I groped for my father's thick hands. They were there. Then I looked down at my father's legs.

Both legs. A new wave of emotion overtook me as I realized that my father was intact and not at all the wreck my brother, Hans, had been. Silent tears fell as numbness settled and I closed my eyes. I no longer was the head of the household, responsible for Mother and my brothers.

"*Vater*," I choked, "you look great."

"I feel good." My father's blue eyes shone with tears. "It's so good to be back."

With that, he held out one arm to hug Mother, who was smiling and crying at the same time.

Every day I followed my father through the house. Just to make sure he was real. The place at the head of the table had been empty for a long time. I kept turning toward it, expecting it to be vacant. Blue eyes met mine. We looked at each other in silent understanding, my father nodding as if to say, I know, I can't believe it myself. I'm finally home.

I often found myself in tears when I saw a man with limbs missing. There were many, some in wheelchairs, some with canes and crutches. For a change, I didn't care about my tears, didn't care what anyone thought. I was amazed I could feel such joy when darkness covered our country.

Germany had been destroyed physically and emotionally. So many millions were dead or maimed that just about every family had losses. Millions more had been displaced. All major cities and most smaller ones lay under rubble. There were no infrastructure, no services, no production left. The famine worsened despite the allied efforts of organizing a new ration system.

As my father adjusted to home life, a new frenzy took over. Glass replaced cardboard windowpanes, firewood piled high next to the stove, furniture was repaired and the garden weeded.

But food was nearly impossible to find. The British military government turned out to be ill equipped to supply an entire country with food. The new ration cards were worthless as long as the supply chain remained broken.

The *Reichsmark* was losing value as soon as it was printed. A loaf of bread cost sixty marks on the black market, an amount that would have seemed ludicrous just a few months ago. Yet, the inflation was so rapid, people used cigarettes as currency.

"We've got to trade," my father said one evening. *Hamstern,* the search and collection of food in exchange for bartered goods, had become a means of survival for many families who had a few valuables and were fit enough to travel.

I looked at Hans who sat motionless at the kitchen table and didn't seem to hear. My father followed my gaze.

"Just the two of us will go. One man has got to protect Mother and Siegfried, right Hans?"

My brother mumbled something and walked off in the living room.

"Good idea," I said loudly, "Never know who's running around the neighborhood. Where will we go?"

"North. The bombers spared some of the farm country."

That left the issue of finding valuables worthy of bartering. Our good leather sofa had been worth two hundred kilos of potatoes. These were nearly gone.

"We'll take the silverware." My father looked at Mother as if he were waiting for her protest. She remained silent. "As soon as the factories reopen I'll go back to work." Solingen's steel industry had ground to a halt, either factories had been destroyed or they had been shuttered by the British.

The next afternoon my father and I set out toward the station. We carried a camera, brass candlesticks and an assortment of famous Solingen cutlery.

As we neared the main train station, my heart began to pound. Crowds clogged the front of the station. Like us they carried sacks and battered suitcases, their faces gray with sunken cheeks and despair in their eyes.

"Stay close," my father said, pulling me into the crowd. Somewhere beyond the human walls, tracks screeched, announcing the arrival of a train.

The shoving intensified.

Pressure clasped my chest like an iron vise. I was back in the bunker, people squeezing and jostling.

My father, already ten feet ahead, bobbed in and out of sight. *Leave,* my mind urged. The panic grew as I became wedged between two men, their cases digging painfully into my knees and hips. The air around me grew too thin to breathe, the edges of my vision blurred, became translucent.

"Günter!"

My father's face swam in front of me, his eyes filled with concern. "I've got you." An arm wrapped around my shoulder, creating a few inches of space. My breathing eased until I was able to move my feet. I felt my father's gaze, but there was no time to explain. A whistle blew, warning people about the approaching train.

The pressure of the crowd increased the closer we got to the tracks, but my father's chest was an icebreaker in the arctic. As my father pushed through the last row, pulling me with him, the cars stopped with a shudder.

I stared.

Like looking at an overstuffed aquarium, people's limbs pressed against wagon windows from the inside. They sat on fronts and back, on steps and in the entrances. They hung from the sides, using ropes to keep from falling off. More had found spots on the roof. The crowd on the ground grumbled. Nobody was getting off to allow new passengers on.

"Günter, listen," my father whispered. "We'll have to do this differently. The roof is the only option."

"How?" I asked. We might as well try to climb Mount Everest. I'd heard of horrible accidents where people had lost their footing and fallen under the trains, cutting off arms and legs or losing their lives.

"Walk with me." My father pushed on down the platform, until we were almost at the end of the snaking wagons. Here fewer people lingered, many resigned to wait for the next train.

He pointed at an old signpost. "Right here. You go first."

With that he hoisted me up on the post. "Step on the train window."

I stretched my right leg and when I made contact, my father gave me a push. Both feet on the window ledge, I tried to climb up, but the surface was slippery and there was nothing to grab. If the train started, I'd tumble off the side.

Out of nowhere, arms grasped my shoulders and I was pulled to the top. A boy about my age whose face was powdered black with soot, grinned. "Slippery as my grandpa's bald head," he said, patting the surface next to him. "Better sit."

A loud bang reverberated through the roof as the wagon beneath me trembled. Then lurched. I slumped down fast.

"Catch." My father's voice drifted up from below. Our

precious suitcase of trade items flew upward. I snatched it from the air and laid it next to me. Another rumble, and the train started to move. Father!

I got on my knees as a sea of faces looked up at me, watching the spectacle.

My father clung to the top of the signpost. But the window I'd stepped on had moved away with the rolling train. He'd never make it.

Fighting down panic I yelled at the boy, "Help me." As we skivvied back and toward the edge, a black cloud of coal exhaust wafted across, temporarily blinding us.

If my father fell, he'd get his legs cut off. I glanced back at the suitcase, wondering if I'd make it back down. *You're going to break something.*

At that moment my father let go…flying through the air as the boy and I adjusted our position. My father's feet hit the rim of the roof, his momentum too slow. His arms flailed as he tried tilting forward. About to loose his balance, we grabbed his arms. Another man jumped to help and we crawled toward our suitcase.

"Fine plan you had," I panted. "You almost didn't make it."

"But I did!" My father's eyes sparkled. I'd never seen him act so reckless.

"Prepare yourself to lie flat," the boy said. "The train shifts a lot. There're tunnels."

With apprehension, I slid lower to face into the wind. Luckily, the weather was nice and clouds kept the roof from sizzling. Within an hour, we'd become one with the crowd, our faces black as miners. Every station looked the same as people tried to force their way into the cars. Fists flew. People screamed insults. We remained on the roof, glad fewer people attempted the climb.

The landscape turned flat with bogs and low-growing heathers, reed-covered roofs and whitewashed buildings.

"We should get off at the next station," my father said as the train slowed. "I'll help you down. Then I'll throw our case. Don't let it out of your sight."

"What about…?" My question was drowned out by brakes squealing and the shouts of hundreds of people.

"Hurry!" My father nodded toward the edge.

The ground below seemed impossibly far. I laid flat on my

stomach, feet sliding first toward the rim. I tensed my legs until I felt the ledge under my soles.

"Easy now." As my father slid on his bottom toward the rim, I scooted across the edge, legs dangling in the void. People passed below me, oblivious to our plans. I kept sliding, the metal edge digging into my thighs.

A whistle blew. The train lurched as I let go. Landing squarely on the concrete, I caught our suitcase. The conductor walked by, ignoring my father clinging to the roof. Nobody paid for fares and he no longer cared.

"Hurry," I yelled, but my father had already jumped.

On landing, he rolled to his side and straightened with a grin. "Not bad for an old man. Now let's find ourselves some food."

In the heat of day, the path was deserted, leading between rows of hedges on both sides, framing us in green splendor. Tall and thick, the hedges were covered in honeysuckle, its sweet scent heavy and dizzying.

Rumor had it that a large farmer was buying items while offering a fair trade of food. We'd exchanged the camera and candle sticks and assembled a small collection of air-dried sausages, black bread, a few cigarettes and precious pieces of chocolate, all of which we carried in an old flour sack.

Our most valuable good—the silverware—was left. My father hoped to trade it for a large amount of food.

"I want to go home," I said. "I'm tired of running around in a circle."

"All in good time," my father murmured. His pre-war impatience, often paired with a sudden outburst of anger, had vanished.

I sighed. I wanted to argue but knew it wouldn't do any good. At least we were safe now. My stomach growled, and I looked forward to a nice pan of fried potatoes. Most farmers offered them free or in trade, and sometimes, when we were lucky, we got an egg.

"We should be there soon." My father shaded his eyes against the harsh sun, trying to catch a glimpse of the farm ahead.

"You!" a deep voice yelled. Within a split second, three

men surrounded us. They looked to be in their thirties with dark beards and stubby hair.

Somebody grabbed my wrists. Another man poked the barrel of a handgun into my father's neck. The man's eyes, narrowed into angry slits, were dark as thunderclouds above a broad and crooked nose and thick lips.

"What do you have?" he said, his accent Russian or Polish. He tore the cloth sack from my shoulder and swung it through the air. Instead of unknotting the bag, he smashed the sack on the ground and savagely drilled his knife into the fabric.

As our provisions spilled into the dirt, my father said, "It's food." His voice was curiously calm. "Trying to support our family at home."

"What in there?" The third man pointed at the suitcase now sitting on the ground. He looked the most intelligent, his clothes less mangled and cleaner.

I kept staring at the gun barrel at my father's neck, its tip digging into the skin. Hands yanked at my pockets, almost pushing me to the ground. Out of the corner of my eye, I saw my knife disappear in the thug's pocket. The man grinned, his upper front teeth missing.

I clenched my teeth to keep from shaking. I wasn't going to show my fear nor was I going to make a sound. *Why weren't there people on the road?* Fingernails dug into my wrists, my arms stretched behind my back, making my shoulders scream in their sockets. But all I could do was watch my father. It was hypnotic because he looked totally relaxed, didn't even breathe hard. Our eyes met, my father's nod imperceptible. I blinked. It was enough to sustain me.

"May I?" Keeping his hands in sight, my father opened the case. Old leather belts and scraps spilled out of the top.

"You shoemaker?" the man with the pistol said.

"Yes," my father said quickly.

I suppressed a grunt. If they took our things we'd be finished. We'd not even have food for the trip home. Or would we become another casualty? I'd heard about gangs roaming the country full of former laborers Hitler had forced into slavery to replace Germany's dwindling workforce. They were without homes and fuming mad. On some level, I didn't even blame them for taking matters into their own hands.

The leader looked at the suitcase. The black-eyed thug still pointed the gun at my father, but it no longer touched his neck. The leader said something, and the man with the gun seemed to argue.

He swung his barrel through the air right in front of my father's chest. I zoomed in on the thug's forefinger. The leader's voice grew louder, and the gunslinger stopped moving.

"You go." The leader nodded.

Quickly, my father closed the suitcase. I sucked in my breath and kept my eyes on the ground, not to let the thugs see my relief. One of them collected our food.

"Let's go," my father said as we watched our provisions disappear in the bushes.

We walked off in silence. I imagined the eyes of the men on my back, imagined them taking aim. Sweat trickled beneath my collar and I suppressed the urge to run.

"You think they would've killed us?" I asked after a while.

"Absolutely." My father swallowed loudly. "Good thing we didn't have much."

"They took my pocket knife, the one with the elephant engraving, even my handkerchief."

"I know, son." My father put an arm around my shoulder. "We are lucky to be alive. We'll get another knife. And," he whispered, "We still have our cutlery."

Bile rose from my stomach then. Our hard-earned food was gone and we had to start over. I wanted to shout, no, scream insults, punch somebody in the face. Instead I walked on silently, trying to feel thankful for being alive. All I felt was fury.

Only when I glanced sideways and saw my father's cool, did I relax a little.

A large outbuilding came into view. Most barns were built of wood, but this one was made of red brick. Our step quickened as we entered the large *Hof.* This had to be the place. An oak tree shaded the lawns, its silver-green leaves rustled in the wind. It was more than ninety feet tall with a thick trunk and gnarly bark, branches stretching toward the sky.

Nothing moved except for two white hens cackling in the tall grass near a manure pile. All looked as it had been here for a hundred years, as if no war had ravaged the country.

My father knocked on the farmhouse door. Made of oak and more than eight feet across it looked as massive as a fortress.

Impatient for something to happen, I headed across the courtyard to the open stalls. Animals stomped and chewed. "Anybody home? *Hallo?*"

"What do you want?" A voice said from the gloom.

"Excuse me." My resolve wavered.

"What?" The voice was deep and rather impatient. "Spit it out. I don't have all day. Cows need milking."

A broad-shouldered man in his fifties appeared out of the dark. He seemed menacing, his face gruff and unfriendly. Deep lines furrowed from his mouth to his chin as if he had frowned for decades.

"I...we...my father and I are wondering if you might want to trade," I said, wishing my father would join me.

"Trade, trade, everybody wants to trade. I have the house full of things I can't use."

I opened my mouth to speak, but nothing came to mind. I hadn't expected this kind of reception. Most of the time farmers were nice. They understood about the hunger and one look at me told them that I'd been starving for a while.

"We have cutlery from Solingen," I blurted, waiting for a response. When none came I hurried on. "Great quality. My father is in the trade."

"Let's see it then." The farmer's huge belly jiggled and his shoes dragged across the gravel as he scanned my hands. His pants were covered in manure and I smelled an unwashed body underneath. Even when water was sparse and we were on the road, I'd at least tried to get baths or go swimming.

"My father has the suitcase. *Vater?* Where are you?" I yelled, making no attempt to hide my dislike.

"Günter?" My father stepped around the corner of the massive homestead. "*Guten Abend.*"

He smiled at the farmer.

"You got things to trade? I've got animals to feed."

"We have high quality silverware from Solingen."

"Your son already said that."

Ignoring the man, my father opened the case and threw out the belts and leather bits. He carefully unwrapped several beautiful serving pieces, knives and large spoons with engraved handles. The silver gleamed in the evening sun.

"Hmmm." The farmer touched one of the ladles. Filth

189

crusted his hands, the tip of his thumb split and the groove filled with dirt. "How much you want?"

"We'd like food we can carry," my father said.

"Let's take a look what we have." The farmer hurried toward the house and ushered us inside.

As my eyes adjusted to the gloom, I stared. Heavy oak and cherry cabinets, a piano, thick wool rugs, china and crystal filled the living room. Three layers of carpets covered the parquet, their colors soft with flower and animal patterns. Since they were at least an inch thick each, the furniture on top appeared to be on a podium.

Colorful bowls and vases covered the table, their blue and gold designs drowned in excess. It looked wrong somehow like a warehouse, and nobody seemed to have cared to arrange it nicely and use it for living. Flies buzzed, sitting and twirling their legs, the window glass soiled with dark specks.

The farmer didn't seem to notice. "This way," he droned.

I followed my father and the farmer to the basement. What had seemed opulent upstairs, now turned to utter amazement. In the semi-darkness of the cellar, smoked sausages looped across rafters like garlands. Chunks of meat and several halves of air-dried hams hung from the ceiling. Two huge barrels were filled with sauerkraut, their stone lids barely closing. In the corner potatoes piled five feet high, three more compartments held beets, carrots and onions. Shelves bowed under jars of fruit, pears, apples, blackberries and jams. Canned beans, cauliflower and tomatoes lined the walls.

I had trouble focusing, the smell of the sausages making my stomach churn. I'd taken hundreds of trips through the neighborhoods and farmlands near my home and what had I found? Almost nothing. What lay here would have lasted five years. I only half listened as my father began negotiating.

"What are you willing to offer?" he said.

"For the whole thing?"

"Yes."

The farmer didn't speak. His eyes scanned the silver pieces, their intricate designs and engravings. He picked one up again, weighing it in his hand, an expression of unchecked greed on his face.

Nobody spoke and I wondered why my father remained

silent. A minute passed. I closed my eyes, trying to ignore the smoky flavor on my tongue and the gurgling in my stomach.

"I'll give you six sausages and canned vegetables. And three loaves of bread. It's upstairs."

The farmer blinked, tearing his eyes away from the goods.

"That's not going to work. This is solid silver, not some cheap plated stuff." My father bent to repack.

I wanted to say, but wait, I'm starving. Some food is better than nothing. Instead I stood, the silence between us expanding until I thought I'd blow up. What would we eat tonight?

The suitcase snapped shut. To my surprise the farmer remained and scrutinized my father.

"Not so hasty," he suddenly said. "What do you want?"

My father straightened and set down the case. "A dozen sausages—the big ones—twenty-five pounds of wheat, six loaves of bread, five pounds of cheese and two bottles of schnapps. And I'd like a few jars of jam."

"That's too much."

"I know it's a lot. But I have no choice. I'll trade what I have as single pieces and get more for it that way."

I watched my father, thinking back at his stories of Enar, the Norwegian shopkeeper. When my father had been stationed in Norway, he'd met Enar in the village. It turned out that Enar loved schnapps...my father's schnapps to be exact. At the time, the German soldiers received weekly schnapps rations and since my father didn't drink, he traded his bottles for food in Enar's shop. That's how we'd received those amazing care packages.

Within minutes, we found ourselves back outside with three bags of food and grains.

"We can stay here tonight," my father said.

"I'm starving."

"I know, Günter. We can eat from our provisions. This fellow wasn't very nice and didn't offer to share any dinner, but he'll let us sleep in the hay."

We made our way to the huge barn that stood about a hundred fifty yards to the side of the house.

Despite the grime in the stalls and the oppressive farm, the barn smelled nice. Hay was stuffed everywhere. I loved barns but was too hungry to explore. My father threw down his coat and opened one of the sacks.

"I can't believe he gave you everything you asked for," I said, feeling almost delirious enjoying the wheat bread with butter and smoked sausage.

"I know." My father ripped a chunk of bread from the loaf with his teeth. "But when I saw the man's greed, I knew I had him."

"Do you really get more if you trade the pieces one at a time?" I couldn't keep from grunting as I chewed.

"Nope, but I wasn't about to give away our valuables. I mean the man can't eat what he has in ten years. It'll go to waste before he'll part with anything."

"I'm glad we got some of it."

"The wheat berries will make bread and pancakes." My father grimaced, rubbing the red welt on his neck.

"Are you all right?"

"Fine, son.

The air smelled of summer and careless adventure as we wandered outside. Birds trilled the last evening songs, swallows swooped low to land on mud nests underneath the overhanging roof. All was quiet except for an occasional stomping of hooves or a snort from the stalls. We took turns washing at the old-fashioned pump.

My father patted me on the back, suppressing a yawn. "Let's get some sleep."

"I'll go upstairs." I climbed the bales to the top and nestled into the hay. It had been a very long day indeed. I was asleep in a minute and didn't hear the farmer outside.

I awoke with a start. In my dream bandits had circled us like a pack of wolves, their eyes red, they drooled, flashing knives and handguns. I was bathed in sweat.

A faint noise reached my ears. Voices. Then a scream, followed by yelling. Then another scream. It was that second scream filled with terror that made me gasp and scramble down the hay bales.

"Vater, where are you?" I whispered. "Wake up! Something terrible is going on outside."

"Ouch, careful."

I'd landed on my father. "Sorry, I—"

192

"Shhh."

The noise outside grew. Rough voices shouted. Glass shattered.

My father grabbed our precious bags. "Let's leave, be very quiet."

"*Vater*, what—"

"Not a sound," my father whispered as we crept to the barn door. "Shit," he said under his breath.

"What?"

"We're locked in. I bet the farmer was afraid we might steal from him." My father's voice was grim.

Outside, somebody hollered in triumph, high pitched and eerie. Then we heard the farmer's voice, but what had sounded so unfriendly and angry last night now quivered with fright.

"No, please," he begged.

"You swine, you lousy pig," a menacing voice said. "Here have a bite." The farmer's voice gurgled. "Pig shit for our swine." Rough laughter followed. By the sound of it, there were several men.

More crashes. Then the same menacing voice said, "Lousy Nazi Schwein, got rich while we're starving. Look what he kept from us. The country is in ruins and he's rich. We should hang you."

The mob chorus yelled in agreement. "Hang' em, hang' em," they shouted.

Whimpering sounded, then a woman's cry. "Please spare me. I didn't know. Please." The voice turned into a high pitch. More rough laughter.

"What do we do?" I whispered.

"We have to find another way out. They might burn everything. It's escalating."

"I saw an opening upstairs earlier. Maybe we can climb out?"

"Let's try." I carefully crawled upward across the stacked hay bales. My father had more trouble, pulling the wheat sack and bags with him.

Outside the chorus continued. "Hang him...kill him."

Painfully slow, we crawled across the hay. It was too dark to see, and the bales were unstable. The upstairs had a partial floor, but it was impossible to tell where it began or ended.

I groped around for the wooden floorboards, the idea of being locked in making my chest tight.

"I see the sky," I murmured over my shoulder. "Over here."

The opening in the hayloft was six by eight feet with a roof overhang outside that allowed additional air to reach the hay, keeping it from getting damp. We couldn't see the mayhem below since the window was on the other side of the building and away from the main farmhouse and courtyard. In the low light, I made out a large pulley under the overhang. Some of the hay was hoisted up this way. But the rope was missing.

I peered through the opening. "How high do you think it is?" The ground below was covered in darkness, but I knew even without seeing that it was a lot higher than a train roof. "I'll jump and open the barn door for you."

"Listen." My father patted my arm. "Hang from the ledge. Then you're already half down. If you hurt yourself, I won't be able to get you."

I crawled out the window, fingers grasping for the edge. If there was equipment below and I fell on something sharp or made noise, the mob would find me. They were liable to hang us without asking questions.

The frenzy in front of the farmhouse reached a fever pitch. Footsteps crunched, wood splintered. The woman's voice wailed, but the farmer was silent. I tried to ignore everything and concentrate on my task... let go... and roll to the side. To my relief, the soil was soft. As I crawled to the corner of the barn, the noise grew louder still. I cringed.

Several fires burned, orange shadows dancing across the lawns and house. Men ran in and out of the stately building, carrying bottles and kegs, furniture and carpets. Some of the loot was on fire. Glass broke. The men were emptying the basement. In the dancing lights, I made out the farmer under the oak tree, a woman by his side. Both had ropes around their necks. They were standing between several men with guns.

One of them smacked his rifle butt into the farmer's legs. Something cracked and the farmer screamed as his knees buckled and he fell to the ground.

Another man stood in front of the woman. She was nearly as large as her husband with ample breasts and large hips. I heard a tearing sound followed by rough laughter. The woman's breasts were exposed, pale flesh in the firelight. The man laughed again, taking hold of one breast. He savagely pulled, making the woman come close to him. A curdling scream rang out as metal flashed. The man cut off her breast with a knife and held it up for all to see. More hollering.

I turned away to look for the barn door. I had to get rid of the image in my head. I had to remain calm and concentrate. My father was heavier and might hurt himself. Our jars would break. I couldn't let that happen.

Head low, I crawled along the barn wall. Near the house the fires flickered brightly. *Just when I need darkness.*

That's when I heard footsteps.

I ducked lower and froze.

"You think anybody hides in the barn?"

"Let's find out," a second voice said.

"That will make a great fire," the first voice chuckled.

There was no time to retreat. I melted into the walls of the barn, my ankles scraping against the rough wood. They would find me any second.

"Tomas, get over here!" The voice came from far away, back by the courtyard.

The footsteps stopped. "We want to look at the barn."

"First things first," the voice said from the courtyard. "Get a couple chairs to hang these Nazi swine."

"What's another few minutes." The voice near the barn tried to sound dismissive but there was a shimmer of uncertainty.

"Tomas! Get over here now!" The voice from the courtyard seethed. A rifle cocked. I remembered to breathe as the footsteps turned away and I made my way to the door.

A safety latch looped around the handle, the hook linking the two barn doors together. I slid off the lock and pulled slightly, a shiver trickling down my back like ice water. I was in full view of the yard and its intruders.

The door creaked in its hinges and my father pushed past me, pulling me to the ground in the process. We crawled around the corner, my father dragging our sacks. We continued crawling fifty more yards and then ran, stumbling into the darkness. At last, my father called to stop.

As we lay there in the middle of a field, flames shot from

the farmhouse, illuminating the night sky. In the dancing light, the old oak stood as it had for a hundred years. From it, two bodies hung, partially naked, their clothes shredded. Men swarmed, throwing things, waving bottles and hollering with glee.

As bile filled my mouth, I heard my father's breathing next to me and felt the tears coming.

CHAPTER TWENTY-TWO

Lilly: May 1946

I will always remember the day we received the postcard. It was yellow and had a red cross in the top left corner. But that wasn't the most shocking thing that happened that day.

The day after we returned from the city, I stopped visiting Vati's photo next to Mutti's bed. I realized he'd lied to me in the worst possible way. He'd chosen someone else over me—someone who'd turned out to be a monster.

Even now, a year after learning about Vati volunteering, I distracted myself whenever I felt the urge of longing for him.

"Lilly, don't you see the living room needs cleaning? And wipe down the table." Mutti had come home upset and frustrated about her visits to the baroness. We still knitted, but the baroness gave us less work.

I scowled, tired of Mutti's moods. "I just did it three days ago."

Don't get me wrong. I enjoyed working, even the trips to the woods didn't bother me because they distracted me from seeing my mother and brother together, and the fact I intruded into their precious lives.

"Then do it again. If you'd done a better job, it wouldn't be necessary."

I ripped a dust cloth from the drawer and stomped off into the living room. Every surface I touched was already clean, so I just sat down at Vati's desk and gazed out the window.

The birch tree blazed burgundy, calling me, so when Mutti left to pick up rations, I ran outside and climbed as high as I dared, hugging the bark, feeling its strength keep me from crumbling. And while I'd grown to tolerate her doting on my brother, the resentment I felt kept bopping to the surface, making my yearning for Vati even more painful.

The city had offered no more help. If Vati was declared dead, we would be eligible for support from the government. But we had no proof whether Vati was alive or dead. It was too 'early.' Many men vanished and then miraculously reappeared from one of the camps or out of hiding. The western allies had dozens of POW camps. Most men in captivity could be traced.

But camps in Poland and Russia were numerous—Stalin's preferred way of dealing with undesirables was throwing them into gulags. At one time Russia had more than 40,000 prisons.

"I have a lot of homework," I told Mutti.

"You can do that later. I need your help now. I have guests tonight."

"But you had guests yesterday."

"It's none of your business," Mutti barked. "Besides, it's the weekend."

"Luise? Are you home?" Karl Huss was yelling and knocking at the same time.

Mutti yanked open the door. "I'm busy. What do you want?"

Karl held up a card waving it in front of her. "Look at this! It's addressed to you. Guess what it is."

"Karl, please give it to me." Mutti tried grabbing the card.

"Why aren't you a little nicer?" Karl's face was close. "I thought we were *good* friends." He was much taller and held the card above her reaching hand. An expression of lascivious hunger crossed his face.

"*Hallo* Herr Huss," I said, slipping behind Mutti. I'd watched Huss's game from the doorway.

His face twisted into a half smile. "*Hallo* Lilly."

Mutti held out a hand. "Will you please give it to me? I'm tired. Lilly, go and take care of your brother."

Huss lowered his arm and offered Mutti the card.

"Mutti, what is it?" I remained in the hallway as Mutti closed the door with a bang.

"I need better light."

"Let me see." I tried catching glimpse, but Mutti hurried past me to the kitchen window. Thanks to Herr Baum, we'd gotten one new windowpane, allowing natural light.

I crowded next to her. Several stamps and splotches scattered over the paper. Tears welled up in Mutti's eyes.

"Is it from Vati?" I felt my own eyes sting.

"I don't know. The script isn't in his handwriting."

Dear Familie Kronen,

We regret to inform you that Wilhelm Kronen, Pioneer Hauptmann, was detained by the Russian government. He has been moved to one of the camps in Eastern Russia. Exact whereabouts are unknown due to repeated relocations. We will provide additional information if and when it becomes available.

The German Red Cross/Tracing Service

I began to cry. I wanted to be happy. I was happy. Vati was alive. They didn't know exactly where he was, but surely he'd come home soon. Many of my former classmates had their fathers return from POW camps.

I couldn't wait to see him.

We'd have a big party and invite all the neighbors. Except Herr Huss. He didn't have any part in my celebration. I hoped Huss would leave and find another place.

If I'd thought the postcard would slow down Mutti's partying, I'd been wrong. She placed the card into the top drawer of the kitchen cabinet and carried on as usual. If there was any doubt, she never let on.

By evening, the living room was clean and smelled of furniture wax. I'd polished Vati's desk, remembering the ink pen and leather pad that were no longer there, and the scent of his cologne. All I detected now was lemon scent and stale smoke from downstairs. His handwriting had been just as neat as his clothes, and though I couldn't read at the time I would watch him fill page after page of notes.

"Lilly, it's time for you to go to your room," Mutti said.

"Why can't I meet your guests? I shouldn't have to go to

bed so early. I'm almost fourteen."

"Hush, young girls shouldn't be up late." Mutti wore the red dress and matching lipstick, a departing gift from Captain Marks, and had her hair pulled back.

"Why do I have to disappear when Burkhart gets to meet everyone?" On several occasions, I'd heard Mutti introduce my brother. I couldn't hear much else with the door closed, except the low mumble of strangers.

"You don't need to concern yourself with your brother." Mutti inspected the glasses, dishes and silverware I'd piled on the table. Our dishes consisted of a mishmash of plates in different sizes, the remains of our china cabinet after the bombings. Sometimes, guests brought their own china, I discovered during dishwashing in the morning.

"Go on," Mutti said when the doorbell rang. "I don't want to hear any complaints."

I stomped off, throwing the door closed behind me as giggles and murmurs floated through the walls, finally relaxing me to sleep.

In my dream, Vati returned and we celebrated. He looked different, and I couldn't figure out why. Yet, I knew it was him. A sound made me open my eyes and for that split second I thought my dream had come true.

A man stood by my bed, gazing at me. But even in the dark I knew he was not my father. His presence made me go cold.

"Hallo sweet girl," he muttered, alcohol laying its cloak around me and taking my breath.

"What is it?" I tried sitting up. "Is it Mutti?"

He sat down heavily. "Your mother is fine," he chuckled. I couldn't figure out what was so funny.

"Please go. I'm tired."

As I racked my brain how to get rid of the man, laughter erupted in the other room.

"Why aren't you a little friendlier, little girl? I don't bite. Come on, give me a kiss." He leaned over my face.

His breath was horrible, alcohol mixed with potato salad— I smelled onions—and something greasy.

The moment I decided to scream, wetness swallowed me. The man's tongue pushed into my mouth like a slimy snake. I kicked and writhed, but he was huge and much stronger. He pinned down my arms, trying to kiss me again.

"Leave me alone," I coughed, trying to slap at the man's arms and face.

"Feisty, aren't you," he panted as I felt my blankets pulling away. The man seemed suddenly distracted and let go of one of my hands.

"See what I have for you."

"Leave me alone. Mutti!" I yelled before the man clamped his fingers over my mouth.

His other hand grabbed my arm and pulled it toward his middle. "Isn't this nice?"

I felt a strange form between my fingers. Despite my disgust I looked down. The penis was gigantic. The man grew frantic, yanking on my nightshirt. When my gown gave way and exposed my belly, I panicked.

"No!" I yelped. The man only grunted as he climbed on top. Huge and heavy like a wardrobe, his body buried me, immobilizing my arms. His shoulder dug into my face. Fabric covered my mouth. I spit, trying to free my face. His hands were busy below. A sharp rip and my underpants gave way as his shoulder ground into my face.

I bit down as hard as I could. My teeth cut through the man's shirt into his flesh. A gurgling scream rang out, a deep growl. The man's torso yanked away, his eyes meeting mine in the dim light. They were livid.

"What are you doing, Gerhard?" Mutti's voice was shrill. The man on top of me froze.

"Just a little visit. Nothing happened," he wheezed, climbing off the bed and massaging his shoulder. I caught a last glimpse of flesh disappearing behind folds of cloth. Mutti pulled him away, one firm hand under his elbow.

"You should be ashamed of yourself," she whispered. At the door she turned. "Go back to sleep, Lilly. Tomorrow this will have been just a bad dream."

The door closed. I was wide-awake.

Alcohol and tobacco lingered. Though it was the middle of summer, I was cold. A wave of laughter drifted through the closed door, Mutti's voice among them.

I turned toward the wall and tried to sleep. But sleep would not come. The last guest left in the early morning. I waited until Mutti had gone to bed and quietly rose. In the kitchen I picked up the water bucket. Without a sound, I opened the door and slipped out.

I needed air, lots of fresh air. Why had I ever thought the end of the war would bring *me* peace?

CHAPTER TWENTY-THREE

Lilly: June 1946

You would have thought that a year after the biggest war of all time was over, we'd be better off. The opposite was true. The winter of 1945-1946 had been horrific, our apartment a frozen landscape with the kitchen the only room we could tolerate.

We huddled around the stove and wore hats and coats while we ate, worked, and napped. At night we sought escape from the cold and each other in our icy beds, waiting for spring and a glimmer of normalcy.

All winter we'd even washed in the kitchen, my brother, now eight-years-old, still oblivious to the shame of being naked in front of us.

How I welcomed the warmth of the sun and the chance to get away from Mutti's prying eyes It was a brilliant day in early June, just getting light, when I got up. Tomorrow would be my 14th birthday. The birds were already busy, the air fresh and new.

Since we were out of water—Mutti had wasted it all on Burkhart's bath last night—I made my way to the communal well. A stonewall, dark with moss, grew tall in front of me. Water ran constantly from a brass spigot into a ten-foot long stone trough, its runoff trickling toward a small pond, cool and green with water lilies and other plant life. A chorus of frogs croaked their morning concert. Flecks of mottled light played across the ripples.

I shivered. It was cool here and always a little scary, but the frogs made me feel welcome. My buckets filled, I hurried home.

On the first floor, curtains moved in the breeze. My neighbor's door opened as I entered the hallway, sending my stomach into free fall.

"What are you doing up so early?" Huss's body shone pale in the dimness of the corridor. He only wore shorts, black hair like a disgusting growth on his soft stomach. His chest looked sunken and anemic.

"Just getting water," I said, my mind busy calculating how I could get around Huss or whether my screams would wake Mutti.

"You should be in bed, Lilly."

"I like to be up early."

As Huss moved toward me, the panic inside made my thighs soft and I couldn't feel my toes. Only my heartbeat pounded like a drum.

"Why don't I help you carry?" His fingers stretched my way.

In my distress I lifted my arms out in front. Immediately, the pails, now between us, grew too heavy, and I had to lower them. His eyes raked across the thin shirt I'd thrown on this morning, now wet and showing the outlines of my nipples beneath.

"It's no problem." Huss's voice was soft. "I'll carry the buckets for you." He bent low, his scalp visible through the thinning hair.

"Mutti is waiting."

"Is she? I thought she was partying late." Huss scanned the ceiling. "There was lots of noise overhead last night." His eyes returned to my face and then my chest. "This is heavy. You're a strong girl."

I looked at the buckets in his hand, weighing whether to run without them. I wanted the water.

"Will you carry them upstairs then?"

"Of course." Huss took hold of the pails and climbed the steps, water sloshing and dripping. I followed a few feet behind. As he lowered the pails in front of my door, I squeezed past him along the handrail. My heart was hammering again and it wasn't from the stairs. There was no room on the landing and Mutti would not hear me.

Before I could twist the door handle, Huss gripped my chin.

"You're so cute. Why don't you come and visit me? I've

got lots of food."

"Maybe another time." I abruptly turned my back on him, worrying he might grab hold of my breast from behind. To my relief, the door gave easily and I pushed it open all the way. "Thanks, Herr Huss," I shouted.

Huss peeked inside our little foyer. It was quiet. Too quiet. He hesitated, scratching his chest where red blotches appeared immediately.

Then he followed me, stepping across the buckets as if this were his home and he had a right to be here.

I considered screaming. Surely, Burkhart would hear me. Maybe Mutti, though she slept like the dead after her parties. And yet, not a sound escaped me. A frozen, mortifying shroud enveloped me—the same helplessness I'd felt during the bombings.

Huss's hand landed on my bare shoulder, covered only with the thin straps. He stepped closer as his fingers slid down the front of my shirt. I shuddered and forgot to exhale. Despite my growth spurt, he was much taller and I couldn't see past him.

He cut off escape to the stairs below. Why hadn't I immediately slammed shut the door?

Huss's breathing quickened, a high-pitched wheeze.

"Lilly?" Burkhart's sleepy voice came from the bedroom door.

Huss caught himself. *"Guten Tag."* He abruptly turned and moved toward the stairs.

"It's fine, go back to sleep," I said, reclaiming my buckets and closing the door. Only after I turned the key and disappeared in the bathroom, did I remember to inhale.

I slid to the floor, my legs as soft as overcooked noodles. Nothing stirred below.

With a sigh, I straightened and began to scrub my body until my skin burned and a puddle covered the floor. At that moment I realized I had to do something about Huss.

Or die trying.

I pulled on a clean dress, my only other dress, and moved into the living room.

Ashtrays overflowed, empty beer and wine bottles stood on the floor and table. Plates and silverware piled high with flies buzzing atop. Bowls with scraps of food and half eaten fruit pie spoke of a successful party. Most guests brought dishes and alcohol as gifts and I couldn't help myself for being glad about leftovers.

Vati's desk was littered with empty bottles. Cigarette ashes flaked across the wood and stuck to rings of dried liquid where bottles and glasses had stood. Stale alcohol mixed with the acrid smell of cold cigarette butts. I gagged. How I loathed Mutti's parties—the smells, the laughter, the merriment of strangers and most of all, Mutti's loud voice, shrill and edgy.

I carried the bottles into the kitchen, waiting for the open windows to clear out the stink. I scrubbed and washed, using more precious soap than I should. I didn't give a damn it was wasteful.

At last, the oak of Vati's desk gleamed once more. A couple of pale rings showed where wet glasses had stood. I needed fine steel wool and wondered if Herr Baum had any. I vowed to visit him again soon. I couldn't wait to see what Erwin had written. He and Herr Baum had begun regular correspondence.

Sniffing my hands, I detected more smoke. Or maybe it was in the walls. Surely, the heavy paper had taken on the odor by now.

"I wonder where Vati is right now," I whispered as the sun peeked across the horizon, bathing the kitchen in orange.

CHAPTER TWENTY-FOUR

Lilly: July 1946

If I'd been careful about my excursions to the basement and outhouse, I was now on full alert. No matter what the time, I always listened before I made my move. And for the most part, I was successful, often asking Burkhart to go with me to 'help' with a basement chore or keep me company.

I knew Mutti hated the fact that Huss was looking for ways to get close to me, but I also knew she wouldn't do anything drastic to protect me. If I wanted things to happen, I had to do them myself.

Except I couldn't think of one single thing. Huss wasn't going to move, and I didn't have any weapons to protect myself. I'd thought about carrying our breadknife, but chances were, he'd wrestle away the knife or worse, use it against me.

And so I grew more and more frustrated, feeling like nothing was ever going to change. Deep down I'd hoped for Vati to return by now. Somehow in my muddled and naïve brain, I'd thought he'd magically appear for my birthday.

Of course, he didn't. My birthday was a muted affair with a bit of honey cake and a reconstituted dress from Mutti. The dress was too wide in the waist, but I still welcomed the improvement to my wardrobe. Six years ago I'd wished for a doll, and now all I wanted was Vati, clean socks, and a new pair of shoes. Of course, what I really wanted was a sense of normalcy.

Since our visit to Dr. Fenning, Mutti had been more

subdued than ever. That is, she was subdued with me, her moods swinging between anger and impatience. I think she was taking out her frustration about Vati's secret decision to join the war on me. Strangely, at the time I wasn't that upset about it. Not yet.

That anger would grow as I grew, with the understanding that he'd chosen Hitler over us. It soon became clear that the Third Reich had had nothing but disdain for its citizens, and that women were considered breeding stock.

Years later, I found out that even as late as the spring of 1945, Hitler had suggested the war would end soon and because there were four to five million men *missing*, every remaining German man should 'marry' at least two women with whom he should produce lots of children.

And there was the sickness of the mother cross. Women who had four children were awarded a bronze cross, mothers with six children received a silver cross and women with eight or more kids a gold cross. Hitler had intended for us to supply soldiers for his cause for eternity.

Nor did he feel remorse for sending the last kids and elderly into battle when it was long clear that the war was lost. Hitler was a certified madman—and my father had chosen him over us?

"Don't they know Vati is in Russia?" Mutti hurled the newspaper on the table.

"What is it?" I asked, reaching for the pages.

As part of the denazification, the British administration requires all adults aged 18 to 65 to complete a survey. Pick up as follows:
Last names beginning A-H July 8-10
Last names beginning I-O July 9-11
Last names beginning P-Z July 10-12
All surveys must be completed and dropped off as follows:
Last names beginning A-H July 15-16
Last names beginning I-O July 16-17
Last names beginning P-Z July 17-18
Noncompliance is punishable by law.

I let the paper sink. "What does it mean?"

"All of us have to declare what we did during the war. If we were in the party or worse…" Mutti sighed. "They're trying to clean up the people who were involved."

Like Vati, I wanted to say. But I remained quiet as an idea began to sprout in my mind.

"You say everyone fills this out?"

Mutti nodded. "Especially if someone works for the city or in a leadership role."

The lines of the newspaper article in front of me blurred. "What does Herr Huss do these days?"

Mutti threw me a quick glance and began rummaging in the empty cupboards. A year after the war, we pretty much had no food except for a few white beans and a couple of onions Herr Baum had shared. I longed for the cherries in the backyard to ripen faster.

"He works for some kind of association. Not sure." Curiosity swung in her voice.

I felt her eyes follow me around the room. I knew that she worried about Huss ever since he'd caught her with the American. She never said a word, but she no longer visited downstairs and it seemed that she tried to stay out of his way. Just like me. But then the wall between us had been fortified over the years and we both remained silent.

That night I forced myself to stay awake, listening to the faint bells of the Lutheran church. One gong meant 15 minutes after the hour, two gongs 30 minutes and so on. When I heard the bells chime eleven plus two extra gongs I got out of bed. Mutti had gone to bed shortly after me and Burkhart always slept hard. I listened to his regular breaths interrupted by an occasional rustling when he turned over.

I was desperate, and desperation makes you do crazy things.

I quietly put on my dress and tiptoed barefoot to the entrance door. The key stuck in the lock and I twisted it, willing it to be quiet. A slight scrunching noise ensued as the lock disengaged. I slipped down the stairs, briefly stopping near Huss's door.

The curtain in the glass inset was dark, no fresh cigarette smoke squeezing through. Huss had recently begun working outside the house and I hoped he kept more regular sleeping hours.

He left the house every morning at seven-thirty and didn't get home till five or six.

I felt my way to the basement door. It was never locked, and I carefully climbed downstairs. I'd left my shoes to be quieter, but now the cold stones seeped into my heels and up my legs. Worse was my breathing. I huffed like a locomotive, the blood rushing through my head in waves.

After listening again and hearing nothing but my own gasps, I turned on the single bulb in the laundry room. To my right were the two private cellars, one for each family. Ours was empty except for some rags and wooden shelves, but through the slatted walls of Huss's space I saw boxes and cartons stacked high.

To the right of his door near the ceiling was a ledge. After being cornered by Huss, I'd gotten into the habit of stopping on my way back from the outhouse and peeking through the window. Once I'd caught him hide a key up there.

I hurried to get a bucket, turned it upside down and climbed on top.

The key was there. It felt clammy in my hand, or was it because my fingers shook so badly? The key twisted smoothly in the old-fashioned padlock as if it had been oiled.

I quickly opened the slatted door and stole inside. The room was five or six feet wide and twelve feet long. The entire wall was covered with boxes, some hidden under oilcloth. Again I stopped to listen. The house was quiet except for an occasional creak in the wooden joists.

"Come on, hurry up," I mumbled. I lit a candle stub and opened the first box closest to the door.

It was filled with kitchen utensils and china. Huss had kept his stuff safe when the bombs fell. I moved on to the next box. More household goods, a frying pan and vases. I wondered briefly where all this had come from. Most of us, my uncles included had few personal items, our kitchens as bare as our closets.

I opened another carton, this one filled with stacks of shirts. They smelled musty and slightly smoky, making me gag.

My frustration grew as I worked through the stacks. Some containers were huge and I couldn't lift them off the ones underneath. Things were taking way too long, my nerves making me shiver though I was sweating under my dress.

In the corner beneath an empty shelf stood a wooden

chest. The padlock on it was broken, and I carefully set it aside. When I opened the lid, my heart jumped against my ribs.

As I suspected Huss, had kept his collections from his national-socialist activities. There was the brown uniform, wrapped in tissue paper, I'd seen him wear years ago. There were several arm bands with the swastika symbol of the SS. There were flags with swastikas and assorted documents. Even Hitler's *Mein Kampf* was stuck in the corner. I picked a couple of items, but when I wanted to close the box, the wooden top slid out of my hand and came down with a thud.

I listened for a moment, the shakes now going up and down my arms. I blew out the candle, rushed out of Huss's cellar and threw shut the door. Just as I attempted to turn the key in the padlock, I heard the basement door.

And froze.

For that split-second of terror my insides turned to mush and my mind drained of thoughts. There was nothing but sickening emptiness and that old inability to move.

When the light in the staircase turned on, I sprang back to action. Re-depositing the key, I took the bucket and ever so quietly rushed behind the brick washbasin. I gasped for air, the sound roaring in the stillness, and stuck my face into my dress to squelch the noise.

Please don't let it be Huss.

"Anyone down here?" Huss said. "Luise? Is that you?"

I remained crouching behind the basin, when I remembered the documents and armband I'd lifted from Huss's box. They were tucked into my underpants, the paper subtly crackling against my skin.

On the other side of the basin, Huss felt for his key and opened the padlock.

"What the..."

He'd noticed the broken padlock I'd forgotten to reattach in my haste. He knew somebody had been in his cellar or maybe he smelled the extinguished candle. Either way, my blood pressure spiked until I saw spots in front of my eyes. There'd be no telling what he'd do if he caught me now.

I didn't hear the rest of Huss's outburst, flying past his cellar up the stairs. I heard Huss yell something, steps following... his labored breath. He was a lot quicker than I'd expected.

I don't know how I made it to the top of the stairs into my apartment. The last thing I saw was Huss's reddened face coming up the stairs, his eyes blazing. I threw the door shut and locked it.

Then I slowly sank to the ground, waiting for my breath to return, feeling Huss's presence on the other side of the wall, feeling for the first time his uncertainty.

Sometime later, I tucked the armband and documents beneath my pillow and climbed into bed. That's when things got really bad. My body began to tremble so hard, I heard the mattress rattle against the frame below me. What had I done?

I was a thief...again. I'd sworn to myself to always be honest and forthright because my parents were not. Now I'd fallen into the same trap—had become one of them.

But you had to, the other part of my mind argued. How else could I stop Huss? I knew it was only a matter of time before he cornered me again, and I'd already had bouts of constipation from fear of going to the outhouse.

I balled my right fist and pushed it against my lips until my jaws hurt. No, I had to do this. I was tired of being afraid and tired of being molested.

I got back out of bed and turned on the light to study the documents I'd stolen. They were from the local SS office and the NSDAP party, memos and letters, telling about new rules and ways to control and scare us.

There was a memo from the NSDAP about new types of food, dated April 5, 1945. It said the rations were below a maintenance minimum and that a famine was imminent. People were supposed to embrace the following foods: rapeseed, rapeseed cakes, chestnuts, acorns, fodder beets, wild berries, roots and mushrooms, clover and Lucerne. For protein, people should consider eating frogs, snails and fish. And to get vitamins, a hot brew of pine needles was recommended.

Another memo from September 21, 1944 said this:

The Führer has ordered that, since the battle is now fought in large swaths of German territory and German cities and villages have become battle zones, our fight must become fanatical. In every battle zone, our fight must be increased with utmost toughness using every battle-fit man. Every bunker, every neighborhood in German towns and every German village must become a fortress, on which the enemy will bleed.

There is only holding the position or annihilation.

I ask the Gau leaders to influence the citizens that they're aware of the necessity for this fight and its consequences. The severity of this fight can force them to sacrifice their belongings, even destroy their own. This fight for life or death of the German people will not stop in its severity for monuments and other cultural values.

Even then, at barely fourteen, a beanpole of a girl with starvation printed on my face, I understood the insanity of this note. It spoke for everything the Third Reich had stood for. Use and, if necessary, kill everyone...destroy everything. My eyes blurred, thinking about the terrible suffering, the waste of human lives. The immensity of it all. For what?

I didn't know why Huss had all those papers, but it was clear he'd been quite intimately involved with the Nazis.

For the first time in months I smiled.

The next afternoon, I waited for Huss in the front yard. I'd made sure Mutti was home and the windows were wide open.

I heard him before I saw him, the slight pause in his shuffling step as if he had to think about moving forward.

"Hallo Herr Huss," I shouted as soon as he rounded the corner.

"Hallo Lilly." He squinted at me, his gaze showing that uncertainty again.

"From now on," I said, my voice a bit shaky despite the pep talk I'd given myself, "You'll leave me alone. I've got something of yours, something that proves you were with the Nazis. So, unless you want me to tell people, your bosses or the Brits, you'll leave me be."

Huss had moved past me as if he didn't care what I said. But now he stopped and faced me.

"You little witch," he seethed. "Want to destroy me?" He opened his mouth, but thought better of it or maybe couldn't come up with something threatening.

"All I ask is that you leave us alone." How that 'us' had slipped in there, I didn't know. But somehow I wanted Mutti and

Burkhart included in the group.

Huss didn't respond and unlocked the front door.

"I hid it somewhere safe," I yelled after him.

As the garden returned to peacefulness, I climbed into the beech tree. I leaned my head back against the rough bark, patting the giant limb I sat on, imploring it to infuse its strength into me.

CHAPTER TWENTY-FIVE

Günter: Winter 1946/1947

Bending low against an icy wind, I hurried after Helmut. From afar, we looked like scarecrows, our jackets ill-fitting and patched together, our pants ending above the ankles. I wore socks of indefinable color, darned by Mother with a mosaic of yarns.

"I've got nothing tonight," I said, letting my hands wander through my pockets as if I could uncover a hidden treasure.

Helmut held up a burlap sack. "Onions and carrots from grandmother." He cleared his throat. "I wish I had a cigarette."

I made a face. Smoking was like throwing your money into a fire. Five cigarettes bought a kilo of bread—*if* you could find a baker. "I wish we had food. The war has been over for a year and still we have nothing." I navigated around a pile of bricks in front of a bombed-out house. "How's work? You still see that girl, Gerda?"

"Work is fine."

"What about Gerda?"

"She's fine."

"Are you getting anywhere with her?" I said.

"What do you mean?"

"Isn't she eighteen?"

"Yes, why?" Helmut looked straight ahead.

"That's old enough to lose your virginity."

Helmut turned pink. "*You* haven't done it yet, have you?"

"I still have a few months until my birthday. I'll try it

215

soon." I didn't think my birthday had anything to do with sex, but it was a good excuse. After all, Helmut had been going steady with Gerda for more than a year while I hadn't met anybody I was too interested in. Who had time for a girl anyway?

"How about Sabine, Gerda's friend?" Helmut said. "She seems to like you well enough."

"She's screwed half the town. Probably infected. Besides, I saw her with a British soldier."

It was dusk by the time we arrived at *Grünewald*, a neighborhood on the south side of town. Down the street, the red-bricked buildings of Henckels Twin factory loomed. In the shine of a single light bulb wrapped in barbed wire, people had set up shop in an empty lot.

A bucket of potatoes sat next to a camera and three cutting knives, their serrated blades gleaming with grease, a sure sign they were plain metal and would rust the instant they became wet. A gruff-looking man with a shaven head and a scar blooming across his cheek presided over chunks of meat, wrapped in bloodied strips of newspaper. He stared at his goods, his eyes darting toward the street once in a while. Two dozen men and women mingled, looking for bargains. An older woman offered chunks of butter. One of her customers held out a scruffy chicken for inspection. It clucked softly as the butter vendor inspected its feathery chest.

Helmut held out his bag. "Do you want to try? You're better at it."

With a shrug, I grabbed the sack and headed toward the back corner where assorted glass bottles sat in the mud. Lounging behind it were two boys our age.

"It's real schnapps," one of them said as I drew near. Even in the gloom, he looked filthy, his hair greasy, the dirt in his face competing with pimples. His eyes shone but he looked washed out and sickly.

"You have to taste it," Helmut whispered. "They could've added water."

"What do you mean?" the pimply boy huffed. "It's good stuff. You can't taste it. Otherwise we'll have nothing left."

"How do we know you aren't lying?" I felt strangely angry.

"Why would we lie? We come here all the time."

"I wouldn't buy from you." I turned abruptly to scrutinize

the butter seller.

"How about some meat?" Helmut said.

Without warning, the pimply boy gripped my arm. "You shouldn't come here if you don't buy."

"Leave me alone!" I yanked free, pushing the boy backwards. I was turning toward Helmut when the boy's fist landed squarely on my cheek, instant pain spreading across my face. As the second youth jumped on Helmut, I blocked my face and bounced back and forth like I'd seen in the boxing ring. My fist shot against the opponent's chin. The boy's head jerked as he flew to the ground.

I grunted. "Come on. Want some more, right here." I pointed to my face.

The boy's matted hair hung across his face. He stood up with effort, shook his head and lifted his arms. "Liar," he sniffed through the blood dripping from his nose. He jumped forward, digging his knuckles into my stomach.

Fighting the urge to double over, my fist made contact with the boy's eye socket. The boy stared in disbelief and sank to his knees.

Several whistles blew at once.

"Stop!" someone yelled. "Don't move." A shot exploded.

I looked up. Men in British military uniforms were fanning across the market. "Helmut. Now!"

"I just about got him," Helmut panted, throwing another punch.

"Police. Let's go!"

Around us, buyers and sellers scattered, dragging their wares with them. The pimply boy staggered, rubbing his eye. Helmut's opponent looked dazed. Quickly, I grabbed two bottles.

And stopped.

There was no way out.

The man with the scarred face was lying facedown in the dirt, his arms pinned back by an officer. More police were cutting off access, the street now clogged with trucks and jeeps. In the back an eight-foot brick wall loomed—too high to climb. The house on the south side had a side door. I doubted it was open.

Trust was a thing of the past. People, even formerly honest ones, stole every day. Besides, we'd have to cross the entire market and give the Brits ample opportunity to catch us. Visions of myself in jail, my father's angry face drifted into my mind.

Fighting rising panic, I pulled Helmut toward the ruins of the apartment house on the north side. The roof was missing, its walls partially collapsed into itself. The stucco had cracked and peeled away. I darted behind a pile of bricks and cement, the remains of an entrance. Along the back wall a basement window, broken since the citywide bombing two years ago, gaped open.

Ignoring the glass shards and splintered wood, I dropped to my knees. The window was no more than a foot high and three feet wide, hiding what was beyond in shadow.

Around the corner, more whistles trilled. My heart pounded in my neck. Any second, the military police would see us. I had no choice. "In here."

Dropping on my stomach I squeezed through the opening. Helmut followed.

Inside, the damp air carried a faint burn smell. I could make out debris and half-collapsed walls.

"Get away from the window," Helmut whispered from somewhere in the darkness.

I felt the familiar tightening in my throat. The inky void was reaching out to grab me. I couldn't move.

"Do you have a light?" I croaked. Chances were Helmut had neither matches nor a lighter, but it distracted me from the increasing terror of remembering the bunker, the sense of suffocating. The fear and tight space, the whimpering of my neighbors had driven me insane. Now the same ghostly hands were choking me.

"If they shine a light in here, they'll see you," Helmut whispered.

"I don't hear anything." I opened my eyes as wide as possible, but the pressure on my chest remained. I leaned against the wall beneath the window, yearning for a whiff of fresh air.

"They may wait for us." Helmut's voice was hollow in the gloom.

Fighting the fog in my brain I listened for sounds, willing the police to be gone. I wanted out.

"I say we try it. They must have gone by now."

Without waiting for an answer I clambered through the window, my palms bleeding by the time I straightened outside. *Breathe* I ordered myself...in, out, in, out. I crept to the corner—

and sighed. The space was deserted.

"I know where we can go," I said when Helmut appeared next to me. I patted my jacket. The bottles were safe.

On the side of an abandoned villa, an isolated bomb had carved a fifty-foot crater, collapsing the house walls on one side. The hole in the earth looked endless in the dark. We climbed inside one of the ground-floor windows, the gas lantern across the street throwing long shadows.

Glass crunched as we searched for a place to sit. The room, its ceiling sloping down toward the back, had been stripped down to the concrete subfloor, the floor planks long torn off for cooking and heating.

I handed Helmut a bottle, slumped to the ground and took a deep swig. The sharp liquid burned as it traveled through my throat, etching a pattern of heat into my stomach.

"They sure were stupid."

"Who?" Helmut's gulp echoed through the room.

"The boys with the liquor."

"Sure were."

I smacked my lips. "This is pretty good." My mouth felt warm and the alcohol numbed my tongue. Heat spread across my face, making me forget the bruise the boy had given me.

"Who'd have thought?" said Helmut.

"They looked like thugs. Could've been water."

"Could've been." Helmut slid across the floor to rest his back against the moldy remnants of wallpaper. "I wonder who lived here."

"I wish we could make a fire."

"That'd be nice."

"You think those boys got arrested?"

"Who?" Helmut took a sip. The bottle sloshed and clanked against the concrete floor.

"The boys with the schnapps."

"Don't know."

"Served them right." I drank again. I felt comfortable now. The heat had spread to my fingers, the pain in my cheek subsided. I wiggled my toes inside the boots. They were tight.

"Wonder where they got the stuff."

"Wonder."

It grew quiet except for the glass clinking between

swallows. The room shrank, became warmer, its shadows familiar. People had lived here, sat on the sofa and listened to the radio. It was hard to imagine. I thought about Hans. He was still tightlipped most of the time, but he'd managed to secure an apprenticeship with an electrician. I guess the quiet, mostly solitary work suited him.

I sat up straight. "Why haven't you done it with Gerda?"

Silence. Helmut lifted his bottle. The liquid sloshed as he drank.

"Helmut?"

"What?"

"You heard me," I said.

Helmut took another swig, setting down the bottle hard. He mumbled something but I couldn't hear.

"What?"

"Why do you want to know?" Helmut said. He sounded irritated.

"Just curious."

More silence.

"Helmut?"

"I don't want to talk right now."

"Fine," I said, "sorry I asked. A fire would be nice."

Helmut leaned over, inspecting an opening in the wall. "Looks like they used to have a stove. I'd love a nice coal fire."

"And something to roast on top." I took another sip. Schnapps dripped down my chin and I wiped at it with a sleeve. Numbness settled, turning my legs and arms heavy, like the earth was pulling me down. I relaxed, feeling almost cheerful.

Quiet settled again. Thoughts went through my mind but they seemed hard to hold on to. The memories of Rolf Schlüter and little Paul, the fact every single classmate was still missing, grew remote, our struggles of finding food among the desolation less urgent.

Every time I wanted to speak, the sentence slipped away. I no longer felt the cold emanating from the concrete.

"We sure showed them," I yelled, feeling the urge to jump up.

Helmut's snort hollered up from the ground. "We sure did!"

I burped. A burping contest ensued. Giggles rang through

the darkness.

"I declare myself the winner," Helmut howled, scrambling to his knees. "I've got to piss."

"You are the burp *meister*. Me too." As I turned the room began to spin. I laughed again, groping for the wall. Misjudging the distance, I fell forward and caught myself on the window sill. "This place needs to stop moving."

"You know why I haven't done it?" Helmut's voice had an edge.

"Done what?"

"Sleep with Gerda, you dumb ass."

"Why?" I only half listened because of the whirling in my head. It was as if I were outside my body, looking in, watching my thoughts disintegrate like crumbling rock in the desert.

Helmut was quiet for a moment. "I don't have condoms. Gerda won't do it without *protection*."

"Heck, if that's all it is, let's find you some rubbers." I climbed through the window. "Man, I'm dizzy."

"Easier said than done. I've tried but …it's embarrassing. *Hey, you got any condoms?*" he squawked. "I sure don't want my parents to know."

"What about the pharmacy?"

"They have nothing. You're lucky to get Band-Aids."

"Shit."

"What?"

"I'm drunk," I said.

Helmut crawled across the window ledge. "I don't feel a thing."

"Yeah, right."

"I can't get up." Helmut sat on the sill, one leg inside, one out.

"You stay here," I sniggered. "I'll pick you up tomorrow."

"Why don't you help me?" Helmut slurred, straining against the hold.

"Fine, I'm coming… to the rescue." I pitched forward and fumbled behind Helmut's back. "Try it now."

A tearing noise followed. "*Scheisse.*"

I bent over laughing as Helmut felt his rear where a patch of fabric had ripped from his bottom. "Idiot. Why didn't you help me?"

"I did."

"I tore my only pants. Mother will kill me."

"Who cares?" I staggered to the edge of the bomb crater. "Let's see if we can hit bottom."

"Man, I need to piss," Helmut said, nearly plunging into the hole.

It grew quiet except for the sound of splattering.

I buttoned my trousers. "Shall we go home? I'll get the bottles."

Helmut remained silent as I scrambled back inside the house. The room began to spin and I tripped. Glass crashed and alcohol vapors wafted in the air.

"What happened?" Helmut's voice seemed to come from far away.

"Don't know. Must've kicked the bottle. It's gone." My voice seemed muffled as if I were speaking through a giant cotton ball. "Where's yours?"

"Don't remember. You know where the vegetables are?"

"I thought you carried them. I can't find the bottle." I sank to my knees and suddenly felt sick.

"You had the sack, remember. You were going to trade."

"I must've dropped them when we fought. Why don't you help me find the bottle?"

Helmut climbed back in. "All right, I'll find it. Why did you leave the food? Now I have nothing to take home."

"Take the rest of the schnapps," I said. "I need to sit a moment." My last words were strange in my ears, my mouth uncooperative.

Helmut slumped to his knees, scooting across the floor. "Here it is. I knew it. Shall we go?"

Sweat beaded on my forehead and I leaned against the wall. I felt hot and cold at the same time. I wanted to rest, close my eyes for a while. Ears ringing, I grew aware of my rattling breath. It seemed to echo across the room while my head floated like a balloon. I forgot what I wanted to do, that I wanted to leave. Life retracted, turned fuzzy around the edges and swallowed me. Nothing mattered as I drifted off.

Just before dawn, when the night was at its coldest, I awoke. A sledgehammer gyrated through my head. I tried to swallow, but my tongue was thick and rigid. A fire burned in my stomach yet my legs and back ached with cold. Nausea spread across my middle, sending bile to my mouth. I crawled toward the window and vomited, bending over in pain. Another heave. I leaned back, waiting for the pounding in my head to subside.

"Get up," I whispered, forcing myself to speak despite the sour dryness in my throat.

Helmut muttered but didn't move.

I pulled myself up and stumbled toward the window. "Let's go."

"Let me sleep."

"I'm freezing."

"Wait, I'll come—just let me wake up."

It was still dark when we arrived in our neighborhood. As Helmut disappeared around a house corner, I entered our apartment. Shivering, my head pounding, my stomach empty and bitter, I crawled into bed.

Drifting off, I felt as thin and hollow as a ghost.

CHAPTER TWENTY-SIX

Lilly: June 1947-June 1948

"You must find work and help support us. You're old enough."
Mutti leaned in the door to the kitchen.

"I want to continue school or get an apprenticeship," I
said. To my frustration, high school was finished. Counting the
war, missing school, I'd completed eight years.

"You know very well we can't afford it."

We could if you worked. I bit my lower lip and said nothing.
At fifteen, I was too young to get a regular job. For us women, the
government had dreamed up a year of compulsory community
service, typically spent scrubbing the house of some wealthy family.

I looked at the woman who was my mother. I scolded
myself for still craving her approval and love when I knew she
didn't deserve it. She'd aged and yet, in her thinness, she looked
good. There was something in her eyes and her demeanor that
attracted men like bees to clover.

"I already spoke with Frau Schneider, the owner of Café
Schneider. They need someone to take care of their baby. They
want you to interview tomorrow at eleven."

I remained mute as I rinsed my nightgown in the sink. I
was afraid if I said something I'd explode into a tirade about the
direction my life was taking. I was fed up with menial work and
furious Mutti only cared about money and putting me to work.

"What if I don't want to go?" I mumbled against the wall.

"What did you say?"

"Nothing!" I slammed the door and carried the wet clothes to the basement to dry. Huss's door was shut, the curtain still. He hadn't bothered us once since I'd stolen his swastikas.

I took the bus to *Widdert*, a small suburb on Solingen's south side. Schneider's café was popular on the weekends. From here, hiking trails led into the hilly woods and the *Wupper* valley below. Afternoons, café Schneider lured with *Kaffee* and *Kuchen,* Germany's favorite pastime. On Friday and Saturday evening, it was the place to be for a dance. Live music helped people forget—along with free-flowing postwar beer. People paid with cigarettes and ever-growing amounts of *Reichsmark.*

Other than dealing with Mutti, things had been quiet at home. Every day after my theft I breathed a little easier. In the beginning, I'd often worried about repercussions, some way for Huss to get even. But I guess the hold of his filthy past was powerful enough to make him stay out of our way. I never said anything to Mutti, and I sometimes wondered what she thought about Huss leaving her alone.

As far as I was concerned, I'd been given a new life. I felt stronger inside, with a new sense of control I'd never had before. It was a heady thing, and it made my life almost tolerable except for the lack of food. Two years after the war ended, we still had nothing to speak of. Black markets were overrun with searching, haggling people, looking for the barest minimum of sustenance while giving away their family heirlooms.

The lack of nourishment and the daily search for food dragged me down, the constant gnawing inside me like a ghost that followed me. How I hated rationing every morsel. I wanted to eat until I was full, not measure each bite and move around spoonfuls, alternate them with drinking water to give my stomach an illusion of fullness.

It was almost as bad watching my brother. He'd gotten gaunt, too, his cheekbones sharp and his shoulder blades sticking out under this shirt.

Secretly I hoped my new job at the café would provide opportunities for extra rations. It was one reason, so I told myself, why I had agreed to go.

My hands were sweaty as I approached the café. I'd

dressed carefully, wearing my best dress with the starched white collar. It was difficult to look good when you had nothing nice or new to wear.

My feet hurt. The only fashionable shoes I possessed, flats with scuffed tips and worn-down heels, were half a size too small.

"*Bitte sehr?*" The girl behind the counter looked at me expectantly, her eyes skipping across my face. They lingered a bit too long on my dress, which was too short by any fashion standards.

"I have an appointment with Frau Schneider," I said, putting force into my voice I didn't feel.

Frau Schneider, the owner of the café, was in her thirties, but cakes and pastries had left their mark on her roundish waist. While most Germans had been starving for years, the Schneider's seemed to lack nothing.

"You're Lilly?" Frau Schneider eyed me carefully. "Your mother tells me you're a neat housekeeper. Is that true?"

"Yes," I said, suppressing the urge to roll my eyes. Frau Schneider's gaze had strayed to my feet.

"You seem awfully young." Frau Schneider sounded doubtful. "Do you have any work experience?"

"I've been taking care of my little brother and our apartment."

"I see." She paused. "Let's try it for a few weeks. I'll show you the house."

The *Schneiders* lived behind and above the café. A small door led to the kitchen and living room while the bedrooms were upstairs. The rooms were large yet stuffy with an assembly of couches and chairs. Dark green and beige wallpaper added gloominess while the heavy cherry wood credenza contained an overload of unmatched glasses and pottery.

I wondered how the *Schneiders* had kept their china from breaking during the bombings. The kitchen had enough room for a table and chairs, but the counters were filled with pots, pans and unwashed dishes. Flies swirled in the pre-summer heat.

"Do you think you can keep our home?" Frau Schneider asked.

I took a deep breath. "I thought I was supposed to watch a baby." There was no sign of children, though judging by the stroller and toys littered across the rug, a child lived here.

"We need help around the house, too." Frau Schneider carelessly stepped across a pile of clothes and shoes, strewn on the floor. "If you can't handle it, we'll find someone else."

"I'll do it." Only when I'd left did I remember that the subject of pay had never come up. I was too embarrassed to go back.

I arrived at the Schneider's at eight the next morning. Like the kitchen, the other rooms were a mess. No, worse. I started cleaning the main bedroom, which was dominated by an oak bed frame so enormous I had to crawl on top to reach the pillows.

Clothes covered every surface and lay in piles on the floor. It looked as if nothing had been dusted in months. The air was musty and I opened the windows wide, taking deep breaths. It was a pretty day. The wind carried the smell of early summer from the garden.

"What are you doing?" Frau Schneider stood in the door while she assessed the room. The beds had been made, the clothes sorted and hung neatly. The dressers were free of dust.

I stood and curtsied. "I'm airing out the room."

Frau Schneider's face scrunched into a frown. "Is that really necessary?"

I shrugged unsure of how to answer. How could I say the room reeked of unwashed clothes and beds? "I had to get the dust out," I stammered.

"I see. Do the bath next."

My heart sank as I walked into the bathroom.

After an hour of scrubbing, Frau Schneider called me down to lunch. It consisted of stale cake from the day before and slices of white bread. I sat silently, chewing the pastry and bread. The soft dough stuck to the roof of my mouth. The cake made me thirsty and I gulped two glasses of water.

While the baby was coddled by Frau Schneider or one of the grandmothers, I was sent to the cellar where a mountain of dirty laundry waited.

After I added more from the bedrooms, it looked like I'd spend the rest of my life down here. First, I had to make a fire under the washbasin—a huge stone pot—to heat the water. Then I sorted laundry by color and type, prepared the wash water, soaked and rinsed the garments. It was nearly six by the time I had everything clean. My arms ached and felt numb from the strain.

Tomorrow, everything would have to be hung outside to dry.

"I'm going now," I said, stopping by the kitchen.

The Schneider's were sitting at dinner, the smells of roasted potatoes and beef stew making me dizzy. My stomach rumbled. The sugary lunch had not lasted past the afternoon and I was ravenous.

"We'll see you tomorrow," Frau Schneider called after me. "Don't be late."

My first payment for two weeks work was the equivalent of a trip to the grocery—not much, considering the runaway inflation. Mutti immediately took the money and rushed to the store. Tomorrow, it'd be worth less. She'd asked every day and when I finally returned with my earnings, Mutti counted it carefully, the bills disappearing inside her apron pocket.

In addition, I received day-old pastries. In the beginning, this was a welcome treat, but after a few weeks sweets and cakes made my stomach hurt. Only Burkhart seemed to crave the unending flow of treats. I would've much preferred a nice piece of *Schwarzbrot*, black rye bread with butter.

"I'll have guests tomorrow, so I need to get a few things." Mutti rifled through the bills. "Why is it less this time?"

I remained silent. I'd hid a couple bills, enough to buy a small loaf of rye bread.

"Yes, I didn't do as much laundry."

"I see."

While Mutti entertained the next night, I handed Burkhart a piece of bread. "Here, something good to eat."

Burkhart sniffed. "Mmmh."

"Don't tell Mutti. I brought it from the café."

Most of my duties consisted of cleaning, washing and mending. Though I worked hard, the Schneider's seemed to attract dirt. Only the bathroom needed less attention since I kept it wiped down every day. But no matter how much I did, I never made progress.

The basement, with its mountains of dirty laundry, was worst. My arms grew strong and muscular from the strain of turning the hot garments with a long wooden ladle. The physical labor burned far more calories than I took in, and I grew even thinner.

"We need your help at the counter," Frau Schneider said one day, appearing in the basement. "You can do the laundry tomorrow. I'll give you an apron."

I wiped the soap off my hands and followed Frau Schneider to the café. Gabi, the girl in charge of the cake counter looked sour.

"Lilly will support you," Frau Schneider said, ignoring Gabi's long face. "I can't help if Lena is sick."

"But she doesn't know anything," Gabi said, throwing me a nasty sideward glance. "I bet she can't even count."

Frau Schneider shrugged. "Then you need to show her."

Several customers lined up in front of the display case and stared at us.

"Watch me." Gabi turned toward the waiting line and plastered a smile on her face. "Bitte schön?"

Seething inside, I vowed to outdo her. She'd obviously eaten too much leftover cake, her black skirt stretching tightly across her back.

Strawberry cake, *Butterkreme* Torte, walnut pies and chocolate éclairs slipped past me in exchange for *Reichsmark*, cigarettes and ration coupons. After the disastrous Third Reich ration system, the British government had created a new scheme that didn't work most of the time either.

We had coupons and cards for all sorts of food, every German was entitled to 1550 calories a day except most of the time, we had a third or less. More than two years after WW2 had ended, the stores remained stubbornly empty.

If you looked around, you weren't surprised. Like most cities, downtown Solingen remained buried under rubble and ashes. The cleanup was excruciatingly slow, the infrastructure broken. Many farms had been destroyed, and not enough workers were available to handle what was left.

The runaway inflation didn't help. Most stores like café Schneider, adjusted prices every day and sometimes twice a day.

"I can do it," I said after watching for a few minutes.

"Better not mess up." Gabi squinted, her chubby face pulled together like bread dough. "I'll tell Frau Schneider and you'll lose your job."

I swallowed a choice comment and went to work.

I got the hang of things pretty quickly, adding up ration

coupons and *Reichsmark*, packaging cake and prepping in-house orders, setting out plates and cups, pouring coffee and tea.

Frau Schneider seemed to be happy, and I became a regular at the counter. It saved the café another serving girl, more money in their pockets and it beat the laundry, but I knew it'd just wait for me. In the beginning I'd hoped to permanently move into the café, but the cleaning and laundry never stopped.

A year later, nothing had changed. Though the café flourished as more people found work and the first factories resumed production, Frau Schneider never raised my pay.

One day, I opened the top dresser drawer in the upstairs bedroom to put away laundry when I found it filled with stacks of *Reichsmark*. It was more money than I'd ever seen. I said nothing and closed the drawer. I could've easily argued that stealing from the *Schneiders* was just as necessary as stealing Herr Flug's wallet and Huss's dirt. But I knew it wasn't the same. And on the walk home that night I came up with another idea.

Picking up rations, I'd met a girl who lived in the neighborhood. Her name was Gerda and she was always friendly without being overbearing. She wore nice clothes and had thick brown hair with matching brown eyes. I liked her a lot. Gerda worked at Ullrich printing company and seemed to enjoy it.

"I need your help," I said when I met Gerda on the street the following evening. It'd been another long week. "I saw in the paper that Ullrich is looking for help. My year is up, and I hate working at the *Schneiders*." I sighed. "Could you put in a good word if I apply? I can learn whatever they need me to. And I'm really strong."

Gerda laughed, pinching my bicep. "I believe it. I'll ask Helmut. He's been there a while." Helmut was Gerda's boyfriend, and she mentioned him all the time.

"That would be wonderful."

I started at Ullrich Printing four weeks later. The interview had been easy. I was able to explain my previous work and why I wanted to leave. They offered a spot in bookbinding but hinted at other things if I did well.

Every morning, I rang Gerda's doorbell and we walked together to work.

"I want you to meet Helmut," Gerda said the first day. "He starts at four in the morning since he's a typesetter. It's an important job." Gerda's voice rang with pride. "He's really good at spelling."

The young man with the mop of sand-colored hair met us at lunch. He was different from what I'd imagined. Tall and thin, he looked much older. His hairline was receding above a crooked nose, but he beamed at me with encouragement.

"Great to meet you," he said, extending an ink-stained hand. "No fear, the color doesn't come off."

Gerda giggled. "Only with special soap."

"Thanks for helping me get the job," I said, watching my hand disappear inside his.

"No problem, it was mostly Gerda." Helmut slung a lanky arm around Gerda's shoulders.

"Let's go out sometime." Helmut looked at the clock on the wall. "I've got to go back to work."

Mutti said little about my new job, especially since my income had increased and I was paid weekly. I kept a bit of money to buy groceries and share them with Burkhart while Mutti continued investing in schnapps and entertainment.

Rumors were flying that our currency, the *Reichsmark*, would change soon. Several people at work had been talking, and I listened carefully.

"You probably heard about the demonstration they had in front of city hall last year," Lotte, one of my other colleagues said. "There were thousands. We protested the horribly low food rations. The British administration is trying to find the hoarders and arrest black market traders. I just know that most stores hide their wares, even the basics like potatoes and coal."

"They say we'll have a new currency and everyone gets new money," another woman said.

"How much?" I asked, thinking of the meager amount of Reichsmark in my wallet.

"Every person is supposed to receive forty *Deutsche Mark*. And they'll exchange your savings, but it's ten to one."

I calculated quickly. Not that I had any savings, but the money would come in handy. I'd finally be able to buy new shoes—if I could find any.

The day the *Deutsche Mark* was introduced, the city changed overnight. After standing in line for two hours, I was the proud owner of forty *Marks* in brand-new bills. The paper crackled in my fist and I sniffed it. All I wanted were shoes and extra food.

"I need your share," Mutti said as soon as I arrived home.

"My feet hurt."

"What about our family?"

What family? If we were a family, I was the Queen of England.

I hesitated, weighing whether it was worth mentioning Mutti's weekly schnapps purchases, which swallowed all our leftover cash. "I'm going to buy shoes, and you'll get the rest."

For once Mutti kept quiet, and I went shopping the next day after work. My eyes about fell out of my head because every store window I passed was filled with goods.

For nine years, the German economy and its citizens had suffered through dwindling rations and starvation. Hundreds of thousands of shops had closed, all production capacity directed toward prolonging the war. Now shelves bowed under the unaccustomed weight of bread, noodles, chocolate, jams, meats and cheeses.

Vegetables and potatoes spilled from buckets as people watched in awe. Clothes for men and women, fashionable hats, gloves and wallets filled displays. Books, pots and pans, even camera equipment were available.

Ebert, the shoe store on *Hauptstrasse,* had more shoes than I'd seen in ten years. It took me two hours, not because I tried on every pair in the store, but because of the people waiting in line. My shoes were black leather—real women's pumps with an inch heel, low enough for me to walk easily. Just two months ago I'd seen used boots for four hundred *Reichsmark* on the black market. I'd paid twenty-four Deutschmark.

By fall, prices for consumer goods would double, demand much higher than supply. Still, it was the beginning of a new economy.

Returning home and thrilled about my purchase, I was surprised to see Mutti sitting at the table staring out the window, her hands in her lap.

"Mutti?"

She turned to face me, her eyes returning from a faraway place.

"Vati wrote." She handed me a piece of paper, covered with Vati's neat script. The vision of him sitting at his desk flooded me, the memory sending a spasm through my gut.

The writing was small to make use of every inch.

Dear Luise, Lilly and Burkhart,

It has been a long time, and I'm finally able to write. I'm in a Russian camp in ~~Northern Siberia~~. Last winter, I became ill and was moved to a much better labor detail. I'm doing fine now. We work in a kitchen that supplies the camp with food. Most of the cooking is simple. We only get scraps and leftovers, but I eat more often. I think of you every day and wonder how you are holding up.

The children must be growing. I'd love to see photos, maybe you could try to send one. I hope they'll let me keep it. I added an address on the envelope and hope you can write. I want to know everything you're doing. We get no news here and it's difficult to imagine what goes on at home. I so hope you're doing all right.

Nothing has been mentioned about my release. We often get new prisoners but they are ~~political prisoners~~, mostly Russians and Poles. Few people leave and we never know where they go and if they were truly released. I'm hopeful that I get to leave soon. I can't believe it's been three years since my arrest. Time goes very slowly here.

I must hope you're managing without me. You've had to be so strong. I look forward to your letter. It will be the best day in years when I get it.

I miss you all so much.

Willi, Vati

Tears streamed as I read. Forgotten was my fury at him for deserting us.

I wiped my face with my forearm, careful not to drip on the letter. Vati was alive! Memories jumbled through my mind, shreds of scenes long ago. Vati walking home from work with his briefcase, in uniform, smiling at me the morning he left. His hug on the train the last time I'd seen him.

I wondered what he looked like now and if the Russians would let him go soon. The Americans, Brits, and French had long released their prisoners.

I wondered what he thought of the war now. I knew so

little about the man, just superficialities like the job he'd had, how he liked to dress in suits, always immaculate, always perfect. But I didn't know the man himself.

I tasted bile, the old anger rising again. I couldn't understand him and wanted to set him down to ask him what in the world he'd thought. How he could have been part of the madness. What he'd done.

Of course, nobody spoke about such things these days. The denazification had turned into a farce. People like Huss who'd been in the NSDAP party or SS, who'd cheered the regime and supported it, worked in it to hammer us into submission—those same people were going back into leadership positions.

They got what was called a Persilschein. Persil was a laundry detergent, and the same people who'd killed Jews and communists had found a way to whitewash their pasts.

Everyone was eager to forget, but I couldn't.

I could neither forget nor forgive Vati for leaving me, not just because we'd been alone, but because he'd made it possible for Huss and Mutti's boyfriends to abuse me.

And so with every passing year, my loathing grew equally with my longing to see him home.

"I'm going to write," I said, jumping up to rummage through Vati's desk for pen and paper. Except for the wood stains, it was one of the few pieces of furniture left unharmed.

After "*Lieber Vati*" I stopped. The paper began to blur as I stared and tried to think of things to say. Nothing was suitable. I thought of Mutti's visitors, Herr Huss. I thought about the country, the terrible crimes committed and the millions dead, my questions for him.

What did you do? Why did you leave us?

"What should I write?" I looked at Mutti who still stared out the window, her eyes wide but dry.

"I don't know."

"What's the matter?"

"I'm fine." Mutti straightened herself and began unpacking her grocery basket she'd thrown to the floor.

"Aren't you going to write?" I looked at my still blank page.

"Sure, I will. I just won't do it now."

"But we should write immediately."

"We won't even know if he'll get the letter."

"But we have to try."

"Didn't I say I'd write?"

I gripped my pen, urging my brain to come up with things I could safely say.

CHAPTER TWENTY-SEVEN

Lilly: June 1949

On my 17th birthday I moved to the administrative department at Ullrich. It was a proud moment in my struggles for decent employment and the first time I felt I'd accomplished something on my own. Of course, I did count Huss getting off our backs as a success, albeit a secret one.

"Let's celebrate this weekend." Gerda, as tall as me, had her brown hair in fashionable curls. She was four years older, and I often admired her.

"Where do you want to go?"

I knew I sounded skeptical when I was supposed to be excited. Solingen's cleanup was slow and tedious as materials were sorted and recycled, but many citizens had taken up hiking and riding bicycles to the newly opened restaurants and cafes in the countryside.

While I was eager to get away from Mutti, I didn't care to spend the evening in a bar or café with a bunch of strangers when I could hardly afford one drink.

"Haven't you heard?" Gerda's voice trembled with excitement. "There's a fair in town this weekend."

"Oh." Sometimes I felt like I was living under a rock. Mutti kept me busy with an endless list of chores. Even on weekends I had to knit for hours despite my fulltime job.

To escape the boredom, I daydreamed. I thought about

moving out and what my home would look like. Sometimes I thought about boys. One had always stopped at the Schneider's café. He'd winked at me at first and getting bolder, had asked me to go out with him. I'd refused, too shy and worried about Mutti's comments.

There were others, like the man who lived down the street from us and worked where Vati had once been head engineer. He was ancient with thinning hair and a puffy face, but Mutti kept hinting he was interested.

Gerda linked her arm with mine as we walked home from work. "I'll pick you up at three tomorrow?"

"What shall we bet Mutti will have some urgent errand that can't wait. I'm so tired of spending my weekends cooking and cleaning."

"It's your birthday!" We were almost to Gerda's house.

I sighed. "That never stopped her in the past."

"Helmut and I are going to see a movie tonight. Want to come?"

I thought about my meager pocket money. "What's playing?"

"*Bergkristall*, something about a mountain farmer. It's supposed to be good."

"Can't afford it. I'll see you tomorrow." As I turned to leave, Gerda yelled after me, "You won't mind if Helmut joins us?"

"Of course not." I knew Gerda was fond of Helmut. She always talked about future plans as if they were already married.

A hazy Saturday sun promised heat as I prepared to go out. I'd inherited another dress from Mutti. Buying new was out of the question. Since the currency reform, prices had more than doubled. So, I'd made a few alterations, cutting off the long sleeves, adding white lace and voila, my dress was ready. Dark blue with a wide skirt, it accentuated my waist and swirled around my legs.

Thankfully my body had finally arrived, coinciding with the currency reform. Where I'd been flat before, I now had modest curves. I'd grown my hair out to shoulder-length and thanks to some natural curls didn't have to do much to it.

I scrubbed the bathroom and prepared lunch. Mutti still didn't cook much, so I'd become a creative chef with the few ingredients we were able to afford, mostly soups with beans and lentils or eggs and potatoes.

When I met up with Gerda, she looked at me admiringly. "You look pretty!"

I smiled. "You look nice, too."

Gerda wore a bright green skirt and white blouse. "Thanks. I hope Helmut likes it."

I took Gerda's arm. "Where is he?"

"He'll meet us there." We walked downtown to catch the streetcar to *Gräfrath*, an old part of Solingen that had escaped most of the bombings.

The air was warm and breezy and the fair in full swing. A cobblestone road, squeezed between shale-shingled houses and pubs, led to the *Marktplatz*, an open area now filled with tents and carnival rides.

Red, green and blue garlands danced above us as people milled and laughter pealed. The aroma of popped corn and caramel mixed with women's perfumes. Couples walked hand-in-hand, children ran and screamed—some carried colorful wads of white and pink spun sugar. A sense of excitement lay in the air and I felt a tingling in my veins.

This is what I'd been missing, what all of us had been missing. Music and decent food, people laughing without fear. Friends and a sense of normalcy. My hands trembled as I gripped my purse tighter. I was determined to have fun today.

Gerda cranked her neck to see over the crowd. "I don't see him."

The throng was especially thick around the booths offering beer and schnapps. Voices swelled and a cloud of alcohol thickened the air.

"Let's go there," I said, pointing at stone steps leading toward the old church. Half-way up we stopped to scan the crowd.

"I see Helmut." Gerda rushed back down and dove into the throng. I followed, a bit breathless about the recklessness around us, the atmosphere charged with a sense of purposeful enjoyment.

Rudi Schuricke's *Capri-Fischer* blared from some loudspeaker as we made our way toward a beer tent. Several young men squeezed around a cocktail table, an assortment of empty and half-empty glasses between them. The noise was deafening. Helmut waved, his eyes glassy as he pulled Gerda into a hug.

"Hallo, *meine Damen*," he shouted. Several pairs of eyes studied me and I felt my breath quicken with nerves. Helmut didn't seem to notice and yelled over the din, "This is Günter, a friend of mine. And his brother, Hans." The young men, beer in hand, leaned forward and nodded.

I stole a glance at Günter, the fellow next to me. His hair was dark, almost black, and cut short in the back. A tuft on top dangled on his tanned forehead. He was a bit shorter than Helmut and almost as thin.

For the briefest moment our eyes met. Something knotted inside me and I looked away. What was the matter with me?

"Let's have a drink, shall we?" Helmut waved us to the counter. "My treat. It's pretty good."

"Prost!" We toasted, glasses clinking together. I glanced at the stranger next to me while trying to think of something smart to say. Nothing came to mind so I kept watching the crowd. Helmut and Gerda shared a kiss.

After a round of bratwurst and fried potatoes, we began to wander around the grounds. A carousel with screaming riders twirled, and a Ferris wheel circled in slow motion.

"Who's going on the *teeter-totter* with me?" Günter looked around our group which had grown since we first arrived. I recognized one of Helmut's friends from work and a couple of women from our neighborhood.

Gerda and Helmut looked at the wild swinging boat-shaped contraption. At one point it looked as if the swing was jumping out of its holding, the people inside pushing against the top.

"No way," Gerda said. "That looks positively scary."

Helmut shook his head. "You're on your own."

"You are all chicken. It's fun," Günter laughed.

"I'll go with you," I said. *Where had that come from?* A dozen pairs of eyes turned on me and I felt my breath quicken once more.

"You sure about this?" Gerda said.

I produced a smile. "No, but I'll try."

Günter grinned and grabbed my hand. "Let's go."

His fingers felt warm and dry, holding mine. They were strong and knew things, causing the bugs in my stomach to do somersaults. Time stood still as we walked. The noise around me faded as I tried to match my step to his.

He slowed to squeeze between people, taking care to make room for me. Our eyes met fully and I noticed they were hazel with bits of sparkly brown around the iris.

As Günter let go of my hand to pay the cashier, the void was immediate. I longed for his hand. He jumped into the boat, taking my elbow to help me in.

"Thanks," I managed, trying to keep my voice steady. I was more nervous than during my interview at Ullrich.

The boat-shaped swing was thirty feet long and made of wood. At each end, mounted bars offered the swingers handholds. Günter stepped to one side, pulling me with him.

More people joined us on each side. A whistle blew and the swing started moving. We took turns pushing our feet into the boat, creating momentum. I grabbed a couple of handles next to Günter and pushed hard. Our fingers almost touched, and the knowledge of him being so close sent delicious currents through me.

"This is great!" I yelled as the boat rocked higher.

Günter grinned at me, and I felt my palms turn clammy. Back and forth we went, the wind blowing my hair and skirt.

From the corner of my eye I kept watching Günter, who seemed nimble and balanced easily. At one point the boat rocked so hard, our feet nearly left the ground. I was flying.

I wouldn't have cared to ever return to earth. As the swing hit the rubber stop at the top, I yelled out with the crowd. Only when the conductor applied his brakes, did we slow down.

"That was fun," Günter said as the teeter-totter came to a stop. He offered me his arm on the climb off the boat and I gladly took it.

"Thanks for inviting me."

"My pleasure. We'll do it again sometime."

Out of breath and smiling we joined our friends. Still, I couldn't stop from feeling disappointed when he let go of my hand. *Don't be ridiculous. You hardly know the man.*

"What shall we do now?" While he'd directed his question more toward me, Helmut answered instead.

"How about exploring the new pub up the street?"

Günter shook his head. "I won't be able to join you. I'm completely broke."

Helmut turned to Gerda and me. "What about you two? What do you want to do?"

"We could stay a while longer." I looked at Günter and started blushing.

"How about we leave in thirty minutes," Gerda said. "It's getting late anyway and Lilly needs to be home by nine."

I nodded.

"That's pretty early, isn't it?" Günter commented.

"Especially since it's her birthday today," Gerda said.

"My mother is strict," I said.

"What? Why didn't you tell us?" Günter looked at me, shaking his head in mock despair.

"What am I going to say? Hey everyone, it's my birthday," I quipped.

"Why not?" Günter laughed. Noticing my discomfort, he added, "Gerda should've told us. It's a bit late for a celebration now. That means we'll have to party another time to make up for it."

I smiled, the flutter in my belly turning into a storm.

Dusk settled and warm lights sprang up all over the grounds. Bing Crosby sang *Far Away Places*.

All I wanted was to hold Günter's hand again, walk with him for hours. But Günter mounted his bike and with a longing I'd never felt before, I looked after him until he disappeared up the street.

Helmut grinned. "He's nice, isn't he?"

I nodded worried what was written on my face.

"He and I are best friends," Helmut said. "We did a lot of stuff together during the war. If you have any questions about him..."

"I better head home," I said feeling my cheeks blaze again.

"Let's go," Gerda said, sensing my discomfort. She grabbed Helmut by the arm. "We'll miss the streetcar and Lilly will get into trouble."

It was long after midnight, and despite my exhaustion I couldn't sleep. With my eyes closed, I relived the evening over and over, wondering if I'd said the right things and what Günter thought of me.

My stomach hitched as I thought of his hands, his dark hair, and nice tan. He was tall, too, and very fit. A bit skinny, but so was everybody else. I'd asked Gerda on the tram and found out he was almost twenty-one. He probably saw lots of girls. My heart pounded against my ribs. Why would he be interested in me?

Feeling hot, I threw my blanket aside, my eyes open. We had new glass here too, and shadows from the street lantern played across my bed. Lace curtains gently swooshed against the sill and I felt the breeze caress my skin.

My nightshirt had pulled up exposing my legs. I lay on my back, fingers tracing the shape of my breasts and for a moment I imagined they were his. My breath quickened as I explored between my legs, pleasure mounting into climax.

I wanted to see him again.

CHAPTER TWENTY-EIGHT

Lilly: September 1949

The fall weekend announced itself with cloudless skies and warm evenings, and I accompanied Gerda and Helmut to café Mais, another local dance spot. In my mind I went over the letter I'd written to Vati. I knew it word for word.

> *Lieber Vati,*
>
> *We were so happy to learn you are doing all right. I miss you so much. I'm working in the bookbinding department of a printing company. It's much better than the housekeeping I used to do. My friend, Gerda, helped me. She's very nice, you'd like her. There's a lot more food now and we have enough to cook.*
>
> *Vati, it's been so long since I've seen you. I hope you are managing and that you will get to come home really soon. Please take care of yourself.*
>
> *Your daughter,*
> *Lilly*
> *P.S. Please come home soon!*

The noise of the café brought me back to the present. Hundreds of people seemed cramped inside, their voices mixed with the blare of music, the smell of beer and cigarette smoke.

Every weekend, Solingen's youth descended here to lose themselves in long-missed entertainment. The country and its people wanted everything. We hungered for light bulbs and coffee cups, underpants and socks, sofas and table cloths. We especially wanted schnapps, beer and wine. We wanted to party and forget we hadn't had a youth.

"That's a surprise," Helmut said when Günter materialized at our table. "I thought you had to work today."

Günter grinned. "Worked till seven."

For a moment, his gaze rested on my face. Too shy to hold eye contact, I looked down quickly. By the time I raised my head, he'd turned to Helmut.

"I'll see if I can find a chair."

"Günter, how are you?" A young woman with light blonde hair poked Günter in the chest. "Good to see you," she said, her blue-shadowed eyes looking smoky and mysterious.

"Elisabet, wie geht's?" Günter smiled at the blonde. I watched as the girl whispered something into his ear. He grinned and nodded.

I felt heat rising from the middle of my breast, up my throat into my face, an angry torridness that choked me.

Since the fair, I'd only seen Günter once when I'd gone with Gerda and Helmut to the movies. He'd stood a few feet away, watching the show, and I caught myself more than once staring in his direction, contemplating whether I'd have the nerve to move closer. Of course, I didn't. Even in the dark, in the flickering lights of the film I'd noticed a streak of wildness that equally attracted and terrified me. Since the movie had run till almost nine, I'd rushed off afterwards.

"I'll be right back," I croaked, running off toward the bathrooms. Checking my eyes and lipstick, I stared at myself in the mirror. My face looked blotchy, spots rising from the open collar of my blouse. I'd been excited about buying it, especially because it had a deep neckline.

Now I wished for a turtleneck. How could I've thought Günter was interested in me? I felt small and insignificant.

Slipping into one of the bathroom stalls, I sat and waited for my skin to calm down.

"Lilly. Are you in here?" Gerda pounded on the bathroom door.

"Yes," I sighed.

"Are you all right? You've been gone for ages." Gerda sounded exasperated.

"I'll be there soon. I must've eaten something bad." The

last thing I wanted to do was confide in Gerda, who might tell Helmut.

When I returned, I found Gerda and Helmut at the table. Günter was nowhere to be seen. The music pounded, playing a fast piece about love and summer heat, the singer's voice soaring.

Dozens of couples swooshed around the dance floor. An even thicker throng crowded the bar, clouds of cigarette smoke and alcohol vapors swirling above.

Reflected by floor-to-ceiling mirrors, the flashes of movement and lights blinded me. I'd turned invisible, contemplating whether to go home before everybody noticed my dark mood and the splotches on my skin.

"Do you want to dance?" One of Helmut's friends, Uwe Reiner, appeared next to me. Uwe was extremely tall, over six feet, and often bent down to speak to people. As a result, his shoulders seemed permanently hunched.

I forced a smile, half of me resolved to dance, the other ready to run. "Sure, why not."

When the song ended, we headed for the bar where dancers crowded to snatch up refreshments. I sipped a brownish beer, the color from a shot of malt, making it slightly sweeter than regular brews. Uwe remained by my side as Gerda nuzzled close to Helmut.

The music changed to a slower pace, the lights dimmed. Couples shuffled around in circles, bodies pressed together. I hoped Uwe wouldn't ask me.

"Are you enjoying yourself?" Günter play-punched Helmut in the arm.

"Looks like you're having a good time," Helmut said.

"Love the music." Günter's face looked as flushed as my throat. "Do you want to dance?"

I looked up, temporarily at a loss for words. "Ehem, I guess," I heard myself say.

"Let's go." Günter took my arm and led me to the dance floor. "Are you mad at me?"

"Why should I be mad at you?" I tried keeping a straight face, feeling his eyes sink into mine.

"You disappeared so suddenly that I thought..." Günter shrugged, holding out his hand to dance pose.

"My stomach hurt. I'm fine now." *Why was I talking like an imbecile?*

I tried breathing normally as his hand burned a hole into the small of my back, willing my feet to follow his. The music was louder here or maybe it was my heightened sense of awareness. A couple near us was kissing, arms entwined and bodies meshed together. I looked away, struggling to come up with something witty to say. His hands on my body made it impossible to think.

"I'm glad you're better."

I wanted to ask if he'd been with the blonde all this time. Instead I said nothing, convinced he considered me a bore. All too soon the song ended. The next dance was fast and Günter led me back to the bar to join our friends.

That's when I remembered the time. Almost nine o'clock. Mutti's pinched face appeared in my vision.

"I've got to leave."

"Your mother?"

I nodded, embarrassed about my ridiculous curfew.

"Hold on. I'll be right back." Without waiting for an answer, Günter disappeared in the throng.

"I can take you home." Uwe, his eyes glassy, hovered over me.

Against all reason I'd hoped, Günter would offer to take me. To avoid answering Uwe, I turned to Gerda who'd promised to walk home with me. But when I saw her so happy with Helmut, I changed my mind. Helmut had just ordered another beer and I knew he didn't want to leave yet.

Somebody started a drinking song and several people joined the howling. The crowd locked arms and swayed back and forth, shiny eyes turned to the ceiling. Glasses clinked, beers sloshed, followed by raucous laughter. A boy tried climbing onto the bar, yelling something about the top of the world before he was pulled down by his friends.

Uwe put his long arm around my shoulder. "Come on, I'll take you home."

"Fine," I managed.

As I hugged Gerda good-bye, Günter reappeared next to us. "Something wrong?"

Gerda shrugged. "Lilly needs to head home and Helmut isn't quite ready to go, so Uwe—"

"I can take you." Günter grinned as I tried to wiggle out of

Uwe's arm.

"I thought you'd left." I wanted to sink into the floor.

"It's really no problem," Uwe chimed in.

Günter shrugged and turned away. "Maybe next time."

I could've sworn he looked upset. Could I dare hope he was mad because he thought Uwe meant something to me?

***

It was after nine-thirty when I arrived, our walk home a non-affair. Uwe tried his best to get me talking, but I remained tightlipped and hurried inside before he could grab my hand.

Worried about another tirade, I tiptoed into the foyer when I noticed Mutti sitting at the kitchen table. Her eyes were red.

"What's the matter?" My stomach lurched in the realization that something terrible had happened.

"It's Vati," Mutti's voice broke, sobbing. "He wrote."

"Let me see."

The letter in Mutti's hand was a crumpled mess. But that was nothing compared to the shakiness of my hand.

Dearest Luise, Lilly and Burkhart,

"My heart is heavy as I need to tell you that I had a hearing in front of a judge. I had waited four years and remained hopeful that my time would be over soon. Instead, I was sentenced to twenty-five years of hard labor.

We're working in a gold mine. It's tough but I'm still pretty strong. I will write again soon. I'm so sorry. All I can do is hope. Hope that my time will be reduced, hope that you will wait for me. I miss you so much.

Yours always,

Willi/Vati

Uncomprehendingly, I stared at the twenty-five years. Vati would be in his seventies by then. I hurled the letter on the table and began to cry. We'd never see him again.

Mutti lifted her tear-stained face toward me, attempting a smile. "Like Vati says, there's always hope. We've managed so far and we'll continue to manage."

She resolutely stood as the shutters came down across her expression. She wiped her eyes and I was reminded of the moment in front of our house when we'd learned about Vati enlisting by choice. I didn't doubt she was sad on some level, but I suspected she was mostly mourning the lack of financial support and status,

Vati's high-level job had provided.

In bed I tried to imagine Vati's face when he was handed down this impossible sentence. The twenty-five years kept rolling through my mind.

It was a death sentence.

People had returned from Russian camps in the past. Vati had obviously done a lot to make them mad, to hold on to him for life. By now I knew there were others like him, well over 10,000 German men still stuck in Siberia and the Ural.

I'd read all I could about Russia. I scanned the newspaper every morning when Mutti was reading death notices and missing person announcements. At best, Stalin's gulags seemed random, people arrested for a wrong comment.

But Vati had been guilty. Heat rose into my neck and the fury dried my tears. Fury for Vati, for abandoning us, for becoming a willing contributor to the evilness that overshadowed my existence and everything I cared for…fury for myself, for my inability to forget. I scolded myself for thinking it was easier to cope when someone had died than to worry about him for eternity.

I was mad at him and knew I'd never look at him the same way. And yet, how could I not wish him home? *You'll never look at him again.*

A sob built in my throat and I muffled my cries in my pillow. All this time since the war ended I'd been hoping, a tiny sliver of my heart still listening for the front door.

I struggled to hang on to that hope. That bit in my heart. Nothing could be harder.

CHAPTER TWENTY-NINE

Lilly: September 1949

Despite the beautiful fall weather, I had trouble getting out of bed. Every day seemed worse than the day before as I forced myself to go to work and come to terms with the fact that Vati was lost.

"Lilly, come on." Gerda put an arm around me. "We're going swimming this weekend. It's supposed to be warm, probably the last time this year."

I shrugged. It was hard to get excited about anything.

"Don't tell me you'd rather stay home with your mother and little brother," Gerda smiled. "Who knows, Günter may join us."

"How do you—"

"No need to explain," Gerda chuckled. "It's pretty obvious. You could've had him take you home last weekend, but you screwed it up."

For the first time in days, I smiled. "Please don't say anything to anybody."

"I won't." Gerda placed her hand on her heart. "Not even Helmut."

Sparkling in the sun, the outdoor pool was surrounded by a wide expanse of lawns. The water looked a cool, refreshing blue. I felt self-conscious about the used bathing suit I'd found in a second-hand store. It was all I could afford. While it hugged my figure and was a pretty turquoise-green material, the cut was old-fashioned modest, covering my hips and chest. To my relief, Gerda's suit wasn't much better.

"He isn't here yet," Gerda whispered, catching my anxious glances at the group sprawled on the lawn.

We swam and forgetting my bulky suit I laughed out loud when the men bombed into the water. To my annoyance Uwe Reiner kept staring at me and remaining close.

"Hey." Günter stood at the edge of the pool.

"Come in," we all screamed, splashing him. He quickly stepped back, took aim and hurled himself between us. He came up laughing and sputtering.

"Hallo Lilly, how are you?"

"Pretty good. It's a nice day."

"I heard about your father. I'm so sorry."

I nodded, my throat immediately tight. I didn't trust myself to speak, so I just nodded.

"Sorry to have brought it up. How stupid of me." For a brief moment, Günter put his hand on my shoulder. "Let's swim and get a beer. I'm buying."

Beer in hand, we returned to the lawn where a patchwork of towels and blankets staked our claim.

To my surprise, Günter sat next to me. "We still haven't celebrated your birthday."

"You didn't forget," I said.

"Of course not. Birthdays are important. How old are you anyway?"

"Seventeen."

"Almost a grown woman," Günter chuckled, his gaze sweeping across my chest.

"I guess so," I breathed, a storm of bugs unleashing inside me.

"Hey, you two," Helmut said, "How about some soccer?"

Günter jumped up. "Want to play? He held out a hand, pulling me to my feet."

I watched as Günter dribbled across the field and maneuvered the ball. Sometimes, our eyes met and he winked at me. Uwe lurked nearby and I turned the other way, hoping he'd leave me alone.

"I've got to go home soon," I said once we'd returned to our towels.

"I'll walk with you," Günter said. "I need to help my father tonight."

The forest felt cool after the day in the sun. Last year's leaves rustled in the mottled light, ferns swayed. My skin burned from the sun and the excitement, every fiber aware of the man next to me. His breath sounded as easy as if we'd sat at the kitchen table while my heart thumped hard and loud.

"Would you like to go out tomorrow?" Günter asked as we approached my house.

"I don't know, I have to ask," I whispered, glancing at the curtains on the first floor. "Let's go to the door," I said, pulling him into the entrance and out of sight.

"Your mother is pretty strict?"

"She's difficult."

"Should I stop by tomorrow? I can always go home."

"What time do you want to be here?"

"How about three?"

"Good."

Entering the hallway, I heard my name.

"Hey," Günter whispered.

"What?" I leaned back outside.

His face was close now, tanned, his eyes dancing. Warm hands took my forearms as he pulled me toward him. I closed my eyes, his lips soft on mine, aromatic with something spicy.

The bugs inside my belly reared.

"I'll see you tomorrow," he said.

I jumped with the knock on the door. I'd been ready for thirty minutes and had restlessly paced the floor. My palms were damp, not exactly suitable for knitting or shaking hands.

"Hallo," I said opening the door, suppressing my panting breath.

Günter grinned. "Are we all right or should I take off running?"

"We're fine." I grabbed my handbag and shut the door behind me as Günter tried to peek inside.

"Is your mother home?"

"She's been gone all day. Honestly, I don't know where she is or when she'll be home. She does this all the time." Burkhart had gone with her and I suspected they were visiting her brother, Uncle August.

"Seems a bit strange, but then, that means you get to go out, too." Günter took my arm under his. "You look nice today." I felt his eyes wander across my figure like a caress, and I could've sworn the air sizzled.

I'd agonized over my blouse, the one with the low neckline, but I had few things that looked decent.

"Where are we going?"

"Have you heard about the new café near *Grünewald*? They're supposed to have fabulous cakes."

Café Kohnen's counters sparkled with an assortment of blueberry and mixed fruit tortes, marzipan and nougat rolls, cheesecakes, mocha and almond pies. The air carried aromas of coffee and chocolate, the smells so intense, my mouth watered.

"You pick whatever you want," Günter said. "Happy birthday."

My eyes began to skip between the apple and chocolate cream pies. I'd not seen such abundance since the years before the war when I'd gone to visit town with Vati.

Günter pulled out his wallet and unfolded a brand-new twenty-mark bill. "We'll eat till we drop."

"What would you like?" The girl behind the counter wore a ruffled white apron and matching headband.

"I'll have the chocolate butter cream." I hadn't eaten anything with butter in eight years.

"Make that two!" Günter ordered. "And a couple hot chocolates."

"Mine with whipped cream," I added.

"*Bitte sehr*," the serving girl curtsied. "I'll bring it right out."

"This is so good." The rich chocolate melted in my mouth and I closed my eyes.

"How come you earn so much money?" I said, scraping bits of buttercream off my plate. "I thought you were going to school."

"I'm going to school as part of an apprenticeship. I work and study on the side. Do you want another piece?"

I nodded, the idea of eating two slices of cake so foreign

and so decadent, I couldn't stop grinning.

Günter signaled the waitress and continued, "I make jewelry on the side."

"What kind of jewelry?"

"I melt scraps of silver from the factory and work them into rings and bracelets."

"I'd love to see your work."

"I can show you later."

I nodded as another piece of pie disappeared inside me. The feeling of fullness accompanied by the rich chocolate flavor was making me dizzy.

"If you want, we can stop by my house on the way," Günter said as he watched me eat. "I'll show you what I made for my aunt."

"Sure, if we have time. I have to be home—"

"I know."

"Sorry, I'm sounding like a broken record. I just don't want to be yelled at."

"I understand. We'll make sure you get home for dinner."

"I don't think I can eat anymore tonight," I laughed.

Günter took my hand into his as we walked. It seemed natural, the touch of his skin on mine warm and comforting.

"I'm just up the street from you," he said. "We moved in with my grandmother four years ago. She has a nice garden."

It was normal for adult children to remain at home. The housing situation was still precarious. Few apartments were available and it was close to impossible to find anything affordable on apprentice wages.

"I share a bedroom with Hans, my older brother. He's getting married soon."

"What does he do?"

Günter's eyes clouded over. "He's an electrician. Just got finished last year."

"Something wrong?"

"Nothing. I just...he had a hard time after the war. Was a POW with the Brits and almost died."

I'd seen that kind of look many times, so I took Günter's hand. "I'm glad he's doing better."

After a quick introduction to his parents, Günter pulled me into his room. Luckily Hans wasn't home. Günter unfolded several wads of tissue paper. Pieces of silver, fashioned into a pendant and matching bracelet, glittered inside.

"This is for my uncle."

"How pretty!" I carefully touched the silver pendant with a swirly pattern. "You're so talented."

"Not really, just handy. It helps to get some extra income."

Günter stepped closer and placed his arm around my shoulder, pulling me toward him. "You look really pretty today."

Blood roared through my head like crashing waves as I leaned into him. "Do I?"

"Yes," he said, gently touching my chin. His lips were soft on mine, his body firm.

"Are you two staying for dinner?" Günter's mother called from the kitchen.

Günter sighed. "I'm taking Lilly home in a few minutes," he yelled.

Without a word, his lips found mine again. I wrapped my arms around his neck, pulling in close, unleashing a wave of electrical currents.

His hands wandered along my back, sending more delicious sensations down my spine. Our breaths quickened, bodies heated and tingly. I forgot where I was, forgot everything but the feeling of being embraced, my body shivering with happiness.

Günter's mother's voice drifted in from the kitchen. "Soup's ready."

I looked around the room. "What time is it?"

"Almost half past six."

"Just one more kiss," I whispered. "I don't care if I'm late."

CHAPTER THIRTY

Lilly: July 1950

We spent more and more time together. We hiked the woods, went swimming and dancing with Günter's friends and hung out at beer gardens and pubs on the weekends.

I was elated, having found a way out of the house away from Mutti, away from the memories of Vati's absence. I loved Günter, and for the first time in my life I was happy.

That is…most of the time. There was still Mutti and the fact I was stuck.

"I can't go," I said, my voice rising in frustration. Not only had Mutti made a long list of chores for the weekend, I felt paralyzed not having any transportation. All our friends and Günter had bicycles and they were planning to spend the weekend swimming and camping at one of the lakes.

"I can't do your chores, but I can help you get a bike."

"How are you going to do that?" I yanked my hand from his, charging ahead.

"Slow down." Günter reclaimed my arm. "We'll save money and buy it."

"Impossible, it'd take me ten years to save enough. Besides, I wouldn't even know where you'd find one."

"I earn money, and the bike shop in town has one sitting in the window."

"You can't be serious."

"If we save for a few weeks we can do it."

"Nobody has ever bought me something this big."

"So I'll be the first." He grinned and hugged me to him.

"And it's really selfish of me because I want you to go with me."

I jumped into his arms and nuzzled my face against his neck. "It'll be the best gift ever."

Günter picked me up after work and we headed downtown. The bicycle in the shop window was a beautiful, metallic burgundy red, shimmering in the light.

"What do you think?" he said.

"It's too much. You didn't tell me it'd be one hundred fifty marks. That's crazy." I shook my head.

"Nonsense. Why else did we stay home for three weeks? Not spend a single *Pfennig*?"

"I know but I can get something cheaper."

Günter gripped my shoulders, his eyes glued to mine. "I'd like to give you this present."

I nodded as an intense feeling of warmth flooded me. For the first time in my life I felt valued...cherished. In all the years since Vati left I hadn't felt this good and my heart opened to embrace Günter. At that moment I threw away my reservations, accepting Günter's recklessness just as I accepted his generosity.

After the purchase, we picked up Günter's bike at his house and met Helmut and Gerda at the beer garden. The restaurant's lawn, crammed with benches and long tables, was overflowing with people. An old man played accordion underneath an awning laden with purple clematis. I kept glancing at my new bike. I still couldn't believe it.

"Are you coming with us tomorrow?" Helmut eyed my treasure.

"We can go next weekend," Günter said, watching Helmut take a sip of beer. "We'll have money again on Friday."

I smiled when I heard the 'we.' "I don't have any gear," I said.

"My brother, Hans, has a tent," said Günter. "He'll let me borrow his stuff. We won't need much else. Some blankets maybe."

"Where will we go?" I asked, anxious about explaining my trip to Mutti and what may happen when I was alone with Günter.

"The Rhine." Gerda blushed, looking at Helmut.

"What do you think?" Günter asked me, a bit of that same anxiety in his eyes.

I nodded, determined to make it happen.

"To the Rhine we go, prost!" Helmut clinked his glass to mine.

I worried all week, getting more anxious by the day. While our friends collected gear, I was feverishly thinking of ways to broach the subject with Mutti. By Friday, I was a nervous wreck.

We'd leave first thing tomorrow and yet I hadn't found an opportunity to ask. The day at the office passed in painful slowness as words and sentences jumbled through my mind, trying to anticipate Mutti's reaction. I was determined to go no matter what she'd say, but the knots in my stomach were fist-size by the time I arrived home.

"I'm going camping this weekend," I blurted, having decided on a full frontal attack.

Mutti sat on the couch looking at knitting patterns. "You have camping gear?"

"Helmut and Günter do."

"I suppose you'll go anyway even if I forbid it."

"Mutti, please. Everyone is going and now that I have a bicycle—"

"And surely you'll sleep in separate tents." Mutti's voice dripped with sarcasm.

My face grew hot. Mutti had a way of piercing my heart. Günter had been very good and treated me with respect, another reason why I liked him so much. But I knew he was waiting. I wanted to move forward, too.

Of course, Helmut and Gerda were already doing *it*. Gerda had made several remarks, turning pink in the process. I'd wanted to know more, but was too embarrassed to ask. Not sure how everything worked, I'd tried to find books, but the descriptions were vague and the drawings crude.

Mutti got up to leave the room. "Don't forget to get your chores done."

"I'll do them tonight," I yelled after her.

Ever since Vati's letter, Mutti had been different. It was as if she was distracted and didn't care so much what I did. Whatever her motivation, I welcomed my new freedom. Not that Mutti liked Günter. He'd stopped by a few times and I'd introduced him.

"I don't care for him!" Mutti had said. "He's just a worker. He didn't even get an education."

"He's smart and he goes to school to become a dye maker. He earns good wages."

"You know what I mean. You should look for a real man, like Herr Hubert down the street. He is a *Beamter*, like Vati."

"Herr Hubert is old and ugly," I shouted.

"You don't have to raise your voice," Mutti said indignantly. "I just think you can do much better."

I wondered why Mutti went out of her way to be cruel and make me feel bad about everything I did. And somehow deep inside I realized she had to feel so ghastly herself that she tried to pull me to her level.

Well, I wasn't going to let her.

CHAPTER THIRTY-ONE

Lilly: August 1950

The Saturday sun barely peeked over the horizon when we left. The air, fresh and fragrant, misted my skin. I breathed deeply, keeping easy pace with my friends. I'd packed a change of clothes and a blanket. Günter carried our gear, a couple of poles, two pieces of tarp to make up the tent roof and a few lengths of string.

The Rhine ran from Switzerland to the North Sea and was very wide near Düsseldorf. Since there hadn't been any industry for years, the water was clean and sparkled in the sun. A sandy pit formed a perfect beach, its pebbles like colorful pearls. The land rose gently, covered in grasses and wildflowers. If you didn't know better, you could've completely forgotten a war had taken place.

Günter and Helmut swam far out into the stream, but we girls stayed near the shore. I didn't feel too confident about my swimming abilities and preferred to keep my feet on the ground. Gerda didn't swim either, so we jumped up and down in the waves. An occasional barge tuckered past in the distance.

We set up house on an outcropping above a rock formation, the space flat as a table and covered with grass, perfect for camping. The tent roof hung so low we had to crawl on our knees not to hit our heads.

Helmut had scrounged a bottle of schnapps. On the way we picked up fresh *Brötchen,* yeast rolls that gave off a rich aroma of fresh-baked bread and melted in your mouth. We bought strawberry jam, a piece of hard cheese and a bale of straw from the nearby farmer to stuff our tent floors with fragrant bright yellow heaps.

Günter guarded the fire. We told stories and drank the strong liquor.

I was dizzy and excited from my new sense of freedom. I had friends and a great man in my life and for the first time I felt careless. The knowledge of Günter next to me was like an invisible touch, as if his soul somehow reached across space to caress me.

The sky sparkled like diamonds on velvet. I thought of Vati and wondered if he saw the same stars and if he was sick. I felt I would've known if he'd died. No, he couldn't be dead.

"We're going to bed," Helmut said. He got up, rubbing Gerda's shoulders.

Günter looked at me, his eyes unreadable in the flickering light. "Do you want to go to bed, too?"

"I'm pretty tired." Nerves made my knees quiver as Günter arranged the fire within the circle of rocks. Then he straightened and wrapped his arm around me from behind.

"Are you having fun?" he whispered, his mouth finding my neck.

Heat pulsed through me as I pressed against him. "It's so pretty out here."

"Let's go." Günter's voice was soft and deeper than usual.

Like a nest, the straw inside the tent rustled beneath the blankets. In the darkness I sensed his body more than I saw it, its faint glow igniting me.

Günter's lips found mine. "Hi."

The river murmured in the distance as I answered his touch. Günter's hands traveled lower, unbuttoning my blouse, each movement unbearably slow, each touch sending ripples down my spine.

We'd kissed a lot and on occasion hid in Günter's room. This was the first time we were truly alone.

"Are you happy?" he said.

"Mmmh."

A breeze caressed my naked skin, followed by Günter's touch. I unbuttoned his shirt and ran my fingertips across the coarse hairs on his chest. His tremble extended through my arm to my heart.

Wiggling out of my shirt, I pulled him closer, my body

bathing in his nearness. There was so much skin, his warmth meeting mine.

"You sure you want to do this?" he asked, his lips traveling down my collarbone.

"We have to be careful. My mother would kill me if...."

"I'll take you away first," he chuckled.

"Take me away now."

My breath quickened as he explored new ground. I remembered the first time I'd met him, the delicious feel of his hands on mine, those hands that knew things. The worry of Helmut and Gerda hearing us faded as Günter's fingers danced lower.

For a second, my thoughts returned to Huss and his disgusting smell. I sighed.

"Something wrong?" Günter asked.

"I'm fine."

"We can stop."

"I...am fine." I wasn't going to give Huss the satisfaction of ruining my love.

"I'm all right if you want to wait."

My mouth closed over his as I grasped his arm. I was lying on flat ground, yet I felt dizzy as if I were extended over an abyss. Jolts of electricity pulsed down my spine and an ache awoke between my thighs.

Günter continued exploring, tugging at the waistband of my shorts. I lifted my hips and he pulled them down. He tore off his shirt and pants, nearly undoing the tent. A giggle broke from my throat before his naked body made contact with mine. I shivered and went quiet.

"Are you cold?" he whispered.

"No."

I rubbed his back, traveled lower, and across his stomach. I savored this flat and muscular spot, found it unbearably erotic. My fingers wandered on, halting, teasing, for a moment distracted from my own pleasure, our quickening breaths melting.

I remembered the stranger in the dim light of my bedroom. I blinked to make the image go away.

Günter's hands continued their wanderings, circling and teasing, sending waves of excitement through me. "You taste like strawberries," he mumbled against my skin as his fingertips brushed along my inner thighs.

I let go of my thoughts, my fears and worries, my back arching to meet him. I wanted him to hurry. I wanted...

The straw rustled softly as he wandered to the triangle of fleece, private and mine alone. I'd found pleasure here before, but this was different, nothing compared to this. I moaned and my body quivered as he stroked gently. I followed suit, taking hold.

He shuddered and as our bodies grew urgent, I pulled him closer. The world disappeared. Life centered on us with unbearable closeness, the air around us alive and pulsing.

He entered me slowly, pushing against the constriction of my virginity, my body, eager to receive him, giving way, our movements awkward at first, then finding rhythm.

The dull pain lessened. He slowed, his lips soft as feathers, hot breaths on damp skin...unbearable. I forgot where my body began or ended.

Ever higher climbing.

My heart jumped against his ribs, pleasure mounting until finally exploding into climax. Drenched in sweat we lay still, holding hands with fingers entwined.

Stillness surrounded us as if time had stopped. Nothing mattered but our smiling faces in the dark.

I awoke early. All was quiet, the Rhine's whispers comforting in the stillness. In the dimness of early dawn I looked at the man next to me. Günter lay on his back, his mouth relaxed, his dark hair unruly across his forehead. I watched him sleep, molding myself to his side. He muttered something and hugged me closer. I felt safe and at ease, a feeling I'd not experienced since before Vati left. It was so long ago that it felt like a mere shadow of this new thing, this closeness and comfort, this man who had entered my life.

I was in love.

Feeling the urge to pee, I snuck outside and clambered down to the beach. It was peaceful, the water cool, caressing my toes. I strolled downstream, taking in the scenery, throwing my arms into the air, breathing deeply before finding a thicket of bushes to hide behind.

A smile appeared as I remembered last night, followed by more butterflies. The air around me buzzed, the colors vibrant, the lush green interspersed with miniature daisies and dandelions. The Rhine whispered, certain of its destination to the North Sea, purposeful like me. I even heard the pebbles rubbing together beneath the surface, the lapping of the water.

I was alive.

They say happiness is fleeting as hot breath in the wind, but to this day I remember this moment as being unconditionally happy. That part of me I'd hidden away—the part that was too vulnerable to admit how hurtful Mutti's refusal of love was—triumphed. I was no longer rejected, no longer treated coldly. I had somebody in my life who appreciated me and made me feel valued as a human being.

I would've sung, had my voice not been so unaccustomed to rejoicing. Instead I danced a few steps and threw a stick into the water, watching it swim away in the current.

BOOK THREE: JUNE 1952 – SEPTEMBER 1953

CHAPTER THIRTY-TWO

Lilly: June 4, 1952

The party was supposed to start in fifteen minutes and I found myself at the window once more. The walkway below, mostly hidden by the red beech I considered my friend growing up, remained stubbornly empty. Why of all days was Günter late today?

Too excited to remain still, I took another round through the living room. It was shabby, really, the sofa an oversized yellow sponge, the seat cushions shiny like the pate of a balding man. The glasses, though mismatched, lined up in perfect order. Napkins were stacked. Pretzels and breadsticks sat arranged in bowls on the table.

I fought down the momentary panic of welcoming my guests without a drop of alcohol. Seven years after the war, after needing everything and getting nothing, every German got drunk as often and as quickly as possible. It was like a frenzy—a race into oblivion.

I didn't do too well with it. I resented the sensation of being out of control and giddy, my head woozy. The next day I was always sick, my stomach an empty sack filled with bile, my tongue a furry animal ready to choke me. Oh, what I'd give to feel that carelessness my friends showed. To forget and go crazy. Instead I caught myself, an invisible barrier that kept my thoughts in focus, sharp as broken glass when I'd much preferred the fog of a bottle of schnapps.

Smoothing down my new pencil skirt made of light-gray

wool worth my six months allowance, I hurried into the kitchen. We now had a refrigerator, a reconditioned Bosch that cost a fortune, but what luxury. It was stuffed with potato salad, deviled eggs and sausages, but I checked it anyway.

"What are you doing?" Burkhart said. At fifteen, my brother's gangly legs banged against the kitchen table, his feet and hands too large for his body. He was enjoying a roast beef sandwich, his eyes glazed, his cheeks stuffed, bits of crumbs flying out of his mouth. Mutti left him here as a special surprise to spoil my evening.

I resented him infiltrating my party. Yet, I found myself loving the sight of him getting his fill. Six years of starvation were hard to forget.

"Inspecting things," I said in an even voice. It wasn't Burkhart's fault that Mutti used him to punish me.

"You checked it a thousand times already."

I ignored him and wiped down the table one more time.

The doorbell rang. In the reflection of the hall mirror, my lipstick glowed a dark red, setting off my early summer tan. I'm not kidding myself. I'm no beauty, the nose I inherited from Mutti—she calls it the *Kirschbaum* nose after her family—too strong, but tonight I was pleased with what I saw.

"Hallo, birthday girl," Günter said when I yanked open the door. He planted a quick kiss on my mouth before he pushed past me. "Got Beckmann Pils plus the schnapps." He placed the case of beer under the table and showed me the three bottles of clear liquid. "Real corn, none of that post-war Fusel." A grin spread across his face, though I could tell he was tired. Working sixty to seventy hour weeks was wearing on him, and it was only Wednesday.

I was about to hug him, nuzzle my face into that soft spot on his neck when he took a step back, his gaze on Burkhart. "What is *he* doing here? Is your mother—"

"Mutti is visiting Uncle August. She left Burkhart." I shrugged helplessly. Arguing with my mother was like trying to sink an iceberg. Impossible.

"I've got school tomorrow," Burkhart chirped in, chewing loudly.

"You'll be in bed by nine," I said.

Burkhart made a face before turning his attention to the

plate of ham and cheese rolls.

At last, Günter pulled me into the living room, where we had a chance to kiss. I leaned into him, drinking in his warmth and stubble of evening beard. He's thin, almost bony, and several inches taller, dark hair flopping across his forehead. I especially love his eyes, hazel with specs of green and brown around the iris.

"Happy birthday," he said, placing a tiny box on my palm.

My hands shook as I lifted the lid. For a brief moment I wondered if it contained what I was waiting for. Just as fleeting, the thought was gone. A silver pendant in the shape of a teardrop lay nestled in paper, a tiny blue stone wedged in the wide part of the shape.

"I love it," I said...and I did. When I returned from the bedroom with the pendant around my neck, the doorbell rang again.

Helmut and Gerda bustled into the foyer, followed by Günter's older brother, Hans and his new wife. Our apartment filled quickly as I took jackets and handed out drinks. Secretly I wondered if Peter Neumann would show up.

It wasn't what you think. I met him by chance when he dropped off his research paper for printing and when I saw what he was writing about I *had* to ask. We'd talked a few times and I was convinced he could help me with Vati.

The room choked with smoke and vapors of schnapps and beer. Günter sauntered past me and leaned out the window. He hadn't joined the singing.

I followed and squeezed his hand as Zarah Leander's *Wunderbar* boomed from the radio. Behind us, couples swayed.

"How about a dance?"

Günter shook his head. "Too tired."

As if he'd heard me, Helmut shouted, "Let's dance." He threw his shoes in the corner and pulled Gerda off the couch. "I want to dance, dance, dance," he yelled.

I smiled. "Helmut, your voice makes the milk go sour."

"I don't care." Teetering, Helmut caught himself on the radio and twisted the knobs.

I hardly heard the doorbell over Frank Sinatra's crooning and hurried to the door.

"Sorry I'm so late. Had a meeting with my professor and missed the train," Peter Neumann said, thrusting a bouquet of lilacs in my hand. The heady scent mixed with party fumes.

"Good of you to come," I said, taking in my late guest. He was a couple of inches taller than Günter, his eyebrows permanently arched, giving him a studious look. I had a thousand questions and contemplated asking him about his research right this minute, when a crash followed by a scream and cursing came from the kitchen.

I mumbled "sorry" and "give me a moment" before heading to investigate. By the time I arrived, Burkhart picked himself off the floor amidst shards of blue and orange porcelain.

"What happened?" As I steadied Burkhart's shoulders, he stumbled against me and burped. I grabbed hold of his chin to get a look at him. "How much did you drink?"

His red-rimmed eyes and boozy breath said it all. "Mutti's best china bowl," I mumbled and broke out in a cold sweat.

Peter appeared by my side, his hand, long white fingers with bits of blond hair, reassuring on my forearm. "Can I help?"

"I've got to get him sobered up." Where was Günter? I forced a smile, hoping to hide my annoyance of him being absent when I most needed him.

"Let me help," Peter offered. I nodded, collecting the shards.

"I want to tango, too," Burkhart slurred as Helmut called from the living room for everyone to dance. Surely, half the neighborhood could hear us.

"The only place you tango is to bed," I said.

"How about some water?" Peter applied the same reassuring grip to Burkhart's shoulder.

"I'll be right back," I said to Peter. Despite the mess, I grinned. Could this evening get anymore surreal? The living room rocked with *Blue Tango* and I felt my feet twitch. "Have you seen Günter?" I yelled over the din.

"He probably went to the bathroom," Gerda said, trying to place her hand over Helmut's mouth to keep him from singing.

"Lilly, please turn down the music." Mutti stood in the door, her mouth pinched flat, the way she did when she was irritated. "Your brother needs to get his sleep, and so do the neighbors."

"Sorry, Mutti." I jumped to lower the volume, scolding myself for not hearing her come in.

"Apologies, *Frau* Kronen," Helmut said. "It's my fault. I wanted to dance."

Before I had time to check on Burkhart and warn Peter, Mutti headed for the kitchen. I followed, trying to catch Peter's attention, trying to warn him, but it was too late.

"What happened to Burkhart?" Mutti threw an angry glance at Peter and bent over my brother. "Oh, *Liebling,* what did they do to you?"

Burkhart threw her a crooked grin.

Peter straightened and moved past me. "I better go," he said. "I'll be in touch."

"Please stay for a drink and some food." I inwardly cringed at the mess on the table. Bowls and platters looked like a herd of sheep had grazed them.

"Another time perhaps?"

I mouthed 'thanks,' frustration clogging my throat. I had so hoped to have a few minutes and pick his brain. Worse, I was embarrassed he witnessed my brother and... Mutti accusing him of making Burkhart drunk.

Great party.

Fun had left the building like air a punctured balloon. The music was turned low and people were talking quietly.

Before Mutti had another fit, I navigated Burkhart to his bed.

When I returned Helmut lounged on the couch. "Have a drink with me," he said, aiming at the half-empty schnapps bottle on the table. "Come on, just one."

I sagged next to him and took a sip, watching my guests.

Lydia, my old friend from elementary school, was in deep conversation with her new boyfriend, Kurt. Hans and his wife chatted with Gerda, their cheeks flushed with too much drink.

"I can't believe you're twenty," Helmut said into my ear. "Our baby is growing up."

I made a face. "Very funny." I was tired of being treated like I couldn't make my own decisions.

"Oh, come on. I didn't mean it." Helmut looked rueful for a moment before breaking into song. "*Hoch soll sie leben, hoch soll sie leben, dreimal hoch.*"

The others fell in and I emptied the schnapps glass, the liquid edging a fiery path to my stomach.

"You look very pretty tonight," Helmut said, forever the charmer. "Want another?"

I shook my head and bounced off the couch. The alcohol crept into my head and heated my cheeks as the image of Mutti stewing in the kitchen faded.

When I opened the window for more fresh air, I made out Günter standing in the shadows of the red beech in the front yard. Not wanting to shout, I slipped downstairs.

"Why don't you smoke inside?" I asked. Something bothered me about the way he leaned against the fence. I knew I was sort of a straight shooter, sometimes too straight, courtesy of Vati, so this sort of pulling away didn't sit well with me. Lately, we did nothing but get drunk every weekend.

Günter's eyes sparkled in the darkness. "I needed air."

"What's wrong?"

"Everything is fine," he laughed, but even in the dark I detected his cynical tone.

What was the matter with him? "Oh, come on," I joked. In the back of my mind something else registered. Günter was lying. Yet, all I said was, "Don't be a goose. Besides, you missed Mutti finding my drunk brother."

"Aren't I lucky." He took a drag and leaned back against the fence. "Who was that fellow in there?"

"I told you I met Peter at work. He is doing a research paper on soldiers missing in action. He may help me with Vati."

Günter patted my arm. "You go on in. I'll join in a minute." He pecked a kiss on my cheek as his hand slipped to my waist and then off. I longed for it to stay there, those knowing fingers. For a moment I contemplated pulling him into a dark corner. We made love in secret whenever we had a chance, though never at my house.

I wanted to ask why he looked so dejected when everybody else was having a good time, but something stopped me. It was getting late, and everyone had to work in the morning.

"You can sleep on the couch if you like."

Günter nodded. Now that I looked closer, I realized how drunk he was. His eyes had trouble focusing. In fact, he didn't really look at me at all. Tilting heavily against the fence post, he stared into the night sky. Why hadn't I paid attention to him? But then, why hadn't he helped me with our guests?

I rubbed my aching forehead. By now Mutti had surely found the shards of her prized bowl.

I was up at five, scrubbing the kitchen, putting away dishes and wiping down tables. The first birds chirped through the open windows and I bathed in the fresh air of early morning.

I leaned back to check my progress. No matter how I cleaned, the place was worn to the bone. Something unyielding emanated from it as if the room had shrunk and though it was now clean, it showed the deterioration of a hard life, the table narrow and bare, paint cracked along the edges, scuff marks on its legs. The chairs, straight-backed—rigid wood, had dug holes into the linoleum.

I washed the floor on my knees, but there were tears in front of the stove and yellow stains by the window. A strange light filled the room, gray as November sky despite the early sun glowing in the east.

Günter left after six, his eyes bloodshot, his forehead clammy with sweat. He gave me a tight hug, a stale cloud of alcohol wafting my way. No time to talk. He had to be at work in an hour and still needed to go home to wash and change.

Burkhart dragged himself into the kitchen around seven, his face pale as the walls.

"I'll never drink again."

I placed a cup of chamomile tea and a piece of dry bread in front of him. "Eat. I fixed you your school sandwich."

He chewed with closed eyes as I grabbed my coat and shoes. Time for work.

In the evening, when I rushed out of Ullrich, I wasn't surprised Günter was absent. He'd been working 12-hour shifts and was either still at work or at home taking a nap.

I smiled to myself, looking forward to seeing him, feeling his embrace, his lips on mine.

When his parents were outside in the garden, we sometimes made quick love on his bed. I admit that the chance of being found out added to the excitement. It was a precarious affair, considering we couldn't lock the door, so I straddled him with my clothes still on. I was always self-conscious about my glowing cheeks, convinced Günter's parents knew exactly what we were up to. Once we sneaked into the attic and pushed against the peeling plaster beneath the window, our breaths melting into each other while Günter's parents and grandmother were having coffee and cake downstairs.

Since we didn't discuss our plans for today, I decided to stop by his place on my way home.

Günter's mother, Grete, opened the door. "Lilly." She was a small woman, her hair graying at the temples.

I tucked at my dress—my favorite with blue and white stripes. "How is he? He drank too much. Well, most of us did."

Instead of an answer, Grete studied my face. "I was hoping you'd know why he missed work," she finally said, waving me into the kitchen.

Something icy curled inside my stomach. "What do you mean he missed work? Is he sick?"

"He was home this morning, but then he left. He acted a bit strange and packed clothes in his satchel."

I frowned. "Why would he take clothes to work?"

"He told me he wanted to visit his friend, Fredi, in Düsseldorf," Grete continued.

A lump formed in my throat the way it does before I cry. I swallowed it away. "What in the world is he doing? He didn't say anything to me."

"Honestly, Lilly, he was rather irritable. Did he not talk to you?" Grete patted my arm. "I thought you two might have planned a spontaneous excursion."

My eyes blurred. "I don't understand. We didn't have a fight and he never—" My voice refused to go on.

"I'm sure he'll be back tonight."

"But he didn't have vacation at work."

"Günter has always been quite independent. He had to be. During the war, he took care of us."

I nodded. That was one of the things I loved about him. He always took care of me.

"Don't worry." Grete stirred the soup simmering on the stove. "Do you want to stay for dinner? We'd love to have you."

I looked up, trying to control my shaky legs.

"I suppose, if you don't mind." I wasn't hungry, but I

never turned down a meal. The years of hunger during and after the war were imprinted on my mind and body like an invisible brand.

"*Guten Abend.*" Hans entered the kitchen. "Wonderful party yesterday, Lilly. Why so somber? It's a nice evening," he said, looking back and forth between his mother and me.

"Günter has disappeared." Grete nodded toward me. "And he didn't tell Lilly about his plans."

"My brother again." Hans shook his head. "He sometimes gets these ideas…" Looking at me, he swallowed the rest of his comment.

Feigning chores, I dragged myself home after the meal, almost expecting to see Günter's bicycle parked in front of our house. But there was only my neighbor's rusty pre-war contraption.

"You're home early." Mutti sat on the couch knitting, the smell of Peter's lilac heady and thick in the room. "Did you have a fight?"

"I'm going to bed."

But no matter how tired I was, I couldn't sleep. My stomach gurgled with the undigested soup, and every time I closed my eyes, a tiny voice whispered in my head. A voice I thought I'd forgotten.

What could've possibly possessed him? And worse, what if he leaves you like your father?

It was morning…early dawn, two days since Günter left. I lay on my back and stared at the ceiling. The wallpaper was flaking, faded shreds curling next to specks of fly poop. In the recesses of my mind, I registered the need to clean up there.

The thought was fleeting and I settled on reviewing what happened at my birthday party. What clues did I miss? Did Günter say something I forgot because of the schnapps? Did I say something to make him mad? Is he jealous of Peter Neumann, the man who may help with Vati?

Nothing came to mind except Mutti's meltdown and Peter leaving as quickly as he could. I craved Günter's embrace, felt the void of his body next to mine.

Today was Friday…movie day, if the weather held, maybe a trip to the lake tomorrow. Since we met three years ago we've gone to the lake or Rhine River every summer. Günter now owned a pup tent and we got straw from the farmer. A shiver ran through me. Not counting Günter's room where his mother could come knocking any moment, camping was the only time we had total privacy.

I was glad Mutti still slept when I got ready for work. I wanted to be alone with my thoughts of Günter, the gravelly feeling in the pit of my stomach that was neither hunger nor fullness.

I forced down a slice of *Graubrot,* the rye bread I bought on sale for *42 Pfennig* every week, scraped with butter and strawberry jam, fixed another for lunch and packed a thermos of peppermint tea.

"Morning," Burkhart slurred. He rubbed his pajama sleeve across his eyes and sagged on a chair.

"How are you feeling?" I asked. He looked much better than yesterday, the memory of his drunkenness renewing my guilt for not supervising better.

He threw me a crooked grin. "Like new. Will you make me a sandwich?"

I slid the butter knife his way and straightened. "Quit being a baby. Time for me to go."

As soon as I stepped outside, my thoughts were back. I hardly noticed Gerda waiting for me at our usual spot at the corner of *Brühler Berg* and *Wachtelstraße.*

"Good morning, sunshine," she said, looping her arm through mine.

I managed a clipped greeting and charged ahead. This morning I wished she'd take the streetcar and let me walk alone. It was a forty-minute hike to Ullrich, plenty of opportunity to ask questions.

"What's your mother up to this time?"

I felt Gerda's concerned glance on my temple, but didn't turn my head. "Nothing, just had a bad night." Secretly I wondered why I wasn't telling Gerda about Günter.

"Cheer up. It's Friday, movie day."

I nodded and for a while we walked in silence, two friends who didn't need constant chatting. I was thankful Gerda was the quiet type. This morning I could use it.

The day was crammed with print orders, returns and service requests. Helmut stopped by for a minute on his lunch break, his hands black as coal.

"Tell Günter we're going to see *Ein Amerikaner in Paris*. It won an Academy Award in March." Helmut swallowed the last of his sandwich and carefully folded the paper into his pocket.

What was I going to say to Günter tonight? Did I want to be angry or forgiving? All I knew right now was that my heart ached for him not telling me about his excursion.

"...did you hear what I said?" Helmut's face appeared in my vision.

"What, sorry?" I forced my mouth into a smile. "*An American in Paris*... sounds good."

"I said we meet at seven-thirty at Kino *Zentral*. They've got the place all restored." Helmut threw a glance at the clock and straightened. "I better go."

When I stuffed my half-eaten sandwich into the drawer, a strip of paper with Peter's address slid out from underneath my notepad. I placed it on the desk and eyed the phone mounted on the wall. My lunch break wasn't over for another five minutes—plenty of time to call.

Peter Neumann knew things about prisoners of war. What if he wanted to meet tonight or tomorrow when I'd be with Günter? My hand sank back to my lap. *Chicken!*

In truth I was embarrassed about my party...about Mutti. I couldn't wait to move out and get a place with Günter.

All afternoon, the clock above the door mocked me, its hands stuck in tar. I swore I heard every tick the minute dial made. It echoed through my head, bounced off my forehead, surrounded me. All I wanted was to be done and see Günter, yet I was trying to concentrate on my order lists, transcribing perfect numbers representing printing paper and inks in the inventory book.

What was I going to ask Günter? Where were you? What did you do? Why didn't you tell me you were going to visit Fredi in Düsseldorf, spending the night...two nights?

I was as overbearing as Mutti. My mind got going in one direction and refused to look at alternatives. It was a dreadful thing I wanted no part of, and yet it showed itself like an ugly version of Mutti.

At five o-clock I hurried outside so I could be alone when I reached the gate.

"Is Günter going to pick you up tonight?"

I swallowed a curse as Gerda grabbed my elbow from behind and walked with me toward the exit.

Avoiding her eyes, I charged ahead. What if Günter wasn't there?

He wasn't.

My heart slammed against my ribs as I walked on, hardly noticing Gerda's small talk. I pushed air into my throat and formed some words.

"...working late," I heard myself say.

As Gerda headed off to shop for a new skirt, I feigned chores and went home. By the time I was close, I decided to stop by Günter's home after dinner.

Thoughts whirled as I approached our house. Even after all this time, my gaze first wandered to the ground-floor window. I dismissed Huss as soon as I grew aware of my lingering apprehension, unlocking the front door. He didn't deserve any of my attention.

After a mumbled greeting, I disappeared in my bedroom. My brother had long moved into Mutti's room where he slept on a narrow cot. In better times we would've moved to a place with separate bedrooms, but all we could do was scrape by every month.

I changed my clothes, hung up my dress to air out, and began to pace. Through the open window I heard neighbors chatting. Herr Baum was mowing his lawn.

Mutti clattered in the kitchen. It was my invitation to join and help her make dinner. To say she wasn't fond of cooking was an understatement. Though I worked all day and Mutti stayed home, I often fixed our meals anyway.

Undoubtedly, she'd ask me about my evening plans. It was an hour and a half until we met Gerda and Helmut at the cinema Zentral. The question was, would Günter come and pick me up, or should I surprise him?

"Isn't it payday?" Mutti said when I entered the kitchen. Mutti held the record in passive-aggressiveness. She was stirring a pot, something with lentils or beans. At least she was good at cooking soup.

I thought you'd never ask, I wanted to say. Instead I held out a couple of bills. I earned twenty-five marks a week and Mutti demanded it all. For the rent and the food.

"Here." She handed me three marks—my allowance.

I took it without comment and headed for the door. Good thing Günter paid for most of our outings.

"You not eating with us tonight?" Mutti said at my back.

"Don't wait up."

It was a seven-minute walk uphill to Günter's place and when his house came into view I could hardly breathe.

I considered the possibility that he may still be gone. His mother had mentioned yesterday how independent he was during the war. What would Mutti say if I stayed home tonight? I hadn't been home on a Friday in two years. It was unthinkable. My eyes burned with unshed tears, imagining myself on the couch next to Mutti. Her curious stares. Everyone's curious stares. *What was wrong with Lilly? Günter left her.*

Stop that, I scolded. He was going to be home tonight. I knew it.

I decided to yell at him, tell him he couldn't just run off to visit his friend without telling me. My fingers trembled on the doorbell.

I always loved to visit because Günter had a real family with a mother *and* father.

I liked Artur in particular. He was much shorter than Vati, his eyes the light blue of an early summer sky. But he was strong because he worked with his hands in the factory and in the garden at home. His fingers were thick and swallowed mine when we shook hands, unlike Vati's which were always manicured perfectly. As I pushed away thoughts of Vati, my earlier anxiety returned with a vengeance.

I cranked my neck to see if Günter's bike leaned against the back corner of the house, just as Artur appeared with a shovel.

"Lilly, how nice to see you. Come back here, we're in the garden."

I smiled, following him. Isn't it strange how the heart takes the smallest wink, the tiniest poke to feel encouraged? For that split second I allowed myself to feel excited, even happy.

My face fell as soon as we rounded the corner. It was a beautiful evening, the air mild and fragrant with flowers and grass clippings. Even before anyone talked, I knew Günter wasn't back.

"Is he…" I stopped not trusting my voice. It had gotten into the habit of shaking. I despised myself for feeling weepy once again.

Grete shook her head. "I thought he'd return by now, but nobody has heard from him."

"I'm quite upset." Artur wiped mud from his hands with a towel. "I've made excuses to his boss, but if he isn't back on Monday, he'll lose his job." He sat down next to Grete, avoiding my gaze. "I don't know what got into him."

"You don't think…what if something happened?" I managed. Visions of Günter covered in blood in some ditch appeared in my head.

"Surely, we would've heard," Grete said, but I could tell she was worried by the way she massaged her temple.

"He could've hit his head, lost his memory," I said.

Artur nodded. I knew he doubted it. So did I.

"He never said anything to you?" Grete asked.

"Not a word." For the hundredth time I went back to the night of my birthday. "He was tired and drunk, but…" I remembered the way he didn't look at me, the peck on the cheek. It wasn't the real Günter. Something had been wrong, but I was too busy to notice.

I shuddered. Of course I had noticed. I scolded myself for not asking him why he'd lied.

What if he planned to leave all along? What other signs had I missed or worse…ignored?

I declined another meal and walked off into the evening. Alone. The air hummed with the first bees and birds happily chirped. I pushed away the guilt of Helmut and Gerda waiting at the movie theater. How could I answer their questions if all I had were questions?

I wandered down the street and headed left to the little park where we used to fetch water after the bombing. Unable to take another step, I sagged onto a tree stump.

I couldn't go home and face Mutti. I couldn't go anywhere. I was stuck in my head, my limbs disconnected from my body, my mind churning. Fresh worry grabbed my insides and jumbled my stomach. Günter could be injured or dead. There were millions of acres of woods and deserted roads all over Germany.

A new thought entered. What if somebody had attacked him, took his money? Whether by accident or on purpose, Günter may have been murdered and buried in a shallow grave. I remembered Günter telling me about his classmates who, in the last weeks of the war, vanished without a trace. Every single one of them. Those boys' parents never heard another word, just like I may never know…may never see him again.

A sound startled me. It was my own breath lurching from my body in a loud gasp. It couldn't be. Not this. Not after surviving the horrible war, the years of starvation.

"Don't be ridiculous," I muttered. "He's quite capable of taking care of himself. Always has."

Dusk settled as I straightened, a new resolve taking over. Tomorrow I'd tell Gerda because Günter would be back on Sunday.

And after a bit of yelling, I'd forgive him.

On Monday, I awoke early. My head buzzed as if a swarm of bees were trapped inside. My body felt heavy, too heavy to move. Not even to one side. I lay on my back with my eyes open, staring at the wallpaper on the ceiling, the flyspecks and loosened seams along the edge of the wall.

I was in the war again—the world I knew had shifted. The rubble under my feet made me stumble, and when I looked up all I loved had vanished.

Günter had not returned yesterday.

I saw myself as an old spinster still living with Mutti in this stuffy worn apartment with these stuffy old chairs and the desk— the desk that once held Vati's memories, the desk that had been stripped of everything now. I remembered scenes of Günter's recklessness and the way his gaze wandered off at times, his mouth pinched. It wasn't a new thing, this expression of wariness, he displayed when he thought himself unobserved. Even the first time we'd met at the fair, he'd been this way. I mean who spends their last *Pfennig* knowing he'd be broke for a week? Even in my worst days I'd been careful to hold back a mark or two…just in case.

On a whim, I scurried into the living room and sagged on Vati's chair. The rings on top of the desk reminded me of scars, impossible to remove. How often had I sat here, first on Vati's lap, and once he was gone, alone, trying to get a whiff of his scent, trying to conjure his presence? The expensive leather pieces and ink pen had long disappeared, bartered away years ago.

It was light already and heavenly air floats in through the window. I had to move now. It was almost six-thirty and I had to leave for work in less than an hour.

Tiny sounds emanated from below, a door opening and closing. A cough. Huss was up and about. I suppressed a shudder. Why couldn't *he* disappear?

Two weeks had passed since my party, and I was beyond anxious. People didn't just disappear. Not now, anyway. During the war, people vanished by the thousands as if the earth had swallowed them. But this was 1952. The war had been over for seven years.

Well, for others it had. For me it continued.

Mutti stuck her head in the door. "What's going on?"

I coughed, my throat thick with mucous like fingers choking me.

Mutti came in and touched my forehead. I inwardly cringed and at the same time loathed myself for craving her touch. I couldn't remember the last time we hugged. Her skin was cool on my hot forehead.

"You have a fever."

I turned toward the wall. I didn't want to see her. The accusatory eyes that said "Günter was no good. I told you so." Mutti knew how to communicate without words. Though silent, they had a way of screaming in my head.

When Günter didn't return after the first weekend, I told Gerda. I had to tell someone. Ever since, as we walked to and from work we went over the events of my birthday party, discussed reasons for Günter's disappearance.

In the beginning, Gerda kept cheering me up. "He'll be home any day, you'll see. He probably got sick or ran out of money and couldn't get home."

I'd nodded, wanting to believe her, wishing for it to be true. But there was that pressure behind my forehead, the unease that spread to my bones like an ache. Gerda was lying. She probably thought something bad had happened to Günter.

I asked myself what Gerda would do if Helmut

disappeared like that. But then, it didn't happen to her, it happened to me. The longing for Günter returned like a hot poker stirring up my insides.

My mind whirled from the sickness. But the worry topped it all. And despite my misery, I was missing him physically. My skin yearned for his touch, our secret lovemaking. The weather was perfect. Helmut and Gerda, Günter's brother, Hans, and his new wife were camping every weekend.

The morning breeze slipped across my body like gentle fingers, and for a moment I daydreamed of Günter's hands on my skin, sliding down my throat to my breasts. My nipples responded to his teasing until I urged him on. Lower... The noise of my breath catching brought me back like plunging through ice into a pond.

I rolled over to face the room where my dress from yesterday hung to air next to my stockings. I only had three pairs, and they were all darned to death, heels and toes crisscrossed with brown yarn. Gerda wore real *Perlon* nylons that were smooth and silky and showed off her skin. They were expensive, but she could afford it because her mother didn't bleed her dry every week.

Günter would buy some for me if I asked...I pulled my knees to my chest as the awareness that Günter was missing came crashing back.

I leaned out of bed to grab my purse. I brought home the slip of paper with Peter's address. I decided to write a note and mail it. Explain Vati's sentence and imprisonment in Russia. That I needed help.

"You staying home?" Mutti asked from the doorway, pulling me back to my miserable present.

"Just today," I croaked.

"I'll make tea." Mutti closed the door as I listen to her chat with Burkhart, her tone light and encouraging. They laughed.

I dug beneath the cover to keep from shivering.

When did we build this wall? An invisible barrier, smooth as glass yet impenetrable.

It was Friday afternoon, sixteen days since Günter's disappearance. I'd made it through another week. Now that I looked back, I didn't know how I could've kept a straight face. But I did.

Actually, everyone knew Günter was missing. The girls in my office threw me sideways glances, their eyes filled with expressions equally glib and pitying. Their whispers faded when I approached, and they pretended nothing was going on. Helmut patted my hand during lunch breaks and Gerda's hugs had grown longer. I wanted to ask Helmut if he understood Günter, whether he'd ever contemplated running away himself. But then I never did. The look at Gerda's happy face had a way of stopping me.

I fought for control not to pass by Günter's house. I couldn't face another meeting with his parents, who looked more somber than I'd ever seen them. Artur was furious that Günter abandoned his job at Dohle.

Günter did his apprenticeship as a dye maker there, designing patterns for cutlery. I'd always been patient, but I couldn't imagine working on a single piece of steel for weeks and months. He used all these little tools to hammer and carve until some design emerged. Flowers and lines and swirls. That's why he was so good making jewelry. I fingered the pendant on my neck as if I could establish some kind of electromagnetic contact with him.

Günter's parents went to the police and filed a report, but no action had been taken. The police said it was too early, that a million soldiers were still missing from the war, that this was nothing, just one young man gone away inexplicably.

The thing they didn't mention was that hundreds of thousands of people traveled during the summer. Ever since the new currency introduction, the post-war youths had been bicycling cross-country to party, drink and eat like there was no tomorrow. What I witnessed for the first time at the fair where I met Günter has grown into a national phenomenon. Germany's youth was going crazy after missing out.

The more I thought about it, the more I suspected Günter had joined them. I grew cold imagining him in some bar drinking and dancing with blondes. My hair had always been an unremarkable brown and the idea he was out there with someone else filled me with anger. Jealousy was a deep boiling thing, and it was worse because I couldn't define what I was jealous about.

"Lilly? May I have a word?" My boss, Herr Keller, waved at me from the door of his office.

I rushed over, my cheeks burning with guilt. Surely, he'd seen me daydream.

"Have a seat." Herr Keller smiled at me, making his lips appear jagged. From the collar of his shirt rose a landscape of shrapnel scars. He had a glass eye which only partly matched his left good one.

As Herr Keller studied a folder, the room sank into silence. I braced myself for a reprimand. Somewhere in the background printing presses chomped. I sat with my fingers twisted, wishing to be away, wishing to leave my body and this ridiculous existence. Just hover like the wind between worlds, without thoughts and feelings.

I couldn't imagine how life had to be for my boss, whose disfigurement was there for the world to see. Not much older than Günter, he'd never mentioned a word about his injuries. Of course, hardly anyone spoke about the war. They wanted to forget who joined the Nazi party, who cheered Hitler's advances. As if it were that easy.

"You've been with us for...?" Keller's good eye rested on my face. At least I thought that's where he was looking.

"Three years."

He nodded and tapped a finger on his misshapen chin. "Looks like you've learned well." He closed the folder with a snap. "We'll give you a raise. Two marks a week." The crooked smile was back.

I mumbled "thank you," discreetly wiping my palms on my skirt.

"I'm sorry about your boyfriend," he said as I made my way to the door, "Just don't let it affect your work."

Back at my desk, I breathed again as I absentmindedly rubbed the shred of paper with Peter's address. I still hadn't written. What was I waiting for?

When Herr Keller disappeared down the hall, I dashed to the phone. Just this one call before I got back to work.

After three rings, Peter's slightly breathless voice came on. "Hallo, Peter Neumann?"

"It's Lilly." The line remained silent and I wondered if he hung up. "You came to my party..." I cringed. Nice going to remind him of the disastrous meeting with Mutti.

"I remember."

"I wonder if we could meet to talk about my father." Again the line went silent. Why didn't phones have screens so I could see Peter's face? "He's in Russia. Alive."

"I…didn't know."

I rolled my eyes. Did he think I'd called him to flirt when I was after his research into prisoners of war? My fingers, clamped around the phone, trembled with embarrassment.

"How about tomorrow, Café Kersting, ten a.m.?" he said. "I heard they reopened after the bombing."

I checked the wall clock as if it'd show me an excuse for Mutti of why I'd leave so early. "Yes," I said. I'd think of something.

I hardly noticed when five o'clock rolled around, my thoughts on my meeting with Peter, a part of me watching for Günter's figure at the gate. It'd been sixteen days since Günter went missing. Nine years since I'd seen Vati.

I wouldn't tell Mutti about the raise.

Café *Kersting* was jam-packed. Everyone wanted to see the new place. My heart galloped in my chest as I made my way to Peter's table along the wall.

"It was all they had left," he said, shaking my hand.

"Hallo," I said, glad I could sit. The table was so narrow, I worried bumping knees.

"So, tell me about your father," Peter said.

Before I could answer, the waitress in a black dress and white apron appeared. "*Bitte schön?*"

I threw a glance at the fancy new menu. I wanted coffee, a delicacy I only had a few times in my life. My mind rattled through the coins in my wallet. 60 Pfennig is a lot, so I decided on peppermint tea.

"My treat," Peter said at that moment. He turned to the waitress. "A cup of coffee for me."

"Same," I said. "Thank you."

The waitress disappeared, and I wondered where to settle my eyes. Memories flashed through me like scenes from a film. Memories of Vati.

"We know he was taken in Courland in May 1945. As of 1944 Germany had occupied the area, taken it from the Russians."

Peter nodded. "Up northeast of Poland."

"He's some place in Siberia. I don't know…"

"You heard from him?"

"Not in a while, though he's written a few times."

"The gulags frequently move their prisoners."

"I thought you may know what I can do..." Until this moment I wasn't sure what I wanted from Peter. But now it was clear. "You did research on German prisoners."

"My paper is about all prisoners of World War Two. I do know a fair bit about Russian gulags." Our coffee had arrived and he took a sip.

"It's just...I worry. He'll be fifty-five in September. I was hoping you'd know what the Russians are planning."

"I doubt even Chancellor Adenauer knows what Stalin is up to." When he saw my face he went on. "Surely you've contacted the Red Cross."

"We did in 1945 when Vati didn't come home. And then again in 1950."

"Your father is one of 14 million search requests."

"I just thought you may have some other way."

"I've been to the Red Cross central search data center in Munich." He shook his head. "It's overwhelming. All these people just missing...gone. At least you know he's alive."

How much longer? How long did a man in his fifties survive a Russian gulag in Siberia where the average temperature in winter was minus thirteen? I took a sip of the coffee, the aroma so heady I closed my eyes.

Peter misinterpreted, and I felt his hand on top of mine. "I don't mean it this way. I have a few contacts, former prisoners who were in Russia. It's just...finding the needle in a field of haystacks would be easier. Even if you knew his location, there's nothing you or any of us can do."

"I understand." Peter was right. Vati was gone and remained gone. Why did I even worry? He lied to us, he lied to everyone. I grew up without a father and I hated him for that, for what he'd done. And yet, I needed closure.

I wanted to be like normal people. Even now, I never asked anybody I met about their father, brother or husband. Most of us didn't. Yet, I worried people would ask me about Vati and I'd have to admit that for me the war continued and with it the waiting, the wondering, and the anger.

"Here." Peter shoved a piece of paper across the table.

"Write down his information. I'll ask around."

Walking home, I decided to spend the remaining weekend with Mutti and Burkhart. I was tempted to stop by Günter's house, but my legs stubbornly marched to our apartment. If he was back, he'd have to come to me.

Was it my pride or the refusal to face another confirmation Günter hadn't returned? In the back of my mind, the thoughts scraped painfully. What if he'd never return? What if he was dead?

I slipped into the kitchen, where the smell of fried meat still clung to the air. Mutti cooked a roast last night as if she wanted to celebrate Günter's disappearance. I opened the window and leaned outside, breathing deeply.

The rhythmic banging of a hammer smacking wood reverberated from next door. Herr Baum was already in his garden.

In hindsight, I was convinced he saved my sanity.

In my dream, Günter was back. I ran to him as he stood waiting in front of Ullrich. Only when he turned toward me, I saw that the left half of his face was covered in craters and scars. He neither smiled nor frowned, he just stood there as if I were invisible. Then he turned again, his good side to me, and walked off.

I woke up bathed in sweat. Three weeks, and still no word. I was growing more convinced something terrible happened. When Vati didn't return after the war, I knew he wasn't dead—even if Mutti acted like he was. But with Günter, I didn't feel anything. It was like a giant nothingness, a hole in my heart that left me clueless. During the day I managed to keep my head together, wanting to show Herr Keller that the raise was well deserved. He'd been stopping by more than usual, giving me little compliments. Secretly, I wondered if he was sweet on me. I hoped not.

I didn't consider myself cruel, but the man's injuries were so sad. He was probably torn up all over his body. Besides, I loved Günter. Now that he was gone, I realized how much I missed him. I realized how I'd taken him for granted. We'd been dating for three years and he was so much a part of my life that not having him around felt like an amputation. Unlike with Vati, it was a physical thing, a pain that burned through me.

Or did I forget the way I waited every night for Vati's return? How my eighth birthday came and went without a doll. Weeks turned into months and years.

The way I missed Vati was like a numbness in my heart—a dull toothache. You knew it was there, but it didn't disrupt your life. You were used to it, the thoughts of him hidden away in the attic of your mind. You didn't go there because you knew you'd meet a ghost.

When I made it into the kitchen, Mutti sat by the window. She was never up before nine and on weekends she slept even later.

"Bad night?" I asked.

"A migraine. Leave the light off."

I wet a washcloth and placed it on her forehead. At forty-eight, she was still a good-looking woman, her hair prematurely white, her cheekbones high.

"Any news?" she said.

I knew exactly what she meant. For the past twenty-one days I'd been home every night. I couldn't answer because my throat seized up, tears threatened.

She turned abruptly. "Isn't it time you let him go?" When I numbly shook my head, she went on. "Maybe he's long home and doesn't want to see you. Or something happened to him. Either way..."

Move on like you moved on, I wanted to say. Instead I blindly filled the kettle and fixed a sandwich for lunch. I had to think of something else. Anything.

Despite my mother's cruelty, my stomach rumbled.

It was a strange thing...hunger. Nowadays people ate well, and the stores were stocked. We were experiencing *Wirtschaftswunder*, the economic wonder of a new German Republic. Everyone made a decent living, enough to pay the bills. At least families with working men. Single women were another story.

There were years, three years during the war and three years after, when hunger followed me like the grim reaper follows the dying. I couldn't shake it. True hunger gnaws constantly, and though it starts in your stomach it soon engulfs your thoughts, your entire being.

It was hard to explain how it felt to find something unexpected like an onion or a shriveled potato. Your mouth watered as you weighed it in your hand. You sniffed it. Eat it raw, right now, just to feel food slide through your throat, occupy the juices in your stomach? Or make a fire and roast it? But that took precious firewood, and your arms were full of lead. Finally, you remembered Mutti and Burkhart who were waiting at home, your little brother hollow-eyed, his collarbone poking through his skin. With a sigh, you pocketed your find and headed home.

Twenty-four days after Günter's disappearance, I finally slept well through the night. The pain of missing him was always present, but I managed it as long as I didn't look at Mutti. Weekends were especially bad, and I savored my time at the grocery store.

It had been a week since I met with Peter and he hadn't called or written. But then why would he? It took months and years to find somebody. The chances of learning more about Vati were like winning the national lottery.

"Lilly!" Günter's mother rushed up the aisle, the basket in her hand swinging. "I'm glad to see you. I was about to stop by your home today." Her eyes were filled with gladness, a certain shine that comes from joy.

"*Guten morgen,*" I said reluctantly. I really wanted to grab and shake her, so I knuckled down on the grocery cart and my purse.

"I heard from Günter," Grete said, fumbling in her coat pocket. "This came yesterday." She thrust a card in my face.

I took it, vaguely aware my fingers were shaking as my eyes strained to focus, not on the pretty landscape of the stream and snow-capped mountains, but on the words. There were few.

"Dears,
I'm heading to Switzerland. The weather is great, have been sleeping in barns. The cherries and peaches are delicious down here.
Viele Grüße, Günter"

I read again and a third time. There was no mention of my name. Nothing. When I finally looked up, I'd forgotten that I was in a grocery store and that Günter's mother stood in front of me.

"He's all right," I whispered and handed back the card.

I turned and marched down the store aisle without saying

good-bye. I couldn't, because if I opened my mouth, I was going to scream. Günter was riding his bike to Switzerland without a care in the world. Certainly without a care about me, his girlfriend. *You aren't his girlfriend anymore,* the voice in my head said. *He hasn't written to you. Only his parents.*

I dropped the basket by the front door and hurried outside. I needed air, lots of air, so I didn't suffocate.

The war did something to him. Nothing obvious like a lost limb or Herr Keller's cratered face. No, something inside, buried deeply. An injury of sorts that refused to heal. Had I ignored the tension in Günter's shoulders, the lengthening frown between his brows when he considered himself unobserved?

I didn't know how I got to the park. In the summer drizzle, my arms were too heavy to open the umbrella. In a way I was glad, because the rain camouflaged my tears—as if my body were crying.

Günter was alive. The relief of knowing he was all right made me want to sing. The fact he left without word and didn't bother to write or call replaced my joy with the cold and black of a dank cave.

What – was – he – doing? What made him this cruel? For three years I'd considered him the man to marry. The one who took me away from the lifelong prison of Mutti's unkindness. Thinking something happened to him was easier than this new truth.

I grew aware of my sandals amidst a puddle. Like two islands they were disconnected from land. Like me. Why did I wear sandals in the rain?

My bowels gurgled as nausea swept up my throat. I folded over until my right cheek met my knee. Rain pelted my back. Never in my life had I felt this lonely.

By the time I came out of my stupor, the light had changed. A feeble sun peeked through the clouds. I was shivering and hot at the same time.

Something had to happen.

The hope of finding mail drove me home, but when I got there, I found nothing waiting for me. I realized Günter had not felt it necessary to contact me, and the pain of that new truth was worse than anything I'd ever experienced. I wanted to scream. And then I wanted to cry. I did neither.

Instead I pretended to meet Gerda when in reality I took off into the woods.

Scenes jumbled through my head...Günter bending over me for our first kiss, Günter handing me a brand-new bicycle after saving his entire allowance for three weeks, a hundred fifty DM, more than I make in a month. And he gave it to me because he wanted me to be able to join him and his friends on rides. Was this the same man? Was it all a dream?

The memories kept coming, pouring through me in a tidal wave until I felt dizzy.

After the postcard, I couldn't pretend any longer. He didn't see fit to let me know about his plans and instead let me worry my head off.

I wasn't important to him one bit. He was cruel and thoughtless. Just like Vati.

I picked up a stick and smacked it against a tree trunk so hard, it gouged my palms and catapulted into bushes. The coldhearted bastard. After all our time together.

I yanked the classified section of the newspaper from my pocket. I was going to move. I wouldn't tell him and I wouldn't tell Mutti. I just wanted out...from the habits of the past three years, from Mutti's dictatorship...from my love.

My forefinger ran down the column. A two-room flat was advertised. New construction, near downtown and streetcar stops. I circled it. I found three more and circled them. Monday after work I'd go to check them out. I was going to show him.

I made three appointments. The forth place was already rented. I told Mutti I was helping Gerda find a new dress.

The apartment house was brand-new, one of hundreds of houses being built in downtown Solingen. Construction debris, pieces of concrete, and wood scraps lay helter-skelter in the front yard. It had taken five years to remove the debris from the bombings. After the war there wasn't an intact building within a couple of square miles—just endless rubble and ruins, partial walls, bent steel, and dead bodies.

Getting through downtown now was like traveling through a maze. Paths ended, blocked by stacks of brick and concrete blocks. Bomb craters were partially filled with water. Men whistled and yelled through windowless walls high above. Saws screeched, hammers pounded. It was a madhouse of new structures...department stores, apartments, banks, clothing and grocery stores.

My gaze traveled up the neatly painted walls of the five-story house as I imagined myself living here. I'd get a couch and matching table, take my bed. Maybe I could make extra money cleaning apartments. Do what I did for Mutti, but get paid for a change. It was hard to believe I actually cleaned our place every week after work and on Saturdays. As if I had to earn the right to live there.

My steps echoed in the staircase, the smell of paint sharp in my nose. Third floor, apartment B.

The door stood open.

Every available square meter was filled with people. Young couples opening and closing doors and cabinets, gazing out the windows.

"May I help you?" The man gave me the once-over.

"I'm Lilly...Kronen. I had an appointment."

He gave me a fleeting smile and checked his clipboard. "Ah, yes. Is your husband joining you?"

"No...he is working."

"I see. Feel free to have a look around. We take applications tonight only. As you can see, there's a lot of demand. No wonder," he chuckled, "eighty marks a month is a steal." He hurried off to point out the tiles surrounding the tub. "Isn't it beautiful...so easy to clean."

I stood frozen, the number eighty bouncing around in my head. Eighty...eight...zero. That was almost as much as I made in a month. I'd have nothing left to live on. I was doing silent calculations in my head as a young woman squeezed past me.

"Here is our application," she chirped. "I sure hope we'll be chosen. Heinz makes good money as an electrician." The man in question smiled brightly at the salesman who frantically scribbled on his clipboard. I wanted to smack her in her perfectly painted mouth.

I slipped out the door. My steps were hollow as I descended, but not as hollow as my thoughts.

The next apartment was the same, eighty-five marks, eleven couples and a single woman—me.

Back on the street, I almost jumped at the sound emerging from my throat. I was laughing. A woman sweeping her sidewalk stared. I stuck my tongue out at her. Heck, why not? My entire life had unraveled. Who cared what was proper? Why had I tried so hard to do the right thing when there was no honor left in this world? At least none for me. I was going to be a spinster jailed in Mutti's apartment.

My heart raced in my neck, heat spreading across my chest. After the terrible bombing in November 1944, I'd expected that nothing could ever scare me like this again.

Had Günter spent time in the bunker, he and I would've met at some point. He lived just a few minutes from the same bunker in the neighborhood Brühl.

From my house, I could be there in less than three minutes. In 1944, these three minutes stretched into eternity. Every second ticked by in slow motion and I remembered everything about that weekend.

What I remembered most was the fear. Fear, growing inside you until all you wanted to do was cry and curl up in a dark hole. It was hard to describe what happened to a person when they were afraid for their lives. I think the worst part for me was that I didn't know what to expect. I only knew what people or what was left of them looked like afterwards.

I was afraid again.

Günter had been gone for a month. Now that I knew he was alive, I no longer worried for his safety. I only loathed his absence. I clung to the idea that a postcard would eventually arrive, at least a few words to show he still remembered me. The mailbox remained empty.

Off and on during the day, my eyes spontaneously filled with tears. I carried a handkerchief in my sleeve at all times, tucking it away soggy. I'd quit wearing eye shadow. It just caked into a mess and made it even more obvious that I cried. What really got me was that I had no outlet for my anger. I wanted to yell at Günter, pound my fists at his chest.

All I had was silence.

I went to see Helmut at lunch the other day and finally asked him if he'd heard anything. He threw me a funny look.

"Not a word," he said, chewing his sandwich, always Gouda cheese and butter.

"Why do you think he's doing it?" I asked.

He shrugged. "I wish I knew." When I remained silent, he continued. "He'll be back. What else is he going to do? His family is here. You're here." He squeezed my hand, his ink-stained fingers comforting. "You didn't even have a fight."

What if he no longer wants me?

"I'll kick him in the behind for you," he continued. "Especially for not writing to you."

Mutti hadn't said much, but I detected the occasional smirk. She was glad Günter was gone. I wanted to hit her. And now my plan of leaving wasn't working out either. I didn't realize that Solingen, like most German cities, was experiencing a new wave of apartment seekers.

Stalin was mad that Germany had chosen to align itself with the western allied forces. They signed a contract, the *Deutschlandvertrag*, to reconnect the U.S., Britain and France with the new German Republic. Stalin answered by building walls across Germany to separate east from west. People from Poland and soviet-occupied Germany were fleeing over here in droves because they worried they'd get stuck with Stalin's dictatorship.

That explained why the man with the clipboard was so glib. Even if I could afford it, they'd give all the apartments to couples and families.

That's when it hit me.

Gerda.

She made more money than I did, and together we could afford it. She was living with her mother.

"How about it?" I said, forcing some brightness into my voice. It was Saturday afternoon and Gerda and I were sitting on the new bench in the little park by the well.

"I've got to think it through," Gerda said. "I'm saving a lot of money living at home. You know…for my dowry." She cringed, obviously feeling guilty for bringing it up.

"Your mother doesn't rob you blind like Mutti."

"What if Helmut…?" Gerda shook her head and gripped my forearm. "Never mind. Tell me more about the apartments."

I smiled, talking faster and faster about the places I'd seen. "It may take a while, but we'd be free and much closer to work. We could entertain, have Helmut and..." my voice fizzled. I jumped up. "I just need to do something. I'm going crazy."

"I know."

Gerda threw back her brown curls and laughed. "What the heck, why not?"

"Really?" I grabbed her hands and pulled her off the bench. "Wait here. I'll get the ads. I'll tell Mutti I'm looking for bargains. She'll never suspect it."

I wanted to skip and sing, arranging furniture in my mind. Mutti would be mad, of course, but she'd just have to get a job herself instead of continuing that silly knitting. It hardly made any money.

When I rushed into my house, my neighbor's door opened. I cringed, the scenario on how I could avoid a meeting replaying like always. Unless I turned around quickly, I was stuck in the corridor and forced to face the man who'd terrorized my childhood.

"Fräulein Lilly, good morning," Huss said with a fake smile. His hair with strings of gray had receded, showing a plate-sized bald spot on top.

"Morning."

I considered turning around, but Huss was faster. He disappeared in his apartment, leaving behind a cloud of cigarette smoke.

I smiled grimly and slipped upstairs.

The week crawled by. Every day I secretly perused the classifieds when Mutti was still in bed. I'd made a list of nine possibilities, with appointments lined up for tomorrow.

"Lilly, phone call for you." One of my colleagues pointed at the phone. It was Friday afternoon again, and my thoughts automatically wandered to Günter. Something had happened. He'd been in an accident. Then I caught myself, wanting not to care.

"Hallo, Lilly Kronen?"

"It's Peter."

As usual, his voice sounded a bit breathless. I was equally excited and relieved, my stomach quieting.

"I found someone who knew your father. I thought you could talk to him."

"Yes, of course." I wanted to ask a thousand questions. "When?"

"Tomorrow, ten o'clock at Café Kersting..."

My mind whirled. I'd made appointments. "How about noon? I'm sorry, I'm looking for a place."

I hung up the phone, growing aware again of my office. People were returning from lunch. Girls chattered, desk drawers rattled, doors opened and closed. Normal sounds I'd heard a thousand times. Except there was depth to them now as if they were full of secrets. I felt giddy. Tomorrow I'd learn something about Vati and find a way out of my misery.

"Lilly?" Gerda materialized in front of my desk. Her cheeks were flushed, her eyes bright. I smiled at her and she must have seen something in my eyes because she cried, "what happened?"

"Nothing," I said. "You first."

"I'm sorry." She leaned against the desk as if to gather strength. "I...Helmut proposed." Her voice hitched and she cleared her throat.

"Congratulations," I cried. "What great news. I know you wanted to..." I remembered the moment of Günter handing me a little box for my birthday, my own hopes shattered. I hurried to her side and hugged her. "I'm very happy for you."

Gerda gripped my hands. "I'm so sorry. About tomorrow..."

That's when it hit me. With Helmut proposing, there wouldn't be an apartment hunt. Gerda would wait for Helmut, save her money to get married soon.

"Oh," was all I managed. I swallowed my disappointment, the lump like a grapefruit in my throat. I was all done crying. It didn't do any good.

"Helmut thought...he'd planned to propose next month, but when he heard we were going to hunt for an apartment, he... Maybe you'll find someone else."

The door to our room opened and Herr Keller limped into his office. Not him.

As Gerda returned to her station, I heard her joyous voice telling everyone about the engagement. I dropped my gaze, glad I'd gotten a mountain of order lists to go through. I couldn't face anyone right now.

Like last time, Café Kersting was a madhouse. Peter waved from a corner table.

"Herr Stuber, meet Lilly Kronen." We shook hands as I slid into the chair. "*Guten Tag.*"

Stuber was in his mid-thirties with thick auburn hair and a checkered dress shirt. His gaze wandered between Peter and me, his hands fluttering. The nervous tick beneath his right eye pulsed like a tiny heartbeat.

"Herr Stuber lives in Wuppertal," Peter said. "Why don't you tell Lilly what you know?"

Stuber nodded and tucked at the collar of his shirt as if it were too tight. "It was May eleven, 1945. I remember it clearly," he said without preamble. His chin sank and his voice was so soft, I had to lean forward to hear him over the hubbub. "You know, a few days after Germany surrendered. We were running, all of us. *Hauptmann* Kronen, your father, was not the last in the group. In fact, he was right in front of me.

"The Russians were in pursuit, shooting. One of our men was hit, so we helped him into the boat. The others were already loaded. I stumbled and almost fell. It was crazy, us running, shouting…the shots. I didn't look up until I was in the boat." Stuber glanced at me as if to gather strength. "When I raised my head, I saw your father still on the beach. Five or six Russian soldiers were approaching, rifles pointed at him. They were shouting. Somebody pushed off the boat." Stuber paused again. "I don't know what happened. One second he was right in front, and then he was gone."

"What then?" It took effort to force air through my throat. By May eleventh, the war had been over. Germany had surrendered on May eight. Had Vati not known? Had he thought he'd do the honorable thing in hopes the Russians would play nice?

"I looked up and saw the Captain with his arms raised. He stood at the bank. He must have been the one pushing us off. We were yelling for him to jump into the water, but he didn't seem to hear. We were just trying to get away…to stay alive. The last thing I saw were the Russians surrounding him, yanking away his gun, pushing him until he collapsed." Stuber fell silent. "I think he gave himself up."

Peter patted my hand. I looked at it like it wasn't mine, just somebody's fingers on the table, a foreign object.

"I had my contact at the German Red Cross check the files," he said. "There's nothing new. From what it looks like, he's still some place in Siberia."

I nodded numbly, trying to imagine the scene on the beach in Courland. My father's face when his buddies swam out of sight.

"Bitte schön?" The waitress held her notepad at the ready.

"*Kaffee*, right?" Peter said, patting my hand again.

I nodded, trying to draw Peter's face into focus. Deep inside, a terrible fury began to brew. I saw the hand on the table shake as something bubbly forced its way out of my throat. A laugh burst from my insides like a roar.

Peter exchanged a glance with Herr Stuber. They had no idea. They had no idea how stupid my father was. Even then, even after the war was lost when his buddies went home, my father took it upon himself to do the honorable thing. What a fool. How could he feel honor about participating in this war? Leaving his family?

All the way home, I steamed. After Stuber left, Peter had repeatedly asked me if I was all right.

Sure, I was all right.

As all right as you could be, knowing your father willingly left you and then willingly stayed behind after the war was *over*. What a farce.

It would've been easier if he were dead. My friend, Lydia, lost her father in Stalingrad. Like other war children, she put things behind her.

For me it continued. Like an idiot I was still looking for answers. When the whole world had moved on, Germany was a new republic in the midst of *Wirtschaftswunder*, I was still asking why my father abandoned us for an evil dictator.

My skin on fire, I entered the apartment. Mutti was on the couch, knitting yet another outfit for the baroness or one of her rich acquaintances.

I wanted to tell her about the soldier in the café. But I couldn't. My throat had closed up. I was afraid if I started I'd go crazy. Mutti didn't need to know. Not now. After seven years, she was still upset about finding out about Vati leaving his job...and us. It was the one thing we had in common.

I did my usual sweep around the apartment, wiping down furniture, scrubbing floors and windows. I went on autopilot, the smells of soap and the feel of warm water on my hands soothing.

"Can you help me?" Burkhart bent over a book, pencil in hand. He was in ninth grade, one year past what I considered my last decent year of school.

I gripped my dust cloth harder and looked over his shoulder. Numbers and letters were scribbled in varying patterns. I'd never learned algebra. Nor a foreign language. I couldn't do much of anything because Mutti hadn't allowed it. She was afraid I'd know more than her.

I'd wanted to go to school so badly. I wanted to study to get my Abitur, learn a real job.

"Sorry." I patted him on the back and swallowed my envy. I was glad he was learning new things. At least one of us could.

Wiping down the sink and putting away my buckets, my thoughts turned to Gerda's engagement party.

It wasn't that I begrudged them their happiness, but I rather preferred time alone. Built up my nerve to visit Günter's parents again. It had been two weeks since I saw Günter's mother at the grocery store. Since the postcard. As far as I knew, Günter was still away.

Why did I hang on to men who left me?

The sun burned my scalp as I made my way to Gerda's and Helmut's party. I wore my favorite blue and white striped dress with a wide skirt and a narrow bodice. It was way too hot for hose, so I wore my sandals, hoping I wouldn't get blisters.

It was a ten-minute walk to Helmut's place in the neighborhood Unnersberg. Narrow half-timbered homes that had escaped the bombings leaned toward me as if in greeting, some so tiny, you could almost touch both corners with your fingers. Their green shutters reminded me of my old neighbor Herr Baum's house. Geraniums winked at me from flowerpots, coloring the stark black and white of the siding. Couples strolled in the sunshine. Kids played soccer on an empty lot.

"Come in. So good to see you," Helmut said. He hugged me tightly, his eyes filled with concern. "Is that idiot still not back?"

I shook my head and produced a smile. "Idiot is right."

"Lilly." Gerda pulled me into the group. Their parents were here along with a few of our friends, Lydia and Kurt, and a couple of colleagues from Ullrich. Whispering congratulations, I handed Gerda my gift, a white ceramic vase I'd bought Friday after work.

Somebody handed me a glass of sparkling wine. I took quick sips, the liquid bubbly in my throat. For once, I didn't mind getting tipsy. The rooms were tiny, crocheted doilies covered tables, fresh flower bouquets loaded down shelves. The doorframes were so low, Helmut tucked his head when he passed through.

The alcohol hit my brain like a fogbank the *Wupper* River. The light grew sharp around the edges, the chatter of voices turned softer and fuzzy like speaking through a wall.

I stood with Lydia and Kurt but couldn't concentrate on their discussion. It was something about the Stalin Note, in which he suggested creating a combined east-west Germany. Of course, Chancellor Adenauer had other ideas. Kurt said something about East Germany becoming Russian while Lydia argued against it.

A commotion erupted at the entrance. Hans, Günter's brother and his wife had arrived and clinked glasses with Helmut. The first schnapps made the rounds.

Helmut headed over, handing me a shot glass. "Prost."

I took a nip, the vapors floating straight to my brain. I felt my cheeks and forehead burn.

"Lilly, it's good to see you." Hans materialized next to me with his wife in tow. "Did you hear from Günter?" he said, his voice too low for others to hear. He was shorter than Günter, so we were eye-to-eye.

"Nothing."

Hans shook his head. "He needs to grow up." He grabbed my elbow and pulled me into the kitchen. "We got another postcard yesterday."

I tried to keep a straight face, tried to mouth the words 'what did it say.' But my head buzzed and tried to comprehend Hans's words, the fact that Günter had sent two postcards to his parents and zero to me.

The sound in my ears grew into a waterfall, splashing and rushing through my head. Obviously, Hans didn't notice my distress because he went on.

"He wrote he'll be back soon because he's out of money."
Hans smiled as if that was something to make me happy.

Instead I stared as the turmoil in my head spread to my limbs. I swayed because all of a sudden Hans grabbed my shoulders and called for help. He exchanged a glance with Helmut and something in their expression told me that escape had been on their minds as well. That they admired Günter.

I sank onto a bench, trying to keep the furniture in focus. Everything wobbled as if we were on a ship. I thought about asking Helmut again about Günter. Over the past three years I'd heard many stories—the horse slaughter, wandering through the woods, Günter's and Helmut's escape from the SS. While I spent my days in our torn-apart flat, at least I still had a home while for 47 days Günter and Helmut had gone through hell.

Helmut handed me a glass of water while Gerda shoved a plate of food in my lap. "Eat. You're skin and bones. I bet you haven't had anything since breakfast."

She was right. As of late, the act of eating was a chore. I couldn't taste anything and didn't feel hungry most of the time. Surprising, considering how a few years ago hunger had kept me in its bony clutches.

I've got to get out of here. Think about this bit of news. Two postcards, none for me. Günter coming home soon. What is soon?

I'm not sure how I got home. Hans walked next to me, supporting my elbow like I was some old lady with brittle joints. He said good-bye at the front door. Mutti's legendary reputation had undoubtedly reached Hans, and he didn't want any part of her.

"Don't you worry, I'll talk to him," he offered, turning away.

'Don't,' I wanted to say, but the words only formed in my head. If he wasn't showing up on his own free will, he might as well stay away.

Everyone chattered excitedly as we hurried out of the office. The weekend lay ahead, and for once I was in a hurry, too. Peter had asked me to meet him tomorrow so I was going to get the new lipstick I'd had my eye on for months. Thanks to my secret raise, I could finally afford it.

If I were sensible, I'd save for new pumps. The heels of my work shoes were worn and the repair shop had kept them going past reason.

Gerda grabbed me from behind and we walked outside arm-in-arm. Since the engagement she was excited as a kid finding its boot filled with chocolate on *Nikolaus*.

The group of women scattered at the gate and there, hands in his pockets, stood Günter.

"Hallo Lilly," he said as if it were the most normal thing in the world. As if he always stood here picking me up.

"Hallo." My face turned into a mask, my features frozen. I could neither smile nor frown, I just stared.

"I'll go ahead and meet you later unless you want me to stay," Gerda said, giving my forearm a squeeze. I could tell she didn't want to be witness to our meeting.

I shook my head up and down, eyes on the man in front of me.

Günter tried a smile. "*Wie geht's Dir?*"

You know how you look at somebody when you haven't seen him or her in a while. You notice the smallest things—the dimple in the right cheek, the tan lines around the neck. Günter looked taller than I remembered, the belt on his waist cinched tighter. The tops of his hands were brown as cocoa, offset by the white of his palms. He must've gotten his hair cut because pale lines edged the top of his forehead.

"Fine."

"I'm sorry."

I didn't make a move, nor did I speak. We just stood there like two boulders in the stream as people spilled out of Ullrich, passing by us with curious looks. Herr Keller limped past.

All this time, six weeks I'd thought about the things I wanted to say to him. Now that he was here, my throat was locked up, the pressure behind my eyeballs increasing.

I set my jaw until I felt my back molars grind together. If there was one thing I wouldn't do it was cry.

Not anymore.

"May I walk you home?"

"Fine."

"I'm sorry," he said again. His gaze was on mine, rueful yet relaxed.

"You already said that." I looked straight ahead as we took off.

"I mean it."

My pace quickened. "Not good enough."

"I'm here to stay now."

"How nice of you."

"What can I do to convince you that I want you?"

"You want me?" I stopped, facing him, my voice rising, and I recognized the shrillness I knew from Mutti's tirades. There were people walking on the sidewalk, carrying shopping bags, chatting and laughing. The weekend started, and everyone was supposed to have a good time. There were dinners to prepare, parties to go to and schnapps to drink. "You sure have a way of showing it."

"I want you. Only you."

"I'm flattered." I forced my legs back into motion. I wanted to get home, away from the curious stares.

"Lilly, let me explain."

"That ought to be interesting."

"I've been a complete idiot. I needed to take a break, get away, see something else. I was tired of working, tired of never having privacy, tired of the same routines."

I wanted to ignore his words, his excuses, yet all I could do was stop again. "Tired of me?"

"Not tired of you. I just—" Günter shook his head.

"You'll have to do better than that," I said. "You were gone for six weeks. SIX. Not a letter, no note, not even a postcard. Nothing. Shame on you!"

"I know, I thought about writing. I wanted to."

I hurried faster and he scrambled after me.

"Lilly?" His voice had a thin quality as if the wind tore it apart. "Please wait. I want to make it up to you. Please!"

I slowed down just a bit. Why was my body overriding my mind?

"I love you! I know I was an idiot, cruel and self-centered. I can't explain it but I've always wanted you. You're the one."

"You have a strange way of showing it."

"Please give me a chance." Günter grabbed my hand and pulled me to a stop. "I don't care how long it takes. I'll wait. Please forgive me." His face was close, so close I wanted to touch his cheeks, run a finger along the edge of his lips. My body began to wobble in the most unreliable way. I felt like leaning forward, into him, and drinking in that warm spot near his neck where I used to find solace. Where I felt peace. *Stop it!*

"I have to think about it."

I didn't remember much about the rest of the way. At some point, I practically ran. My heart hammered, and my throat was sore when I arrived home. Günter was no longer behind me.

All this time I'd waited—for some sign of life, for a postcard, for anything—I was preparing a speech in my head. Now that the day had come, I didn't know what to say or do.

Not only that. I didn't know what to feel.

CHAPTER THIRTY-THREE

Günter: June-July 1952

To say I didn't enjoy Lilly's birthday party is an understatement. I felt strangely detached, our friends, even Helmut getting on my nerves—and Lilly, especially Lilly, distracted by the useless search for her father.

All I knew was that I was tired. No. Exhausted. Sort of thin on the inside like that morning I got drunk on the stolen schnapps with Helmut a million years ago. I was tired of working so many hours, tired of the cramped living conditions at my parents' house and the lack of privacy when we wanted to make love. Lilly's mother was such a pain. I couldn't stand being in her house and felt stifled when I visited.

Every week, Mother asked for rent, and I had to hand over a chunk of my earnings. I couldn't afford to move and even if I could, housing was impossible to find.

My chest constricted, and I realized I was stinking furious. All I ever remembered doing was working and taking care of others. But it was more than that. It was as if rage engulfed me like a cloak, a darkness I couldn't see beyond.

It was early in the morning as I trudged toward my house, head pounding with a vengeance after the countless shots I'd poured into myself, my throat like sandpaper. I was parched. Drinking several cups of water, I cooled my aching forehead under the faucet. I shivered as sweat dripped down my armpits.

I straightened with a groan and forced myself to search for my work shirt. My vision blurred and I sat back on the bed, trying to focus my brain and grapple the thought, the idea that had lurked in my head for a while. I'd arrived at a stopping point. I couldn't see a straight way ahead. The path that everyone else took—engagement, marriage, working sixty hours a week and getting drunk on weekends—it no longer held any appeal. I wanted to choose a path, right or left, and the indecision was driving me equally crazy as the knowledge that neither path would make me happy.

I stuck my head into the kitchen, where Mother was prepping red currants for jam.

"I'm taking the day off," I mumbled. "Probably going to visit Fredi. He owes me money." Not feeling like talking, I ran out without waiting for a reply.

Taking deep breaths to blow away the cobwebs, I pedaled toward *Düsseldorf.* It was cloudy and cool this early, and the exercise revived me. I rode through small villages where life went on as usual, people constructing buildings, heading to shops and work.

"Fredi is in Switzerland," Fredi's mother said when I rang the doorbell.

"What is he doing down there?"

"Working. I don't expect him back until Christmas."

Disappointed, I continued to the Rhine River near Fredi's house. I couldn't go home. Just couldn't. Sitting down on the levy, I watched the Rhine pass by in oblivion. The water whispered as I stared, the hammering in my head reduced to a dull pounding. I rubbed my stiffening neck and ate the bread and cheese I'd picked up on the way. Still, I sat.

I was surprised when it turned dark. Resigned to spend the night, I took my blanket and rolled up under the stars.

The next morning, I was still no wiser. All I knew was that just the thought of going home made me steam. I needed another day. It was Friday, anyway.

I headed south, only stopping when my legs refused to go on, when I was hungry or needed a bathroom break. The exercise and fresh air made me ravenous. I took off my shirt and rode bare-chested, picking up food from local farmers and sleeping in barns. One day turned to a week, then two.

The Rhine valley formed an open trough, middle-age

castles and ruins dotted the ridges and grapevines covered the hills in neat rows.

With every pedal stroke, I felt more relieved, the ghosts of my past a little less vivid. There were Rolf Schlüter, little Paul, the communist neighbor's wife sitting dead in her kitchen, Hans looking like death, the man digging for his wife, Birdsnest and Harald, the SS men in the pub, and…and. I squinted against the sinking sun, glad the wind dried my eyes. I'd survived, yet I was empty. There was a hollowness inside that included my heart.

Lilly's face, her eyes serious in contemplation, floated into my mind. I pushed it away.

It was early evening when I arrived in the old Rhine city of *Rüdesheim*. Swarms of bicyclists crowded roads and sidewalks as if the entire German youth were on the move. I arranged a room at the youth hostel and proceeded to investigate the town.

Music blared from bars and outdoor cafes and I decided to try the "Old Baron" tavern along a cobblestone road near the center. Surrounded by rose bushes, a beer garden invited with long benches. A band of accordion, guitar and drum players strummed furiously, belching out common tunes.

It was crowded, and I wedged myself into an open spot. Around me a wild party was in full swing. I ordered beer with brats and potato salad, watching the loud singing men and women wave steins back and forth with the music.

"You here alone?" a blond chap yelled across the table.

I mouthed "ja," unsure the fellow heard me above the noise.

"Where you from?" the blond man slurred.

"Solingen." I took a deep swig from my mug, some kind of pilsner with a hoppy flavor.

With nothing in my stomach, it went straight to my brain.

A girl next to me turned her head. "Isn't that where they make all the metal stuff? Knives and things?" She had brown hair and was very tanned with small high breasts. Her legs were long and muscular and barely covered by a ripped pair of capris.

I grinned. "That's what I do for a living."

"That's so cool." The girl smiled at me, and I noticed her white teeth. "My name is Elke." The girl held out her hand.

"Günter."

The voices along the tables grew louder as the sun went

down. Small lanterns along the walls twinkled soft light across the garden. The brunette and I discussed our experience on the road. I'd lost track of time and floated. The blond man across the table slept, head resting between mugs and dirty plates.

"Do you want to go for a walk?" Elke's face was close.

"Sure." I took her hand and led her through the gate outside.

Elke squeezed my fingers. "Pretty wild in there, isn't it?"

Beneath the old promenade the Rhine murmured. "I love this river," I sighed, the girl's voice fuzzy in my ears.

"Look how it glitters." Elke ran to the water's edge, throwing off her sandals. Wading in the shallows she laughed. She moved like a dancer with smooth long steps. It was like watching a film.

"Look how *you* glitter."

"What are you waiting for?"

"I'd rather stay dry."

"Then I'll have to come to you." She left the water and stopped in front of me. Almost as tall as I, her lips touched mine. "Hi."

Her breath smelled of beer and something sweet, our kiss hot and sensual. Sinking into the still warm grass, I lost myself in the stranger. Elke pulled up her shirt, her nipples tiny pink blossoms on white. I leaned over, flicking my tongue across.

Other couples were near us, engrossed in each other—I was intoxicated to be out here, exposed and uninhibited. There were no more rules, nobody to tell me anything.

When the girl whimpered and tugged at my pants, I tore open my shorts. Her eyes flashed hunger as she lifted her hips and responded eagerly to my movements. I was in some sort of twilight zone, between worlds. Nothing was real and yet, everything was more real than I'd ever experienced.

I rolled into the grass, too numb to say anything and passed out.

I awoke in the middle of the night. The girl was gone. Scrambling toward the road, my stomach lurched and I threw up, hanging across a fence. I needed to find my room.

In the morning, my mouth cotton and my bowels gurgling, I headed outside taking deep breaths. Walking up the street I recognized the brunette, at least I think it was her, and remembered last night—vaguely.

She saw me and smiled. "You don't look so well."

"I'm not."

"Want some tea?"

"Sure."

Her companions sat on the outdoor terrace, the blonde chap crumpled, his face tinged green. I slumped down as Elke poured tea.

"We're staying another day," she said, her eyes searching my face. "Do you want to come along?"

"What are you doing?"

"Probably going to swim and pick cherries from the farmer up the street." Elke smiled another brilliant smile. "Come on, go with us."

Too weak to make a decision, I nodded.

We spent the day and evening together, drinking more beer and making love in the grass after dark. I felt odd in this group of strangers. They all knew each other well, several couples and Elke, who seemed unattached. She was cute and always laughed, flashing her teeth, much different from Lilly who was mostly serious and focused. I couldn't think of her here.

"Why don't you come with us?" Elke sat up to face me.

I stared at the night sky. "I'm leaving in the morning."

"Do you want to meet later?" I nodded, but the more my buzz wore off, the more I knew I'd never write. I hadn't told Elke about Lilly.

"I won't have much time once I get back to work," I sighed. "If there's work."

Elke put her chin on my chest. "You'll lose your job?"

"I'll find something."

I hit the road at six in the morning, wanting to put as much distance between me and Elke as possible. I never intended to get involved and now this girl expected me to write or worse, visit?

I pedaled and breathed the fresh morning air—free again—the thought of home far away. In fact, my entire life's history was turning hazy like a dream you barely remember. My bicycle was holding up well, my body rejoicing despite some of the grueling hills.

For a while, I followed the Rhine. Another week passed as the thought of needing to write a note nagged at me. My parents were waiting. So was Lilly. Yet, every time I passed a kiosk with rows of colorful postcards, I hurried along. What was there to write? How could I explain? Drenched in sweat from sun and exercise, I rode bareback and jumped into the river when I found suitable spots along the banks.

With every mile I grew lighter as if I were stripping away my memories. The roads and taverns were filled with bicyclists, but other than small talk, I kept my distance. To save money, I slept in barns and haystacks, paying a few *Pfennig* for a breakfast of bread, fried potatoes, and eggs. In the fourth week I finally wrote a quick card to my parents. I bought a second card for Lilly, but when I thought of what to say, no words came to mind. She was undoubtedly frantic...expecting an explanation. Nothing like that fit on a card. So, I stuck the card into my satchel and continued south.

Nearing Lake Constance, the land turned flat and the lake stretched in front of me like a silvery band. To the south, the Swiss Alps rose, their tops white under permanent snow. Orchards hugged the shores with fruit stands offering cherries, peaches, and strawberries.

A group of bicyclists had stopped at an intersection and, judging by the deep tan, had been on the road a while.

"*Wie geht's?*" I yelled as I approached. They were obviously arguing and I jumped back on my bike. I didn't have any use for baggage.

"Where are you from?" One of the girls heard me despite the shouting.

"Solingen." I nodded over my shoulder as if home were right around the corner.

"That's quite a ways, isn't it?" the blonde said. "We came from Hannover but now, as you can see, we can't decide if we want to go further south or start circling back."

"I'm going south."

"Where to?" The young man next to the blonde was speaking now. The arguing had stopped, all eyes on me.

"Switzerland," I blurted. Somehow it sounded good, now that it was out.

"That's another day," the young man said. "Are you

running away from something?"

I smiled. "I've got to think things over."

The blonde winked, "Sounds like girl trouble to me."

Her long hair was tied into a ponytail. She wore black shorts and a pink shirt she'd tied around her waist, revealing a trim stomach. Of course, being trim was nothing special. Most everyone who'd survived the war and five years of starvation was thin.

"Why don't we go with this fellow for a while longer?" she said, giving me the onceover. "Looks like he could use some company." Without waiting for an answer from her friends, the blonde mounted her bike. "You don't mind if we run along? By the way, I'm Rita."

"Günter. I still have a couple hours left in me."

The group followed, once in a while one of them rode alongside. Cars were sparse and we had the roads to ourselves most of the time. We exchanged information about places we'd visited, friendly farmers and grumpy barkeepers. Near the Swiss boarder we stopped at a *Hof,* a two-story farmhouse with large window boxes, brimming with flowers that spoke of a well cared for interior.

Surrounded by several low-lying buildings, hay bales were neatly stacked. Healthy looking horses and cows grazed contentedly nearby. An older man in blue coveralls, whose bowlegged legs made him appear much shorter, walked up from the barn.

"What's your business?" he yelled.

We looked at each other, unsure who should speak. "We'd like dinner and maybe a place to sleep for the night," I said. "Of course, we'll pay for it."

"Will you?" The farmer scratched his chin, assessing us. "Wait here, let me talk to my wife." He disappeared into the house.

"You think he'll let us?" Bernd said. I rubbed my backside where heat and sweat had turned into ache.

"You're in luck," the old man said. "The wife is in a good mood."

"I'll take bread and jam if you have it," I suggested. "We can sleep up there." I nodded toward the opening above the barn doors, where hay had been stacked high.

"That's fine for tonight," the old man said. "But you may come in for a real dinner—if you clean up."

Rita, the blonde from Hannover, rummaged through her bag in search of clean clothes. "Thanks so much. Where can we wash?"

"Over there, see the barrel? It's clean water and you can use the pump next to it for more. We'll see you shortly."

"Thanks so much, Herr...?" I said. The man reminded me of the old man who'd fed Helmut and me while we hid from the SS.

"Klein, my name is Klein."

"*Danke*, Herr Klein. That is mighty kind of you." I turned to follow the others.

"Don't forget to take off your shoes," Herr Klein called after us.

Soon we sat around a huge oak table in the kitchen. Shelves with blue and white pottery and an old hutch with assorted glassware rimmed the room. Herr and Frau Klein were in their sixties but appeared fit and healthy.

Large quantities of fried potatoes, thick slices of bread, butter, strawberry jam, homemade sausage and a huge apple pie were competing for space. For a while nobody talked. The old couple smiled as we devoured everything in sight. I chewed and swallowed, yet couldn't keep my eyes from roving across the table. It'd been years since I starved, but I never passed up the opportunity to stuff myself. Even if I'd be uncomfortable for hours.

Despite her friendliness, I noticed deep lines in Frau Klein's face. Shadows surrounded her eyes while her movements appeared labored as if it took too much effort. Several times I felt her watching me.

"Eat," she said every so often.

"That was wonderful." Bernd stood up, rubbing his stomach. "We'll go outside and walk around, if you don't mind."

"Sure," the old man said.

"I'm staying in for a bit." My legs were heavy tonight. It'd been a long day—almost five long weeks. "This must be your family?" I said, nodding toward the sideboard where photographs of young men stood in silver frames.

"We had two sons." Herr Klein leaned back in his chair to blow puffs of fragrant smoke from a pipe. He glanced at the sink where his wife and the two girls were washing dishes. "We lost them in the war," he continued quietly.

I bit my lip. "I'm so sorry." I was an idiot for sticking my nose in other people's business.

"It's all right, son. Except we have nobody to continue the farm."

Unsure what to say, I nodded.

The farmer pointed his pipe toward the kitchen. "She likes to have some young blood around."

"I'd be happy to help for a day or two…" I said. "I can't speak for the others, but I'm not in a hurry."

"We could use some help with the stalls. It's getting difficult to take care of everything."

"It's a deal."

I was exhausted when we finally crawled into the hay. It smelled of summer and earth and was warm to the touch. The farmer had even supplied us with extra blankets to keep the pokey stalks out of our clothes.

I thought of the time I was locked in the barn with my father, the Nazi farmer being hung under the oak, the madness of the night.

Animals snorted below, soft comforting sounds. I dozed, my last thought on the young men who used to live here, farming the land, never doubting their place in life.

"Shhh," a voice whispered into my ear as I emerged from deep sleep.

"What is it?" I felt a hand on my stomach. It was very dark.

"It's me, Rita."

"Something wrong?" I whispered, rousing myself as Rita's fingers traced a path across my chest.

"I thought you liked me," Rita murmured. "Bernd is asleep, don't worry."

"But we… you shouldn't," I mumbled as her mouth closed over mine. Instinctively, I returned the kiss.

"Mmmh, you taste so good." Rita pressed her body into my side. "Come on, nobody will know." Soft lips, sweet like strawberries and vanilla, touched mine.

My mind tried to focus, to will my hands to push her away. Instead my body responded, eager and oblivious to the struggles in my head. Her tongue probed and mine joined the dance. Her hand wandered under my shirt, her fingers nimble and warm. I meant to pull them out, to tell her to stop and leave me alone. Yet, I did nothing, not even when she straddled my legs and I detected the heat of her crotch against my thigh. She rubbed herself, little moans against my neck.

"Touch me," she whispered, placing my hands on her breasts. I remembered how full they were, how they strained against the fabric of her shirt. As my fingers brushed her hardened nipples, she moaned again and something inside me let go. I rolled toward her, pulled up her shirt and buried my face against her heated flesh.

My tongue found her, sucking, teasing, and circling. Her body writhed as she pulled me on top, her breaths quick and urgent. I'd never experienced this kind of intensity, my pelvis pushing into oblivion. She answered my moves, squeezing until nothing mattered, the sensations taking me away.

I emerged breathless, blood pounding in my head. Somebody moved nearby as I slid off Rita's body. My skin was damp with a sudden chill. Groping in the dark, I found my blanket and lay back, staring into the dark. All was quiet, the girl moved away. As I drifted off to sleep, a dull ache spread across my neck where the girl had bit me.

In the morning I found myself alone, the heap of blankets empty. I scrambled across the hay, pulling sticks and blades from hair and clothes. After a quick birdbath, I entered the house.

"Hallo?"

"*Guten Morgen!*" Frau Klein, carrying a plate heaped with slices of homemade bread, smiled at me.

The group sat whispering. When they looked up, I knew something was wrong. With a pang, I remembered last night. It felt as unreal as a dream, my fingers wandering to my neck where a dull ache persisted. Bernd got up, though Rita tried to pull him back on his chair.

"No, Bernd! Don't!"

But Bernd yanked free and stepped in my way. "Be glad we're guests here or I'd kick your ass." He clenched his jaw and looked ready to pop me in the chin.

As I tried to assess the situation, details of last night came flooding back. "I'm sorr—"

"You poor son of a bitch, I'll give you sorry." Bernd

grabbed my shirt, his face inches away. His friends jumped up to restrain Bernd's arms.

"Let's go," Rita urged, not meeting my eyes. Bernd abruptly turned and the others walked out after him. Through the window, I watched them talk to the old farmer who was listening and shaking his head. My cheeks burned with embarrassment as the group mounted their bikes.

"*Junge.*" Frau Klein patted my back. "Don't worry about it. They were no good."

I searched for the right words. "I'm so sorry. I'll leave right now if you want. But I'm still willing to help you today. I promised, and I feel bad that we didn't keep our word."

"Nonsense," Frau Klein said, "of course you can stay. We'd love to have your help." She moved into the kitchen. "I fried potatoes. Better eat, you'll need your strength."

After piling a mountain of potatoes, eggs and onion on the table, Frau Klein sat down to face me. "I don't know where you are in life, if you have a girl, but that Rita, I watched her. She was chasing you with her eyes the entire time." Frau Klein shook her head.

Where had I been that I never noticed? Embarrassed once more I jumped up. "You have a very nice home."

Frau Klein chuckled grimly. "It used to be a joy when we had our boys. We worked hard so they could go on and..." Frau Klein's eyes glinted. "Nothing matters more than your family and the people you love."

I stood, unsure what to say, uncomfortable and wishing for something to do.

To my relief Herr Klein entered. "Let's talk about your day."

The cows watched as I cleaned stalls. The manure didn't bother me. Somehow it smelled right, of healthy animals, straw, hay and grains. After lunch, I worked in the vegetable garden.

I dug and hacked, the earth fragrant under my touch. Rows of carrots, their spidery tops a juicy green, lined the dark earth next to sections of onions, beans, cabbages and lettuce. In my mind appeared the image of Lilly scrubbing carrots. She bent low above the sink in the kitchen, her eyes dancing. I sighed, the memory so vivid, I could've sworn she was right next to me.

The raised bed with an assortment of kitchen greens

reminded me of Mother's herb garden. I breathed deeply, enjoying the sun on my back. For a moment, I imagined living here, helping the Kleins work the land, taking their sons' place. *Nothing matters more than the people you love.*

After dinner, my stomach bursting, I crawled into the hayloft. But despite my tired body, sleep refused me. Dinner had been scrumptious with homemade bread and butter, pork steaks, potatoes and carrots. Frau Klein baked a rhubarb pie with butter crumbs, and I ate most of it.

Something was bothering me and it wasn't my full stomach. It was hot tonight, and I couldn't get comfortable. Lilly's face drifted by, smiling and sweet. I wondered what she was doing.

Dawn was breaking when I awoke. I shivered. Not from the cool air, but from Lilly's eerie laugh still ringing in my ears. I'd waited to pick her up at work but she took the arm of Peter Neumann and gave him a kiss. Then she laughed and turned her back on me, Peter's arm firmly around her shoulders.

During my second day in the fields, I planted bits of potatoes for the fall crop. As I dug into the earth, my eyes blurred with visions of Lilly: our first encounter at the fair and how she joined me on the teeter-totter, our first kiss, and making love in my tent.

What had I done? I'd run off as if being chased by the SS, without telling anyone, without telling Lilly. I hadn't written, the second postcard going to my parents. What had Frau Klein said? Nothing matters more than the people you love.

I let out a sigh. I loved Lilly, her earnestness, her strength amid all the adversity, her mother's coldness and cruelty. Until now I'd been sure she loved me too. I was her way out. I knew that.

What if Lilly no longer wanted me? What if she'd hooked up with that Peter Neumann? For the first time in many years, I was afraid. I knew she was the sincerest human being I'd ever met, someone who saw the truth.

I marveled at her inner strength. Judging by her mother, she should've been a nutcase. Instead, she somehow managed to protect that bit of her. She kept it hidden, that piece of the heart that is not only capable of love, but of offering warmth and caring to another.

Me!

My insides twisted painfully. After what I'd done and seen,

it would've be so easy to let go of what was left of my morals. Lilly had been the one who allowed me to continue living, who showed me that life was worthwhile, that being honest and true was a good thing. She allowed me to see past the shadows of my past, had shaven away the calluses so I could feel again.

How could I have been so blind?

During lunch, I was still deep in thought. Not even Frau Klein's gaze on me got me talking. The ghosts of my past had evaporated and I no longer understood why I'd left. Well, I did understand, but the urgency was gone.

By going away, I was now able to return. For good.

Frau Klein kept glancing at me. "It's probably time for you to head home." Her eyes were shiny again.

Clearing my throat, I nodded. "I'll leave tomorrow."

CHAPTER THIRTY-FOUR

Lilly: July 21, 1952

I stared into the distance where Günter had long disappeared. What just happened? The gates of the print shop had emptied and I stood, unmoving, shreds of our conversation whirling like wisps of clouds, soft and shapeless, impossible to hold on to. I heaved, the sound loud in my ears. The life I'd prepared for was no longer. There wouldn't be an engagement or a wedding. There was no more going out at night, only endless evenings alone with Mutti.

I didn't know how long I remained there suspended, my mind refusing to acknowledge the inevitable. *You did the right thing. You had to break up with him.* Then why did I feel so lousy, my throat raw and aching from the effort not to cry?

It was Monday evening, and the week stretched in front of me. I'd spent all weekend thinking about what to do. I couldn't decide. In the end I didn't visit Günter.

On Saturday morning, I met Peter downtown, where we discussed Vati's whereabouts and the conditions he likely dealt with. Russian gulags were, in essence, death camps. Escape was impossible, and food and clothing sparse. There was no medicine, and men were forced to labor in mines and cut lumber. Siberia's temperatures in the winter averaged minus fifteen degrees Fahrenheit, but often dropped much lower. How could a fifty-five year old man survive in these conditions?

And why did I keep digging when I was fuming mad at Vati? Finding out that he surrendered *after* the war was already over had renewed my wrath at him. I didn't understand him, this clinging to rules and honor against all reason.

Peter had patted my hand several times, and I was beginning to suspect he wanted to see me for other reasons.

On Sunday I took Burkhart to the zoo in Wuppertal. Mutti paid our train fare and we splurged on ice cream and chocolate éclairs. In the moments when my attention slipped from the animals to Günter, my insides began to hurt. It was an ache so deep, it felt like my soul was diseased.

So, I put up a show and laughed along with Burkhart, watching polar bears and monkeys climb around in their enclosures. The last time I'd gone to the zoo was with Vati when I was six. Burkhart hardly remembered him. The few times Vati was on leave during the war, Burkhart was five or six himself. The other day I saw him study the photo next to Mutti's bed. It was the same image I used to visit when I was afraid I wouldn't remember Vati's face.

I had trouble remembering Günter's after six weeks. Now there was no longer a need.

I wandered home slowly, my legs straining to carry my weight. My feet, still a size ten, were filled with rocks. The evening stretched before me.

It wasn't any different than the previous six weeks.

But it was.

Because I no longer hoped or analyzed. I didn't make up questions about Günter's motives, nor did I wonder what he experienced during his trip. He'd begged me to reconsider, told me he loved me, his eyes filling with tears. When had I ever seen him cry?

It was over. I'd made the decision that I couldn't forgive Günter ...and began to grasp that this was my new life. That this was what I'd endure for eternity.

Numbness settled as I climbed up the stairs to our apartment.

Mutti was in the kitchen, oblivious to my pain. If she knew, she'd rejoice. Dance around the table and sing.

As I put away my purse, Mutti turned toward me, her eyes burning with fury.

"When were you going to tell me?"

"Tell you what?" I was confused, wondering why she wasn't pleased about Günter and me breaking up.

Mutti thrust a slip of paper in my face. "Your raise."

I sank on a chair as the weight of this impossible day dragged me down.

"Aren't you going to say something?" Her voice is shrill. "You know we scrape by every month! You're acting selfish."

I looked at my mother, the way others must see her. The hair pulled away from her face to showcase her cheekbones, the lush mouth glowing with lipstick, the coal lines around her eyes. I saw her for what she was, a middle-aged woman who found validation for her existence in the way men treated her. Who was left by her husband without reason, at least not a reason she understood.

She had little in common with Vati. He was all about honor, however twisted. She didn't know the meaning of the word.

There was a time when I would've done anything to gain the love and acceptance of that woman. I'd tried, God knows I'd tried. Cooked, cleaned, boiled laundry and knitted miles of yarn to get a word of approval, a smile or just a nod. It happened so infrequently, when it did happen, it was like a beam of light hitting my heart. Maybe that was what Mutti was going for. Make me so thankful for her sparse love that I'd forever continue vowing for it.

I opened my mouth, words tumbling out faster than I was aware of them. My head was filled with too much blood and threatened to explode. My heart pounded painfully as if my ribcage were sore from the sadness inside me.

"You call me selfish?" I blurted. "All I do is work. I come home and clean and cook. What else do you want from me?" My voice rang foreign in my ears, a shrill whining that echoed through my skull. "Why don't *you* go work for a change?"

"If your earnings weren't so pitiful..."

"And whose fault is that?"

Mutti shrugged. "The war..."

"You did exactly what Hitler wanted."

Mutti's eyes met mine. Her pupils contracted. I should've stopped arguing, but it was like trying to stop a locomotive with a stick. "Are you mad?"

"Not at all." I took a breath, my voice surprisingly calm.

"He said he wanted girls to be hard working, without an education, without a future other than being mothers. You didn't let me go to school or learn anything while Burkhart... You wanted me dumb and subservient, your personal slave to clean up after you."

"No wonder you can't keep a man happy."

I looked at her, feeling my face turn into a grin. "*I* broke it off."

Mutti's mouth opened, but no sound came out. Was she truly speechless because I pointed out the truth, was she surprised or mad that I'd finally spoken up?

"You've lost your mind. Your father...it's all his fault..." As Mutti launched into a tirade, I pulled myself from the chair and headed for my bedroom. Her words bounced around the room like shrapnel, intent on inflicting maximum damage. But I wore a bulletproof vest, and none of it reached my ears. Somewhere in the back of my mind, I registered Burkhart's expression of shock. He'd never heard me talk like this to Mutti.

Nor had I.

I wanted to slam my bedroom door, but the energy had seeped away like water in sand and I closed it softly. I kicked off my shoes and collapsed on the bed, wishing for the world to come to an end, wishing that one of those bombs in 1944 had found me.

CHAPTER THIRTY-FIVE

Lilly: July 29, 1952

War had been declared in my home. Mutti wasn't speaking, her eyes daggers, the air poisoned with her thoughts. I felt them pelting off my skin. My brother had taken Mutti's side, at least when she was around. He left me little snippets of paper notes.

I was determined to stand my ground. I wouldn't give up the few marks that provided me the merest hint of independence. With Günter no longer helping, I couldn't afford even the most basic items like gloves or stockings for winter.

I washed all my clothes by hand to keep them nice, but there were stains on some, and the material had grown thin on others.

My fingers rested in the soapy water, the tiny bathroom mirror foggy with steam. It was just as well. I didn't want to look at myself. I didn't want to look at anything.

I thought my life was unbearable when the bombs dropped on us and we fixed grass soup. In a way, this was worse. People had to be happy. The country was experiencing a "wonder." Everyone worked and earned money—money that bought things in stores. People invested in radios and fancy sofas. We all wanted this new Germany to become strong. We wanted to be normal again.

All this busyness kept us from thinking about our worries of an angry Russia dividing our nation. We were progressive, a new Republic with a new name that distracted us from our past.

Only nobody truly put their past behind them. Certainly not this country, and certainly not me. We just pretended to move ahead. On the surface, we were building new homes and filling our apartments with things once more. Beneath, we mourned our dead and chewed on the terrible guilt about what Germany had done to the world. To the Jews, to the Russians, to the gypsies, to the British and the invalids. But also what we did to ourselves and what the Third Reich did to its children.

Us.

"You about done in there?" Mutti's voice cut through the silence. "I'd like to take a bath."

"Five minutes," I said, wringing out the laundry and piling it in the basket.

I headed past her to the yard, deep in thought as I hung up my blouses and underthings.

"Lilly, is that you?" Herr Baum's feeble voice drifted over the fence.

The guilt over not visiting the old man in months made me rush over. "How are your knees?" Herr Baum had severe arthritis and hobbled most of the time.

"About the same," he said, his face half shadowed by his slouchy yard hat. I couldn't remember ever seeing him without it. He squinted at me. "Will you indulge an old man for a few minutes? Just made myself a pot of bean stew."

I glanced at the windows behind me. Why go inside when there was nothing but the arctic?

"I'll be right over," I said as I pushed my mouth into a smile.

I headed to the street and found Herr Baum waiting by his back gate. He'd shrunk since I last saw him, a little old man with a face full of wrinkles. Guilt grabbed me, so I rushed forward to pat his arm. My forced smile turned into a real one.

"It's been too long." My words were hollow as an old tree stump.

He nodded at me, his eyes a bit teary among the folds.

"Sit, sit," he said, motioning me toward the little table on the patio. "I'll get the soup."

"Let me help you."

I followed Herr Baum into the house, through the basement, up the stairs. It took several minutes as the old man

322

crept up each step.

His gnarled fingers clenched around the walking stick. "I hate using that thing," he huffed. "All my life I've taken care of myself. Now look at me. My muscles have atrophied like drying jellyfish in the sun, and my legs wobble as if they have a mind of their own."

I wanted to support his arm to get away from the basement. This is where Anna had lived.

We never talked about Anna, the rabbit. How one day she was gone and Huss had a feast. Just the memory of that night when I smelled the roast made me gag. It had been his revenge for stealing from him. I'd stopped him from hurting us, but he'd found a different way to get to me... and the old man.

Because the day after I'd stolen the swastikas and documents from Huss, I'd taken them to Herr Baum, who'd promised to keep them safe. He'd never asked why, but as far as I knew, he still had them.

My throat tightened even now, six years later. A sigh rang out in the cool damp air of the basement as we carried our bowls outside. I couldn't even tell if it was mine or his. Regret blurred my vision. After Anna disappeared, I didn't see Herr Baum for a long time.

"What's the matter?" Herr Baum said as we reemerged in his yard.

"Nothing." I was unable to meet the old man's eyes. He'd always had a way to look into my soul and I was afraid what he'd find right now.

"You've hardly said a word." Herr Baum leaned back with a grunt as we took our seats in the yard. I could tell he was in pain. "Erwin sends his regards. He's been promoted."

I strained to smile, but even the memory of saving Erwin couldn't pull me out of my hole. "Is there anything I can do? Get you a pillow?"

He laughed. "I wish a pillow would do it. I need a new body and some extra muscles and bones."

I tried another smile.

"See. That face of yours bothers me. I better get you some chocolate."

I wanted to say no, I've got to go home, but Herr Baum was already heading for the stairs.

What did I have to rush home for? There was nothing that couldn't wait. Especially Mutti's fury.

"There, try that." Herr Baum unwrapped a bar of milk chocolate. My favorite. He patted me on the head before slumping back into his chair.

As I reached for the sweets, out of nowhere my throat clamped shut. I pried open my eyes to keep them from blurring, but it wasn't working. My body turned into a shaky mess as I began to cry.

Herr Baum said nothing, just sat there and let me weep. Minutes passed. I had no idea how long it took before I was able to catch my breath. A finely pressed handkerchief appeared in my vision. I took it and mopped my face.

When I looked up, Herr Baum's gaze met mine. He still didn't speak, just nodded as if he knew my life was over and my heart had gone into a deep freeze.

I opened my mouth and began to speak. Out came Günter's disappearance, my worries and yearning. My failed attempt to move out, our breakup, the war with Mutti.

"And then I find out that Vati let himself be arrested. After he abandoned us. I can't ever forgive him. Or Günter."

I looked at Herr Baum, but the consolatory expression from earlier had been replaced with something like contemplation. His eyes glittered with unshed tears.

"Let me tell you a story," he said. He took a sip of mineral water and hunched lower into his chair. "I had a daughter once."

"I never saw her."

"She died of tuberculosis. But that's not why I'm telling you this." Herr Baum rubbed the back of his hand across his face. "I stopped seeing her when she began meeting a man from the SS. I refused to speak to her even when she got sick. Even after her husband had been killed in the war. I couldn't forgive her for getting involved with Hitler's evil. I didn't hear from her again until the letter arrived."

Another sigh rattled the stillness. It sounded more like a sob. "I still remember where I was that day, splitting wood in the backyard, when the mailman rang the doorbell. He never rang, but this time he clutched a paper in his hand.

"'You need to sign for this one,'" he said. I carried the letter inside. I didn't get much mail those days. Just a few bills every month for the water and electricity. Nobody knew I existed. My sister in Cologne never wrote. Nor did my nephew or any of my former colleagues from high school where I taught history for forty years. For all I knew, they were dead.

"I slumped down at the kitchen table where the remnants from breakfast still stood, a mug, the same mug I use every day and a plate with crumbs. I took the kitchen knife to open the envelope, all the while guessing why some lawyer in Stuttgart had written me."

A lone tear appeared on Herr Baum's cheek. "The letter said, 'Dear Herr Baum, we regret to inform you that your daughter, Annemarie Lister, born Baum, passed away peacefully on March 16, 1944. Her will stipulates you as the sole heir. Please contact us at your earliest convenience so we can take care of Frau Lister's effects. Sincerely, Manfred Timmermann, Attorney at law.'

"I'd pushed the memory of Annemarie from my conscience until that day. But here is the thing." Herr Baum abruptly leaned forward and patted my hand, his fingers as gnarled as oak bark.

"I made a mistake. I was stupid thinking I could ignore something so close to my heart. But that's impossible because this thing, this love is part of you. You can't run from it, just as you can't shed your skin.

"After the letter, I wanted to die myself. All these lost years I could've shared with my daughter. Especially after her husband, the SS officer had died."

"Why didn't she visit?" I asked.

"She did." Herr Baum's chuckle was grim. "'Hallo Papa,' she said, her face pale as a cloud." A sigh that sounded more like a cry escaped the old man. "I sent her away. 'I don't let Nazis into my house,' I said and shut the door in her face.

"Eventually she left, but not before pleading. 'I'm not a Nazi. Please, Papa. I'm not well. Can you not forgive me?'

"I leaned on the door from the other side, sensing her presence, her trembling limbs through the thick oak door. I even sensed her tears."

Herr Baum looked at me, but I wasn't sure he actually saw me. "Now she's gone. Forever. And the bitter taste in my mouth refuses to go away."

Without a word I pushed the chocolate across the table.

Herr Baum needed it more than I did.

CHAPTER THIRTY-SIX

Lilly: September 24, 1953

"I mean it." Peter leaned into me as we shared a bench in front of the new ice café in town, both of us enjoying one of the new waffle cones.

I closed my eyes against the bright sun, savoring the creamy vanilla on my tongue. It always amazed me how much pleasure I got from something as simple as ice cream. It was as if I had to pinch myself that I was able to eat something this delicious.

"I've got plenty of space." Peter turned toward me. "A private room if you like." I felt his hand on my forearm, those long fingers as pale as ever. I knew this wasn't what he wanted. What he wanted was for me to move in with him and share the house he'd inherited from his parents. "Your mother can't expect you to hang around forever."

He was right, of course. Mutti and I acted like strangers. "She'd have to find a job," I said, more to myself than to Peter.

"It's about time."

I knew Peter was mad about the way Mutti treated me. I also knew he loved me. I opened my eyes and caught a glimpse of his expression, a mixture of anger and devotion. He was a nice man. When I broke up with Günter a year ago, Peter offered me a way to distract myself. He'd been there for me, endured my anger outbursts and my bouts of depression.

He wasn't bad looking, either—smart and better educated than Günter. Yet, I couldn't make myself love him.

While Günter was on his trip and I was looking for a new place, I would've jumped at the opportunity. Now that it presented itself, I was struck with indecision.

It wasn't that I didn't recognize a first love. I did. It was magical, and then it died. It was just that my heart felt frozen in place, sitting in the dark and not moving. My thoughts roiled in circles, going nowhere, my legs and arms numb and useless like I operated in a vacuum, an emptiness.

On the upside, I'd learned a lot about Russian gulags. Peter was reluctant to share because he worried about me. Still, I made him. From what he told me it was amazing anyone survived for more than a year. The arctic temperatures were minor when you considered the conditions in the mines and labor camps.

Prisoners were tortured and kept in single cells for years until they went mad. The rest worked until they collapsed. Most normal Russian peasants didn't have enough to eat—in fact, a famine in 1947/1948 killed a million citizens—so the government certainly didn't provide adequate food or clothing for their prisoners. Nobody knew how many people died in gulags, but the numbers were in the millions. Vati would be one of them soon.

"Promise me to think about it?" he said, letting go of my arm.

Suddenly, I was unable to sit another minute. "I'm sorry. I've got to go home."

The doorbell rang shortly after I arrived at the flat.

"I'll get it," I yelled, running to open the door.

I'd changed and put on a new shade of pink lipstick that highlighted my tan. Summer had turned into glorious fall. Even this late in September, the weather was warm, the air filled with the earthy fragrance of fallen leaves. I didn't tell Peter that Gerda was picking me up and we planned to go to the *Biergarten* later. There were things I couldn't explain. This was one of them.

A policeman in a green uniform stood at the door. He took off his cap and tucked it under his arm.

"Is Frau Kronen home?" He looked at me strangely, a mix of sympathy and professional indifference. My head began to spin and my stomach cramped into a fist-sized stone. I couldn't catch my breath and felt tears burning in the back of my throat.

Something bad had happened.

I mumbled a greeting and steadied myself on the doorframe. *Breathe.* My first thought was Günter, but then I remembered he was no longer in my life. The realization that this man was here because of Vati hit me like a cement block. Mutti was reading the obituaries in the newspaper. I opened my mouth. Except nothing but a heavy sigh came out.

"Is Gerda not going?" Mutti said without looking up.

Barely trusting myself to speak I stumbled, "Mutti."

"What's the matter?" She sounded irritated, but as she met my gaze there was something else in her eyes. Maybe a shred of compassion or some kind of recognition that this moment was bigger than our quarrels.

"A police man is here."

Without a word, Mutti hurried out of the room. I followed.

The officer nodded. "Frau Kronen?"

"Yes?" As Mutti's hand shot to her head, confirming each lock was in place, I stared at the man, willing him to speak.

He looked official, his hair in a crew cut and his uniform immaculate. "I've got news about your husband, Wilhelm Kronen. We received word he'll be released."

I stared at the officer but didn't hear what else he said. His mouth opened and closed like a fish out of water.

Vati is coming home.

I watched Mutti, her face pale, her eyes filled with excitement, panic, and regret. I wondered what went through her head. If she was worried or happy. What she remembered of her husband, a man she hadn't seen in ten years and who'd been gone from our house for thirteen.

I was suddenly under water, a heavy weight on my chest. I had trouble breathing, remembering the Jews Hitler put into concentration camps. If they didn't die, they were near death, just bones with skin and huge eyes that had seen too much.

Vati was part of that regime. Even if he didn't do the jailing, he'd believed in Hitler, the madman who declared war with 37 countries, took all our manpower, resources and knowhow, our boys and men, and fed them into the war machine. He'd stolen our youth. I would hate the man and his Reich until eternity.

And a little bit of this hate was reserved for Vati.

Yet, I couldn't help myself for feeling excited. Now that I thought about it, I had hoped for his return every day.

"Lilly?" Mutti stared at me. "Did you hear what he said?" Coming up for air I shook my head.

"Herr Kronen is scheduled to arrive on Thursday," the policeman said, turning his attention to me. "He can be picked up in *Friedland*, the refugee camp near *Göttingen*."

I nodded, the lump in my stomach now in my throat where it threatened to burst.

"We are happy to assist you," the officer said. "The city has offered to send a car."

"Thank you." Mutti was breathless, her eyes shiny.

I didn't listen anymore. Vati would be home in five days.

At once I worried about not recognizing him, walking past him in the crowd. Most of all I worried about Vati finding out about Mutti.

The news of Vati's pending arrival created a firestorm of inquiries from family and friends. Everybody wanted to see the man who'd survived nine years in Russian gulags.

They were eager to visit. Newspapers called to set up interviews.

I spent hours trying to remove scratches and moisture rings from Vati's desk. Several remained like scars of my life.

The drive to *Friedland* took forever. Mutti actually tried to convince me I should stay home and wait there. Work some more, clean some more. Why should I ride in a car with them to reunite with my father? The woman knew no shame. I wouldn't have it. Not this time.

Mutti sat in front, her new hat uncharacteristically lopsided. Burkhart lounged next to me, none of us speaking as the landscape outside flew by. Off and on he ran his palms along his knee-long shorts and I suspected he was as nervous as I felt.

"You excited?" I asked.

He nodded, not meeting my eyes. But then he leaned in closely and whispered into my ear. "What do you think he looks like?"

"Don't know," I said quietly. I'd been worrying about the same thing. What if Vati lost his leg or worse... I couldn't see my brother's face, but his right knee wiggled up and down, making our seat vibrate.

Outside the countryside showed the ruins of houses. Like decayed teeth they remained between new homes in various stages of construction. Piles of bricks and debris, overgrown with weeds and bushes, stacks of roof tiles and framing crowded yards and sidewalks.

Empty stretches of road followed colorful stands of trees. Not the mature trees that once grew here, but new trees with thin trunks and branches, eager to grow and fill the void of burned and chopped down forests. They covered the ground with new growth, their leaves now vibrant with yellow and orange.

The train station in *Friedland* overflowed with people. They were of all ages, but mostly women and some children, throwing anxious glances toward the tracks. Many held signs with a man's name, some carried photos.

Have you seen Heinz Schnabel, last heard of June 10, 1943? Albert Weinart, born November 5, 1910, missing in Russia. There were hundreds and the walls of the little station house were plastered with hundreds more. Signposts lined the perimeter with photos of soldiers. Gray uniforms turned pale, faces faded along with memories.

Many women returned here every week. We'd been warned that the men weren't always on the trains, that Russian communication was unreliable. Vati may not come after all.

Many of the waiting people carried flowers, fancy little bouquets and unruly wild flowers, their dresses and skirts colorful patches against the gray block walls of the station.

Mutti returned from the information booth. "The train is late," she said. "I guess they always are."

I looked in the direction of the tracks snaking away in the distance, entangling themselves with other tracks. My eyes watered as I stared, willing my brain to look beyond what could be seen, willing the train to arrive.

On the other side of the tracks, barracks lined up between patches of grass and dirt roads, ready to house those that needed a place to stay. My heels hurt in the new pumps. I wore a gray wool suit with a red and black checkered silk neckerchief. It was too warm today, but it was the only formal outfit I owned.

Murmurs arose, turning into shouts.

The crowd shifted and people pushed forward to catch a glimpse of the end of the tracks. Drawn into the frenzy, I forced my way past arms and shoulders, pulling Burkhart with me.

In the distance, the gray speck of a train grew steadily larger as the rails in the station began to hum and vibrate. The train seemed to move at a snail's pace while the pushing of the crowd intensified. The noise had died down, a collective holding of breaths, the whistle from the conductor jarring my ears.

A loudspeaker crackled. "Step back from the curb. Make room." More whistles and commands followed as we moved slowly sideways and back.

He's coming. I fought back tears and elbowed my way toward Mutti. I might not recognize my father.

The train was gray and dirty, most of the windows blind with filth. Some glass was missing or broken, and some had been patched with wood. Somebody had written on the train walls in chalk, *Willkommen in der Heimat.*

Like ghosts, the outlines of faces were visible within. Some men leaned out of the open windows, smiling, waving, their faces haggard, their eye sockets hollow.

The wagons screeched and rumbled to a halt as silence settled on the platform. People waited and stared, trying to recognize a loved one, digging into their memories to identify a husband, a brother, or a father.

I scanned the men exiting the train. They waved now and shouts broke out in the crowd. When somebody pushed from behind, I stood my ground. These men looked old, much older than they could be. These were not the proud men who once left our homes to fight in a war.

Somebody screamed. A middle-aged woman waved her arms frantically as she shoved past me.

"Here, here," she yelled. "Theo, I'm here!"

A man who appeared to be in his fifties scanned the sea of faces, looking surprised but mostly bewildered. As the woman reached him, they embraced. One arm enfolded her, the other hung uselessly by his side. The couple remained linked, unmoving. Two or three other women crowded around the man, touching him.

Someone pulled on my sleeve. "I'm looking for my husband." The woman was pale, her cheekbones glowing with too much rouge. "Have you seen him? His name is Walter Stein." She thrust a wrinkled photograph of a man in uniform in my face. The man in the picture smiled and waved.

"I'm sorry, I'm waiting for my father."

As the woman mumbled something and pressed onward, asking again and again, more men spilled onto the platform. I leaned against the throng that wanted to tear me away from the train and the men.

More people cried out and quiet scenes of joy unfolded. One man stood alone, more than six feet tall, towering above us. He looked forlorn, unsure what to do and where to go. Nobody was picking him up.

"That's him…" Mutti's voice broke as she charged toward a figure in the back of the crowd.

I followed with Burkhart, not caring that I stepped on feet and bumped elbows.

Mutti stopped in front of a gray-faced man with a stubble of beard. "Willi?" His hair was cut short and receded. He wore glasses, old-fashioned horn-rimmed with metal sidebars. His eyes seemed shrunken, a dull blue behind round lenses.

Red, spidery veins covered his nose and cheeks. His face was lean and drawn, and folds of skin disappeared into a collar that was too wide. His clothes were ragged and loose.

Upon hearing his name, he turned to focus on us.

"Luise." Vati grimaced as he opened his arms to embrace Mutti. Tears spilled through his closed eyes and rolled down his cheeks.

I anxiously watched Vati's face, trying to memorize its lines, a face I hadn't seen in more than a decade.

Our eyes met.

"Lilly." He leaned toward me. The world stopped as I listened to his breathing and felt his arms wrap around my waist.

I sighed. He was using both his arms. I closed my eyes and for a moment, I heard nothing. I just touched this man who was my father and a stranger. I sank into his embrace as I traveled back in time, the sensation so powerful, I swayed.

For the briefest moment, I was small again, without fear and worries, with simple wishes like a doll and a few minutes of reading, just a little girl hugging her father. He smelled of dry sweat and I remembered the cologne and Vati's neatness. I searched for something familiar in his hug, a memory from long ago. I could not find it.

As we drew apart, I watched his face. Behind the tears, his eyes were worn, almost empty. I wanted to ask him things, about his life in Russia, about survival. Mostly I wanted to know why he'd left us all these years ago. What he thought about the war now, Hitler's murderous reign. How much had he even heard about it?

I felt myself choke. I couldn't ask this man anything.

Burkhart wiggled between us, and I let go.

"Burkhart!" Vati hugged my brother as we leaned against him, an island of four in a sea of bodies.

"Oh, Willi!" Mutti touched Vati's mouth where a gaping hole had replaced his front teeth. It was a tender gesture and as she took his hand and he put an arm around her waist, I realized that both of them had lost a great deal, too.

"Let's go home," I said.

On the way to the car, I claimed his other arm. He moved slowly, his feet too heavy to lift, his steps careful and deliberate.

"Here, Vati, you sit in front." I held his elbow as he sank to the seat.

He smiled at me, not the careless smile I remembered, but a smile built of sadness, unconvincing. I fought the urge to crawl on his lap and hold him close.

Vati turned back toward us, his voice barely reaching. "How far is it?"

Mutti patted him on the shoulder. "A few hours, not too bad."

Vati's mouth twisted into a smile but his eyes didn't keep up. They were busy scanning us, the strangers that were once his family. I wondered what he remembered about the girl that turned into a woman or about the baby boy with blond locks and a soft face that now showed the first signs of beard. What did he know about Mutti who looked old with lines edged around her eyes and mouth?

"What are a few hours after all this time?" he said.

It surprised me how slow he spoke. As if it took too much effort to form the words and push the air through his voice box. My brother was studying a father he didn't remember.

"How big you are, Burkhart. What grade are you in?" Vati asked.

"Tenth," Burkhart said, obviously glad to have something to talk about. "My favorite subject is math."

"Good boy!" Vati reached back to pat Burkhart's knee, awkwardly, more like a man patting a dog. He searched for something else to say, but no words came out, and he closed his mouth. Silence settled.

After a while, Vati turned toward me. "You're a grown woman." He grasped my hand and held it. His fingers were cold and dry, like bones left overnight in the desert.

I smiled and wiped a fresh tear from my face. The fist-sized lump in my throat was back.

"Come now, don't cry. I'm home," he said.

I nodded, but the tears kept coming. Vati was much smaller than I remembered. It wasn't his thinness. Rather he looked shrunken, almost transparent against the black leather seat.

"There...will be a reception," Mutti said.

Vati remained quiet.

"Our neighbors and family want to see you. They...we want to welcome you home."

"I wish..." Vati began and shook his head.

"What?" Mutti said.

"Nothing, I'm just tired."

"If they stay too long, we kick them out," I said.

As we pulled in front of our house, Vati fumbled for the car door and straightened himself on the sidewalk. Birch branches with white ribbons fluttered in the wind along the entrance, the wrought-iron fence and garden.

Mutti took his arm. "Let's go inside." I hurried to his other side, leading him toward the house. Neighbors came running. They had to have lain in wait.

Herr Huss leaned in the entrance, staring at the procession. Vati and Huss were the same age, but despite his puffiness, Huss appeared much younger. An odd expression passed across his face, as we approached. It spoke of familiarity, of ownership, as he first stared at Vati, then at Mutti. Vati followed his gaze and Mutti, turning red, pulled Vati into the house.

"*Willkommen zu Hause*," Huss called after them. I glanced at him in disgust before following my parents.

Vati turned, noticing the dread and loathing on my face.

This wasn't the time to explain years of abuse, so I smiled.

"*Komm*, Vati, let's go upstairs and get you settled."

Yelling and clapping erupted as we entered. The living room and kitchen were filled with people...neighbors, family and former colleagues. They sat and stood, some smoking, holding beer and wine glasses, smiling, their eyes on Vati.

"Have a seat," Uncle August boomed. "How about a smoke? Cigarette, cigar?"

Vati shook his head. Someone slapped Vati on the shoulder and he froze.

"How about a beer?" A woman from across the street offered a tall glass. Vati took it and sat down. He looked at the glass, the fine carbonation and foam on top as if he'd never seen anything like it.

Our eyes met and I nodded. He returned to stare at the glass in his hand.

Laughter pealed as one of the guests told a joke. Platters of pickled onions, peppers and cookies cluttered the top of the desk. I wiped away drops of beer. Mutti joined the crowd, her face pale next to the red lipstick, her eyes guarded. She watched Vati like the others, waiting for him to speak, to explain himself.

The doorbell rang and Vati jerked, spilling some of the beer on his leg. Herr Baum limped into the room, his feet scraping across the carpet. He looked ancient and leaned on his cane.

"Good to see you home at last," he said, shaking Vati's hand and slumping into a chair. "What a mess," he said to no one in particular. "Hitler made us all criminals. The world hates us."

"It was my duty," Vati said, taking in the old man.

I wanted to shake him, this man who I didn't know anymore. What duty, I wanted to scream? Why didn't you see through it? Günter did. Even at sixteen, he knew more and refused to become part of the madness. It almost cost him his life.

Günter.

The memory of him nearly pulled me over. My heart wrenched and I felt my throat tighten. I realized I longed for him as much now as on the day I broke up with him.

No. More.

All this time I hesitated to accept Peter's offer to move in, get away from Mutti. All this time I thought I hesitated because of Mutti.

It wasn't so. It was because I couldn't forget Günter.

His hazel eyes swam in my vision, smiling and then turning serious. I'd forever lost my chance to be with the man I love. Because I refused to forgive him.

I looked at Vati. After all these atrocities and hardships, could I find the strength in me to forgive? Not forget, but get over what he'd done?

Herr Baum and I exchanged glances. He nodded and gave me that desolate half-smile, reminding me of the story about his daughter.

You lose everything if you cannot move on. Hitler and his cronies, the greatest evildoers of history, win. You're one more victim in their murderous plan.

"No," I shouted. My breath labored, and I felt my heart hammer against my ribs.

"Everything all right?" Uncle August's blue eyes were filled with concern.

I nodded, growing aware of my surroundings. The noise had swelled as more people arrived, their eyes curious and staring. They shook Vati's hand, patted his arm and said words of welcome. Vati leaned back awkwardly, said a greeting or two and fell silent again.

"That's what they wanted you—all of us—to believe," Herr Baum said after a while. "Look what it did to you. Thirteen years wasted." His raspy voice was grave.

Vati shook his head. The beer in his hand looked like pee now, the foam evaporated and the carbonation flat. "At the time, it seemed like the honorable thing to do."

At that moment, I realized Vati wasn't lying about that. He actually believed he did the right thing. He only lied to us, the people who should've mattered most.

Herr Baum continued. "It was insanity. Millions killed, Jews exterminated, the destruction of everything we ever knew, our heritage, our culture, and our reputation. All gone."

"Oh, Herr Baum, why don't we talk about something positive," the woman from across the street said.

"That's right, nobody wants to talk about what really happened." Herr Baum's eyes squeezed nearly shut behind the folds of loose skin. "Let's bury the past and pretend it never took place." His voice cut through the buzz, the room turning silent. Outside the open window, a black bird squawked as if to add its disdain.

Vati swallowed several times as if he were choking. His lips moved and I bent lower. "I did what I was told," he mumbled. I looked at him, wondering about the virtues of obedience. The Third Reich was good at creating organized groups from Hitler Youth to the Association of German Girls, moving on to mothers with crosses, soldiers, SS, SA and Gestapo. Each group had hierarchies, people who told other people what to do. At what point did we have a moral duty to ignore obedience and laws and think for ourselves?

I moved toward Herr Baum and took his hand. "We better let Vati rest a while."

He smiled at me, but he had that look on his face, the same look he had when he told me about losing his daughter. He must think about her every day.

I realized that I was lucky because thinking about Vati somewhere in that prison had sustained me. Or maybe it was the wish for an explanation, the hate I'd felt. I watched my father and couldn't quite hold on to the hate because the life I'd lost and mourned, our family life, was gone. No matter what I did, I would never recapture it.

And if I didn't forgive him now, I would forever remain with one foot in the war.

Mutti moved next to Vati. They were holding hands, and I imagined how they must have been years ago when they were my age, all that love and their plans of raising a family, spending their lives together. They'd lost out, too.

At that moment I knew that my love was something precious, something to be preserved. No matter what happened, there was still warmth in my heart...for Vati...and...

I abruptly straightened. There was an urge in me, a terrible longing. I'd been a blind fool and a stupid, stubborn idiot. Why hadn't I seen it before?

I raced downstairs, out the front door, up the yard into the street. I wore heels, but I ran anyway...all the way uphill, a hundred yards, two hundred. I panted, my lungs aching with each step. I couldn't slow down. I mustn't.

Günter's house sat on a street of identical homes, all two stories with pointed roofs and red clay tiles. It had been recently painted, the stucco a fresh white. I massaged my ribs as I hurried to the door. It was late, after nine o'clock and a light shone in the front window where Günter's parents had their bedroom.

I rang the doorbell anyway, hardly able to breathe.

"Lilly?" Artur stood in the doorway in shirttails. "What happened? What's wrong?"

I realized that my face had to be red-hot and my hair was a mess. "It's...Vati is home."

Artur took me firmly by the arm and guided me into the foyer. "That is great news," he said.

My legs didn't work so well and I was teetering just as Günter came down the stairs. The hall was a bit dark, but I felt his eyes sink into mine like a strong wind taking hold of a leaf.

"What's going on?" he said.

"I...made a terrible mistake." I swayed again and Günter rushed to my side, putting an arm around my waist.

The next moment we were alone.

"I'm so sorry." I struggled to keep my balance, afraid of Günter's rejection. I knew he didn't have a girlfriend, Gerda had mentioned as much, but he might no longer want me.

Günter pulled me to him, his arms warm and strong on my back.

"I've been stupid," I said. "I—"

Günter's lips found mine and I no longer teetered.

I was strong and purposeful, our kiss full of promise. I drank in his closeness, the warmth of his chest and neck. And I knew now that Günter had to go away. That, in a way, he didn't have a choice. And while he was guilty of leaving without an excuse, I'd been stronger. I'd endured and survived so I could end up right here in Günter's arms.

When Günter rode off, he left behind the claustrophobic memories of war and the claustrophobic demands of post-war Germany, his job, his parents...me.

The trip cleansed him just as Vati's return cleansed me. That, and the realization that I was strong and capable of taking care of myself. I'd gotten rid of Huss, and now I'd gotten rid of the burden that accompanied me for all these years.

I could breathe again. And I'd do it together with Günter. My love.

THE END

EPILOGUE

May 26, 1954

I awoke with a start, my first gaze toward the window to check the weather. A tentative sun rose behind the stand of juniper trees and the cloudless blue above promised a beautiful day. I smiled.

Ever since Günter picked me up from Ullrich a few weeks ago, I'd been anxious, worrying about the weather, because today was my wedding. To save money, we were celebrating at Günter's house—more precisely, in his garden.

His grandma had offered us a place in her house, a single room on the second floor and a bedroom in the attic. I wasn't so sure I liked living with his parents and grandmother, but this was the best we could do. After Mutti, it was paradise.

Solingen had no apartments. At least none we could afford, just long waiting lists. I thought back at my attempts at securing a flat almost two years ago. It was worse now. Every day more people were moving from the east. I thought about the man with the clipboard and the woman with the perfect lipstick, her arrogant stare. I wondered if she lived in that apartment now.

I smiled again. I didn't care. Let her be with her electrician. I had Günter, and I loved him. And as of tonight I would no longer *share space* with my parents. Never again.

I grew aware of my surroundings, the faint rustling of a human presence on the other side of the wall, murmurs, water running inside a pipe, a door opening and closing. My parents were up. My parents...how strange that sounded. I hadn't thought of them together since I was a little girl.

For thirteen years I didn't use that word. It was always Mutti.

Since Vati's return, I hadn't seen much of the father I once had. Maybe I'd been too young when he left, but the man in the kitchen looked distant, his skin glowing red from the years of heavy frost exposure, his hands spotted gray and brown over thickly-corded veins.

His voice was deeper, and he spoke slowly most of the time. He hardly smiled. I'd tried to talk to him about the war, but he refused. He only spoke of the camps, the things he'd been made to do in the dozens of Russian gulags he survived.

Worse was how my parents acted. Yes, acting is the right word. They played the roles of a married couple. When I was around, they were polite, said thank you and please. But they showed little emotion and no connection, like two adults meeting on a cruise and sharing breakfast as perfect strangers.

I couldn't wait to be gone from the iciness that threatened to spill over into my heart.

My gaze returned to my wardrobe, where my suit hung waiting. Black, with wide lapels, it was made of light wool and looked formal and sensible. Günter helped pay for it.

It was frivolously expensive and just right because my new life began today. I got up and ran my fingers over the lacey white blouse, its collar shaped like a star because I was going to be in heaven.

When Vati first returned, I thought he'd soon relax and become more talkative. But months later, and despite the six-week vacation and spa rehabilitation that the city paid for, he remained quiet, his eyes often far away.

The city finally recognized that Vati existed and because of the long and horrible imprisonment and his status as *Beamter,* the city offered him his job back. For the time between 1945 and 1950, he received one Mark for every day and two Marks for the years between 1950 and 1953. He studied every night to catch up on the new systems and technologies the city had been implementing.

Mutti was subdued. I didn't know if she felt truly guilty or if she just didn't have anything to say. Her new occupation was shopping. She invested in hats and gloves and all manners of elegant dresses and matching shoes as if they could somehow conceal her shameful past.

And yet there was part of me that acknowledged Mutti's excesses were not that unusual. War wives not only had affairs, many divorced their husbands and remarried. What I couldn't get over weren't her lies or her men, but her refusal to love me when I'd most needed her.

My parents had made it clear I was on my own for the wedding. Vati didn't like Günter either. Like Mutti, he thought Günter wasn't good enough. There had been a time when I'd have done anything to be on his good side and his negative opinion would've devastated me.

I'd hated him for what he'd done, and at the same time yearned for his love. In the end, I was going with neither. All I could do was forgive on my terms. The love I'd envisioned from him was not to be had. My fury has been replaced with pity and acceptance, maybe a bit of resignation.

He'd chosen obedience to a twisted ideal over his responsibility for his family. That sort of blind obedience had made it possible for Hitler to gain power because this blindness stopped Vati from seeing the truth that there was a choice. Though Vati had been a soldier in two wars and survived eight years of gulags, I didn't consider him brave.

But what was worst to me was how he and Mutti considered me less worthy than my brother even now because I was a girl and because Hitler had *special* plans for girls. And to think there had been a time when I thought I'd done something to deserve all this. A puff of air escaped me. What buffoons.

I wanted to laugh, but it felt dangerously close to crying. Considering what had happened, I was lucky. What did they do to young Jewish women? Had them strip naked, pierced them with needles, performed experiments, took out their ovaries...My eyes filled with tears, and for a while I was blind to my surroundings.

Vati's coughing brought me back. Günter and I planned and financed the party, but even that didn't matter. I knew Günter would take care of me just as I'd take care of him. He was industrious when many gave up, organized and created things seemingly from thin air. He'd seen through the Nazis and he stuck around to help his family. He may not be a *Beamter*, a senior official, but to me he was by far the smarter man.

Forcing myself away from the wardrobe, I entered the

kitchen where Vati sat reading the newspaper.

"*Guten Morgen,*" I said, patting him on the shoulder. A little bit of the girl was back, looking for his attention and I couldn't help but smile. I smiled because deep down I thanked him for the memory he'd instilled in me. However flawed, however warped, it was this memory that sustained me through Mutti's neglect. *You don't walk out of your family because it's part of your soul.* Herr Baum was right. The chance of expunging your past and the love that binds you is as great as shedding your skin.

Vati looked up, his gaze on me soft as if he couldn't quite believe he had an adult daughter. "Ready for the big day?" His face glowed as if he were holding his breath.

"I am." I looked at Mutti, who silently ironed a shirt, her expression unreadable.

When I passed by her, she touched my cheek. "Your last day," she said, her eyes glittering.

Thankfully, I wanted to say, but all I did was nod and pour myself a cup of coffee. My mother's capacity for sentimentality was amazing. Or did she finally realize she was about to lose her daughter? Despite the cold anger in my heart, I fought the urge to turn around and hug her. We'd been through a lot together, most of it horrible. It bound us just as my longing for Vati and my love for Günter. And somewhere inside me was still the need to please her. Maybe in time I'd learn to forgive.

I sagged next to Vati, taking in my old home. The kitchen was as shabby as ever, the linoleum cracked beneath the table, burn stains in front of the stove. To me it was no longer dreadful because now, despite its ugliness and scars, it was part of my past.

"I guess, I better start cooking—the roast will take a while." I smiled, realizing that as of today, I'd be slipping between the folds of their lives to find my own.

Garlands and bouquets of white carnations greeted us as we arrived at the reception. The civil ceremony at the courthouse was simple, only our parents attended while Gerda, Helmut and Hans remained behind to set up the garden.

They assembled chairs and tables and prepared the buffet. Rich butter cream cake—a special request from me—followed generous helpings of beef roast, potatoes, green beans and cauliflower, salad and bread along with beer and Mosel wine.

Herr Baum sat on a garden bench watching the merriment. He waved me over and my hands disappeared in his gnarly ones.

"Here," he said, as I felt something on my palm. "You and Günter go on a honeymoon." He smiled, and it was the happiest expression I could remember.

In my fingers lay a crisp hundred-mark bill. I heard myself gasp. "Oh, Herr Baum, that's too much!"

"Child, I don't need it. Time for you to have some fun." I gave him a hug and felt him chuckle.

"I'll visit you soon," I said.

He patted my arm. "You do some living now, you hear."

As if on cue, Helmut began to sing, "*Hoch soll'n sie leben,*" and our raucous friends joined in, swinging glasses, toasting and hollering. Fruit brandy, corn and cigar vapors mixed with the excited chatter of guests.

Back with Günter, I laughed until I watched my parents leave in silence, several feet of space between them.

Vati embraced me earlier, wishing me a wonderful future. I suspected he meant well. I hugged him back, the spot in my heart alive again, but not as bright. I loved Vati, but I did not admire him. I was happy to see him home safe and back at the work he used to enjoy.

I was free of him now, free of the burden of his absence. And with that freedom came a new lightness. It was as if I could fly if I flapped my arms.

"You never have to go back there," Günter whispered as our last guests left arm in arm singing.

I let it sink in, this new truth.

"Time for bed, Frau Schmidt." He kissed my nose. "And welcome home."

I smiled. Life had begun.

HISTORICAL TIMELINE

September 1, 1939
Germany attacks Poland under the guise that Poland has attacked a German office, killing several men. In reality, Hitler has planned the war on Poland for years. The attack at the German office has been staged by the SS and actually begins at least an hour earlier than announced. Two days later, France and Britain declare war against Germany. Within two weeks Poland is overrun, and is divided up between Germany and the USSR.

Spring 1940
Emboldened by the quick victory, Hitler attacks Denmark and Norway. France is invaded next. Both offensives require many troops, siphoning German men away from homes. First attacks on German ground occur; Hitler dictates the building of additional bunkers.

May 11, 1940
The British Royal Air Force (RAF) begins attacks on Germany

1941
Hitler breaks his agreement with the USSR and attacks.

Dec 11, 1941
Germany declares war on the U.S.
May 30, 1942

The RAF bombs Cologne with more than 1,000 bombs, 262 attacks will follow.

Sept 13, 1942
The battle for Stalingrad begins.

1942/1943
The winter of Stalingrad turns the tide, ultimately leading to Germany's doom and the loss of WWII. More than 700,000 people, Russians and Germans die during the battle.

Feb 2, 1943
The German army surrenders in Stalingrad. Large-scale air attacks bomb and devastate German cities. The civilian population, mostly women and children, without food or heat, seek refuge in bunkers and cellars.

Feb 18, 1943
National Socialist propaganda minister Goebbels declares "total war" – the Third Reich's reaction to the defeat at Stalingrad

April 19, 1943
The Warsaw ghetto's remaining Jews start to fight the German SS and resist until May 16.

1943
To scare the German civilian population, British and American Air Forces execute large scale bombing attacks, carpet bombs cover large areas. The German flak anti aircraft fire, in charge of protecting the homeland, is unable to reach the high flying planes.

June 6, 1944
The Allied Forces land in France

June 22, 1944
Dissention erupts within Germany's military leadership to end Hitler's regime

July 20, 1944
Oberst Stauffenberg attempt to assassinate Hitler fails

Sept. 11, 1944
The Allied Forces enter Germany.

Oct. 16, 1944
The Red Army enters Germany.

Nov. 4/5 1944
Solingen is leveled and burns for a week. The bombing on November 5 lasts 18 minutes and leaves 100 large, 300 middle sized and 500 small fires. 921 tons of bombs and air mines, followed by 138 tons of phosphor bombs fall. Thousands die and more than 20,000 people lose their homes. On November 5, 1944, the British radio announces: "Solingen, the heart of the German steel industry, a destroyed, dead city!"

Jan. 1945
As the German Army lacks ammunition and food and soldiers retreat on all fronts, families are asked to sacrifice yet again. In what has been called the "final war", boys and grandfathers are drafted. The Allies move across Germany to finish the job, no longer expecting much opposition. Air attacks blanket the country. The Red Army liberates the Concentration Camp (KZ) Auschwitz—most of the prisoners have died in SS-organized gas chambers and during death marches.

Feb 13, 1945
RAF and USAAF bomb Dresden, burning it to the ground, killing 18,000-25,000 civilians.

March 1945
In the desperate last wave of the *Volkssturm,* Hitler orders all boys, born 1928 and 1929 as well as old men to defend the 'fatherland.' With Russians and Americans already on German ground, the German government threatens to execute anyone who displays white sheets or flags as a sign of surrender.

April 16/17, 1945
American troops arrive in Solingen. Its citizens surrender without a fight.

April 21, 1945
Battle of Berlin, 2.5 million Red Army soldiers surround the city, fighting one million German soldiers. The last fanatics, SS, Hitler youth create stand-up desertion tribunals, shooting surrendering German citizens on the spot.

April 30, 1945
Hitler commits suicide.

May 2-8, 1945
The German government surrenders.

Summer 1945
British and American military release German prisoners while the USSR continues filling its camps.

1945-1948
With its infrastructure and production facilities destroyed, the German population starves. Families go on barter trips, trading and stealing to survive as run-away inflation and black markets emerge throughout the country.

1946
US, British and French occupation governments pass "Denazification" laws, trying to stop former affiliates of the Third Reich to reenter leadership positions. Most adult Germans are required to complete a 130-question survey about their involvement with the Nazis.

June 1948
The Deutsche Mark (DM) is introduced. Every German receives DM 40. Stores that have hoarded for months fill with merchandise overnight. Black markets disappear.

1950s
The *Wirtschaftswunder*, the Economic Wonder of post-war Germany begins, drastically improving standard of living for West Germans within a few years.

May 1952
Against Stalin's wishes of a unified Germany, the West-German part of the country aligns itself with the western allies by signing the Germany Contract with the U.S., France and Great Britain. As a result Stalin begins erecting borders to formally divide east and west Germany.

March 1953
Stalin dies.

1954-1955
The last prisoners of war "The last 10,000" are released from Soviet camps.

SOLINGEN, NOVEMBER 1944-COURTESY STADTARCHIV SOLINGEN

GALLERY OF CHARACTERS

LILLY (HELGA) 1932-2004

After marrying Günter, Lilly, whose real name was Helga, became a homemaker and had two girls, Barbara and Annette (the author). In 1970, she returned to work, first as an office assistant and later at Deutsche Bank. Here she remained until the early nineties and retirement. A nurturing mother, she took great pride in raising her daughters, allowing them to succeed and supporting them through college. Without-a-doubt she kept the most immaculate house in the city. She subscribed to a healthy lifestyle, didn't drink and ate organic food. Always busy, she enjoyed knitting, cross-stitch, her garden and travel. She also loved her five grandchildren. In 2004, one month before her fiftieth wedding anniversary, she suffered a brain hemorrhage and fell into a coma. She passed away six months later at the age of 72.

GÜNTER 1928-

Günter became a master dye maker and ran his own company for seven years. In 1970, he joined Hugo Pott, a world-renowned silverware company and became a lead designer. His unique expertise, a combination of artistry and technical knowledge, made him a sought-after employee all his life. He retired at age 70. Always figuring he'd be the first to die, he was devastated when Helga fell ill. After her death, he struggled to find meaning in his life, but the grit that accompanied him all his life saved him. He remains independent, still lives in the same house and is active with his nature ponds and garden. Günter has found a companion in Helmut's widow Gerda. They share visits and the occasional trip.

WILHELM (WILLI) 1897-1989

Willi recovered and returned to work fulltime at the city of Solingen in 1954. He retired at seventy and maintained an active lifestyle. He learned about Luise's affairs through anonymous letters and contemplated divorce. It is unclear why he remained with her, but they lived together until his death at age 92.

LUISE 1904-1997

Luise remained critical of Lilly all her life. Up to her death at a retirement home—Lilly refused to take her in—Luise could be seen parading through Solingen in hat and gloves, her permed hair tinged purple in perfect curls.

ARTUR 1902-1987

Artur returned to work in Solingen's steel industry until his retirement. He loved gardening and remained married to Grete for more than fifty years, sharing the house with Günter and Lilly and their grandchildren. Artur suffered from chronic bronchitis which worsened as he aged, but passed away peacefully in his sleep at age 83.

GRETE 1904-1989

Grete enjoyed many quiet years as a homemaker. After Artur's death, she remained in the same house with Günter and Lilly. They cared for her when she fell ill from liver cancer until her death five months later.

HELMUT 1928-1992

Helmut worked as a typesetter and had two children with his wife Gerda. A heavy smoker all his life, he contracted lung cancer and died in 1992. Günter and Helmut remained casual friends all their lives.

GERDA (HELGA) 1928-

Gerda's real name is also Helga. In the book the author changed Helga's name to Gerda to avoid confusion. Gerda became a homemaker and had a daughter and son. She lives in a retirement community near Günter's home and they often visit each other.

HANS 1927-2001

Hans became a commercial electrician and traveled often on business. He married another Helga – a popular name in the twenties and thirties – and had one daughter. After his wife passed away from a heart condition, he retired near Günter's home and married a second time. An avid cook and wine connoisseur, he passed away from liver disease.

SIEGFRIED 1936-

Siegfried married and had two boys with his wife, Silvia. He emigrated to Switzerland where he is now retired.

BURKHART 1937-2001

Burkhart joined the German military and became a helicopter pilot. He married Maria and had two children. Due to his public service, he was able to retire in his fifties. Lilly expressed regret never developing a closer bond with her brother, a separation their mother, Luise, nurtured a lifetime. A strong smoker for many years, he developed lung and prostate cancer and passed away at age 64.

Karl Huss

Karl Huss is a fictitious character merged of two factual individuals. Family history confirms that Luise had an affair with a neighbor whose name is unknown. Willi's brother, Eugen who served in the military and had multiple behavioral problems, spent much time in the basement and molested Lilly.

Herr Baum

Also a fictitious character, Herr Baum provides a voice of reason during the insanity of the Third Reich.

AUTHOR NOTE

Historians of wars tend to cover the obvious. There are aggressors and there are victims. In the case of World War II, Hitler and his Nazi regime represented an evil so great, many consider it the vilest period in human history.

Gestapo, SS and SA officers terrorized Jews and minorities, brought war and destruction to many countries across the world, and over several years killed six million Jews alone. It is easy to see why many people despised Germany and its citizens.

Between 55 and 80 million people lost their lives, the most destructive war ever fought. More than half of them were civilians. By the time the war ended, thousands of European, Russian and Asian cities were ruined. Germany's infrastructure and economy were annihilated. Germany had been evil and had received its punishment.

Yet, wars affect more than the soldiers fighting in them. Wars are all encompassing and life changing for everyone involved. This was the case then as it is today—and for nobody more than for children.

The reasons I wrote this book are three-fold. First, I wanted to preserve the personal history of our family. Often, the past dies with the oldest generation. All we are left with are photos, names and family trees. Though my parents were in no way extraordinary people, their lives and circumstances, measured by today's standards, were exceptional. They were neither Nazis nor soldiers, but they were German when Hitler attacked Poland. Their lives, along with those of millions of other children were hidden within the atrocities of the Third Reich.

My mother was seven when World War II began. Her father joined the army within months, leaving her with a cruel mother who favored her brother. She endured a life most of us would think impossible. My father was eleven and soon became the "man of the house," responsible for supporting his family, mostly on an empty stomach. They were innocent victims of circumstance, yet they never saw it that way. They never complained, always worked and never questioned. They created things out of nothing, slowly and patiently.

Second, this book is my way of adding rarely covered details of wartime and post war Germany to the large picture of German history and the finer brushstrokes that happened behind the scenes.

Thirdly, I wanted to draw attention to the victims of war, particularly children who often have no voice. It seems a world without war is impossible to achieve. From wars in Iraq and Afghanistan to civil conflicts in Syria and genocide in Darfur, wars are a staple of human nature or rather, governments with an evil purpose. Like my parents endured then, millions of children suffer today.

It is time to let them speak.

ABOUT THE AUTHOR

Annette Oppenlander is an award-winning writer, literary coach and educator. As a bestselling historical novelist, Oppenlander is known for her authentic characters and stories based on true events, coming alive in well-researched settings. Having lived in Germany the first half of her life and the second half in various parts in the U.S., Oppenlander inspires readers by illuminating story questions as relevant today as they were in the past. Oppenlander's bestselling true WWII story, Surviving the Fatherland, has received multiple awards, including the 2017 National Indie Excellence Award, the Indie B.R.A.G. Award and a Readers' Favorite Book Award. Her historical time-travel trilogy, Escape from the Past, takes readers to the German Middle Ages and the Wild West. Uniquely, Oppenlander weaves actual historical figures and events into her plots, giving readers a flavor of true history while enjoying a good story. Oppenlander shares her knowledge through writing workshops at colleges, libraries and schools. She also offers vivid presentations and author visits. The mother of fraternal twins and a son, she lives with her husband and old mutt, Mocha, in Bloomington, Ind.

"Nearly every place holds some kind of secret, something that makes history come alive. When we scrutinize people and places closely, history is no longer a date or number, it turns into a story."

From the Author: Thank you for reading SURVIVING THE FATHERLAND. My sincere hope is that you derived as much entertainment from reading this story as I enjoyed in creating it. If you have a few moments, please feel free to add your review of the book at your favorite online site for feedback. Also, if you would like to connect with previous or upcoming books, please visit my website for information and to sign up for e-news: http://www.annetteoppenlander.com.

Sincerely, Annette

CONTACT ME

Website: www.annetteoppenlander.com
Facebook: www.facebook.com/annetteoppenlanderauthor
Twitter: @aoppenlander
Pinterest: @annoppenlander

ALSO BY ANNETTE OPPENLANDER

A Different Truth
Escape from the Past: The Duke's Wrath (Book One)
Escape from the Past: The Kid (Book Two)
Escape from the Past: At Witches' End (Book Three)
47 Days: How Two Teen Boys Defied the Third Reich (Novelette) – Excerpt
from Surviving the Fatherland
Everything We Lose: A Civil War Novel of Hope, Courage and Redemption
Where the Night Never Ends: A Prohibition Era Novel

68715888R00208

Made in the USA
Middletown, DE
17 September 2019